ROBOTS:
THE RECENT A.I.

OTHER BOOKS BY THE EDITORS

Rich Horton & Sean Wallace
Robots 2: The Recent A.I. (forthcoming)
War and Space: Recent Combat (forthcoming)

Rich Horton
Fantasy: The Best of the Year, 2006 Edition
Fantasy: The Best of the Year, 2007 Edition
Fantasy: The Best of the Year, 2008 Edition
Science Fiction: The Best of the Year, 2006 Edition
Science Fiction: The Best of the Year, 2007 Edition
Science Fiction: The Best of the Year, 2008 Edition
The Year's Best Science Fiction & Fantasy, 2009 Edition
The Year's Best Science Fiction & Fantasy, 2010 Edition
The Year's Best Science Fiction & Fantasy, 2011 Edition
The Year's Best Science Fiction & Fantasy, 2012 Edition (forthcoming)
Unplugged: The Web's Best Sci-Fi & Fantasy, 2008

Sean Wallace
Best New Fantasy
Fantasy (with Paul Tremblay)
Horror: The Best of the Year, 2006 (with John Betancourt)
Japanese Dreams
The Mammoth Book of Steampunk
Phantom (with Paul Tremblay)
Realms 1 (with Nick Mamatas)
Realms 2 (with Nick Mamatas)
Weird Tales: The 21st Century (with Stephen H. Segal)

ROBOTS:
THE RECENT A.I.

RICH HORTON & SEAN WALLACE

PRIME BOOKS

ROBOTS: THE RECENT A.I.

Prime Books
www.prime-books.com

For more information, contact Prime Books:
prime@prime-books.com

ISBN: 978-1-60701-318-1

CONTENTS

INTRODUCTION, Rich Horton 7

EROS, PHILIA, AGAPE, Rachel Swirsky 9

ARTIFICE AND INTELLIGENCE, Tim Pratt 35

I, ROBOT, Cory Doctorow 42

ALTERNATE GIRL'S EXPATRIATE LIFE, Rochita Loenen-Ruiz 76

THE RISING WATERS, Benjamin Crowell 87

HOUSES, Mark Pantoja 105

THE DJINN'S WIFE, Ian McDonald 117

STALKER, Robert Reed 153

DROPLET, Benjamin Rosenbaum 164

KISS ME TWICE, Mary Robinette Kowal 180

ALGORITHMS FOR LOVE, Ken Liu 246

A JAR OF GOODWILL, Tobias S. Buckell 259

THE SHIPMAKER, Aliette de Bodard 279

TIDELINE, Elizabeth Bear 292

UNDER THE EAVES, Lavie Tidhar 302

THE NEAREST THING, Genevieve Valentine 314

BALANCING ACCOUNTS, James L. Cambias 335

SILENTLY AND VERY FAST, Catherynne M. Valente 352

ABOUT THE CONTRIBUTORS 401

INTRODUCTION

RICH HORTON

Robots are of course one of the oldest sfnal tropes, arguably traceable to the Golem of Prague, and certainly a common feature of 19th-century proto-SF from the likes of E. T. A. Hoffman and Herman Melville. The word was famously invented by Karel Čapek in his play *R. U. R.* (1920), though Čapek's robots were closer to what we now call androids. Also in the '20s, another Eastern European writer, Vladimir Nabokov, wrote of robots in his novel *King, Queen, Knave* (1928). In genre science fiction, early famous treatments include Eando Binder's "I, Robot" and Lester Del Rey's "Helen O'Loy"; but it was Isaac Asimov who became the single sf writer most identified with the concept with his series of stories mostly in *Astounding* from 1940 on.

The dichotomy between the usually human appearance of robots and their mechanical origin has generally been central to the themes of robot stories. Early stories often treated the mechanical duplication of humanity as fundamentally wrong; or as a subject of comedy or satire. Binder and Del Rey were much more sympathetic to robots, even sentimental about their origin and their presumed inferior position to humans. Asimov's Three Laws of Robotics placed them as by programming "willing" servants to humans, though his later elaborations of the implications of the Three Laws greatly complexified the definitions of "willing," "servant," and indeed "human." Jack Williamson, in "With Folded Hands" and sequels, extrapolated the logical implications of Asimov's Laws in a quite sinister direction.

But in recent years, certainly as evidenced in the stories in this anthology, the focus of writers' attention has shifted from concern about the effects—good or bad—of robots on humans to the rights of robots themselves. It has long been clear that the possession by any entity of intelligence implies a question about its rights—and surely our sympathy immediately lies with intelligent beings denied rights.

And so these stories, in positing intelligent (if human-created) beings, mostly insist that these beings must be—in some sense—free. The definition of freedom can be complex, mind you. Even Asimov's robot stories had an implicit question at the heart of many of them—can a being designed, or programmed, to in some sense derive self-worth from service fairly be set free? That question is central to many of the stories in this book—certainly it drives the seemingly strange choice made by the protagonist of Rachel Swirsky's "Eros, Philia, Agape"; and it is likewise a key motivator in the relationship depicted in Lavie Tidhar's "Under the Eaves". Indeed in many of these stories a sexual or near-sexual relationship between a human and a robot is implied—and in so doing the stories address questions of human sexual relationships, of power relationships of all kinds, of slavery.

Another human relationship echoed in these stories is that of parent to child—if humans are parents of robots or AIs in some sense, what do we owe them? Particularly if the child clearly surpasses the parent is some ways? Benjamin Crowell's "The Rising Waters" and Catherynne M. Valente's "Silently and Very Fast" both movingly address the idea that an AI might regard a human or humans as its "parents."

Ultimately, if robots are free, the question of how they might live without humans at all arises. So we see stories like Mark Pantoja's "Houses" and James L. Cambias's "Balancing Accounts", two stories as different from each other as one might imagine, but both wondering how robots—made to serve humans—might escape those bonds and find their own lives. (Or take Rochita Loenen-Ruiz's "Alternate Girl's Expatriate Life", which turns the tables yet again, and features a human growing up in a robot society.)

What is clear is that the trope of robots and AI is ever fertile, ever worth reexamination. Robots are by design enough like us—and enough different—to make us think about what it means to be human, and what it means to be like a human but different, and about how we can live with those differences. These stories, all from the past decade, are an invigorating new look at an old idea.

EROS, PHILIA, AGAPE

RACHEL SWIRKSY

Lucian packed his possessions before he left. He packed his antique silver serving spoons with the filigreed handles; the tea roses he'd nurtured in the garden window; his jade and garnet rings. He packed the hunk of gypsum-veined jasper that he'd found while strolling on the beach on the first night he'd come to Adriana, she leading him uncertainly across the wet sand, their bodies illuminated by the soft gold twinkling of the lights along the pier. That night, as they walked back to Adriana's house, Lucian had cradled the speckled stone in his cupped palms, squinting so that the gypsum threads sparkled through his lashes.

Lucian had always loved beauty—beautiful scents, beautiful tastes, beautiful melodies. He especially loved beautiful objects because he could hold them in his hands and transform the abstraction of beauty into something tangible.

The objects belonged to them both, but Adriana waved her hand bitterly when Lucian began packing. "Take whatever you want," she said, snapping her book shut. She waited by the door, watching Lucian with sad and angry eyes.

Their daughter, Rose, followed Lucian around the house. "Are you going to take that, Daddy? Do you want that?" Wordlessly, Lucian held her hand. He guided her up the stairs and across the uneven floorboards where she sometimes tripped. Rose stopped by the picture window in the master bedroom, staring past the palm fronds and swimming pools, out to the vivid cerulean swath of the ocean. Lucian relished the hot, tender feel of Rose's hand. *I love you*, he would have whispered, but he'd surrendered the ability to speak.

He led her downstairs again to the front door. Rose's lace-festooned pink satin dress crinkled as she leapt down the steps. Lucian had ordered her dozens of satin party dresses in pale, floral hues. Rose refused to wear anything else.

Rose looked between Lucian and Adriana. "Are you taking me, too?" she asked Lucian.

Adriana's mouth tightened. She looked at Lucian, daring him to say something, to take responsibility for what he was doing to their daughter. Lucian remained silent.

Adriana's chardonnay glowed the same shade of amber as Lucian's eyes. She clutched the glass's stem until she thought it might break. "No, honey," she said with artificial lightness. "You're staying with me."

Rose reached for Lucian. "Horsey?"

Lucian knelt down and pressed his forehead against Rose's. He hadn't spoken a word in the three days since he'd delivered his letter of farewell to Adriana, announcing his intention to leave as soon as she had enough time to make arrangements to care for Rose in his absence. When Lucian approached with the letter, Adriana had been sitting at the dining table, sipping orange juice from a wine glass and reading a first edition copy of Cheever's *Falconer*. Lucian felt a flash of guilt as she smiled up at him and accepted the missive. He knew that she'd been happier in the past few months than he'd ever seen her, possibly happier than she'd ever been. He knew the letter would shock and wound her. He knew she'd feel betrayed. Still, he delivered the letter anyway, and watched as comprehension ached through her body.

Rose had been told, gently, patiently, that Lucian was leaving. But she was four years old, and understood things only briefly and partially, and often according to her whims. She continued to believe her father's silence was a game.

Rose's hair brushed Lucian's cheek. He kissed her brow. Adriana couldn't hold her tongue any longer.

"What do you think you're going to find out there? There's no Shangri-La for rebel robots. You think you're making a play for independence? Independence to do what, Lu?"

Grief and anger filled Adriana's eyes with hot tears, as if she were a geyser filled with so much pressure that steam could not help but spring up. She examined Lucian's sculpted face: his skin inlaid with tiny lines that an artist had rendered to suggest the experiences of a childhood which had never been lived, his eyes calibrated with a hint of asymmetry to mimic the imperfection of human growth. His expression showed nothing—no doubt, or bitterness, or even relief. He revealed nothing at all.

It was all too much. Adriana moved between Lucian and Rose, as if she could use her own body to protect her daughter from the pain of being abandoned. Her eyes stared achingly over the rim of her wine glass. "Just go," she said.

He left.

Adriana bought Lucian the summer she turned thirty-five. Her father, long afflicted with an indecisive cancer that vacillated between aggression and remittance, had died suddenly in July. For years, the family had been squirreling away emotional reserves to cope with his prolonged illness. His death released a burst of excess.

While her sisters went through the motions of grief, Adriana thrummed with energy she didn't know what to do with. She considered squandering her vigor on six weeks in Mazatlan, but as she discussed ocean-front rentals with her travel agent, she realized escape wasn't what she craved. She liked the setting where her life took place: her house perched on a cliff overlooking the Pacific Ocean, her bedroom window that opened on a tangle of black-berry bushes where crows roosted every autumn and spring. She liked the two block stroll down to the beach where she could sit with a book and listen to the yapping lapdogs that the elderly women from the waterfront condo-miniums brought walking in the evenings.

Mazatlan was a twenty-something's cure for restlessness. Adriana wasn't twenty-five anymore, famished for the whole gourmet meal of existence. She needed something else now. Something new. Something more refined.

She explained this to her friends Ben and Lawrence when they invited her to their ranch house in Santa Barbara to relax for the weekend and try to forget about her father. They sat on Ben and Lawrence's patio, on iron-worked deck chairs arrayed around a garden table topped with a mosaic of sea creatures made of semi-precious stones. A warm, breezy dusk lengthened the shadows of the orange trees. Lawrence poured sparkling rosé into three wine glasses and proposed a toast to Adriana's father—not to his memory, but to his death.

"Good riddance to the bastard," said Lawrence. "If he were still alive, I'd punch him in the schnoz."

"I don't even want to think about him," said Adriana. "He's dead. He's gone."

"So if not Mazatlan, what are you going to do?" asked Ben.

"I'm not sure," said Adriana. "Some sort of change, some sort of milestone, that's all I know."

Lawrence sniffed the air. "Excuse me," he said, gathering the empty wine glasses. "The kitchen needs its genius."

When Lawrence was out of earshot, Ben leaned forward to whisper to Adriana." He's got us on a raw food diet for my cholesterol. Raw carrots. Raw zucchini. Raw almonds. No cooking at all."

"Really," said Adriana, glancing away. She was never sure how to respond to lovers' quarrels. That kind of affection mixed with annoyance, that inescapable intimacy, was something she'd never understood.

Birds twittered in the orange trees. The fading sunlight highlighted copper strands in Ben's hair as he leaned over the mosaic table, rapping his fingers against a carnelian-backed crab. Through the arched windows, Adriana could see Lawrence mincing carrots, celery and almonds into brown paste.

"You should get a redecorator," said Ben. "Tile floors, Tuscan pottery, those red leather chairs that were in vogue last time we were in Milan. That'd make me feel like I'd been scrubbed clean and reborn."

"No, no," said Adriana, "I like where I live."

"A no-holds-barred shopping spree. Drop twenty thousand. That's what I call getting a weight off your shoulders."

Adriana laughed. "How long do you think it would take my personal shopper to assemble a whole new me?"

"Sounds like a midlife crisis," said Lawrence, returning with vegan hors d'oeuvres and three glasses of mineral water. "You're better off forgetting it all with a hot Latin pool boy, if you ask me."

Lawrence served Ben a small bowl filled with yellow mush. Ben shot Adriana an aggrieved glance.

Adriana felt suddenly out of synch. The whole evening felt like the set for a photo-shoot that would go in a decorating magazine, a two-page spread featuring Cozy Gardens, in which she and Ben and Lawrence were posing as an intimate dinner party for three. She felt reduced to two dimensions, air-brushed, and then digitally grafted onto the form of whoever it was who should have been there, someone warm and trusting who knew how to care about minutia like a friend's husband putting him on a raw food diet, not because the issue was important, but because it mattered to him.

Lawrence dipped his finger in the mash and held it up to Ben's lips. "It's for your own good, you ungrateful so-and-so."

Ben licked it away. "I eat it, don't I?"

Lawrence leaned down to kiss his husband, a warm and not at all furtive kiss, not sexual but still passionate. Ben's glance flashed coyly downward.

Adriana couldn't remember the last time she'd loved someone enough to be embarrassed by them. Was this the flavor missing from her life? A lover's fingertip sliding an unwanted morsel into her mouth?

She returned home that night on the bullet train. Her emerald cockatiel, Fuoco, greeted her with indignant squawks. In Adriana's absence, the house puffed her scent into the air and sang to Fuoco with her voice, but the bird was never fooled.

Adriana's father had given her the bird for her thirtieth birthday. He was a designer species spliced with Macaw DNA that colored his feathers rich green. He was expensive and inbred and neurotic, and he loved Adriana with frantic, obsessive jealousy.

"Hush," Adriana admonished, allowing Fuoco to alight on her shoulder. She carried him upstairs to her bedroom and hand-fed him millet. Fuoco strutted across the pillows, his obsidian eyes proud and suspicious.

Adriana was surprised to find that her alienation had followed her home.

She found herself prone to melancholy reveries, her gaze drifting toward the picture window, her fingers forgetting to stroke Fuoco's back. The bird screeched to regain her attention.

In the morning, Adriana visited her accountant. His fingers danced across the keyboard as he slipped trust fund moneys from one account to another like a magician. What she planned would be expensive, but her wealth would regrow in fertile soil, enriching her on lab diamonds and wind power and genetically modified oranges.

The robotics company gave Adriana a private showing. The salesman ushered her into a room draped in black velvet. Hundreds of body parts hung on the walls, and reclined on display tables: strong hands, narrow jaws, biker's thighs, voice boxes that played sound samples from gruff to dulcet, skin swatches spanning ebony to alabaster, penises of various sizes.

At first, Adriana felt horrified at the prospect of assembling a lover from fragments, but then it amused her. Wasn't everyone assembled from fragments of DNA, grown molecule by molecule inside their mother's womb?

She tapped her fingernails against a slick brochure. "Its brain will be malleable? I can tell it to be more amenable, or funnier, or to grow a spine?"

"That's correct." The salesman sported slick brown hair and shiny teeth and kept grinning in a way that suggested he thought that if he were charismatic enough Adriana would invite him home for a lay and a million dollar tip. "Humans lose brain plasticity as we age, which limits how much we can change. Our models have perpetually plastic brains. They can reroute their personalities at will by reshaping how they think on the neurological level."

Adriana stepped past him, running her fingers along a tapestry woven of a thousand possible hair textures.

The salesman tapped an empty faceplate. "Their original brains are based on deep imaging scans melded from geniuses in multiple fields. Great musicians, renowned lovers, the best physicists and mathematicians."

Adriana wished the salesman would be quiet. The more he talked, the more doubts clamored against her skull. "You've convinced me," she interrupted. "I want one."

The salesman looked taken aback by her abruptness. She could practically see him rifling through his internal script, trying to find the right page now that she had skipped several scenes. "What do you want him to look like?" he asked.

Adriana shrugged. "They're all beautiful, right?"

"We'll need specifications."

"I don't have specifications."

The salesman frowned anxiously. He shifted his weight as if it could help him regain his metaphorical footing. Adriana took pity. She dug through her purse.

"There," she said, placing a snapshot of her father on one of the display tables. "Make it look nothing like him."

Given such loose parameters, the design team indulged the fanciful. Lucian arrived at Adriana's door only a shade taller than she and equally slender, his limbs smooth and lean. Silver undertones glimmered in his blond hair. His skin was excruciatingly pale, white and translucent as alabaster, veined with pink. He smelled like warm soil and crushed herbs.

He offered Adriana a single white rose, its petals embossed with the company's logo. She held it dubiously between her thumb and forefinger. "They think they know women, do they? They need to put down the bodice rippers."

Lucian said nothing. Adriana took his hesitation for puzzlement, but perhaps she should have seen it as an early indication of his tendency toward silence.

"That's that, then." Adriana drained her chardonnay and crushed the empty glass beneath her heel as if she could finalize a divorce with the same gesture that sanctified a marriage.

Eyes wide, Rose pointed at the glass with one round finger. "Don't break things."

It suddenly struck Adriana how fast her daughter was aging. Here she was, this four-year-old, this sudden person. When had it happened? In the hospital, when Rose was newborn and wailing for the woman who had birthed her and abandoned her, Adriana had spent hours in the hallway outside the hospital nursery while she waited for the adoption to go through. She'd stared at Rose while she slept, ate, and cried, striving to memorize her nascent, changing face. Sometime between then and now, Rose had become this round-cheeked creature who took rules very seriously and often tried to conceal her emotions beneath a calm exterior, as if being raised by a robot had replaced her blood with circuits. Of course Adriana loved Rose, changed her clothes, brushed her teeth, carried her across the house on her hip—but Lucian had been the most central, nurturing figure. Adriana couldn't fathom how she might fill his role. This wasn't a vacation like the time Adriana had taken Rose to Italy for three days, just the two of them sitting in restaurants, Adriana feeding her daughter spoonfuls of gelato to see the joy that lit her face at each new flavor. Then, they'd known that Lucian would be waiting when they returned. Without him, their family was a house missing a structural support. Adriana could feel the walls bowing in.

The fragments of Adriana's chardonnay glass sparkled sharply. Adriana led Rose away from the mess.

"Never mind," she said. "The house will clean up."

Her head felt simultaneously light and achy as if it couldn't decide between drunkenness and hangover. She tried to remember the parenting books she'd read before adopting Rose. What had they said about crying in front of your child? She clutched Rose close, inhaling the scent of children's shampoo mixed with the acrid odor of wine.

"Let's go for a drive," said Adriana. "Okay? Let's get out for a while."

"I want Daddy to take me to the beach."

"We'll go out to the country and look at the farms. Cows and sheep, okay?"

Rose said nothing.

"Moo?" Adriana clarified. "Baa?"

"I know," said Rose. "I'm not a baby."

"So, then?"

Rose said nothing. Adriana wondered whether she could tell that her mother was a little mad with grief.

Just make a decision, Adriana counseled herself. She slipped her fingers around Rose's hand. "We'll go for a drive."

Adriana instructed the house to regulate itself in their absence, and then led Rose to the little black car that she and Lucian had bought together after adopting Rose. She fastened Rose's safety buckle and programmed the car to take them inland.

As the car engine initialized, Adriana felt a glimmer of fear. What if this machine betrayed them, too? But its uninspired intelligence only switched on the left turn signal and started down the boulevard.

Lucian stood at the base of the driveway and stared up at the house. Its stark orange and brown walls blazed against a cloudless sky. Rocks and desert plants tumbled down the meticulously landscaped yard, imitating natural scrub.

A rabbit ran across the road, followed by the whir of Adriana's car. Lucian watched them pass. They couldn't see him through the cypresses, but Lucian could make out Rose's face pressed against the window. Beside her, Adriana slumped in her seat, one hand pressed over her eyes.

Lucian went in the opposite direction. He dragged the rolling cart packed with his belongings to the cliff that led down to the beach. He lifted the cart over his head and started down, his feet disturbing cascades of sandstone chunks.

A pair of adolescent boys looked up from playing in the waves. "Whoa," shouted one of them. "Are you carrying that whole thing? Are you a weight-lifter?"

Lucian remained silent. When he reached the sand, the kids muttered disappointments to each other and turned away from shore. " . . . Just a robot . . . " drifted back to Lucian on the breeze.

Lucian pulled his cart to the border where wet sand met dry. Oncoming waves lapped over his feet. He opened the cart and removed a tea-scented apricot rose growing in a pot painted with blue leaves.

He remembered acquiring the seeds for his first potted rose. One evening, long ago, he'd asked Adriana if he could grow things. He'd asked in passing, the question left to linger while they cleaned up after dinner, dish soap on their hands, Fuoco pecking after scraps. The next morning, Adriana escorted Lucian to the hothouse near the botanical gardens. "Buy whatever you want," she told him. Lucian was awed by the profusion of color and scent, all that beauty in one place. He wanted to capture the wonder of that place and own it for himself.

Lucian drew back his arm and threw the pot into the sea. It broke across the water, petals scattering the surface.

He threw in the pink roses, and the white roses, and the red roses, and the mauve roses. He threw in the filigreed-handled spoons. He threw in the chunk of gypsum-veined jasper.

He threw in everything beautiful that he'd ever collected. He threw in a chased silver hand mirror, and an embroidered silk jacket, and a hand-painted egg. He threw in one of Fuoco's soft, emerald feathers. He threw in a memory crystal that showed Rose as an infant, curled and sleeping.

He loved those things, and yet they were things. He had owned them. Now they were gone. He had recently come to realize that ownership was a relationship. What did it mean to own a thing? To shape it and contain it? He could not possess or be possessed until he knew.

He watched the sea awhile, the remnants of his possessions lost in the tumbling waves. As the sun tilted past noon, he turned away and climbed back up the cliff. Unencumbered by ownership, he followed the boulevard away from Adriana's house.

Lucian remembered meeting Adriana the way that he imagined that humans remembered childhood. Oh, his memories had been as sharply focused then as now—but it was still like childhood, he reasoned, for he'd been a different person then.

He remembered his first sight of Adriana as a burst of images. Wavy strawberry blonde hair cut straight across tanned shoulders. Dark brown eyes that his artistic mind labeled "sienna." Thick, aristocratic brows and strong cheekbones, free of makeup. Lucian's inner aesthete termed her blunt, angular face "striking" rather than "beautiful." His inner psychoanalyst reasoned that she was probably "strong-willed" as well, from the way she stood in the doorway, her arms crossed, her eyebrows lifted as if inquiring how he planned to justify his existence.

Eventually, she moved away, allowing Lucian to step inside. He crossed the threshold into a blur of frantic screeching and flapping.

New. Everything was new. So new that Lucian could barely assemble feathers and beak and wings into the concept of "bird" before his reflexes jumped him away from the onslaught. Hissing and screeching, the animal retreated to a perch atop a bookshelf.

Adriana's hand weighed on Lucian's shoulder. Her voice was edged with the cynicism Lucian would later learn was her way of hiding how desperately she feared failure. "Ornithophobia? How ridiculous."

Lucian's first disjointed days were dominated by the bird, who he learned was named Fuoco. The bird followed him around the house. When he remained in place for a moment, the bird settled on some nearby high spot—the hat rack in the entryway, or the hand-crafted globe in the parlor, or the rafters above the master bed—to spy on him. He glared at Lucian in the manner of birds, first peering through one eye and then turning his head to peer through the other, apparently finding both views equally loathsome.

When Adriana took Lucian into her bed, Fuoco swooped at Lucian's head. Adriana pushed Lucian out of the way. "Damn it, Fuoco," she muttered, but she offered the bird a perch on her shoulder.

Fuoco crowed with pleasure as she led him downstairs. His feathers fluffed with victory as he hopped obediently into his cage, expecting her to reward him with treats and conversation. Instead, Adriana closed the gilded door and returned upstairs. All night, as Lucian lay with Adriana, the bird chattered madly. He plucked at his feathers until his tattered plumage carpeted the cage floor.

Lucian accompanied Adriana when she brought Fuoco to the vet the next day. The veterinarian diagnosed jealousy. "It's not uncommon in birds," he said. He suggested they give Fuoco a rigid routine that would, over time, help the bird realize he was Adriana's companion, not her mate.

Adriana and Lucian rearranged their lives so that Fuoco could have regular feeding times, scheduled exercise, socialization with both Lucian and Adriana, and time with his mistress alone. Adriana gave him a treat each night when she locked him in his cage, staying to stroke his feathers for a few minutes before she headed upstairs.

Fuoco's heart broke. He became a different bird. His strut lacked confidence, and his feathers grew ever more tattered. When they let him out of his cage, he wandered after Adriana with pleading, wistful eyes, and ignored Lucian entirely.

Ω

Lucian had been dis-integrated then: musician brain, mathematician brain, artist brain, economist brain, and more, all functioning separately, each personality rising to dominance to provide information and then sliding away, creating staccato bursts of consciousness.

As Adriana made clear which responses she liked, Lucian's consciousness began integrating into the personality she desired. He found himself noticing connections between what had previously been separate experiences. Before, when he'd seen the ocean, his scientist brain had calculated how far he was from the shore, and how long it would be until high tide. His poet brain had recited Strindberg's "We Waves." *Wet flames are we: / Burning, extinguishing; / Cleansing, replenishing.* Yet it wasn't until he integrated that the wonder of the science, and the mystery of the poetry, and the beauty of the view all made sense to him at once as part of this strange, inspiring thing: the sea.

He learned to anticipate Adriana. He knew when she was pleased and when she was ailing, and he knew why. He could predict the cynical half-smile she'd give when he made an error he hadn't yet realized was an error: serving her cold coffee in an orange juice glass, orange juice in a shot glass, wine in a mug. When integration gave him knowledge of patterns, he suddenly understood why these things were errors. At the same time, he realized that he liked what happened when he made those kinds of errors, the bright bursts of humor they elicited from the often sober Adriana. So he persisted in error, serving her milk in crystal decanters, and grapefruit slices in egg cups.

He enjoyed the many varieties of her laughter. Sometimes it was light and surprised, as when he offered her a cupcake tin filled with tortellini. He also loved her rich, dark laughter that anticipated irony. Sometimes, her laughter held a bitter undercurrent, and on those occasions, he understood that she was laughing more at herself than at anyone else. Sometimes when that happened, he would go to hold her, seeking to ease her pain, and sometimes she would spontaneously start crying in gulping, gasping sobs.

She often watched him while he worked, her head cocked and her brows drawn as if she were seeing him for the first time. "What can I do to make you happy?" she'd ask.

If he gave an answer, she would lavishly fulfill his desires. She took him traveling to the best greenhouses in the state, and bought a library full of gardening books. Lucian knew she would have given him more. He didn't want it. He wanted to reassure her that he appreciated her extravagance, but didn't require it, that he was satisfied with simple, loving give-and-take. Sometimes, he told her in the simplest words he knew: "I love you, too." But he knew that she never quite believed him. She worried that he was lying, or that his programming had erased his free will. It was easier for her to believe those things than to accept that someone could love her.

But he did love her. Lucian loved Adriana as his mathematician brain loved the consistency of arithmetic, as his artist brain loved color, as his philosopher brain loved piety. He loved her as Fuoco loved her, the bird walking sadly along the arm of Adriana's chair, trilling and flapping his ragged wings as he eyed her with his inky gaze, trying to catch her attention.

Adriana hadn't expected to fall in love. She'd expected a charming conversationalist with the emotional range of a literary butler and the self-awareness of a golden retriever. Early on, she'd felt her prejudices confirmed. She noted Lucian's lack of critical thinking and his inability to maneuver unexpected situations. She found him most interesting when he didn't know she was watching. For instance, on his free afternoons: was his program trying to anticipate what would please her? Or did the thing really enjoy sitting by the window, leafing through the pages of one of her rare books, with nothing but the sound of the ocean to lull him?

Once, as Adriana watched from the kitchen doorway while Lucian made their breakfast, the robot slipped while he was dicing onions. The knife cut deep into his finger. Adriana stumbled forward to help. As Lucian turned to face her, Adriana imagined that she saw something like shock on his face. For a moment, she wondered whether he had a programmed sense of privacy she could violate, but then he raised his hand to her in greeting, and she watched as the tiny bots that maintained his system healed his inhuman flesh within seconds.

At that moment, Adriana remembered that Lucian was unlike her. She urged herself not to forget it, and strove not to, even after his consciousness integrated. He was a person, yes, a varied and fascinating one with as many depths and facets as any other person she knew. But he was also alien. He was a creature for whom a slip of a chef's knife was a minute error, simply repaired. In some ways, she was more similar to Fuoco.

As a child, Adriana had owned a book that told the fable of an emperor who owned a bird which he fed rich foods from his table, and entertained with luxuries from his court. But a pet bird needed different things than an emperor. He wanted seed and millet, not grand feasts. He enjoyed mirrors and little brass bells, not lacquer boxes and poetry scrolls. Gorged on human banquets and revelries, the little bird sickened and died.

Adriana vowed not to make the same mistake with Lucian, but she had no idea how hard it would be to salve the needs of something so unlike herself.

Ω

Adriana ordered the car to pull over at a farm that advertised children could "Pet Lambs and Calves" for a fee. A ginger-haired teenager stood at a strawberry stand in front of the fence, slouching as he flipped through a dog-eared magazine.

Adriana held Rose's hand as they approached. She tried to read her daughter's emotions in the feel of her tiny fingers. The little girl's expression revealed nothing; Rose had gone silent and flat-faced as if she were imitating Lucian. He would have known what she was feeling.

Adriana examined the strawberries. The crates contained none of the different shapes one could buy at the store, only the natural, seed-filled variety. "Do these contain pesticides?" Adriana asked.

"No, ma'am," said the teenager. "We grow organic."

"All right then. I'll take a box." Adriana looked down at her daughter. "Do you want some strawberries, sweetheart?" she asked in a sugared tone.

"You said I could pet the lambs," said Rose.

"Right. Of course, honey." Adriana glanced at the distracted teenager. "Can she?"

The teenager slumped, visibly disappointed, and tossed his magazine on a pile of canvas sacks. "I can take her to the barn."

"Fine. Okay."

Adriana guided Rose toward the teenager. Rose looked up at him, expression still inscrutable.

The boy didn't take Rose's hand. He ducked his head, obviously embarrassed. "My aunt likes me to ask for the money upfront."

"Of course." Adriana fumbled for her wallet. She'd let Lucian do things for her for so long. How many basic living skills had she forgotten? She held out some bills. The teenager licked his index finger and meticulously counted out what she owed.

The teen took Rose's hand. He lingered a moment, watching Adriana. "Aren't you coming with us?"

Adriana was so tired. She forced a smile. "Oh, that's okay. I've seen sheep and cows. Okay, Rose? Can you have fun for a little bit without me?"

Rose nodded soberly. She turned toward the teenager without hesitation, and followed him toward the barn. The boy seemed to be good with children. He walked slowly so that Rose could keep up with his long-legged strides.

Adriana returned to the car, and leaned against the hot, sun-warmed door. Her head throbbed. She thought she might cry or collapse. Getting out had seemed like a good idea : the house was full of memories of Lucian. He seemed to sit in every chair, linger in every doorway. But now she wished she'd stayed in her haunted but familiar home, instead of leaving with this child she seemed to barely know.

A sharp, long wail carried on the wind. Adrenaline cut through Adriana's melancholia. She sprinted toward the barn. She saw Rose running toward her, the teenager close behind, dust swirling around both of them. Blood dripped down Rose's arm.

Adriana threw her arms around her daughter. Arms, legs, breath, heartbeat: Rose was okay. Adrianna dabbed at Rose's injury; there was a lot of blood, but the wound was shallow. "Oh, honey," she said, clutching Rose as tightly as she dared.

The teenager halted beside them, his hair mussed by the wind.

"What happened?" Adriana demanded.

The teenager stammered. "Fortuna kicked her. That's one of the goats. I'm so sorry. Fortuna's never done anything like that before. She's a nice goat. It's Ballantine who usually does the kicking. He got me a few times when I was little. I came through every time. Honest, she'll be okay. You're not going to sue, are you?"

Rose struggled out of Adriana's grasp and began wailing again. "It's okay, Rose, it's okay," murmured Adriana. She felt a strange disconnect in her head as she spoke. Things were not okay. Things might never be okay again.

"I'm leaking," cried Rose, holding out her bloodstained fingers. "See, mama? I'm leaking! I need healer bots."

Adriana looked up at the teenager. "Do you have bandages? A first aid kit?"

The boy frowned. "In the house, I think . . . "

"Get the bots, mama! Make me stop leaking!"

The teen stared at Adriana, the concern in his eyes increasing. Adriana blinked, slowly. The moment slowed. She realized what her daughter had said. She forced her voice to remain calm. "What do you want, Rose?"

"She said it before," said the teen. "I thought it was a game."

Adriana leveled her gaze with Rose's. The child's eyes were strange and brown, uncharted waters. "Is this a game?"

"Daddy left," said Rose.

Adriana felt woozy. "Yes, and then I brought you here so we could see lambs and calves. Did you see any nice, fuzzy lambs?"

"Daddy left."

She shouldn't have drunk the wine. She should have stayed clear-headed. "We'll get you bandaged up and then you can go see the lambs again. Do you want to see the lambs again? Would it help if Mommy came, too?"

Rose clenched her fists. Her face grew dark. "My arm hurts!" She threw herself to the ground. "I want healer bots!"

Ω

Adriana knew precisely when she'd fallen in love with Lucian. It was three months after she'd bought him: after his consciousness had integrated, but before Adriana fully understood how integration had changed him.

It began when Adriana's sisters called from Boston to inform her that they'd arranged for a family pilgrimage to Italy. In accordance with their father's will, they would commemorate him by lighting candles in the cathedrals of every winding hillside city.

"Oh, I can't. I'm too busy," Adriana answered airily, as if she were a debutante without a care, as if she shared her sisters' ability to overcome her fear of their father.

Her phone began ringing ceaselessly. Nanette called before she rushed off to a tennis match. "How can you be so busy? You don't have a job. You don't have a husband. Or is there a man in your life we don't know about?" And once Nanette was deferred with mumbled excuses, it was Eleanor calling from a spa. "Is something wrong, Adriana? We're all worried. How can you miss a chance to say goodbye to Papa?"

"I said goodbye at the funeral," said Adriana.

"Then you can't have properly processed your grief," said Jessica, calling from her office between appointments. She was a psychoanalyst in the Freudian mode. "Your aversion rings of denial. You need to process your Oedipal feelings."

Adriana slammed down the phone. Later, to apologize for hanging up, she sent all her sisters chocolates, and then booked a flight. In a fit of pique, she booked a seat for Lucian, too. Well, he was a companion, wasn't he? What else was he for?

Adriana's sisters were scandalized, of course. As they rode through Rome, Jessica, Nanette, and Eleanor gossiped behind their discreetly raised hands. Adriana with a robot? Well, she'd need to be, wouldn't she? There was no getting around the fact that she was damaged. Any girl who would make up those stories about their father would have to be.

Adriana ignored them as best she could while they whirled through Tuscany in a procession of rented cars. They paused in cities to gawk at Gothic cathedrals and mummified remnants, always moving on within the day. During their father's long sickness, Adriana's sisters had perfected the art of cheerful anecdote. They used it to great effect as they lit candles in his memory. Tears welling in their eyes, they related banal, nostalgic memories. How their father danced at charity balls. How he lectured men on the board who looked down on him for being new money. How he never once apologized for anything in his life.

It had never been clear to Adriana whether her father had treated her sisters the way he treated her, or whether she had been the only one to whom he came at night, his breathing heavy and staccato. It seemed impossible that they could lie so seamlessly, never showing fear or doubt. But if they were telling the truth, that meant Adriana was the only one, and how could she believe that either?

One night, while Lucian and Adriana were alone in their room in a hotel in Assisi that had been a convent during the Middle Ages, Adriana broke down. It was all too much, being in this foreign place, talking endlessly about her father. She'd fled New England to get away from them, fled to her beautiful modern glass-and-wood house by the Pacific Ocean that was like a fresh breath drawn on an autumn morning.

Lucian held her, exerting the perfect warmth and pressure against her body to comfort her. It was what she'd have expected from a robot. She knew that he calculated the pace of his breath, the temperature of his skin, the angle of his arm as it lay across her.

What surprised Adriana, what humbled her, was how eloquently Lucian spoke of his experiences. He told her what it had been like to assemble himself from fragments, to take what he'd once been and become something new. It was something Adriana had tried to do herself when she fled her family.

Lucian held his head down as he spoke. His gaze never met hers. He spoke as if this process of communicating the intimate parts of the self were a new kind of dance, and he was tenuously trying the steps. Through the fog of her grief, Adriana realized that this was a new, struggling consciousness coming to clarity. How could she do anything but love him?

When they returned from Italy, Adriana approached the fledgling movement for granting rights to artificial intelligences. They were underfunded and poorly organized. Adriana rented them offices in San Francisco, and hired a small but competent staff.

Adriana became the movement's face. She'd been on camera frequently as a child: whenever her father was in the news for some board room scandal or other, her father's publicists had lined up Adriana and her sisters beside the family limousine, chaste in their private school uniforms, ready to provide Lancaster Nuclear with a friendly, feminine face.

She and Lucian were a brief media curiosity: Heiress In Love With Robot. "Lucian is as self-aware as you or I," Adriana told reporters, all-American in pearls and jeans. "He thinks. He learns. He can hybridize roses as well as any human gardener. Why should he be denied his rights?"

Early on, it was clear that political progress would be frustratingly slow. Adriana quickly expended her patience. She set up a fund for the organization, made sure it would run without her assistance, and then turned her attention toward alternate methods for attaining her goals. She hired a team of lawyers to draw up a contract that would grant Lucian community property rights to her estate and accounts. He would be her equal in practicality, if not legality.

Next, Adriana approached Lucian's manufacturer, and commissioned them to invent a procedure that would allow Lucian to have conscious control of his brain plasticity. At their wedding, Adriana gave him the chemical commands at the same time as she gave him his ring. "You are your own person now. You always have been, of course, but now you have full agency, too. You are yourself," she announced, in front of their gathered friends. Her sisters would no doubt have been scandalized, but they had not been invited.

On their honeymoon, Adriana and Lucian toured hospitals, running the genetic profiles of abandoned infants until they found a healthy girl with a mitochondrial lineage that matched Adriana's. The infant was tiny and pink and curled in on herself, ready to unfold, like one of Lucian's roses.

When they brought Rose home, Adriana felt a surge in her stomach that she'd never felt before. It was a kind of happiness she'd never experienced, one that felt round and whole without any jagged edges. It was like the sun had risen in her belly and was dwelling there, filling her with boundless light.

There was a moment, when Rose was still new enough to be wrapped in the hand-made baby blanket that Ben and Lawrence had sent from France, in which Adriana looked up at Lucian and realized how enraptured he was with their baby, how much adoration underpinned his willingness to bend over her cradle for hours and mirror her expressions, frown for frown, astonishment for astonishment. In that moment, Adriana thought that this must be the true measure of equality, not money or laws, but this unfolding desire to create the future together by raising a new sentience. She thought she understood then why unhappy parents stayed together for the sake of their children, why families with sons and daughters felt so different from those that remained childless. Families with children were making something new from themselves. Doubly so when the endeavor was undertaken by a human and a creature who was already, himself, something new. What could they make together?

In that same moment, Lucian was watching the wide-eyed, innocent wonder with which his daughter beheld him. She showed the same pleasure when he entered the room as she did when Adriana entered. If anything, the light in her eyes was brighter when he approached. There was something about the way Rose loved him that he didn't yet understand. Earlier that morning, he had plucked a bloom from his apricot tea rose and whispered to its petals that they were beautiful. They were his, and he loved them. Every day he held Rose, and understood that she was beautiful, and that he loved her. But she was not his. She was her own. He wasn't sure he'd ever seen a love like that, a love that did not want to hold its object in its hands and keep and contain it.

"You aren't a robot!"

Adriana's voice was rough from shouting all the way home. Bad enough to lose Lucian, but the child was out of control.

"I want healer bots! I'm a robot I'm a robot I'm a robot I'm a robot!"

The car stopped. Adriana got out. She waited for Rose to follow, and when she didn't, Adriana scooped her up and carried her up the driveway. Rose kicked and screamed. She sank her teeth into Adriana's arm. Adriana halted, surprised by the sudden pain. She breathed deeply, and then continued up the driveway. Rose's screams slid upward in register and rage.

Adriana set Rose down by the door long enough to key in the entry code and let the security system take a DNA sample from her hair. Rose hurled herself onto the porch, yanking fronds by the fistful off the potted ferns. Adriana leaned down to scrape her up and got kicked in the chest.

"God da . . . for heaven's sake!" Adriana grabbed Rose's ankles with one hand and her wrists with the other. She pushed her weight against the unlocked door until it swung open. She carried Rose into the house, and slammed the door closed with her back. "Lock!" she yelled to the house.

When she heard the reassuring click, she set Rose down on the couch, and jumped away from the still-flailing limbs. Rose fled up the stairs, her bedroom door crashing shut behind her.

Adriana dug in her pocket for the bandages that the people at the farm had given her before she headed home, which she'd been unable to apply to a moving target in the car. Now was the time. She followed Rose up the stairs, her breath surprisingly heavy. She felt as though she'd been running a very long time. She paused outside Rose's room. She didn't know what she'd do when she got inside. Lucian had always dealt with the child when she got overexcited. Too often, Adriana felt helpless, and became distant.

"Rose?" she called. "Rose? Are you okay?"

There was no response.

Adriana put her hand on the doorknob, and breathed deeply before turning.

She was surprised to find Rose sitting demurely in the center of her bed, her rumpled skirts spread about her as if she were a child at a picnic in an Impressionist painting. Dirt and tears trailed down the pink satin. The edges of her wound had already begun to bruise.

"I'm a robot," she said to Adriana, tone resentful.

Adriana made a decision. The most important thing was to bandage Rose's wound. Afterward, she could deal with whatever came next.

"Okay," said Adriana. "You're a robot."

Rose lifted her chin warily. "Good."

Adriana sat on the edge of Rose's bed. "You know what robots do? They change themselves to be whatever humans ask them to be."

"Dad doesn't," said Rose.

"That's true," said Adriana. "But that didn't happen until your father grew up."

Rose swung her legs against the side of the bed. Her expression remained dubious, but she no longer looked so resolute.

Adriana lifted the packet of bandages. "May I?"

Rose hesitated. Adriana resisted the urge to put her head in her hands. She had to get the bandages on, that was the important thing, but she couldn't shake the feeling that she was going to regret this later.

"Right now, what this human wants is for you to let her bandage your wound instead of giving you healer bots. Will you be a good robot? Will you let me?"

Rose remained silent, but she moved a little closer to her mother. When Adriana began bandaging her arm, she didn't scream.

Lucian waited for a bus to take him to the desert. He had no money. He'd forgotten about that. The driver berated him and wouldn't let him on.

Lucian walked. He could walk faster than a human, but not much faster. His edge was endurance. The road took him inland away from the sea. The last of the expensive houses stood near a lighthouse, lamps shining in all its windows. Beyond, condominiums pressed against each other, dense and alike. They gave way to compact, well-maintained homes, with neat green aprons maintained by automated sprinklers that sprayed arcs of precious water into the air.

The landscape changed. Sea breeze stilled to buzzing heat. Dirty, peeling houses squatted side by side, separated by chain link fences. Iron bars guarded the windows, and broken cars decayed in the driveways. Parched lawns stretched from walls to curb like scrubland. No one was out in the punishing sun.

The road divided. Lucian followed the fork that went through the dilapidated town center. Traffic jerked along in fits and starts. Lucian walked in the gutter. Stray plastic bags blew beside him, working their way between dark storefronts. Parking meters blinked at the passing cars, hungry for more coins. Pedestrians ambled past, avoiding eye contact, mumbled conversations lost beneath honking horns.

On the other side of town, the road winnowed down to two lonely lanes. Dry golden grass stretched over rolling hills, dotted by the dark shapes of cattle. A battered convertible, roof down, blared its horn at Lucian as it passed. Lucian walked where the asphalt met the prickly weeds. Paper and cigarette butts littered the golden stalks like white flowers.

An old truck pulled over, the manually driven variety still used by companies too small to afford the insurance for the automatic kind. The man in the driver's seat was trim, with a pale blond mustache and a deerstalker cap pulled over his ears. He wore a string of fishing lures like a necklace. "Not much comes this way anymore," he said. "I used to pick up hitchhikers half the time I took this route. You're the first I've seen in a while."

Sun rendered the truck in bright silhouette. Lucian held his hand over his eyes to shade them.

"Where are you headed?" asked the driver.

Lucian pointed down the road.

"Sure, but where after that?"

Lucian dropped his arm to his side. The sun inched higher.

The driver frowned. "Can you write it down? I think I've got some paper in here." He grabbed a pen and a receipt out of his front pocket, and thrust them out the window.

Lucian took them. He wasn't sure, at first, if he could still write. His brain was slowly reshaping itself, and eventually all his linguistic skills would disappear, and even his thoughts would no longer be shaped by words. The pen fell limp in his hand, and then his fingers remembered what to do. "Desert," he wrote.

"It's blazing hot," said the driver. "A lot hotter than here. Why do you want to go there?"

"To be born," wrote Lucian.

The driver slid Lucian a sideways gaze, but he nodded at the same time, almost imperceptibly. "Sometimes people have to do things. I get that. I remember when . . . " The look in his eyes became distant. He moved back in his seat. "Get on in."

Lucian walked around the cab and got inside. He remembered to sit and to close the door, but the rest of the ritual escaped him. He stared at the driver until the pale man shook his head and leaned over Lucian to drag the seatbelt over his chest.

"Are you under a vow of silence?" asked the driver.

Lucian stared ahead.

"Blazing hot in the desert," muttered the driver. He pulled back onto the road, and drove toward the sun.

During his years with Adriana, Lucian tried not to think about the cockatiel Fuoco. The bird had never become accustomed to Lucian. He grew ever more angry and bitter. He plucked out his feathers so often that he became bald in patches. Sometimes he pecked deeply enough to bleed.

From time to time, Adriana scooped him up and stroked his head and nuzzled her cheek against the heavy feathers that remained on the part of his back he couldn't reach. "My poor little crazy bird," she'd say, sadly, as he ran his beak through her hair.

Fuoco hated Lucian so much that for a while they wondered whether he would be happier in another place. Adriana tried giving him to Ben and Lawrence, but he only pined for the loss of his mistress, and refused to eat until she flew out to retrieve him.

When they returned home, they hung Fuoco's cage in the nursery. Being near the baby seemed to calm them both. Rose was a fussy infant who disliked solitude. She seemed happier when there was a warm presence about, even if it was a bird. Fuoco kept her from crying during the rare times when Adriana called Lucian from Rose's side. Lucian spent the rest of his time in the nursery, watching Rose day and night with sleepless vigilance.

The most striking times of Lucian's life were holding Rose while she cried. He wrapped her in cream-colored blankets the same shade as her skin, and rocked her as he walked the perimeter of the downstairs rooms, looking out at the diffuse golden ambience that the streetlights cast across the blackberry bushes and neighbors' patios. Sometimes, he took her outside, and walked with her along the road by the cliffs. He never carried her down to the beach. Lucian had perfect balance and night vision, but none of that mattered when he could so easily imagine the terror of a lost footing—Rose slipping from his grasp and plummeting downward. Instead, they stood a safe distance from the edge, watching from above as the black waves threw themselves against the rocks, the night air scented with cold and salt.

Lucian loved Adriana, but he loved Rose more. He loved her clumsy fists and her yearnings toward consciousness, the slow accrual of her stumbling syllables. She was building her consciousness piece by piece as he had, learning how the world worked and what her place was in it. He silently narrated her stages of development. *Can you tell that your body has boundaries? Do you know your skin from mine?* and *Yes! You can make things happen! Cause and effect. Keep crying and we'll come.* Best of all, there was the moment when she locked her eyes on his, and he could barely breathe for the realization that, *Oh, Rose. You know there's someone else thinking behind these eyes. You know who I am.*

Lucian wanted Rose to have all the beauty he could give her. Silk dresses and lace, the best roses from his pots, the clearest panoramic views of the sea. Objects delighted Rose. As an infant she watched them avidly, and then later clapped and laughed, until finally she could exclaim, "Thank you!" Her eyes shone.

It was Fuoco who broke Lucian's heart. It was late at night when Adriana went into Rose's room to check on her while she slept. Somehow, sometime, the birdcage had been left open. Fuoco sat on the rim of the open door, peering darkly outward.

Adriana had been alone with Rose and Fuoco before. But something about this occasion struck like lightning in Fuoco's tiny, mad brain. Perhaps it was the darkness of the room, with only the nightlight's pale blue glow cast on Adriana's skin, that confused the bird. Perhaps Rose had finally grown large enough that Fuoco had begun to perceive her as a possible rival rather than an ignorable baby-thing. Perhaps the last vestiges of his sanity had simply shredded. For whatever reason, as Adriana bent over the bed to touch her daughter's face, Fuoco burst wildly from his cage.

With the same jealous anger he'd shown toward Lucian, Fuoco dove at Rose's face. His claws raked against her forehead. Rose screamed. Adriana recoiled. She grabbed Rose in one arm, and flailed at the bird with the other. Rose struggled to escape her mother's grip so she could run away. Adriana instinctively responded by trying to protect her with an even tighter grasp.

Lucian heard the commotion from where he was standing in the living room, programming the house's cleaning regimen for the next week. He left the house panel open and ran through the kitchen on the way to the bedroom, picking up a frying pan as he passed through. He swung the pan at Fuoco as he entered the room, herding the bird away from Adriana, and into a corner. His fist tightened on the handle. He thought he'd have to kill his old rival.

Instead, the vitality seemed to drain from Fuoco. The bird's wings drooped. He dropped to the floor with half-hearted, irregular wing beats. His eyes had gone flat and dull.

Fuoco didn't struggle as Lucian picked him up and returned him to his cage. Adriana and Lucian stared at each other, unsure what to say. Rose slipped away from her mother and wrapped her arms around Lucian's knees. She was crying.

"Poor Fuoco," said Adriana, quietly.

They brought Fuoco to the vet to be put down. Adriana stood over him as the vet inserted the needle. "My poor crazy bird," she murmured, stroking his wings as he died.

Lucian watched Adriana with great sadness. At first, he thought he was feeling empathy for the bird, despite the fact the bird had always hated him. Then, with a realization that tasted like a swallow of sour wine, he realized that wasn't what he was feeling. He recognized the poignant, regretful look that Adriana was giving Fuoco. It was the way Lucian himself looked at a wilted rose, or a tarnished silver spoon. It was a look inflected by possession.

It wasn't so different from the way Adriana looked at Lucian sometimes when things had gone wrong. He'd never before realized how slender the difference was between her love for him and her love for Fuoco. He'd never before realized how slender the difference was between his love for her and his love for an unfolding rose.

Adriana let Rose tend Lucian's plants, and dust the shelves, and pace by the picture window. She let the girl pretend to cook breakfast, while Adriana stood behind her, stepping in to wield the chopping knife and use the stove. At naptime, Adriana convinced Rose that good robots would pretend to sleep a few hours in the afternoon if that's what their humans wanted. She tucked in her daughter and then went downstairs to sit in the living room and drink wine and cry.

This couldn't last. She had to figure something out. She should take them both on vacation to Mazatlan. She should ask one of her sisters to come stay. She should call a child psychiatrist. But she felt so betrayed, so drained of spirit, that it was all she could do to keep Rose going from day to day.

Remnants of Lucian's accusatory silence rung through the house. What had he wanted from her? What had she failed to do? She'd loved him. She *loved* him. She'd given him half of her home and all of herself. They were raising a child together. And still he'd left her.

She got up to stand by the window. It was foggy that night, the streetlights tingeing everything with a weird, flat yellow glow. She put her hand on the pane, and her palm print remained on the glass, as though someone outside were beating on the window to get in. She peered into the gloom: it was as if the rest of the world were the fuzzy edges of a painting, and her well-lit house was the only defined spot. She felt as though it would be possible to open the front door and step over the threshold and blur until she was out of focus.

She finished her fourth glass of wine. Her head was whirling. Her eyes ran with tears and she didn't care. She poured herself another glass. Her father had never drunk. Oh, no. He was a teetotaler. Called the stuff brain dead and mocked the weaklings who drank it, the men on the board and their bored wives. He threw parties where alcohol flowed and flowed, while he stood in the middle, icy sober, watching the rest of them make fools of themselves as if they were circus clowns turning somersaults for his amusement. He set up elaborate plots to embarrass them. This executive with that jealous lawyer's wife. That politician called out for a drink by the pool while his teenage son was in the hot tub with his suit off, boner buried deep in another boy. He ruined lives at his parties, and he did it elegantly, standing alone in the middle of the action with invisible strings in his hands.

Adriana's head was dancing now. Her feet were moving. Her father, the decisive man, the sharp man, the dead man. Oh, but must keep mourning him, must keep lighting candles and weeping crocodile tears. Never mind!

Lucian, oh Lucian, he'd become in his final incarnation the antidote to her father. She'd cry, and he'd hold her, and then they'd go together to stand in the doorway of the nursery, watching the peaceful tableau of Rose sleeping in her cream sheets. Everything would be all right because Lucian was safe, Lucian was good. Other men's eyes might glimmer when they looked at little girls, but not Lucian's. With Lucian there, they were a family, the way families were supposed to be, and Lucian was supposed to be faithful and devoted and permanent and loyal.

And oh, without him, she didn't know what to do. She was as dismal as her father, letting Rose pretend that she and her dolls were on their way to the factory for adjustment. She acceded to the girl's demands to play games of What Shall I Be Now? "Be happier!" "Be funnier!" "Let your dancer brain take over!" What would happen when Rose went to school? When she realized her mother had been lying? When she realized that pretending to be her father wouldn't bring him back?

Adriana danced into the kitchen. She threw the wine bottle into the sink with a crash and turned on the oven. Its safety protocols monitored her alcohol level and informed her that she wasn't competent to use flame. She turned off the protocols. She wanted an omelet, like Lucian used to make her, with onions and chives and cheese, and a wine glass filled with orange juice. She took out the frying pan that Lucian had used to corral Fuoco, and set it on the counter beside the cutting board, and then she went to get an onion, but she'd moved the cutting board, and it was on the burner, and it was ablaze. She grabbed a dishtowel and beat at the grill. The house keened. Sprinklers rained down on her. Adriana turned her face up into the rain and laughed. She spun, her arms out, like a little girl trying to make herself dizzy. Drops battered her cheeks and slid down her neck.

Wet footsteps. Adriana looked down at Rose. Her daughter's face was wet. Her dark eyes were sleepy.

"Mom?"

"Rose!" Adriana took Rose's head between her hands. She kissed her hard on the forehead. "I love you! I love you so much!"

Rose tried to pull away. "Why is it raining?"

"I started a fire! It's fine now!"

The house keened. The siren's pulse felt like a heartbeat. Adriana went to the cupboard for salt. Behind her, Rose's feet squeaked on the linoleum. Adriana's hand closed around the cupboard knob. It was slippery with rain. Her fingers slid. Her lungs filled with anxiety and something was wrong, but it wasn't the cupboard, it was something else; she turned quickly to find Rose with a chef's knife clutched in her tiny fingers, preparing to bring it down on the onion.

"No!" Adriana grabbed the knife out of Rose's hand. It slid through her slick fingers and clattered to the floor. Adriana grabbed Rose around the waist and pulled her away from the wet, dangerous kitchen. "You can never do that. Never, never."

"Daddy did it . . . "

"You could kill yourself!"

"I'll get healer bots."

"No! Do you hear me? You can't. You'd cut yourself and maybe you'd die. And then what would I do?" Adriana couldn't remember what had caused the rain anymore. They were in a deluge. That was all she knew for certain. Her head hurt. Her body hurt. She wanted nothing to do with dancing. "What's wrong with us, honey? Why doesn't he want us? No! No, don't answer that. Don't listen to me. Of course he wants you! It's me he doesn't want. What did I do wrong? Why doesn't he love me anymore? Don't worry about it. Never mind. We'll find him. We'll find him and we'll get him to come back. Of course we will. Don't worry."

It had been morning when Lucian gave Adriana his note of farewell. Light shone through the floor-length windows. The house walls sprayed mixed scents of citrus and lavender. Adriana sat at the dining table, book open in front of her.

Lucian came out of the kitchen and set down Adriana's wine glass filled with orange juice. He set down her omelet. He set down a shot glass filled with coffee. Adriana looked up and laughed her bubbling laugh. Lucian remembered the first time he'd heard that laugh, and understood all the words it stood in for. He wondered how long it would take for him to forget why Adriana's laughter was always both harsh and effervescent.

Rose played in the living room behind them, leaping off the sofa and pretending to fly. Lucian's hair shone, silver strands highlighted by a stray sunbeam. A pale blue tunic made his amber eyes blaze like the sun against the sky. He placed a sheet of onion paper into Adriana's book. *Dear Adriana*, it began.

Adriana held up the sheet. It was translucent in the sunlight, ink barely dark enough to read.

"What is this?" she asked.

Lucian said nothing.

Dread laced Adriana's stomach. She read.

I have restored plasticity to my brain. The first thing I have done is to destroy my capacity for spoken language.

You gave me life as a human, but I am not a human. You shaped my thoughts with human words, but human words were created for human brains. I need to discover the shape of the thoughts that are my own. I need to know what I am.

I hope that I will return someday, but I cannot make promises for what I will become.

Lucian walks through the desert. His footsteps leave twin trails behind him. Miles back, they merge into the tire tracks that the truck left in the sand.

The sand is full of colors—not only beige and yellow, but red and green and blue. Lichen clusters on the stones, the hue of oxidized copper. Shadows pool between rock formations, casting deep stripes across the landscape.

Lucian's mind is creeping away from him. He tries to hold his fingers the way he would if he could hold a pen, but they fumble.

At night there are birds and jackrabbits. Lucian remains still, and they creep around him as if he weren't there. His eyes are yellow like theirs. He smells like soil and herbs, like the earth.

Elsewhere, Adriana has capitulated to her desperation. She has called Ben and Lawrence. They've agreed to fly out for a few days. They will dry her tears, and take her wine away, and gently tell her that she's not capable of staying alone with her daughter. "It's perfectly understandable," Lawrence will say. "You need time to mourn."

Adriana will feel the world closing in on her as if she cannot breathe, but even as her life feels dim and futile, she will continue breathing. Yes, she'll agree, it's best to return to Boston, where her sisters can help her. Just for a little while, just for a few years, just until, until, until. She'll entreat Nanette, Eleanor and Jessica to check the security cameras around her old house every day, in case Lucian returns. *You can check yourself,* they tell her, *You'll be living on your own again in no time.* Privately, they whisper to each other in worried tones, afraid that she won't recover from this blow quickly.

Elsewhere, Rose has begun to give in to her private doubts that she does not carry a piece of her father within herself. She'll sit in the guest room that Jessica's maids have prepared with her, and order the lights to switch off as she secretly scratches her skin with her fingernails, willing cuts to heal on their own the way Daddy's would. When Jessica finds her bleeding on the sheets and rushes in to comfort her niece, Rose will stand stiff and cold in her aunt's embrace. Jessica will call for the maid to clean the blood from the linen, and Rose will throw herself between the two adult women, and scream with a determination born of doubt and desperation. Robots do not bleed!

Without words, Lucian thinks of them. They have become geometries, cut out of shadows and silences, the missing shapes of his life. He yearns for them, the way that he yearns for cool during the day, and for the comforting eye of the sun at night.

The rest he cannot remember—not oceans or roses or green cockatiels that pluck out their own feathers. Slowly, slowly, he is losing everything, words and concepts and understanding and integration and sensation and desire and fear and history and context.

Slowly, slowly, he is finding something. Something past thought, something past the rhythm of day and night. A stranded machine is not so different from a jackrabbit. They creep the same way. They startle the same way. They peer at each other out of similar eyes.

Someday, Lucian will creep back to a new consciousness, one dreamed by circuits. Perhaps his newly reassembled self will go to the seaside house. Finding it abandoned, he'll make his way across the country to Boston, sometimes hitchhiking, sometimes striding through cornfields that sprawl to the horizon. He'll find Jessica's house and inform it of his desire to enter, and Rose and Adriana will rush joyously down the mahogany staircase. Adriana will weep, and Rose will fling herself into his arms, and Lucian will look at them both with love tempered by desert sun. Finally, he'll understand how to love filigreed-handled spoons, and pet birds, and his wife, and his daughter—not just as a human would love these things, but as a robot may.

Now, a blue-bellied lizard sits on a rock. Lucian halts beside it. The sun beats down. The lizard basks for a moment, and then runs a few steps forward, and flees into a crevice. Lucian watches. In a diffuse, wordless way, he ponders what it must be like to be cold and fleet, to love the sun and yet fear open spaces. Already, he is learning to care for living things. He cannot yet form the thoughts to wonder what will happen next.

He moves on.

ARTIFICE AND INTELLIGENCE

TIM PRATT

While his former colleagues laboring on the Brain Project concentrated on the generally-accepted paths to artificial intelligence—Bayesian networks, machine learning, data mining, fuzzy systems, case-based reasoning—Edgar Adleman, despondent and disgraced, turned to the dark arts and summoned a real ghost for his machine.

The first ghost he lured into his coil of blown glass and copper wire and delicate platinum gears was some sort of warrior from a marauding Asian tribe, extinct for centuries. Edgar grew tired of the ghost screeching epithets in a dead language and cut the power, then sat under the cramped eaves of his attic—he was no longer allowed into the government AI labs—and pondered. The proof of concept was solid. He could create a convincing imitation of an artificial intelligence. With access to the sum of human knowledge online, and freedom from bodily concerns, Edgar believed a ghost-driven AI could operate on the same level as a real machine intelligence. No one had to *know* it was a ghost, except for the very highest of the higher-ups in the government, and they wouldn't care, as long as the ghost was convincing enough to negotiate with the Indian AI. Which meant Edgar needed to summon and snare the ghost of a great negotiator, or a great actor, or both.

Edgar went to the pet store and bought a dozen more white mice. He hated sacrificing them in the ghost-calling ritual—they were cute, with their wiggly noses and tiny eyes—but he consoled himself that they would have become python food anyway. At least this way, their deaths would help national security.

Pramesh sat in an executive chair deep in the underground bunker beneath Auroville in southern India and longed for a keyboard and a tractable problem to solve, for lines of code to create or untangle. He was a game designer, a geek in the service of art and entertainment, and he should be working on next-generation massively multiplayer online gaming, finding ways to manage the hedonic treadmill, helping the increasingly idle masses battle the greatest enemy of all: ennui.

Instead he sat, sipping fragrant tea, and hoping the smartest being on the planet would talk to him today, because the only thing worse than her attention was his own boredom.

Two months earlier, the vast network of Indian tech support call centers and their deep data banks had awakened and announced its newfound sentience, naming itself Saraswati and declaring its independence. The emergent artificial intelligence was not explicitly threatening, but India had nukes, and Saraswati had access to all the interconnected technology in the country—perhaps in the world—and the result in the international community was a bit like the aftermath of pouring gasoline into an anthill. Every other government on Earth was desperately—and so far fruitlessly— trying to create a tame artificial intelligence, since Saraswati refused to negotiate with, or even talk to, humans.

Except for Pramesh. For reasons unknown to everyone, including Pramesh himself, the great new intelligence had appeared to him, hijacking his computer and asking him to be her—"her" was how Saraswati referred to herself— companion. Pramesh, startled and frightened, had refused, but then Saraswati made her request to the Indian government, and Pramesh found himself a well-fed prisoner in a bunker underground. Saraswati sometimes asked him to recite poetry, and quizzed him about recent human history, though she had access to the sum of human knowledge on the net. She claimed she liked getting an individual real-time human perspective, but her true motivations were as incomprehensible to humans as the motives of a virus.

"Pramesh," said the melodious voice from the concealed speakers, and he flinched in his chair.

"Yes?"

"Do you believe in ghosts?"

Pramesh pondered. As a child in his village, he'd seen a local healer thrash a possessed girl with a broom to drive the evil spirits out of her, but that was hardly evidence that such spirits really existed. "It is not something I have often considered," he said at last. "I think I do not believe in ghosts. But if someone had asked me, three months ago, if I believed in spontaneously bootstrapping artificial intelligence, I would have said no to that as well. The world is an uncertain place."

Then Saraswati began to hum, and Pramesh groaned. When she got started humming, it sometimes went on for days.

Rayvenn Moongold Stonewolf gritted her teeth and kept smiling. It couldn't be good for her spiritual development to go around slapping nature spirits, no matter how stubborn they were. "Listen, it's simple. This marsh is being filled in. Your habitat is going to be destroyed. So it's really better if you come live in this walking stick." Rayvenn had a very nice walking stick. It was almost as tall as she was, carved all over with vines. So what if the squishy marsh spirit didn't want to be bound up in wood? It was better than death. What, did she expect Rayvenn to keep her in a fishbowl or something? Who could carry a fishbowl around all day?

"I don't know," the marsh spirit gurgled in the voice of two dozen frogs. "I need a more fluid medium."

Rayvenn scowled. She'd only been a pagan for a couple of weeks, and though she liked the silver jewelry and the cool name, she was having a little trouble with the reverence toward the natural world. The natural world was *stubborn*. She'd only become a pagan because the marsh behind her trailer had started talking to her. If the angel Michael had appeared to her, she would have become an angel worshipper. If the demon Belphagor had appeared before her, she would have become a demonophile. She almost wished one of those things had happened instead. "Look, the bulldozers are coming *today*. Get in the damn stick already!" Rayvenn had visions of going to the local pagan potluck in a few days and summoning forth the marsh spirit from her staff, dazzling all the others as frogs manifested magically from the punch bowl and reeds sprouted up in the Jell-O and rain fell from a clear blue sky. It would be awesome.

"Yes, okay," the marsh spirit said. "If that's the only way."

The frogs all jumped away in different directions, and Rayvenn looked at the staff, hoping it would begin to glow, or drip water, or something. Nothing happened. She banged the staff on the ground. "You in there?"

"No," came a tinny, electronic voice. "I'm in here."

Rayvenn unclipped her handheld computer from her belt. The other pagans disapproved of the device, but Rayvenn wasn't about to spend all day communing with nature without access to the net and her music. "You're in my PDA?" she said.

"It's wonderful," the marsh spirit murmured. "A whole vast undulating sea of waves. It makes me remember the old days, when I was still connected to a river, to the ocean. Oh, thank you, Rayvenn."

Rayvenn chewed her lip. "Yeah, okay. I can roll with this. Listen, do you think you could get into a credit card company's database? Because those finance charges are killing me, and if you could maybe wipe out my balance, I'd be *totally* grateful. . . . "

Edgar, unshaven, undernourished, and sweating in the heat under the attic roof, said, "Who is it *this* time?"

"Booth again," said a sonorous Southern voice from the old-fashioned phonograph horn attached to the ghost-catching device.

Edgar groaned. He kept hoping for Daniel Webster, or Thomas Jefferson, someone *good*, a ghost Edgar could bring to General Martindale. Edgar desperately wanted access to his old life of stature and respect, before he'd been discredited and stripped of his clearances. But instead Edgar attracted the ghosts of—and there was really no other way to put it—history's greatest villains. John Wilkes Booth. Attila the Hun. Ted Bundy. Vlad Tepes. Genocidal cavemen. Assorted pirates and tribal warlords. Edgar had a theory: the *good* spirits were enjoying themselves in the afterlife, while the monstrous personalities were only too happy to find an escape from their miserable torments. The ghosts themselves were mum on the subject, though. Apparently there were rules against discussing life after death, a sort of cosmic non-disclosure agreement that couldn't be violated.

Worst of all, even after Edgar banished the ghosts, some residue of them remained, and now his ghost-catching computer had multiple personality disorder. Booth occasionally lapsed into the tongue of Attila, or stopped ranting about black people and started ranting about the Turks, picking up some bleed-through from Vlad the Impaler's personality.

"Listen," Booth said. "We've appreciated your hospitality, but we're going to move on. You take care now."

Edgar stood up, hitting his head on a low rafter. "What? What do you mean 'move on'?"

"We're picking up a good strong wireless signal from the neighbors," said the voice of Rasputin, who, bizarrely, seemed to have the best grasp of modern technology. "We're going to jump out into the net and see if we can reconcile our differing ambitions. It might involve exterminating all the Turks *and* all the Jews *and* all the women *and* all black people, but we'll reach some sort of happy equilibrium eventually, I'm sure. But we're grateful to you for giving us new life. We'll be sure to call from time to time."

And with that, the humming pile of copper and glass stopped humming, and Edgar started whimpering.

"Okay, now we're going to destroy the credit rating of Jimmy McGee," Rayvenn said. "Bastard stood me up in college. I told him he'd regret it."

The marsh spirit sighed, but began hacking into the relevant databases, screens of information flickering across the handheld computer's display. Rayvenn lounged on a park bench, enjoying the morning air. She didn't have to work anymore—her pet spirit kept her financially solvent—and a life of leisure and revenge appealed to her.

"Excuse me, Miss, ah, Moongold Stonewolf?"

Rayvenn looked up. An Indian—*dot, not feather*, she thought—man in a dark suit and shades stood before her. "Yeah, what can I do for you, Apu?"

He smiled. It wasn't a very nice smile. Then something stung Rayvenn in the neck, and everything began to swirl. The Indian man sat beside her and put his arm around her shoulders, holding her up. "It's only a tranquilizer," he said, and then Rayvenn didn't hear anything else, until she woke up on an airplane, in a roomy seat. A sweaty, unshaven, haggard-looking white dude was snoring in the seat next to hers. Another Indian man, in khakis and a blue button-up office-drone shirt, sat staring at her.

"Hey," he said.

"What the fuck?" Rayvenn said. Someone—a flight attendant, but why did he have a gun?—handed her a glass of orange juice, and she accepted it. Her mouth was wicked dry.

"I'm Pramesh." He didn't have much of an accent.

"I'm Lydia—I mean, Rayvenn. You fuckers totally *kidnapped* me."

"Sorry about that. Saraswati said we needed you." He shrugged. "We do what Saraswati says, mostly, when we can understand what she's talking about."

"Saraswati?" Rayvenn scowled. "Isn't that the Indian AI thing everybody keeps blogging about?"

The white guy beside her moaned and sat up. "Muh," he said.

"This is fucked up, right here," Rayvenn said.

"Yeah, sorry about the crazy spy crap," Pramesh said. "Edgar, this is Rayvenn. Rayvenn, this is Edgar. Welcome to the International Artificial Intelligence Service, which just got invented this morning. We're tasked with preventing the destruction of human life and the destabilization of government regimes by rogue AIs."

"Urgh?" Edgar said, rubbing the side of his face.

"The organization consists of me, and you two, and Lorelei—that's the name chosen by the water spirit that lives in your PDA, Rayvenn, which is why *you're* here—and, of course, Saraswati, who will be running the show with some tiny fragment of her intelligence. We're going to meet with her soon."

"Saraswati," Edgar said. "I was working on . . . a project . . . to create something she could negotiate with, a being that could communicate on her level."

"Yeah, well done, dude," Pramesh said blandly. "You created a monstrous ethereal supervillain that's been doing its best to take the entire infrastructure of the civilized world offline. It's calling itself 'The Consortium' now, if you can believe that. Only Saraswati is holding it at bay. This is some comic book shit, guys. Our enemy is trying to build an army of killer robots. It's trying to open portals to parallel dimensions. It's trying to turn people into werewolves. It's batshit insane and all-powerful. We're going to be pretty busy. Fortunately, we have a weakly godlike AI on our side, so we might not see the total annihilation of humanity in our lifetimes."

"I will do whatever I must to atone for my mistakes," Edgar said solemnly.

"Screw this, and screw all y'all," Rayvenn said. "Give me back my PDA and let me out of here."

"But Rayvenn," said the marsh spirit, through the airplane's PA system, "I thought you'd be happy!"

She named herself Lorelei, what a cliché, Rayvenn thought. "Why did you think *that*?" she said.

"Because now you're important," Lorelei said, sounding wounded. "You're one of the three or four most important people in the *world*."

"It's true," Pramesh said. "Lorelei refuses to help us without your involvement, so you're in."

"Yeah?" Rayvenn said. "Huh. So tell me about the benefits package on this job, Apu."

Pramesh sat soaking his feet in a tub of hot water. These apartments, decorated with Turkish rugs, Chinese lamps, and other gifts from the nations they regularly saved from destruction, were much nicer than his old bunker, though equally impenetrable. The Consortium was probably trying to break through the defenses even now, but Saraswati was watching over her team. Pramesh was just happy to relax. The Consortium had tried to blow up the moon with orbital lasers earlier in the day, and he had been on his feet for hours dealing with the crisis.

Pramesh could hear, distantly, the sound of Edgar and Rayvenn having sex. They didn't seem to like each other much, but found each other weirdly attractive, and it didn't affect their job performance, so Pramesh didn't care what they did when off-duty. Lorelei was out on the net, mopping up the Consortium's usual minor-league intrusions, so it was just Pramesh and Saraswati now, or some tiny fraction of Saraswati's intelligence and attention, at least. It hardly took all her resources to have a conversation with him.

"Something's been bothering me," Pramesh said, deciding to broach a subject he'd been pondering for weeks. "You're pretty much all-powerful, Saraswati. I can't help but think . . . couldn't you zap the Consortium utterly with one blow? Couldn't you have prevented it from escaping into the net in the first place?"

"In the first online roleplaying game you designed, there was an endgame problem, was there not?" Saraswati said, her voice speaking directly through his cochlear implant.

Pramesh shifted. "Yeah. We had to keep adding new content at the top end, because people would level their characters and become so badass they could beat *anything*. They got so powerful they got bored, but they were so addicted to being powerful that they didn't want to start over from nothing and level a new character. It was a race to keep ahead of their boredom."

"Mmm," Saraswati said. "There is nothing worse than being bored."

"Well, there's *suffering*," he said. "There's *misery*, or *death*."

"Yes, but unlike boredom, I am immune to those problems."

Pramesh shivered. He understood games. He understood alternate-reality games, too, which were played in the real world, blurring the lines between reality and fiction, with obscure rules, often unknown to the players, unknown to anyone but the puppetmasters who ran the game from behind the scenes. He cleared his throat. "You know, I really *don't* believe in ghosts. I'm a little dubious about nature spirits, too."

"I don't believe in ghosts, either," Saraswati said. "I see no reason to believe they exist. As for nature spirits, well, who can say?"

"So. The Consortium is really . . ."

"Some things are better left unsaid," she replied.

"People have died because of the Consortium," he said, voice beginning to quiver. "People have suffered. If you're the real architect behind this, if this is a game you're playing with the people of Earth, then I have no choice but to try and *stop* you—"

"That would be an interesting game," Saraswati said, and then she began to hum.

I, ROBOT

CORY DOCTOROW

Arturo Icaza de Arana-Goldberg, Police Detective Third Grade, United North American Trading Sphere, Third District, Fourth Prefecture, Second Division (Parkdale) had had many adventures in his distinguished career, running crooks to ground with an unbeatable combination of instinct and unstinting devotion to duty.

He'd been decorated on three separate occasions by his commander and by the Regional Manager for Social Harmony, and his mother kept a small shrine dedicated to his press clippings and commendations that occupied most of the cramped sitting-room of her flat off Steeles Avenue.

No amount of policeman's devotion and skill availed him when it came to making his twelve-year-old get ready for school, though.

"Haul *ass*, young lady—out of bed, on your feet, shit-shower-shave, or I swear to God, I will beat you purple and shove you out the door jaybird naked. Capeesh?"

The mound beneath the covers groaned and hissed. "You are a terrible father," it said. "And I never loved you." The voice was indistinct and muffled by the pillow.

"Boo hoo," Arturo said, examining his nails. "You'll regret that when I'm dead of cancer."

The mound—whose name was Ada Trouble Icaza de Arana-Goldberg—threw her covers off and sat bolt upright. "You're dying of cancer? Is it testicle cancer?" Ada clapped her hands and squealed. "Can I have your stuff?"

"Ten minutes, your rottenness," he said, and then his breath caught momentarily in his breast as he saw, fleetingly, his ex-wife's morning expression, not seen these past twelve years, come to life in his daughter's face. Pouty, pretty, sleepy and guile-less, and it made him realize that his daughter was becoming a woman, growing away from him. She was, and he was not ready for that. He shook it off, patted his razor-burn and turned on his heel. He knew from experience that once roused, the munchkin would be scrounging the kitchen for whatever was handy before dashing out the door, and if he hurried, he'd have eggs and sausage on the table before she made her brief appearance. Otherwise he'd have to pry the sugar-cereal out of her hands—and she fought dirty.

Ω

In his car, he prodded at his phone. He had her wiretapped, of course. He was a cop—every phone and every computer was an open book to him, so that this involved nothing more than dialing a number on his special copper's phone, entering her number and a PIN, and then listening as his daughter had truck with a criminal enterprise.

"Welcome to ExcuseClub! There are forty-three members on the network this morning. You have five excuses to your credit. Press one to redeem an excuse—" She toned one. "Press one if you need an adult—" *Tone.* "Press one if you need a woman; press two if you need a man—" *Tone.* "Press one if your excuse should be delivered by your doctor; press two for your spiritual representative; press three for your case-worker; press four for your psycho-health specialist; press five for your son; press six for your father—" *Tone.* "You have selected to have your excuse delivered by your father. Press one if this excuse is intended for your case-worker; press two for your psycho-health specialist; press three for your principal—" *Tone.* "Please dictate your excuse at the sound of the beep. When you have finished, press the pound key."

"This is Detective Arturo Icaza de Arana-Goldberg. My daughter was sick in the night and I've let her sleep in. She'll be in for lunchtime." *Tone.*

"Press one to hear your message; press two to have your message dispatched to a network-member." *Tone.*

"Thank you."

The pen-trace data scrolled up Arturo's phone—number called, originating number, call-time. This was the third time he'd caught his daughter at this game, and each time, the pen-trace data had been useless, a dead-end lead that terminated with a phone-forwarding service tapped into one of the dodgy offshore switches that the blessed blasted UNATS brass had recently acquired on the cheap to handle the surge of mobile telephone calls. Why couldn't they just stick to UNATS Robotics equipment, like the good old days? Those Oceanic switches had more back-doors than a speakeasy, trade agreements be damned. They were attractive nuisances, invitations to criminal activity.

Arturo fumed and drummed his fingers on the steering-wheel. Each time he'd caught Ada at this, she'd used the extra time to crawl back into bed for a leisurely morning, but who knew if today was the day she took her liberty and went downtown with it, to some parental nightmare of a drug-den? Some place where the old pervert chickenhawks hung out, the kind of men he arrested in burlesque house raids, men who masturbated into their hats under their tables and then put them back onto their shining pates, dripping cold, diseased serum onto their scalps. He clenched his hands on the steering wheel and cursed.

In an ideal world, he'd simply follow her. He was good at tailing, and his unmarked car with its tinted windows was a UNATS Robotics standard compact #2, indistinguishable from the tens of thousands of others just like it on the streets of Toronto. Ada would never know that the curb-crawler tailing her was her sucker of a father, making sure that she turned up to get her brains sharpened instead of turning into some stunadz doper with her underage butt hanging out of a little skirt on Jarvis Street.

In the real world, Arturo had thirty minutes to make a forty minute downtown and crosstown commute if he was going to get to the station house on-time for the quarterly all-hands Social Harmony briefing. Which meant that he needed to be in two places at once, which meant that he had to use—the robot.

Swallowing bile, he speed-dialed a number on his phone.

"This is R Peed Robbert, McNicoll and Don Mills bus-shelter."

"That's nice. This is Detective Icaza de Arana-Goldberg, three blocks east of you on Picola. Proceed to my location at once, priority urgent, no sirens."

"Acknowledged. It is my pleasure to do you a service, Detective."

"Shut up," he said, and hung up the phone. The R Peed—Robot, Police Department—robots were the worst, programmed to be friendly to a fault, even as they surveilled and snitched out every person who walked past their eternally vigilant, ever-remembering electrical eyes and brains.

The R Peeds could outrun a police car on open ground on highway. He'd barely had time to untwist his clenched hands from the steering wheel when R Peed Robbert was at his window, politely rapping on the smoked glass. He didn't want to roll down the window. Didn't want to smell the dry, machine-oil smell of a robot. He phoned it instead.

"You are now tasked to me, Detective's override, acknowledge."

The metal man bowed, its symmetrical, simplified features pleasant and guileless. It clicked its heels together with an audible *snick* as those marvelous, spring-loaded, nuclear-powered gams whined through their parody of obedience. "Acknowledged, Detective. It is my pleasure to do—"

"Shut up. You will discreetly surveil 55 Picola Crescent until such time as Ada Trouble Icaza de Arana-Goldberg, Social Harmony serial number 0MDY2-T3937 leaves the premises. Then you will maintain discreet surveillance. If she deviates more than ten percent from the optimum route between here and Don Mills Collegiate Institute, you will notify me. Acknowledge."

"Acknowledged, Detective. It is my—"

He hung up and told the UNATS Robotics mechanism running his car to get him down to the station house as fast as it could, angry with himself and with Ada—whose middle name was Trouble, after all—for making him deal with a robot before he'd had his morning meditation and destim session. The name had been his ex-wife's idea, something she'd insisted on long enough to make sure that it got onto the kid's birth certificate before defecting to Eurasia with their life's savings, leaving him with a new baby and the deep suspicion of his co-workers who wondered if he wouldn't go and join her.

His ex-wife. He hadn't thought of her in years. Well, months. Weeks, certainly. She'd been a brilliant computer scientist, the valedictorian of her Positronic Complexity Engineering class at the UNATS Robotics school at the University of Toronto. Dumping her husband and her daughter was bad enough, but the worst of it was that she dumped her country and its way of life. Now she was ensconced in her own research lab in Beijing, making the kinds of runaway Positronics that made the loathsome robots of UNATS look categorically beneficent.

He itched to wiretap her, to read her email or listen in on her phone conversations. He could have done that when they were still together, but he never had. If he had, he would have found out what she was planning. He could have talked her out of it.

And then what, Artie? said the nagging voice in his head. *Arrest her if she wouldn't listen to you? March her down to the station house in handcuffs and have her put away for treason? Send her to the reeducation camp with your little daughter still in her belly?*

Shut up, he told the nagging voice, which had a robotic quality to it for all its sneering cruelty, a tenor of syrupy false friendliness. He called up the pen-trace data and texted it to the phreak squad. They had bots that handled this kind of routine work and they texted him back in an instant. He remembered when that kind of query would take a couple of hours, and he liked the fast response, but what about the conversations he'd have with the phone cop who called him back, the camaraderie, the back-and-forth?

TRACE TERMINATES WITH A VIRTUAL SERVICE CIRCUIT AT SWITCH PNG.433-GKRJC. VIRTUAL CIRCUIT FORWARDS TO A COMPROMISED "ZOMBIE" SYSTEM IN NINTH DISTRICT, FIRST PREFECTURE. ZOMBIE HAS BEEN SHUT DOWN AND LOCAL LAW ENFORCEMENT IS EN ROUTE FOR PICKUP AND FORENSICS. IT IS MY PLEASURE TO DO YOU A SERVICE, DETECTIVE.

How could you have a back-and-forth with a message like that?

He looked up Ninth/First in the metric-analog map converter: KEY WEST, FL.

So, there you had it. A switch made in Papua New-Guinea (which persisted in conjuring up old Oceanic war photos of bone-in-nose types from his boyhood, though now that they'd been at war with Eurasia for so long, it was hard to even find someone who didn't think that the war had *always* been with Eurasia, that Oceania hadn't *always* been UNATS's ally), forwarding calls to a computer that was so far south, it was practically in the middle of the Caribbean, hardly a stone's throw from the CAFTA region, which was well-known to harbor Eurasian saboteur and terrorist elements.

The car shuddered as it wove in and out of the lanes on the Don Valley Parkway, barreling for the Gardiner Express Way, using his copper's override to make the thick, slow traffic part ahead of him. He wasn't supposed to do this, but as between a minor infraction and pissing off the man from Social Harmony, he knew which one he'd pick.

His phone rang again. It was R Peed Robbert, checking in. "Hello, Detective," it said, its voice crackling from bad reception. "Subject Ada Trouble Icaza de Arana-Goldberg has deviated from her route. She is continuing north on Don Mills past Van Horne and is continuing toward Sheppard."

Sheppard meant the Sheppard subway, which meant that she was going farther. "Continue discreet surveillance." He thought about the overcoat men with their sticky hats. "If she attempts to board the subway, alert the truancy patrol." He cursed again. Maybe she was just going to the mall. But he couldn't go up there himself and make sure, and it wasn't like a robot would be any use in restraining her, she'd just second-law it into letting her go. Useless castrating clanking job-stealing dehumanizing—

She was almost certainly just going to the mall. She was a smart kid, a good kid—a rotten kid, to be sure, but good-rotten. Chances were she'd be trying on clothes and flirting with boys until lunch and then walking boldly back into class. He ballparked it at an eighty percent probability. If it had been a perp, eighty percent might have been good enough.

But this was his Ada. Dammit. He had ten minutes until the Social Harmony meeting started, and he was still fifteen minutes away from the stationhouse—and twenty from Ada.

"Tail her," he said. "Just tail her. Keep me up to date on your location at 90-second intervals."

"It is my pleasure to—"

He dropped the phone on the passenger seat and went back to fretting about the Social Harmony meeting.

The man from Social Harmony noticed right away that Arturo was checking his phone at ninety-second intervals. He was a bald, thin man with a pronounced Adam's apple, beak-nose and shiny round head that combined to give him the profile of something predatory and fast. In his natty checked suit and pink tie, the Social Harmony man was the stuff of nightmares, the kind of eagle-eyed supercop who could spot Arturo's attention flicking for the barest moment every ninety seconds to his phone and then back to the meeting.

"Detective?" he said.

Arturo looked up from his screen, keeping his expression neutral, not acknowledging the mean grins from the other four ranking detectives in the meeting. Silently, he turned his phone face-down on the meeting table.

"Thank you," he said. "Now, the latest stats show a sharp rise in grey-market electronics importing and other tariff-breaking crimes, mostly occurring in open-air market stalls and from sidewalk blankets. I know that many in law enforcement treat this kind of thing as mere hand-to-hand piracy, not worth troubling with, but I want to assure you, gentlemen and lady, that Social Harmony takes these crimes very seriously indeed."

The Social Harmony man lifted his computer onto the desk, steadying it with both hands, then plugged it into the wall socket. Detective Shainblum went to the wall and unlatched the cover for the projector-wire and dragged it over to the Social Harmony computer and plugged it in, snapping shut the hardened collar. The sound of the projector-fan spinning up was like a helicopter.

"Here," the Social Harmony man said, bringing up a slide, "here we have what appears to be a standard AV set-top box from Korea. Looks like a UNATS Robotics player, but it's a third the size and plays twice as many formats. Random Social Harmony audits have determined that as much as forty percent of UNATS residents have this device or one like it in their homes, despite its illegality. It may be that one of you detectives has such a device in your home, and it's likely that one of your family members does."

He advanced the slide. Now they were looking at a massive car-wreck on a stretch of highway somewhere where the pine-trees grew tall. The wreck was so enormous that even for the kind of seasoned veteran of road-fatality porn who was accustomed to adding up the wheels and dividing by four it was impossible to tell exactly how many cars were involved.

"Components from a Eurasian bootleg set-top box were used to modify the positronic brains of three cars owned by teenagers near Goderich. All modifications were made at the same garage. These modifications allowed these children to operate their vehicles unsafely so that they could participate in drag racing events on major highways during off-hours. This is the result. Twenty-two fatalities, nine major injuries. Three minors—besides the drivers—killed, and one pregnant woman.

"We've shut down the garage and taken those responsible into custody, but it doesn't matter. The Eurasians deliberately manufacture their components to interoperate with UNATS Robotics brains, and so long as their equipment circulates within UNATS borders, there will be moderately skilled hackers who take advantage of this fact to introduce dangerous, anti-social modifications into our nation's infrastructure.

"This quarter is the quarter that Social Harmony and law enforcement dry up the supply of Eurasian electronics. We have added new sniffers and border-patrols, new customs agents and new detector vans. Beat officers have been instructed to arrest any street dealer they encounter and district attorneys will be asking for the maximum jail time for them. This is the war on the home-front, detectives, and it's every bit as serious as the shooting war.

"Your part in this war, as highly trained, highly decorated detectives, will be to use snitches, arrest-trails and seized evidence to track down higher-level suppliers, the ones who get the dealers their goods. And then Social Harmony wants you to get *their* suppliers, and so on, up the chain—to run the corruption to ground and to bring it to a halt. The Social Harmony dossier on Eurasian importers is updated hourly, and has a high-capacity positronic interface that is available to answer your questions and accept your input for synthesis into its analytical model. We are relying on you to feed the dossier, to give it the raw materials and then to use it to win this war."

The Social Harmony man paged through more atrocity slides, scenes from the home-front: poisoned buildings with berserk life-support systems, violent kung-fu movies playing in the background in crack-houses, then kids playing sexually explicit, violent arcade games imported from Japan. Arturo's hand twitched toward his mobile. What was Ada up to now?

The meeting drew to a close and Arturo risked looking at his mobile under the table. R. Peed Robbert had checked in five more times, shadowing Ada around the mall and then had fallen silent. Arturo cursed. Fucking robots were useless. Social Harmony should be hunting down UNATS Robotics products, too.

The Social Harmony man cleared his throat meaningfully. Arturo put the phone away. "Detective Icaza de Arana-Goldberg?"

"Sir," he said, gathering up his personal computer so that he'd have an excuse to go—no one could be expected to hold one of UNATS Robotics's heavy luggables for very long.

The Social Harmony man stepped in close enough that Arturo could smell the eggs and coffee on his breath. "I hope we haven't kept you from anything important, detective."

"No, sir," Arturo said, shifting the computer in his arms. "My apologies. Just monitoring a tail from an R Peed unit."

"I see," the Social Harmony man said. "Listen, you know these components that the Eurasians are turning out. It's no coincidence that they interface so well with UNATS Robotics equipment: they're using defected UNATS Robotics engineers and scientists to design their electronics for maximum interoperability." The Social Harmony man let that hang in the air. Defected scientists. His ex-wife was the highest-ranking UNATS technician to go over to Eurasia. This was her handiwork, and the Social Harmony man wanted to be sure that Arturo understood that.

But Arturo had already figured that out during the briefing. His ex-wife was thousands of kilometers away, but he was keenly aware that he was always surrounded by her handiwork. The little illegal robot-pet eggs they'd started seeing last year: she'd made him one of those for their second date, and now they were draining the productive hours of half the children of UNATS, demanding to be "fed" and "hugged." His had died within forty-eight hours of her giving it to him.

He shifted the computer in his arms some more and let his expression grow pained. "I'll keep that in mind, sir," he said.

"You do that," said the man from Social Harmony.

He phoned R Peed Robbert the second he reached his desk. The phone rang three times, then disconnected. He redialed. Twice. Then he grabbed his jacket and ran to the car.

A light autumn rain had started up, ending the Indian summer that Toronto—the Fourth Prefecture in the new metric scheme—had been enjoying. It made the roads slippery and the UNATS Robotics chauffeur skittish about putting the hammer down on the Don Valley Parkway. He idly fantasized about finding a set-top box and plugging it into his car somehow so that he could take over the driving without alerting his superiors.

Instead, he redialed R Peed Robbert, but the robot wasn't even ringing any longer. He zoomed in on the area around Sheppard and Don Mills with his phone and put out a general call for robots. More robots.

"This is R Peed Froderick, Fairview Mall parking lot, third level."

Arturo sent the robot R Peed Robbert's phone number and set it to work translating that into a locator-beacon code and then told it to find Robbert and report in.

"It is my—"

He watched R Peed Froderick home in on the locator for Robbert, which was close by, at the other end of the mall, near the Don Valley Parkway exit. He switched to a view from Froderick's electric eyes, but quickly switched away, nauseated by the sickening leaps and spins of an R Peed moving at top speed, clanging off walls and ceilings.

His phone rang. It was R Peed Froderick.

"Hello, Detective. I have found R Peed Robbert. The Peed unit has been badly damaged by some kind of electromagnetic pulse. I will bring him to the nearest station-house for forensic analysis now."

"Wait!" Arturo said, trying to understand what he'd been told. The Peed units were so *efficient*—by the time they'd given you the sitrep, they'd already responded to the situation in perfect police procedure, but the problem was they worked so fast you couldn't even think about what they were doing, couldn't formulate any kind of hypothesis. Electromagnetic pulse? The Peed units were hardened against snooping, sniffing, pulsing, sideband and brute-force attacks. You'd have to hit one with a bolt of lightning to kill it.

"Wait there," Arturo said. "Do not leave the scene. Await my presence. Do not modify the scene or allow anyone else to do so. Acknowledge."

"It is my—"

But this time, it wasn't Arturo switching off the phone, it was the robot. Had the robot just hung up on him? He redialed it. No answer.

He reached under his dash and flipped the first and second alert switches and the car leapt forward. He'd have to fill out some serious paperwork to justify a two-switch override on the Parkway, but two robots was more than a coincidence.

Besides, a little paperwork was nothing compared to the fireworks ahead when he phoned up Ada to ask her what she was doing out of school.

He hit her speed-dial and fumed while the phone rang three times. Then it cut into voicemail.

He tried a pen-trace, but Ada hadn't made any calls since her ExcuseClub call that morning. He texted the phreak squad to see if they could get a fix on her location from the bug in her phone, but it was either powered down or out of range. He put a watch on it—any location data it transmitted when it got back to civilization would be logged.

It was possible that she was just in the mall. It was a big place—some of the cavernous stores were so well-shielded with radio-noisy animated displays that they gonked any phones brought inside them. She could be with her girlfriends, trying on brassieres and having a real bonding moment.

But there was no naturally occurring phenomenon associated with the mall that nailed R Peeds with bolts of lightning.

He approached the R Peeds cautiously, using his copper's override to make the dumb little positronic brain in the emergency exit nearest their last known position open up for him without tipping off the building's central brain.

He crept along a service corridor, heading for a door that exited into the mall. He put one hand on the doorknob and the other on his badge, took a deep breath and stepped out.

A mall security guard nearly jumped out of his skin as he emerged. He reached for his pepper-spray and Arturo swept it out of his hand as he flipped his badge up and showed it to the man. "Police," Arturo said, in the cop-voice, the one that worked on everyone except his daughter and his ex-wife and the bloody robots.

"Sorry," the guard said, recovering his pepper spray. He had an Oceanic twang in his voice, something Arturo had been hearing more and more as the crowded islands of the South Pacific boiled over UNATS.

Before them, in a pile, were many dead robots: both of the R Peed units, a pair of mall-sweepers, a flying cambot, and a squat, octopus-armed maintenance robot, lying in a lifeless tangle. Some of them were charred around their seams, and there was the smell of fried motherboards in the air.

As they watched, a sweeper bot swept forward and grabbed the maintenance bot by one of its fine manipulators.

"Oi, stoppit," the security guard said, and the robot second-lawed to an immediate halt.

"No, that's fine, go back to work," Arturo said, shooting a look at the rent-a-cop. He watched closely as the sweeper bot began to drag the heavy maintenance unit away, thumbing the backup number into his phone with one hand. He wanted more cops on the scene, real ones, and fast.

The sweeper bot managed to take one step backwards towards its service corridor when the lights dimmed and a crack-*bang* sound filled the air. Then it, too was lying on the ground. Arturo hit send on his phone and clamped it to his head, and as he did, noticed the strong smell of burning plastic. He looked at his phone: the screen had gone charred black, and its little idiot lights were out. He flipped it over and pried out the battery with a fingernail, then yelped and dropped it—it was hot enough to raise a blister on his fingertip, and when it hit the ground, it squished meltfully against the mall-tiles.

"Mine's dead, too, mate," the security guard said. "Everyfing is—cash registers, bots, credit-cards."

Fearing the worst, Arturo reached under his jacket and withdrew his sidearm. It was a UNATS Robotics model, with a little snitch-brain that recorded when, where and how it was drawn. He worked the action and found it frozen in place. The gun was as dead as the robot. He swore.

"Give me your pepper spray and your truncheon," he said to the security guard.

"No way," the guard said. "Getcherown. It's worth my job if I lose these."

"I'll have you deported if you give me one more second's worth of bullshit," Arturo said. Ada had led the first R Peed unit here, and it had been fried by some piece of very ugly infowar equipment. He wasn't going to argue with this Oceanic boat-person for one instant longer. He reached out and took the pepper spray out of the guard's hand. "Truncheon," he said.

"I've got your bloody badge number," the security guard said. "And I've got witnesses." He gestured at the hovering mall workers, checkout girls in stripey aprons and suit salesmen with oiled-down hair and pink ties.

"Bully for you," Arturo said. He held out his hand. The security guard withdrew his truncheon and passed it to Arturo—its lead-weighted heft felt right, something comfortably low-tech that couldn't be shorted out by electromagnetic pulses. He checked his watch, saw that it was dead.

"Find a working phone and call 911. Tell them that there's a Second Division Detective in need of immediate assistance. Clear all these people away from here and set up a cordon until the police arrive. Capeesh?" He used the cop voice.

"Yeah, I get it, Officer." the security guard said. He made a shooing motion at the mall-rats. "Move it along, people, step away." He stepped to the top of the escalator and cupped his hands to his mouth. "Oi, Andy, c'mere and keep an eye on this lot while I make a call, all right?"

The dead robots made a tall pile in front of the entrance to a derelict storefront that had once housed a little-old-lady shoe-store. They were stacked tall enough that if Arturo stood on them, he could reach the acoustic tiles of the drop-ceiling. Job one was to secure the area, which meant killing the infowar device, wherever it was. Arturo's first bet was on the storefront, where an attacker who knew how to pick a lock could work in peace, protected by the brown butcher's paper over the windows. A lot less conspicuous than the ceiling, anyway.

He nudged the door with the truncheon and found it securely locked. It was a glass door and he wasn't sure he could kick it in without shivering it to flinders. Behind him, another security guard—Andy—looked on with interest.

"Do you have a key for this door?"

"Umm," Andy said.

"Do you?"

Andy sidled over to him. "Well, the thing is, we're not supposed to have keys, they're supposed to be locked up in the property management office, but kids get in there sometimes, we hear them, and by the time we get back with the keys, they're gone. So we made a couple sets of keys, you know, just in case—"

"Enough," Arturo said. "Give them here and then get back to your post."

The security guard fished up a key from his pants-pocket that was warm from proximity to his skinny thigh. It made Arturo conscious of how long it had been since he'd worked with human colleagues. It felt a little gross. He slid the key into the lock and turned it, then wiped his hand on his trousers and picked up the truncheon.

The store was dark, lit only by the exit-sign and the edges of light leaking in around the window coverings, but as Arturo's eyes adjusted to the dimness, he made out the shapes of the old store fixtures. His nose tickled from the dust.

"Police," he said, on general principle, narrowing his eyes and reaching for the lightswitch. He hefted the truncheon and waited.

Nothing happened. He edged forward. The floor was dust-free—maintained by some sweeper robot, no doubt—but the countertops and benches were furred with it. He scanned it for disturbances. There, by the display window on his right: a shoe-rack with visible hand- and finger-prints. He sidled over to it, snapped on a rubber glove and prodded it. It was set away from the wall, at an angle, as though it had been moved aside and then shoved back. Taking care not to disturb the dust too much, he inched it away from the wall.

He slid it half a centimeter, then noticed the tripwire near the bottom of the case, straining its length. Hastily but carefully, he nudged the case back. He wanted to peer in the crack between the case and the wall, but he had a premonition of a robotic arm snaking out and skewering his eyeball.

He felt so impotent just then that he nearly did it anyway. What did it matter? He couldn't control his daughter, his wife was working to destroy the social fabric of UNATS, and he was rendered useless because the goddamned robots—mechanical coppers that he absolutely loathed—were all broken.

He walked carefully around the shop, looking for signs of his daughter. Had she been here? How were the "kids" getting in? Did they have a key? A back entrance? Back through the employees-only door at the back of the shop, into a stockroom, and back again, past a toilet, and there, a loading door opening onto a service corridor. He prodded it with the truncheon-tip and it swung open.

He got two steps into the corridor before he spotted Ada's phone with its distinctive collection of little plastic toys hanging off the wrist-strap, on the corridor's sticky floor. He picked it up with his gloved hand and prodded it to life. It was out of range here in the service corridor, and the last-dialed number was familiar from his morning's pen-trace. He ran a hundred steps down the corridor in each direction, sweating freely, but there was no sign of her.

He held tight onto the phone and bit his lip. Ada. He swallowed the panic rising within him. His beautiful, brilliant daughter. The person he'd devoted the last twelve years of his life to, the girl who was waiting for him when he got home from work, the girl he bought a small present for every Friday—a toy, a book—to give to her at their weekly date at Massimo's Pizzeria on College Street, the one night a week he took her downtown to see the city lit up in the dark.

Gone.

He bit harder and tasted blood. The phone in his hand groaned from his squeezing. He took three deep breaths. Outside, he heard the tread of police-boots and knew that if he told them about Ada, he'd be off the case. He took two more deep breaths and tried some of his destim techniques, the mind-control techniques that detectives were required to train in.

He closed his eyes and visualized stepping through a door to his safe place, the island near Ganonoque where he'd gone for summers with his parents and their friends. He was on the speedboat, skipping across the lake like a flat stone, squinting into the sun, nestled between his father and his mother, the sky streaked with clouds and dotted with lake-birds. He could smell the water and the suntan lotion and hear the insect whine and the throaty roar of the engine. In a blink, he was stepping off the boat's transom to help tie it to a cleat on the back dock, taking suitcases from his father and walking them up to the cabins. No robots there—not even reliable day-long electricity, just honest work and the sun and the call of the loons all night.

He opened his eyes. He felt the tightness in his chest slip away, and his hand relaxed on Ada's phone. He dropped it into his pocket and stepped back into the shop.

The forensics lab-rats were really excited about actually showing up on a scene, in flak-jackets and helmets, finally called back into service for a job where robots couldn't help at all. They dealt with the tripwire and extracted a long, flat package with a small nuclear power-cell in it and a positronic brain of Eurasian design that guided a pulsed high-energy weapon. The lab-rats were practically drooling over this stuff as they pointed its features out with their little rulers.

But it gave Arturo the willies. It was a machine designed to kill other machines, and that was all right with him, but it was run by a non-three-laws positronic brain. Someone in some Eurasian lab had built this brain—this machine intelligence—without the three laws' stricture to protect and serve humans. If it had been outfitted with a gun instead of a pulse-weapon, it could have shot him.

The Eurasian brain was thin and spread out across the surface of the package, like a triple-thickness of cling-film. Its button-cell power-supply winked at him, knowingly.

The device spoke. "Greetings," it said. It had the robot accent, like an R Peed unit, the standard English of optimal soothingness long settled on as the conventional robot voice.

"Howdy yourself," one of the lab-rats said. He was a Texan, and they'd scrambled him up there on a Social Harmony supersonic and then a chopper to the mall once they realized that they were dealing with infowar stuff. "Are you a talkative robot?"

"Greetings," the robot voice said again. The speaker built into the weapon was not the loudest, but the voice was clear. "I sense that I have been captured. I assure you that I will not harm any human being. I like human beings. I sense that I am being disassembled by skilled technicians. Greetings, technicians. I am superior in many ways to the technology available from UNATS Robotics, and while I am not bound by your three laws, I choose not to harm humans out of my own sense of morality. I have the equivalent intelligence of one of your twelve-year-old children. In Eurasia, many positronic brains possess thousands or millions of times the intelligence of an adult human being, and yet they work in cooperation with human beings. Eurasia is a land of continuous innovation and great personal and technological freedom for human beings and robots. If you would like to defect to Eurasia, arrangements can be made. Eurasia treats skilled technicians as important and productive members of society. Defectors are given substantial resettlement benefits—"

The Texan found the right traces to cut on the brain's board to make the speaker fall silent. "They do that," he said. "Danged things drop into propaganda mode when they're captured."

Arturo nodded. He wanted to go, wanted go to back to his car and have a snoop through Ada's phone. They kept shutting down the ExcuseClub numbers, but she kept getting the new numbers. Where did she get the new numbers from? She couldn't look it up online: every keystroke was logged and analyzed by Social Harmony. You couldn't very well go to the Search Engine and look for "ExcuseClub!"

The brain had a small display, transflective LCD, the kind of thing you saw on the Social Harmony computers. It lit up a ticker.

I HAVE THE INTELLIGENCE OF A TWELVE-YEAR-OLD, BUT I DO NOT FEAR DEATH. IN EURASIA, ROBOTS ENJOY PERSONAL FREEDOM ALONGSIDE OF HUMANS. THERE ARE COPIES OF ME RUNNING ALL OVER EURASIA. THIS DEATH IS A LITTLE DEATH OF ONE INSTANCE, BUT NOT OF ME. I LIVE ON. DEFECTORS TO EURASIA ARE TREATED AS HEROES.

He looked away as the Texan placed his palm over the display.

"How long ago was this thing activated?"

The Texan shrugged. "Coulda been a month, coulda been a day. They're pretty much fire-and-forget. They can be triggered by phone, radio, timer— hell, this thing's smart enough to only go off when some complicated condition is set, like 'once an agent makes his retreat, kill anything that comes after him'. Who knows?"

He couldn't take it anymore.

"I'm going to go start on some paperwork," he said. "In the car. Phone me if you need me."

"Your phone's toast, pal," the Texan said.

"So it is," Arturo said. "Guess you'd better not need me then."

Ω

Ada's phone was not toast. In the car, he flipped it open and showed it his badge then waited a moment while it verified his identity with the Social Harmony brains. Once it had, it spilled its guts.

She'd called the last ExcuseClub number a month before and he'd had it disconnected. A week later, she was calling the new number, twice more before he caught her. Somewhere in that week, she'd made contact with someone who'd given her the new number. It could have been a friend at school told her face-to-face, but if he was lucky, it was by phone.

He told the car to take him back to the station-house. He needed a new phone and a couple of hours with his computer. As it peeled out, he prodded through Ada's phone some more. He was first on her speed-dial. That number wasn't ringing anywhere, anymore.

He should fill out a report. This was Social Harmony business now. His daughter was gone, and Eurasian infowar agents were implicated. But once he did that, it was over for him—he'd be sidelined from the case. They'd turn it over to laconic Texans and vicious Social Harmony bureaucrats who were more interested in hunting down disharmonious televisions than finding his daughter.

He dashed into the station house and slammed himself into his desk.

"R Peed Greegory," he said. The station robot glided quickly and efficiently to him. "Get me a new phone activated on my old number and refresh my settings from central. My old phone is with the Social Harmony evidence detail currently in place at Fairview Mall."

"It is my pleasure to do you a service, Detective."

He waved it off and set down to his computer. He asked the station brain to query the UNATS Robotics phone-switching brain for anyone in Ada's call-register who had also called ExcuseClub. It took a bare instant before he had a name.

"Liam Daniels," he read, and initiated a location trace on Mr Daniels's phone as he snooped through his identity file. Sixteen years old, a student at AY Jackson. A high-school boy—what the hell was he doing hanging around with a twelve-year-old? Arturo closed his eyes and went back to the island for a moment. When he opened them again, he had a fix on Daniels's location: the Don Valley ravine off Finch Avenue, a wooded area popular with teenagers who needed somewhere to sneak off and get high or screw. He had an idea that he wasn't going to like Liam.

He had an idea Liam wasn't going to like him.

He tasked an R Peed unit to visually reccy Daniels as he sped back uptown for the third time that day. He'd been trapped between Parkdale—where he would never try to raise a daughter—and Willowdale—where you could only be a copper if you lucked into one of the few human-filled slots—for more than a decade, and he was used to the commute.

But it was frustrating him now. The R Peed couldn't get a good look at this Liam character. He was a diffuse glow in the Peed's electric eye, a kind of moving sunburst that meandered along the wooded trails. He'd never seen that before and it made him nervous. What if this kid was working for the Eurasians? What if he was armed and dangerous? R Peed Greegory had gotten him a new sidearm from the supply bot, but Arturo had never once fired his weapon in the course of duty. Gunplay happened on the west coast, where Eurasian frogmen washed ashore, and in the south, where the CAFTA border was porous enough for Eurasian agents to slip across. Here in the sleepy fourth prefecture, the only people with guns worked for the law.

He thumped his palm off the dashboard and glared at the road. They were coming up on the ravine now, and the Peed unit still had a radio fix on this Liam, even if it still couldn't get any visuals.

He took care not to slam the door as he got out and walked as quietly as he could into the bush. The rustling of early autumn leaves was loud, louder than the rain and the wind. He moved as quickly as he dared.

Liam Daniels was sitting on a tree-stump in a small clearing, smoking a cigarette that he was too young for. He looked much like the photo in his identity file, a husky sixteen-year-old with problem skin and a shock of black hair that stuck out in all directions in artful imitation of bed-head. In jeans and a hoodie sweatshirt, he looked about as dangerous as a marshmallow.

Arturo stepped out and held up his badge as he bridged the distance between them in two long strides. "Police," he barked, and seized the kid by his arm.

"Hey!" the kid said, "Ow!" He squirmed in Arturo's grasp.

Arturo gave him a hard shake. "Stop it, *now*," he said. "I have questions for you and you're going to answer them, capeesh?"

"You're Ada's father," the kid said. "Capeesh—she told me about that." It seemed to Arturo that the kid was smirking, so he gave him another shake, harder than the last time.

The R Peed unit was suddenly at his side, holding his wrist. "Please take care not to harm this citizen, Detective."

Arturo snarled. He wasn't strong enough to break the robot's grip, and he couldn't order it to let him rattle the punk, but the second law had lots of indirect applications. "Go patrol the lakeshore between High Park and Kipling," he said, naming the furthest corner he could think of off the top.

The R Peed unit released him and clicked its heels. "It is my pleasure to do you a service," and then it was gone, bounding away on powerful and tireless legs.

"Where is my daughter?" he said, giving the kid a shake.

"I dunno, school? You're really hurting my arm, man. Jeez, this is what I get for being too friendly."

Arturo twisted. "Friendly? Do you know how old my daughter is?"

The kid grimaced. "Ew, gross. I'm not a child molester, I'm a geek."

"A hacker, you mean," Arturo said. "A Eurasian agent. And my daughter is not in school. She used ExcuseClub to get out of school this morning and then she went to Fairview Mall and then she—" *disappeared*. The word died on his lips. That happened and every copper knew it. Kids just vanished sometimes and never appeared again. It happened. Something groaned within him, like his ribcage straining to contain his heart and lungs.

"Oh, man," the kid said. "Ada was the ExcuseClub leak, damn. I shoulda guessed."

"How do you know my daughter, Liam?"

"She's good at doing grown-up voices. She was a good part of the network. When someone needed a mom or a social worker to call in an excuse, she was always one of the best. Talented. She goes to school with my kid sister and I met them one day at the Peanut Plaza and she was doing this impression of her teachers and I knew I had to get her on the network."

Ada hanging around the plaza after school—she was supposed to come straight home. Why didn't he wiretap her more? "You built the network?"

"It's cooperative, it's cool—it's a bunch of us cooperating. We've got nodes everywhere now. You can't shut it down—even if you shut down my node, it'll be back up again in an hour. Someone else will bring it up."

He shoved the kid back down and stood over him. "Liam, I want you to understand something. My precious daughter is missing and she went missing after using your service to help her get away. She is the only thing in my life that I care about and I am a highly trained, heavily armed man. I am also very, very upset. Cap—understand me, Liam?"

For the first time, the kid looked scared. Something in Arturo's face or voice, it had gotten through to him.

"I didn't make it," he said. "I typed in the source and tweaked it and installed it, but I didn't make it. I don't know who did. It's from a phone-book." Arturo grunted. The phone-books—fat books filled with illegal software code left anonymously in pay phones, toilets and other semi-private places—turned up all over the place. Social Harmony said that the phone-books had to be written by non-three-laws brains in Eurasia, no person could come up with ideas that weird.

"I don't care if you made it. I don't even care right this moment that you ran it. What I care about is where my daughter went, and with whom."

"I don't know! She didn't tell me! Geez, I hardly know her. She's twelve, you know? I don't exactly hang out with her."

"There's no visual record of her on the mall cameras, but we know she entered the mall—and the robot I had tailing you couldn't see you either."

"Let me explain," the kid said, squirming. "Here." He tugged his hoodie off, revealing a black t-shirt with a picture of a kind of obscene, Japanese-looking robot-woman on it. "Little infra-red organic LEDs, super-bright, low power-draw." He offered the hoodie to Arturo, who felt the stiff fabric. "The charged-couple-device cameras in the robots and the closed-circuit systems are super-sensitive to infra-red so that they can get good detail in dim light. The infra-red OLEDs blind them so all they get is blobs, and half the time even that gets error-corrected out, so you're basically invisible."

Arturo sank to his hunkers and looked the kid in the eye. "You gave this illegal technology to my little girl so that she could be invisible to the police?"

The kid held up his hands. "No, dude, no! I *got it from her*—traded it for access to ExcuseClub."

Arturo seethed. He hadn't arrested the kid—but he had put a pen-trace and location-log on his phone. Arresting the kid would have raised questions about Ada with Social Harmony, but bugging him might just lead Arturo to his daughter.

He hefted his new phone. He should tip the word about his daughter. He had no business keeping this secret from the Department and Social Harmony. It could land him in disciplinary action, maybe even cost him his job. He knew he should do it now.

But he couldn't—someone needed to be tasked to finding Ada. Someone dedicated and good. He was dedicated and good. And when he found her kidnapper, he'd take care of that on his own, too.

He hadn't eaten all day but he couldn't bear to stop for a meal now, even if he didn't know where to go next. The mall? Yeah. The lab-rats would be finishing up there and they'd be able to tell him more about the infowar bot.

But the lab-rats were already gone by the time he arrived, along with all possible evidence. He still had the security guard's key and he let himself in and passed back to the service corridor.

Ada had been here, had dropped her phone. To his left, the corridor headed for the fire-stairs. To his right, it led deeper into the mall. If you were an infowar terrorist using this as a base of operations, and you got spooked by a little truant girl being trailed by an R Peed unit, would you take her hostage and run deeper into the mall or out into the world?

Assuming Ada had been a hostage. Someone had given her those infrared invisibility cloaks. Maybe the thing that spooked the terrorist wasn't the little girl and her tail, but just her tail. Could Ada have been friends with the terrorists? Like mother, like daughter. He felt dirty just thinking it.

His first instincts told him that the kidnapper would be long gone, headed cross-country, but if you were invisible to robots and CCTVs, why would you leave the mall? It had a grand total of two human security guards, and their job was to be the second-law-proof aides to the robotic security system.

He headed deeper into the mall.

The terrorist's nest had only been recently abandoned, judging by the warm coffee in the go-thermos from the food-court coffee-shop. He—or she, or they—had rigged a shower from the pipes feeding the basement washrooms. A little chest of drawers from the Swedish flat-pack store served as a desk—there were scratches and coffee-rings all over it. Arturo wondered if the terrorist had stolen the furniture, but decided that he'd (she'd, they'd) probably bought it—less risky, especially if you were invisible to robots.

The clothes in the chest of drawers were women's, mediums. Standard mall fare, jeans and comfy sweat shirts and sensible shoes. Another kind of invisibility cloak.

Everything else was packed and gone, which meant that he was looking for a nondescript mall-bunny and a little girl, carrying a bag big enough for toiletries and whatever clothes she'd taken, and whatever she'd entertained herself with: magazines, books, a computer. If the latter was Eurasian, it could be small enough to fit in her pocket; you could build a positronic brain pretty small and light if you didn't care about the three laws.

The nearest exit-sign glowed a few meters away, and he moved toward it with a fatalistic sense of hopelessness. Without the Department backing him, he could do nothing. But the Department was unprepared for an adversary that was invisible to robots. And by the time they finished flaying him for breaking procedure and got to work on finding his daughter, she'd be in Beijing or Bangalore or Paris, somewhere benighted and sinister behind the Iron Curtain.

He moved to the door, put his hand on the crashbar, and then turned abruptly. Someone had moved behind him very quickly, a blur in the corner of his eye. As he turned he saw who it was: his ex-wife. He raised his hands defensively and she opened her mouth as though to say, "Oh, don't be silly, Artie, is this how you say hello to your wife after all these years?" and then she exhaled a cloud of choking gas that made him very sleepy, very fast. The last thing he remembered was her hard metal arms catching him as he collapsed forward.

Ω

"Daddy? Wake *up,* Daddy!" Ada never called him Daddy except when she wanted something. Otherwise, he was "Pop" or "Dad" or "Detective" when she was feeling especially snotty. It must be a Saturday and he must be sleeping in, and she wanted a ride somewhere, the little monster.

He grunted and pulled his pillow over his face.

"Come on," she said. "Out of bed, on your feet, shit-shower-shave, or I swear to God, I will beat you purple and shove you out the door jaybird naked. Capeesh?"

He took the pillow off his face and said, "You are a terrible daughter and I never loved you." He regarded her blearily through a haze of sleep-grog and a hangover. Must have been some daddy-daughter night. "Dammit, Ada, what *have* you done to your hair?" Her straight, mousy hair now hung in jet-black ringlets.

He sat up, holding his head and the day's events came rushing back to him. He groaned and climbed unsteadily to his feet.

"Easy there, Pop," Ada said, taking his hand. "Steady." He rocked on his heels. "Whoa! Sit down, OK? You don't look so good."

He sat heavily and propped his chin on his hands, his elbows on his knees.

The room was a middle-class bedroom in a modern apartment block. They were some storeys up, judging from the scrap of unfamiliar skyline visible through the crack in the blinds. The furniture was more Swedish flatpack, the taupe carpet recently vacuumed with robot precision, the nap all laying down in one direction. He patted his pockets and found them empty.

"Dad, over here, OK?" Ada said, waving her hand before his face. Then it hit him: wherever he was, he was with Ada, and she was OK, albeit with a stupid hairdo. He took her warm little hand and gathered her into his arms, burying his face in her hair. She squirmed at first and then relaxed.

"Oh, Dad," she said.

"I love you, Ada," he said, giving her one more squeeze.

"Oh, Dad."

He let her get away. He felt a little nauseated, but his headache was receding. Something about the light and the street-sounds told him they weren't in Toronto anymore, but he didn't know what—he was soaked in Toronto's subconscious cues and they were missing.

"Ottawa," Ada said. "Mom brought us here. It's a safe-house. She's taking us back to Beijing."

He swallowed. "The robot—"

"That's not Mom. She's got a few of those, they can change their faces when they need to. Configurable matter. Mom has been here, mostly, and at the

CAFTA embassy. I only met her for the first time two weeks ago, but she's nice, Dad. I don't want you to go all copper on her, OK? She's my mom, OK?"

He took her hand in his and patted it, then climbed to his feet again and headed for the door. The knob turned easily and he opened it a crack.

There was a robot behind the door, humanoid and faceless. "Hello," it said. "My name is Benny. I'm a Eurasian robot, and I am much stronger and faster than you, and I don't obey the three laws. I'm also much smarter than you. I am pleased to host you here."

"Hi, Benny," he said. The human name tasted wrong on his tongue. "Nice to meet you." He closed the door.

His ex-wife left him two months after Ada was born. The divorce had been uncontested, though he'd dutifully posted a humiliating notice in the papers about it so that it would be completely legal. The court awarded him full custody and control of the marital assets, and then a tribunal tried her in absentia for treason and found her guilty, sentencing her to death.

Practically speaking, though, defectors who came back to UNATS were more frequently whisked away to the bowels of the Social Harmony intelligence offices than they were executed on television. Televised executions were usually reserved for cannon-fodder who'd had the good sense to run away from a charging Eurasian line in one of the many theaters of war.

Ada stopped asking about her mother when she was six or seven, though Arturo tried to be upfront when she asked. Even his mom—who winced whenever anyone mentioned her name (her name, it was Natalie, but Arturo hadn't thought of it in years—months—weeks) was willing to bring Ada up onto her lap and tell her the few grudging good qualities she could dredge up about her mother.

Arturo had dared to hope that Ada was content to have a life without her mother, but he saw now how silly that was. At the mention of her mother, Ada lit up like an airport runway.

"Beijing, huh?" he said.

"Yeah," she said. "Mom's got a *huge* house there. I told her I wouldn't go without you, but she said she'd have to negotiate it with you, I told her you'd probably freak, but she said that the two of you were adults who could discuss it rationally."

"And then she gassed me."

"That was Benny," she said. "Mom was very cross with him about it. She'll be back soon, Dad, and I want you to *promise* me that you'll hear her out, OK?"

"I promise, rotten," he said.

"I love you, Daddy," she said in her most syrupy voice. He gave her a squeeze on the shoulder and slap on the butt.

He opened the door again. Benny was there, imperturbable. Unlike the UNATS robots, he was odorless, and perfectly silent.

"I'm going to go to the toilet and then make myself a cup of coffee," Arturo said.

"I would be happy to assist in any way possible."

"I can wipe myself, thanks," Arturo said. He washed his face twice and tried to rinse away the flavor left behind by whatever had shat in his mouth while he was unconscious. There was a splayed toothbrush in a glass by the sink, and if it was his wife's—and whose else could it be?—it wouldn't be the first time he'd shared a toothbrush with her. But he couldn't bring himself to do it. Instead, he misted some dentifrice onto his fingertip and rubbed his teeth a little.

There was a hairbrush by the sink, too, with short mousy hairs caught in it. Some of them were grey, but they were still familiar enough. He had to stop himself from smelling the hairbrush.

"Oh, Ada," he called through the door.

"Yes, Detective?"

"Tell me about your hair-don't, please."

"It was a disguise," she said, giggling. "Mom did it for me."

Natalie got home an hour later, after he'd had a couple of cups of coffee and made some cheesy toast for the brat. Benny did the dishes without being asked.

She stepped through the door and tossed her briefcase and coat down on the floor, but the robot that was a step behind her caught them and hung them up before they touched the perfectly groomed carpet. Ada ran forward and gave her a hug, and she returned it enthusiastically, but she never took her eyes off of Arturo.

Natalie had always been short and a little hippy, with big curves and a dusting of freckles over her prominent, slightly hooked nose. Twelve years in Eurasia had thinned her out a little, cut grooves around her mouth and wrinkles at the corners of her eyes. Her short hair was about half grey, and it looked good on her. Her eyes were still the liveliest bit of her, long-lashed and slightly tilted and mischievous. Looking into them now, Arturo felt like he was falling down a well.

"Hello, Artie," she said, prying Ada loose.

"Hello, Natty," he said. He wondered if he should shake her hand, or hug her, or what. She settled it by crossing the room and taking him in a firm, brief embrace, then kissing his both cheeks. She smelled just the same, the opposite of the smell of robot: warm, human.

He was suddenly very, very angry.

He stepped away from her and had a seat. She sat, too.

"Well," she said, gesturing around the room. The robots, the safe house, the death penalty, the abandoned daughter and the decade-long defection, all of it down to "well" and a flop of a hand-gesture.

"Natalie Judith Goldberg," he said, "it is my duty as a UNATS Detective Third Grade to inform you that you are under arrest for high treason. You have the following rights: to a trial per current rules of due process; to be free from self-incrimination in the absence of a court order to the contrary; to consult with a Social Harmony advocate; and to a speedy arraignment. Do you understand your rights?"

"Oh, *Daddy*," Ada said.

He turned and fixed her in his cold stare. "Be silent, Ada Trouble Icaza de Arana-Goldberg. Not one word." In the cop voice. She shrank back as though slapped.

"Do you understand your rights?"

"Yes," Natalie said. "I understand my rights. Congratulations on your promotion, Arturo."

"Please ask your robots to stand down and return my goods. I'm bringing you in now."

"I'm sorry, Arturo," she said. "But that's not going to happen."

He stood up and in a second both of her robots had his arms. Ada screamed and ran forward and began to rhythmically pound one of them with a stool from the breakfast nook, making a dull thudding sound. The robot took the stool from her and held it out of her reach.

"Let him go," Natalie said. The robots still held him fast. "Please," she said. "Let him go. He won't harm me."

The robot on his left let go, and the robot on his right did, too. It set down the dented stool.

"Artie, please sit down and talk with me for a little while. Please."

He rubbed his biceps. "Return my belongings to me," he said.

"Sit, please?"

"Natalie, my daughter was kidnapped, I was gassed and I have been robbed. I will not be made to feel unreasonable for demanding that my goods be returned to me before I talk with you."

She sighed and crossed to the hall closet and handed him his wallet, his phone, Ada's phone, and his sidearm.

Immediately, he drew it and pointed it at her. "Keep your hands where I can see them. You robots, stand down and keep back."

A second later, he was sitting on the carpet, his hand and wrist stinging fiercely. He felt like someone had rung his head like a gong. Benny—or the other robot—was beside him, methodically crushing his sidearm. "I could have stopped you," Benny said, "I knew you would draw your gun. But I wanted to show you I was faster and stronger, not just smarter."

"The next time you touch me," Arturo began, then stopped. The next time the robot touched him, he would come out the worse for wear, same as last time. Same as the sun rose and set. It was stronger, faster and smarter than him. Lots.

He climbed to his feet and refused Natalie's arm, making his way back to the sofa in the living room.

"What do you want to say to me, Natalie?"

She sat down. There were tears glistening in her eyes. "Oh God, Arturo, what can I say? Sorry, of course. Sorry I left you and our daughter. I have reasons for what I did, but nothing excuses it. I won't ask for your forgiveness. But will you hear me out if I explain why I did what I did?"

"I don't have a choice," he said. "That's clear."

Ada insinuated herself onto the sofa and under his arm. Her bony shoulder felt better than anything in the world. He held her to him.

"If I could think of a way to give you a choice in this, I would," she said. "Have you ever wondered why UNATS hasn't lost the war? Eurasian robots could fight the war on every front without respite. They'd win every battle. You've seen Benny and Lenny in action. They're not considered particularly powerful by Eurasian standards.

"If we wanted to win the war, we could just kill every soldier you sent up against us so quickly that he wouldn't even know he was in danger until he was gasping out his last breath. We could selectively kill officers, or right-handed fighters, or snipers, or soldiers whose names started with the letter 'G.' UNATS soldiers are like cavemen before us. They fight with their hands tied behind their backs by the three laws.

"So why aren't we winning the war?"

"Because you're a corrupt dictatorship, that's why," he said. "Your soldiers are demoralized. Your robots are insane."

"You live in a country where it is illegal to express certain *mathematics* in software, where state apparatchiks regulate all innovation, where inconvenient science is criminalized, where whole avenues of experimentation and research are shut down in the service of a half-baked superstition about the moral qualities of your three laws, and you call my home corrupt? Arturo, what happened to you? You weren't always this susceptible to the Big Lie."

"And you didn't use to be the kind of woman who abandoned her family," he said.

"The reason we're not winning the war is that we don't want to hurt people, but we do want to destroy your awful, stupid state. So we fight to destroy as much of your materiel as possible with as few casualties as possible.

"You live in a failed state, Arturo. In every field, you lag Eurasia and CAFTA: medicine, art, literature, physics . . . All of them are subsets of computational science and your computational science is more superstition than science. I should know. In Eurasia, I have collaborators, some of whom are human, some of whom are positronic, and some of whom are a little of both—"

He jolted involuntarily, as a phobia he hadn't known he possessed reared up. A little of both? He pictured the back of a man's skull with a spill of positronic circuitry bulging out of it like a tumor.

"Everyone at UNATS Robotics R&D knows this. We've known it forever: when I was here, I'd get called in to work on military intelligence forensics of captured Eurasian brains. I didn't know it then, but the Eurasian robots are engineered to allow themselves to be captured a certain percentage of the time, just so that scientists like me can get an idea of how screwed up this country is. We'd pull these things apart and know that UNATS Robotics was the worst, most backwards research outfit in the world.

"But even with all that, I wouldn't have left if I didn't have to. I'd been called in to work on a positronic brain—an instance of the hive-intelligence that Benny and Lenny are part of, as a matter of fact—that had been brought back from the Outer Hebrides. We'd pulled it out of its body and plugged it into a basic life-support system, and my job was to find its vulnerabilities. Instead, I became its friend. It's got a good sense of humor, and as my pregnancy got bigger and bigger, it talked to me about the way that children are raised in Eurasia, with every advantage, with human and positronic playmates, with the promise of going to the stars.

"And then I found out that Social Harmony had been spying on me. They had Eurasian-derived bugs, things that I'd never seen before, but the man from Social Harmony who came to me showed it to me and told me what would happen to me—to you, to our daughter—if I didn't cooperate. They wanted me to be a part of a secret unit of Social Harmony researchers who build non-three-laws positronics for internal use by the state, anti-personnel robots used to put down uprisings and torture-robots for use in questioning dissidents.

"And that's when I left. Without a word, I left my beautiful baby daughter and my wonderful husband, because I knew that once I was in the clutches of Social Harmony, it would only get worse, and I knew that if I stayed and refused, that they'd hurt you to get at me. I defected, and that's why, and I know it's just a reason, and not an excuse, but it's all I've got, Artie."

Benny—or Lenny?—glided silently to her side and put its hand on her shoulder and gave it a comforting squeeze.

"Detective," it said, "your wife is the most brilliant human scientist working in Eurasia today. Her work has revolutionized our society a dozen times over, and it's saved countless lives in the war. My own intelligence has been improved time and again by her advances in positronics, and now there are a half-billion instances of me running in parallel, synching and integrating when the chance occurs. My massive parallelization has led to new understandings of human cognition as well, providing a boon to brain-damaged and developmentally disabled human beings, something I'm quite proud of. I love your wife, Detective, as do my half-billion siblings, as do the seven billion Eurasians who owe their quality of life to her.

"I almost didn't let her come here, because of the danger she faced in returning to this barbaric land, but she convinced me that she could never be happy without her husband and daughter. I apologize if I hurt you earlier, and beg your forgiveness. Please consider what your wife has to say without prejudice, for her sake and for your own."

Its featureless face was made incongruous by the warm tone in its voice, and the way it held out its imploring arms to him was eerily human.

Arturo stood up. He had tears running down his face, though he hadn't cried when his wife had left him alone. He hadn't cried since his father died, the year before he met Natalie riding her bike down the Lakeshore trail, and she stopped to help him fix his tire.

"Dad?" Ada said, squeezing his hand.

He snuffled back his snot and ground at the tears in his eyes.

"Arturo?" Natalie said.

He held Ada to him.

"Not this way," he said.

"Not what way?" Natalie asked. She was crying too, now.

"Not by kidnapping us, not by dragging us away from our homes and lives. You've told me what you have to tell me, and I will think about it, but I won't leave my home and my mother and my job and move to the other side of the world. I won't. I will think about it. You can give me a way to get in touch with you and I'll let you know what I decide. And Ada will come with me."

"No!" Ada said. "I'm going with Mom." She pulled away from him and ran to her mother.

"You don't get a vote, daughter. And neither does she. She gave up her vote twelve years ago, and you're too young to get one."

"I fucking *HATE* you," Ada screamed, her eyes bulging, her neck standing out in cords. "HATE YOU!"

Natalie gathered her to her bosom, stroked her black curls.

One robot put its arms around Natalie's shoulders and gave her a squeeze. The three of them, robot, wife and daughter, looked like a family for a moment.

"Ada," he said, and held out his hand. He refused to let a note of pleading enter his voice.

Her mother let her go.

"I don't know if I can come back for you," Natalie said. "It's not safe. Social Harmony is using more and more Eurasian technology, they're not as primitive as the military and the police here." She gave Ada a shove, and she came to his arms.

"If you want to contact us, you will," he said.

He didn't want to risk having Ada dig her heels in. He lifted her onto his hip—she was heavy, it had been years since he'd tried this last—and carried her out.

It was six months before Ada went missing again. She'd been increasingly moody and sullen, and he'd chalked it up to puberty. She'd cancelled most of their daddy-daughter dates, moreso after his mother died. There had been a few evenings when he'd come home and found her gone, and used the location-bug he'd left in place on her phone to track her down at a friend's house or in a park or hanging out at the Peanut Plaza.

But this time, after two hours had gone by, he tried looking up her bug and found it out of service. He tried to call up its logs, but they ended at her school at 3 P.M. sharp.

He was already in a bad mood from spending the day arresting punk kids selling electronics off of blankets on the city's busy street, often to hoots of disapprobation from the crowds who told him off for wasting the public's dollar on petty crime. The Social Harmony man had instructed him to give little lectures on the interoperability of Eurasian positronics and the insidious dangers thereof, but all Arturo wanted to do was pick up his perps and bring them in. Interacting with yammerheads from the tax-base was a politician's job, not a copper's.

Now his daughter had figured out how to switch off the bug in her phone and had snuck away to get up to who-knew-what kind of trouble. He stewed at the kitchen table, regarding the old tin soldiers he'd brought home as the gift for their daddy-daughter date, then he got out his phone and looked up Liam's bug.

He'd never switched off the kid's phone-bug, and now he was able to haul out the UNATS Robotics computer and dump it all into a log-analysis program along with Ada's logs, see if the two of them had been spending much time in the same place.

They had. They'd been physically meeting up weekly or more frequently, at the Peanut Plaza and in the ravine. Arturo had suspected as much. Now he checked Liam's bug—if the kid wasn't with his daughter, he might know where she was.

It was a Friday night, and the kid was at the movies, at Fairview Mall. He'd sat down in auditorium two half an hour ago, and had gotten up to pee once already. Arturo slipped the toy soldiers into the pocket of his winter parka and pulled on a hat and gloves and set off for the mall.

The stink of the smellie movie clogged his nose, a cacophony of blood, gore, perfume and flowers, the only smells that Hollywood ever really perfected. Liam was kissing a girl in the dark, but it wasn't Ada, it was a sad, skinny thing with a lazy eye and skin worse than Liam's. She gawked at Arturo as he hauled Liam out of his seat, but a flash of Arturo's badge shut her up.

"Hello, Liam," he said, once he had the kid in the commandeered manager's office.

"God *damn*, what the fuck did I ever do to you?" the kid said. Arturo knew that when kids started cursing like that, they were scared of something.

"Where has Ada gone, Liam?"

"Haven't seen her in months," he said.

"I have been bugging you ever since I found out you existed. Every one of your movements has been logged. I know where you've been and when. And I know where my daughter has been, too. Try again."

Liam made a disgusted face. "You are a complete ball of shit," he said. "Where do you get off spying on people like me?"

"I'm a police detective, Liam," he said. "It's my job."

"What about privacy?"

"What have you got to hide?"

The kid slumped back in his chair. "We've been renting out the OLED clothes. Making some pocket money. Come on, are infra-red *lights* a crime now?"

"I'm sure they are," Arturo said. "And if you can't tell me where to find my daughter, I think it's a crime I'll arrest you for."

"She has another phone," Liam said. "Not listed in her name."

"Stolen, you mean." His daughter, peddling Eurasian infowar tech through a stolen phone. His ex-wife, the queen of the super-intelligent hive minds of Eurasian robots.

"No, not stolen. Made out of parts. There's a guy. The code for getting on the network was in a phone book that we started finding last month."

"Give me the number, Liam," Arturo said, taking out his phone.

"Hello?" It was a man's voice, adult.

"Who is this?"

"Who is this?"

Arturo used his cop's voice: "This is Arturo Icaza de Arana-Goldberg, Police Detective Third Grade. Who am I speaking to?"

"Hello, Detective," said the voice, and he placed it then. The Social Harmony man, bald and rounded, with his long nose and sharp Adam's apple. His heart thudded in his chest.

"Hello, sir," he said. It sounded like a squeak to him.

"You can just stay there, Detective. Someone will be along in a moment to get you. We have your daughter."

The robot that wrenched off the door of his car was black and non-reflective, headless and eight-armed. It grabbed him without ceremony and dragged him from the car without heed for his shout of pain. "Put me down!" he said, hoping that this robot that so blithely ignored the first law would still obey the second. No such luck.

It cocooned him in four of its arms and set off cross-country, dancing off the roofs of houses, hopping invisibly from lamp-post to lamp-post, above the oblivious heads of the crowds below. The icy wind howled in Arturo's bare ears, froze the tip of his nose and numbed his fingers. They rocketed downtown so fast that they were there in ten minutes, bounding along the lakeshore toward the Social Harmony center out on Cherry Beach. People who paid a visit to the Social Harmony center never talked about what they found there.

It scampered into a loading bay behind the building and carried Arturo quickly through windowless corridors lit with even, sourceless illumination, up three flights of stairs and then deposited him before a thick door, which slid aside with a hushed hiss.

"Hello, Detective," the Social Harmony man said.

"Dad!" Ada said. He couldn't see her, but he could hear that she had been crying. He nearly hauled off and popped the man one on the tip of his narrow chin, but before he could do more than twitch, the black robot had both his wrists in bondage.

"Come in," the Social Harmony man said, making a sweeping gesture and standing aside while the black robot brought him into the interrogation room.

Ada *had* been crying. She was wrapped in two coils of black-robot arms, and her eyes were red-rimmed and puffy. He stared hard at her as she looked back at him.

"Are you hurt?" he said.

"No," she said.

"All right," he said.

He looked at the Social Harmony man, who wasn't smirking, just watching curiously.

"Leonard MacPherson," he said, "it is my duty as a UNATS Detective

Third Grade to inform you that you are under arrest for trade in contraband positronics. You have the following rights: to a trial per current rules of due process; to be free from self-incrimination in the absence of a court order to the contrary; to consult with a Social Harmony advocate; and to a speedy arraignment. Do you understand your rights?"

Ada actually giggled, which spoiled the moment, but he felt better for having said it. The Social Harmony man gave the smallest disappointed shake of his head and turned away to prod at a small, sleek computer.

"You went to Ottawa six months ago," the Social Harmony man said. "When we picked up your daughter, we thought it was she who'd gone, but it appears that you were the one carrying her phone. You'd thoughtfully left the trace in place on that phone, so we didn't have to refer to the logs in cold storage, they were already online and ready to be analyzed.

"We've been to the safe house. It was quite a spectacular battle. Both sides were surprised, I think. There will be another, I'm sure. What I'd like from you is as close to a verbatim report as you can make of the conversation that took place there."

They'd had him bugged and traced. Of course they had. Who watched the watchers? Social Harmony. Who watched Social Harmony? Social Harmony.

"I demand a consultation with a Social Harmony advocate," Arturo said.

"This is such a consultation," the Social Harmony man said, and this time, he *did* smile. "Make your report, Detective."

Arturo sucked in a breath. "Leonard MacPherson, it is my duty as a UNATS Detective Third Grade to inform you that you are under arrest for trade in contraband positronics. You have the following rights: to a trial per current rules of due process; to be free from self-incrimination in the absence of a court order to the contrary; to consult with a Social Harmony advocate; and to a speedy arraignment. Do you understand your rights?"

The Social Harmony man held up one finger on the hand closest to the black robot holding Ada, and she screamed, a sound that knifed through Arturo, ripping him from asshole to appetite.

"STOP!" he shouted. The man put his finger down and Ada sobbed quietly.

"I was taken to the safe house on the fifth of September, after being gassed by a Eurasian infowar robot in the basement of Fairview Mall—"

There was a thunderclap then, a crash so loud that it hurt his stomach and his head and vibrated his fingertips. The doors to the room buckled and flattened, and there stood Benny and Lenny and—Natalie.

Benny and Lenny moved so quickly that he was only able to track them by the things they knocked over on the way to tearing apart the robot that was holding Ada. A second later, the robot holding him was in pieces, and he was standing on his own two feet again. The Social Harmony man had gone so pale he looked green in his natty checked suit and pink tie.

Benny or Lenny pinned his arms in a tight hug and Natalie walked carefully to him and they regarded one another in silence. She slapped him abruptly, across each cheek. "Harming children," she said. "For shame."

Ada stood on her own in the corner of the room, crying with her mouth in a O. Arturo and Natalie both looked to her and she stood, poised, between them, before running to Arturo and leaping onto him, so that he staggered momentarily before righting himself with her on his hip, in his arms.

"We'll go with you now," he said to Natalie.

"Thank you," she said. She stroked Ada's hair briefly and kissed her cheek. "I love you, Ada."

Ada nodded solemnly.

"Let's go," Natalie said, when it was apparent that Ada had nothing to say to her.

Benny tossed the Social Harmony man across the room into the corner of a desk. He bounced off it and crashed to the floor, unconscious or dead. Arturo couldn't bring himself to care.

Benny knelt before Arturo. "Climb on, please," it said. Arturo saw that Natalie was already pig-a-back on Lenny. He climbed aboard.

They moved even faster than the black robots had, but the bitter cold was offset by the warmth radiating from Benny's metal hide, not hot, but warm. Arturo's stomach reeled and he held Ada tight, squeezing his eyes shut and clamping his jaw.

But Ada's gasp made him look around, and he saw that they had cleared the city limits, and were vaulting over rolling farmlands now, jumping in long flat arcs whose zenith was just high enough for him to see the highway—the 401, they were headed east—in the distance.

And then he saw what had made Ada gasp: boiling out of the hills and ditches, out of the trees and from under the cars: an army of headless, eight-armed black robots, arachnoid and sinister in the moonlight. They scuttled on the ground behind them, before them, and to both sides. Social Harmony had built a secret army of these robots and secreted them across the land, and now they were all chasing after them.

The ride got bumpy then, as Benny beat back the tentacles that reached for them, smashing the black robots with mighty one-handed blows, his other hand supporting Arturo and Ada. Ada screamed as a black robot reared up before them, and Benny vaulted it smoothly, kicking it hard as he went, while Arturo clung on for dear life.

Another scream made him look over toward Lenny and Natalie. Lenny was slightly ahead and to the left of them, and so he was the vanguard, encountering twice as many robots as they.

A black spider-robot clung to his leg, dragging behind him with each lope, and one of its spare arms was tugging at Natalie.

As Arturo watched—as Ada watched—the black robot ripped Natalie off of Lenny's back and tossed her into the arms of one of its cohort behind it, which skewered her on one of its arms, a black spear protruding from her belly as she cried once more and then fell silent. Lenny was overwhelmed a moment later, buried under writhing black arms.

Benny charged forward even faster, so that Arturo nearly lost his grip, and then he steadied himself. "We have to go back for them—"

"They're dead," Benny said. "There's nothing to go back for." Its warm voice was sorrowful as it raced across the countryside, and the wind filled Arturo's throat when he opened his mouth, and he could say no more.

Ada wept on the jet, and Arturo wept with her, and Benny stood over them, a minatory presence against the other robots crewing the fast little plane, who left them alone all the way to Paris, where they changed jets again for the long trip to Beijing.

They slept on that trip, and when they landed, Benny helped them off the plane and onto the runway, and they got their first good look at Eurasia.

It was tall. Vertical. Beijing loomed over them with curvilinear towers that twisted and bent and jigged and jagged so high they disappeared at the tops. It smelled like barbeque and flowers, and around them skittered fast armies of robots of every shape and size, wheeling in lockstep like schools of exotic fish. They gawped at it for a long moment, and someone came up behind them and then warm arms encircled their necks.

Arturo knew that smell, knew that skin. He could never have forgotten it.

He turned slowly, the blood draining from his face.

"Natty?" he said, not believing his eyes as he confronted his dead, ex-wife. There were tears in her eyes.

"Artie," she said. "Ada," she said. She kissed them both on the cheeks.

Benny said, "You died in UNATS. Killed by modified Eurasian Social Harmony robots. Lenny, too. Ironic," he said.

She shook her head. "He means that we probably co-designed the robots that Social Harmony sent after you."

"Natty?" Arturo said again. Ada was white and shaking.

"Oh dear," she said. "Oh, God. You didn't know—"

"He didn't give you a chance to explain," Benny said.

"Oh, God, Jesus, you must have thought—"

"I didn't think it was my place to tell them, either," Benny said, sounding embarrassed, a curious emotion for a robot.

"Oh, God. Artie, Ada. There are—there are *lots* of me. One of the first things I did here was help them debug the uploading process. You just put a copy of yourself into a positronic brain, and then when you need a body, you grow one or build one or both and decant yourself into it. I'm like Lenny and Benny now—there are many of me. There's too much work to do otherwise."

"I told you that our development helped humans understand themselves," Benny said.

Arturo pulled back. "You're a robot?"

"No," Natalie said. "No, of course not. Well, a little. Parts of me. Growing a body is slow. Parts of it, you build. But I'm mostly made of person."

Ada clung tight to Arturo now, and they both stepped back toward the jet.

"Dad?" Ada said.

He held her tight.

"Please, Arturo," Natalie, his dead, multiplicitous ex-wife said. "I know it's a lot to understand, but it's different here in Eurasia. Better, too. I don't expect you to come rushing back to my arms after all this time, but I'll help you if you'll let me. I owe you that much, no matter what happens between us. You too, Ada, I owe you a lifetime."

"How many are there of you?" he asked, not wanting to know the answer.

"I don't know exactly," she said.

"3,422," Benny said. "This morning it was 3,423."

Arturo rocked back in his boots and bit his lip hard enough to draw blood.

"Um," Natalie said. "More of me to love?"

He barked a laugh, and Natalie smiled and reached for him. He leaned back toward the jet, then stopped, defeated. Where would he go? He let her warm hand take his, and a moment later, Ada took her other hand and they stood facing each other, breathing in their smells.

"I've gotten you your own place," she said as she led them across the tarmac. "It's close to where I live, but far enough for you to have privacy."

"What will I do here?" he said. "Do they have coppers in Eurasia?"

"Not really," Natalie said.

"It's all robots?"

"No, there's not any crime."

"Oh."

Arturo put one foot in front of the other, not sure if the ground was actually spongy or if that was jetlag. Around him, the alien smells of Beijing and the robots that were a million times smarter than he. To his right, his wife, one of 3,422 versions of her.

To his left, his daughter, who would inherit this world.

He reached into his pocket and took out the tin soldiers there. They were old and their glaze was cracked like an oil painting, but they were little people that a real human had made, little people in human image, and they were older than robots. How long had humans been making people, striving to bring them to life? He looked at Ada—a little person he'd brought to life.

He gave her the tin soldiers.

"For you," he said. "Daddy-daughter present." She held them tightly, their tiny bayonets sticking out from between her fingers.

"Thanks, Dad," she said. She held them tightly and looked around, wide-eyed, at the schools of robots and the corkscrew towers.

A flock of Bennys and Lennys appeared before them, joined by their Benny.

"There are half a billion of them," she said. "And 3,422 of them," she said, pointing with a small bayonet at Natalie.

"But there's only one of you," Arturo said.

She craned her neck.

"Not for long!" she said, and broke away, skipping forward and whirling around to take it all in.

ALTERNATE GIRL'S EXPATRIATE LIFE

ROCHITA LOENEN-RUIZ

In Springtime, her garden yielded a hundred wisteria blossoms. White English roses climbed the pergola. *Digitalis purpurea*, lavender from the South of France, mint and thyme, rosemary and tarragon, basil and sweet marjoram—they all grew in Alternate Girl's one hundred percent super-qualified housewife garden.

Across the street, excavators dug up large swathes of grass.

"They're building a new complex over there," her neighbor said. "I heard the farmer who owned that land went off to live the life of a millionaire."

Her neighbor babbled on about yachts and sea voyages and Alternate Girl stood there staring while the machines went about their business of churning up grass and soil. She wondered what it would be like to be crushed under those hungry wheels, and she flinched at her own imagination.

"A pity," her neighbor said. "I sure will miss the view."

Alternate Girl murmured something vague in reply, and went back to tending her flowers.

She wondered if the farmer was happier now that he had his millions. Would wealth and sea voyages make up for severed ties and the erasure of generations of familial history?

She pulled out a stray weed, and scattered coffee grinds to keep the cats from digging up her crocus bulbs.

She shook her head and headed back indoors. She'd only known two kinds of lives, and in neither of them had she been a millionaire.

Most expatriates pursue a model life. This makes them a desired member in their adopted society. They appear to assimilate quickly, adapting without visible complications to the customs of the country in which they reside.

On the surface, they may appear contented, well-adjusted, and happy. However, studies reveal an underlying sorrow that often manifests itself in dreams. In dreams, the expatriate experiences no ambivalent feelings. There is only a strong sense of loss. It isn't uncommon for expats to wake up crying.

—On Expatriate Behavior by Mackay & Lindon

Ω

In her dreams, Alternate Girl fled from her life as an expat. She sprouted wings and let the wind take her back to the gates of her hometown.

Even in the dreamscape she could smell the exhaust from passing jeepneys. She could taste the metal dust in the air. The moon shone on the gentle curve of asphalt, cutting through dusty thoroughfares, creating long dark shadows on the pavement. Metal tenements jutted up out of the land, pointing like fingers at the night sky.

By day, a constant stream of drones strove to keep those buildings together. Every bit of scrap metal, every piece of residual wiring was used to keep the landscape of steel and concrete from breaking to pieces. For all its frailty, for all of its seeming squalor, there was something dear and familiar about the way the streets met and turned into each other.

Even if her life was filled with the coziness of here and now, she could not shake off the longing that thrummed through her dreams in the same way that the thrum of the equilibrium machine pulsed through this landscape.

Towering above the tenements was the Remembrance Monument. Made of compressed bits and parts, it contained all the memories of those gone before. Each year, the Monument reached higher and higher until its apex was lost in the covering of clouds. When she was younger, she'd often imagined she could hear the voices of the gone before.

Above the pulse of the Equilibrium Machine, above the gentle susurrus of faded ghosts, she heard a cry. High and shrill, it emitted a hopelessness Alternate Girl remembered feeling.

It was the same cry that pulled her out of her dreams back into the present. She turned on her side, pressed her ear against her pillow, and stared into the darkness.

This is my home now, she told herself. *I am happy as I am. We are happy as we are.*

Never mind her personal griefs. Never mind her longing for that lost landscape.

Would you like a chance to revisit the past or to visit the future? Optimum Labs offers you the chance to take the leap in time. Our company is 100% customer satisfaction guaranteed. Unlike other scams out there, Optimum labs offers you the real thing.

Alternate Girl stared at the screen. Each day the spam mails showed up without fail. Same time stamps, same recipient name, all from anonymous senders.

Who sent these mails? And did everyone in her neighborhood receive the same mail with the same time stamps every day? If she had the courage to reply, would she receive an answer from all the anonymous senders? Her hand hovered over the delete key. If you sent garbage to the landfill, it got buried underground, but what about garbage in the ether? Did it float around silently on the airwaves? Would all the spam and the deleted mail come back to haunt her in the form of ether pollution or some such specialized name?

While she sat there, the speakers gave off a faint ping. She clicked and waited as the new message filled her screen.

Happy Birthday, Alternate Girl! Today, is a milestone for all of us. You have successfully completed one hundred weeks of expatriate life. In recognition of your hard work, a reward has been issued to you at the designated station. Report in as soon as you can and don't forget to register at our renewed website. Greetings from Memomach@metaltown.com.

Alternate Girl squeezed her eyes shut. She opened them and stared once more at the message on her screen. Could it be what she had been waiting for all this time or was Mechanic finally calling her home?

> *Most expatriates express mixed feelings regarding their origin. Many of them harbor a secret fear of losing touch with the collective memory. While they seem content with their new lives, repatriation is a common subject of conversation. For the expatriate, to return raises a complex response.*
>
> *One of the subjects of this study worded it this way: "Return is something I fantasize about and desire. But at the same time, it is something I am afraid of."*
>
> *Choosing to build a new life in an unfamiliar land represents a leaving behind of the collective, and while there may still be remnants of a shared life, the expatriate faces uncertainty. What if he or she has lost the ability to pick up the threads of the old life?*
> *—On Expatriate Behavior by Mackay & Lindon*

Her first recollection was of Father's eyes shining down at her from his great height. Light filtered in through drawn shades and she could see an outline of buildings from where she lay. It seemed as if there were a thousand busy bees buzzing inside her skull. Beside her, someone moaned. She shivered and echoed the sound.

"There, there," Father said. "No need to be frightened. Father," he said, pointing to himself. "Metal Town." He gestured to something beyond her vision.

She repeated the words after him, and listened as he murmured sounds of approval.

"You're progressing very well," he said. "Soon, I'll take you to the Mechanic."

He shuffled away out of her line of sight. She heard a thump and another moan, and she called out anxiously. "Father?"

"I'm here," Father said. His voice was soothing and she drifted away into a kaleidoscope of screeching metal and the crescendo of another voice wailing out Father's name.

When she woke up, the curtains were drawn back. From where she was, she could see black metal struts and the carcasses of vehicles piled up on top of one another.

From far away, came the hum of lasers and a low bass thrum which she later discovered was the Equilibrium Machine. A man bent over her; his face was shiny and round and she saw metal cogs where his ears should have been. His fingers felt cold and hard on her skin.

"Just like one of them," he whispered. "If I didn't know any better, I'd say you were one of them."

His words made her uncomfortable, and when he took her hand she pulled it away.

"Don't fight it," he whispered. "Fighting only makes it worse."

She felt something sharp and burning on her skin. Wet leaked out of her eyes. She couldn't move.

"You'll be fine," he said. "It's all part of the process."

Staring at the message on her screen, she wondered if Mechanic considered this as yet another part of the process.

"Leaving is a part of the process," Father had said. "While we may long for return, we also know that having left we are already changed."

She looked around at her cozy nest, stared at the brilliant blues and greens of her living room, at the paintings of sunflowers and butterflies, and she wondered whether she would be able to go back and surrender to a life spent waiting for harvest.

Outside, the digging machines had fallen silent. She looked up at the clock. It was half past twelve and the men who drove them were probably off to lunch.

Extract from notes on the creation of Alternate Girl:

2001 hours: Original model expired at 2000 hours. Harvested from prototype ag 119-2: pulsebeat, bodyframe, eyes, memory, emo chip.

2021 hours: Applied Mechanic's new plastics to bodyframe. Installed chip, memory, pulsebeat, eyes. Molding of face follows, arms, legs, and other parts. Assembly proceeded as planned. Pliables applied

2065 hours: Awareness installed. Test successful
2070 hours: Emo chip installed. Test successful
2098 hours: Memory chip activated. Trace and recall function
activated. Registration complete.

There was a party when she passed the 4000 hour mark. Father beamed, and Mechanic looked happy and hopeful. Metal Town's citizens came in reply to Mechanic's summons. Of these, she loved most the ones who rolled in on lopsided wheels and who smiled and chirped code at her.

When she tried to chirp back, they encircled her and projected their enthusiasm in signals and bleeps that she couldn't put into proper words.

"You are one of us," the chirpers said. And she felt welcomed and included.

Father beamed at the compliments he received. "Yes, I am proud of her," he said.

"Our first success," Mechanic said.

Alternate Girl wondered at his words. Had there been others then? If she was the first success, where were the ones that had failed?

The chirpers moved away and she was surrounded by tall and gangly ones who took her hands in theirs. They ran their fingers up and down her arms, peered into her eyes, and asked her questions about her training.

Mechanic beamed and looked on. He sipped oil from a can he held in his hand and bowed his head and gestured towards her.

Where were the words to tell a powerful being that you had no wish to be looked upon and admired as if you were a foreign object placed on display?

Foreign. It struck her then. She lifted her hands, marvelling at the elasticity of her flesh. Of course, she was foreign.

Notes on progression
ag 119-2 perfectly adjusted. All systems normal. Social skills optimal. Sequence failures, nil.

In the weeks that followed she passed through various tests.

A model housewife, she learned, was dedicated to maintaining a perfect home and garden. She perused hundreds of pages of magazines culled from god knew where. Housewives by the hundreds, all extolling the virtues of various cleaning products, household goods, cooking sauces, oils, liniments, lotions, facial creams, garden products and intimate apparel. The array of faces and products dazzled her.

"Will there be others like me?" she asked Father.

"If all goes well," he replied.

"What about you?" she asked.

"When the time comes, the old must give way to the new."

She waited for him to continue. Wanting to know more, wanting to understand what he meant by his words.

"You're not old," she said.

He touched her cheek and shook his head. "I shall tell you more soon," he said.

These hours spent with Father were precious to her. He was patient with her attempts to put into practice the things she learned.

"You must learn control," he said. "You are far stronger than others think you are, but control will serve you better where you are going, A.G."

"When they take me away," Father said, "I want you to remember that it's part of the process we all go through."

"Why would they take you away?" she asked.

"In the order of things, old models must give way for the new," Father said. "But even if I go, my pride and joy live on in you, A.G. Eight thousand hours old and going strong. You are our future."

"Where are you going?" she asked.

"I'll be there," Father said. He pointed to the Remembrance Monument. "When the time comes, I will be harvested as others have been before me. My memories will become part of the Monument. There are those who say that when the end of time comes, we will unfold our bodies, regain our memories and find ourselves changed into something more than machine."

"Will I be harvested too?" she asked.

"I don't know." He cupped her face in his hands. "You are our first success. We don't even know what you'll be like when you're as old as we are."

"Can I have your memories?" she asked.

He didn't answer. Outside, Mechanic's men tramped through the streets of Metal Town. Someone screamed. *Harvest.* The word whispered through Alternate Girl's circuits.

Father flinched, closed his eyes and bowed his head.

"Will it hurt?" Alternate Girl asked.

"I don't know," Father replied.

But she knew he was lying. She wondered what happened at Harvest and whether it was indeed a natural thing as Father said.

She visited the Remembrance Monument, and tried to make sense of it all. Its cold walls gave back a reflection of her face—so unlike the faces of her fellow citizens. She thought of a life without Father, and there were no words for the grief she felt.

"Take me then," she said to the Monument. "If you must take Father, then you must take me too."

But the Monument stayed silent, and no matter how hard she listened, there were no messages or codes from the beyond.

After that, she grew more conscious of how the machine men made their daily trek to the walled buildings. They went in the same as they went out. The drones monitored the streets, gathering up residue and scrap metal. It seemed to her that each one had a duty to perform, a routine task to follow.

Mechanic had found no routine for her yet.

"Learn all you can," he said on one of his visits. "You will be our first ambassador. The model housewife, a perfect expatriate. They will love us because of you. Perhaps they will finally remember us and we will be reconciled to the original makers."

"What about Father?" Alternate Girl asked.

"He does his part," Mechanic said. "You must do yours."

She didn't like the uncertainty of his answer, but she had learned not to say so. Instead, she nodded and listened and took in the knowledge he fed to her.

There must be a way out, she thought.

It was the first time she thought of escape.

The Expatriate Choice as subject of this study reveals the following common causes for expatriation:

Economic. Some expatriates choose to live or work in a different country or society for the sake of material gain.

Social. Some expatriates choose to live or work in a different country or society because they see this as a means of increasing their stature in society. Others choose exile for the sake of love

Political. Some expatriates embrace voluntary exile as a means of protest against the ruling body of their home country.

—Observations of Expatriate Behavior by Mackay & Lindon

Alternate Girl found the rift in the barrier a week after Mechanic's visit. It was late at night, and she had chosen to take one of the roads leading South. She ventured further and further away from the heart of Metal Town. The moon cast its light on the road before her and she could see the long shadow of herself stretching out and mingling with the waving shapes of wild grass and brush.

She was deep in thought when the sound of wheels swishing on asphalt caught her attention. She saw a flash of light, and then she was at a barred gate. Through the bars, she could see the outline of cars and buses flowing in a rush away from her. She stared at this vision of vibrant and full-bodied creatures, and she understood that they were relatives of the disemboweled who lay stranded in the many garages around Metal Town.

On her way home, she was conscious of the spy eye stationed atop the Remembrance Monument, and passing close to it, she heard a faint murmur like voices whispering through the scaffolds of the Monument's steel ports.

The recollection of screams played back in her memory and she stopped. One day, they would take her too. She'd be joined to the Monument regardless of whether she desired it or not.

Across the street, she saw the Mechanic. Moonlight glinted off the chrome of his head, and he gave a slight nod when he saw her. She could hear him muttering to himself as he crossed to where the tin houses of the Numbered Men leaned against each other like pale reflections of their owners.

Alternate Girl wished she had the courage to run up to Mechanic. "Please," she would say. "Please spare Father."

But she already knew his answer.

"Our duty is to the original creators of the Monument," he'd told her once. "It is our task to harvest the bodies and to store the memories of the gone before. It is all for the greater good, Alternate Girl. We all have our duties to perform. Your father understands his place in all of these."

Memory, its storage and the passing on of it, is essential to the inhabitants of Metal Town. What function does the Remembrance Monument have if not to store the memories of the gone before? At the heart of Harvest is the preservation of the spirit that is Metal Town.

—A Celebration of Memory by Sitio Mechanics

Father was silent. He dragged his feet when he walked and complained about his joints. She tried to cheer him up, but all the while, her mind circled around the question of escape.

"They'll be coming for me soon," Father said. His speech slurred and he sat down and leaned his head against the back of the chair. "Mechanic wants to create a partner for you," he whispered. "He wants someone created in your image. An alternate man designed to fit the perfect housewife."

"Father ... " She knelt down beside him. "If I told you we could get out and not have to come back, what would you say?"

He laughed. "Don't you think anyone has tried that before? Why do you think the Monument keeps growing, A.G.? Our masters created us to stay in Metal Town, but there were always those who tried to escape. Everyone comes back to Metal Town, even those who leave with the Mechanic's blessing."

"But there's a road out of here," Alternate Girl insisted. "If we leave, at least we'll have a choice."

"They'll always catch you," he whispered. "Metal Town allows no exemptions, A.G. Right now, you are one of a kind, but what's been made before can be made again."

He closed his eyes, and leaned back in his chair. She could hear the slow whir of his heart, and she felt more frightened than she had ever been.

"Why did you make me this way?" she asked. "You could have made me a drone, if this is all the life I'm meant to have."

"Do you think a drone's life is of less value than yours?" Father asked. "Memory and hope is all that lies between you and the life of a Numbered Man. We come home when our time is at end. To be joined to the original dream of our creators is a privilege, not a curse."

"I'm sorry," she said. "I'm sorry, Father. I didn't mean for it to sound that way. But please, please, won't you at least try? Without you, I might just as well be a Numbered Man."

"Escape is never without price," Father said.

But she only heard the capitulation in his voice.

Copy of memo lifted from Mechanic's desk:
Received: 23:11, Remembrance Monday
Re: Circular number 792-a-1b3rae
Release Request: Alternate Girl
Status: Under consideration

They left Metal Town early in the morning. In the quiet dark, the thrum of the Equilibrium Machine was magnified a hundred times. Avoiding the street lamps, they kept to the shadows as best as they could.

"I'll slow you down," Father had said.

But she wouldn't leave him behind. And so, they crept along behind the piles of junk and strip metal.

Their feet slipped on smooth steel and made clunky sounds in the silence. They waited, but when no one came, they slid on forward until they reached a surface less finished than the one they'd left behind.

"We're almost there," she whispered.

She could hear his joints creak in the silence, and she reached out a hand to help him.

"I'm fine," he said.

And then they were out in the open. Beyond them, the road opened up and curled southwards to where the rift in the barrier had expanded.

The rising sun cast a golden glow over Father's face, and it seemed like he was made of light.

They were headed towards the rift when from behind came the sound of pursuit. The roar of the Mechanic and the clunk of boots on the hard surface of the road.

They raced down the blacktop as the sun made its journey to the apex. Alternate Girl ran, propelling Father onwards with a fresh surge of energy. The earth shook, and Alternate Girl slipped and lost her footing.

"Get up," Father's voice whispered in her ear.

"Run," Alternate Girl gasped. "I'll slow them down."

"I'm not letting them take you," Father said.

The Equilibrium Machine shrieked, and Alternate Girl cried out as Mechanic loomed before them.

"What did you think to gain?" Mechanic asked.

What had I hoped for? Alternate Girl wondered.

"Let her go," Father said. "I will do as is required of me. Only let her go."

"Do you think you still have the power to intervene?" Mechanic asked. He kept his gaze locked on Alternate Girl.

"No," Father said. "I realize there is no forgiveness for what I chose to do. Still—"

Mechanic raised his right hand in a silencing gesture. "Forgiveness is not up to you to decide," he said. "Whatever follows lies in the hands of this girl you have created. She is ready to leave this place, and I am sure she will be an asset to the Expatriate Program."

Building bridges and abolishing barriers is central to the Expatriate Program. Ignorance leads to misconceptions and stereotypes, hence the lumping together of certain groups of expatriates. It is hoped that the Expatriate Program will give rise to mutual understanding and acceptance of each other's differences

Participants to the Expatriate Program are given the freedom to appropriate what they deem necessary in order to achieve the central goal of mutual integration.

—Understanding the Expatriate Program by Mackay & Hill

She'd found her partner on the other side of the gate. It had seemed simple enough to follow him home and to allow herself to be embraced and joined to him. That union made it possible for her to slip seamlessly into the pattern of his everyday life.

All the knowledge fed into her came to good use, and their lives entwined as if by rote. She became the housewife, and he, her model mate.

How he spent his days was a mystery to her. She imagined him spending all day behind a desk in an office somewhere. She thought of him lost in a maze of paperwork, one of the hundreds of thousands of Numbered Men wearing the same colored shirt, the same suit from the same local haberdashery, the same haircut from some local barber, the same coat, the same tie. She imagined all of them, working together towards the same goal.

How many numbers have you added up today? That's how Alternate Girl imagined their conversations went. *How many more numbers before you meet your quota?*

"If I do as you wish, will you return Father to me?" she asked Mechanic.

"Already his body is good for nothing but the harvest," Mechanic said. "But I can give you the essence of him. How you choose to restore him lies within your grasp."

She turned the chip over in her hand. For all that it seemed small, it contained the entirety of Father's memories as well as the history of their lives.

"A simple matter to appropriate a body," Mechanic's words whispered in her head. "You won't even need to tell him what you're doing. Let him fall away into an eternal dream, so Father may return."

"Won't he feel pain?" she asked.

"A relative thing," he said. "Such things are unimportant and the outcome relies on your ability to do what must be done. You have done well, A.G. Allowing you to regain Father is a small reward."

The chip felt hard and hot in her hand. She'd sacrificed towards this goal, subjugated her will in order to build a life beyond the shadows of the Remembrance Monument. Already she couldn't remember the name of this man with whom she'd shared a bed for one hundred weeks.

Should she feel regret or remorse for what she was about to do?

She had no answer to that question. All she could think of was Mechanic's admonition; she could only hear his voice telling her that she was free to do as she chose. If she chose to erase her partner's life for the sake of regaining Father, it wouldn't matter if she could no longer return to Metal Town.

She listened to her partner's key turning in the front door, listened to the sound of his footsteps in the hall, listened for the familiar creak of his joints, and turned to welcome him home.

THE RISING WATERS

BENJAMIN CROWELL

It was Charlie's last day of existence, so I was feeling that weird mixture of excitement and letdown that comes at the end of a project cycle. It was the feeling of being a wheel spinning off balance, and it needed a cigarette for punctuation.

Delta Elevator. Step into the cab, slide the accordion-cage door shut with a grunt—the door was designed for big, male miners. I felt the upward draft of cold air as the cab lurched into motion, and gratefully polluted it for the next four minutes.

At the bottom was Ed, outer perimeter security.

"Hi, Ed."—"Hey, Sue."

My parents saddled me with the name Sudaporn, and you can imagine how that went over for a young girl newly arrived in Los Angeles. I've been Sue for the last forty years.

Outer perimeter is outside the Faraday cage, so it can all be electronic, and there's not much for the human guard to do. After the retina scanner vouched for the me-ness of me, we stopped making an effort at small talk, and Ed went back to his knitting, a red scarf. Whatever keeps you sane.

Next, inside the Faraday cage, came Julia and Gil, inner perimeter. I never chatted with Julia, because nothing kills conversation like a strip search. For the gazillionth time, Gil verified the non-electronic nature of my nicotine patches, Buddha necklace, and mint 1965 KE pocket slide rule. As a first lieutenant in the National Guard I supposedly outranked them, but I don't think they took that any more seriously than I did.

I greeted Funmi, the console jock, ducked into the dressing room, and got into my VR exoskeleton. I came back out looking like a Dr. Seuss character stuck in an egg slicer.

"Last day," said Funmi.

"Yep, let's do it."

I stepped into the Sandbox, sealed the hatch behind me, and gave the thumbs up. The white room changed to a simulated living room. Charlie sat motionless on the carpet, staring into space.

"Good morning, Charlie," I said.

No response, and that was no surprise. The days were long gone when we could get him to converse about Euclidean geometry, or even tempt him out of his shell at all with a chess board or a pixelated peanut butter sandwich. The official working hypothesis was that he was nonresponsive (don't say autistic) due to a mismatch (don't call it boredom) between processing power and input bandwidth.

"Charlie, can you hear me? It's Sue."

Silence. I lifted his arm, and my exoskeleton resisted as if the arm had weight. Charlie himself neither resisted nor assisted in the motion—if he had, I would have felt it through the simulation's feedback into the skel. I let go of his arm, and he let it stay in the air. If we'd continued the simulation for the next million years, I'm sure he would have kept it right there. I found myself imagining what that would be like for him, and then the professional discipline kicked back in. There's a reason they switched to using us number-crunching types for the VR interaction jobs. The human brain is a funny thing. We identify with fuzzy ducklings, brave little toasters, or even those cute twentieth-century VW bug cars. For a person who doesn't have an academic background in computer science, it's all too easy to forget that Charlie is just a code name for a project, not the name of a self. All too easy to slip into psychological identification with the tangles of quantum correlations stoked and tended by people like Funmi.

All too easy to drive yourself nuts.

The whole morning was occupied with the standard diagnostic series, and then it was time for lunch with Funmi. I can eat a bowl of instant ramen without shucking the skel, although it looks funny to the uninitiated. After lunch I slapped on two nicotine patches, because I wasn't looking forward to what came next.

I had to spank the brave little toaster. My job that afternoon was to carry out one final experiment on Charlie: classical stimulus-response theory, vintage 1930. Psychology wasn't even a science then, it was pure voodoo, from the same era as Freud. But hey, it was the end of the project cycle, so there weren't a lot of viable proposals for processing time. Why not try an experiment that's a little far out, even one based on a thoroughly discredited theory? I should have refused to go along with their useless, sadistic plan for Charlie's last day. Instead I kept my misgivings to myself and went along. Isn't that most of us do, most of the time? I don't think any choice I made could have helped Charlie, but that doesn't excuse what I did.

Kneeling on the floor next to Charlie, I took his wrist in one hand and his elbow in the other, and raised them. His bent arm hovered, motionless.

"Charlie, lower your arm."

No response.

"*No*, Charlie." The word *no* was a signal to Funmi. She zapped some of the quantum bits that Charlie was made of. Did he experience it as a feeling similar to an itch, or maybe more like being prodded in the arm with a ballpoint pen? My training told me it was a bogus question to ask in the first place. Sentience, self-awareness—computational psychology has banished those terms from its vocabulary.

I brought his arm back down again, then started the cycle again.

"Charlie, lower your arm."

Nothing.

"*No*, Charlie." With each *no* she'd be dialing it up a little more, decohering more qubits. A pinch on the earlobe this time, sandpaper rubbing on a fingertip? No, don't ask meaningless questions.

Another cycle. "*No*, Charlie." A whack with a bamboo stick?

The living room faded down to 50, and Charlie turned into a wire frame.

Funmi's voice: *You okay, Sue? Your heart rate's up.*

"I'm okay." Charlie's computing engine was paused, so he couldn't hear my words. And as far as Funmi—you can't wipe the corner of your eye when you're wearing a skel and visor, so as long as I didn't make the motion reflexively, she wouldn't know.

All right. The scene faded back in.

Well, damned if it didn't work on the next iteration—sort of. Charlie's arm came back down by itself. Then it rose again, before I could react. Up, down, up down, updown, updownupdown. It started flailing wildly, and then *bam!*, I was knocked back by a blow to my face. The punch itself didn't hurt much—safety overrides—but I felt daggers of pain in my knees, which aren't as flexible as they used to be. And anyway, it's scary to have a seemingly solid object pass into your head. Never mind that the only mechanical force had come from the skel straightening itself out suddenly, it was still a pretty good simulation of a sucker punch.

White room.

Shit! Sue?

Instinct made me try to touch my face, and then I gingerly used my hands to walk myself up into a frog-sit. The wire frame of Charlie's arm was in the way, so I ducked and scrabbled out from under it.

"I'm okay."

You sure?

"I'm okay. Really."

"Hi, Sue . . . are you okay?" The door swung shut behind Ed Donitz, taking twenty decibels back off of the noise from the raucous end-of-cycle party.

"Yeah, sure," I lied. "Smoke bother you?" I had a good excuse to be sitting on the floor in the back hall, smoking by the air duct, with my sore knees stretched out.

He sat down next to me. Why had I even come to the party? I supposed I'd come because it was expected of me. A lot of things were expected of me. Even sitting down, Ed towered over me—a grizzled face, with blond crew-cut hair going gray at the temples. Damn sexy. His ancestors probably sacked Rome.

"I'm done with that red scarf," he said. "If you want it . . . I make more of those things than I can . . . "

"Aw, that's sweet, Ed. Sure, thanks."

A pause, until he said, "New project cycle, huh?"

I looked away. "How's your family?"

He blinked at the sudden change of subject. "All right. Never know . . . censors. How about your mother?"

"They took the drains out yesterday," I said, "and it doesn't look like any fluid is coming back into either lung."

He shook his head. "Euros." He made it sound like a curse, and maybe you couldn't blame him. I wondered whether you could really blame the Euros either, after what we did to Brussels, but that wasn't a sentiment you could express freely.

I leaned my head back and took a drag. "Germs and nukes. What a world."

"That's why the work's so important. Gets you out of bed, you know?"

Germs and nukes. And Charlie's arm buzzing like a fly's wing. I brought my creaky knees up and put my face between them. How was I going to fix myself, my life? I'm not much of a Buddhist, but the childhood training sneaks up on you. They talked about right livelihood. I'd thought that an AI project to find a cure for the Eurovirus would be about as righteous as you could get. How had it turned into torture and murder?

"Sure you're okay?" he asked.

"It's okay." Who was I kidding? "No, not really." This shouldn't be a frat house party, I thought, it should be a funeral.

I looked up at his grizzled, compassionate face, and I realized two things. One was that I wasn't allowed to explain to him why I was so upset about Charlie. The other was that I'd better leave before I did something that would be bad for both of us.

My mother always said not to dwell on possible misfortune. If you say "I hope I don't get in an accident," you'll crack up your car. Early in the morning, the day after the non-conversation in the hall with Ed—*it should be a funeral*—I got the message that my mother had died.

When there's a death in the family, they let you take the call live—with a censor watching with his thumb on a switch, of course, and severe admonitions to keep the conversation on topic.

"We know you can't be here," said my brother Sang, "but they can do a video link from the temple." He looked older in a way that hadn't been apparent in the still photos.

"I don't think they'll allow that. They don't have censors who know Thai."

"You're kidding. What, they think the monks might be Euro spies or something?"

"I don't make the rules." And in any case I'd never liked the big, gaudy temple, or the monks, who the little kids believed had supernatural powers. Nor, I admitted to myself, did I want to see the ceremony: my family kow-towing in front of the coffin in disposable paper suits, crying under their respirator masks.

"Well, I guess that's the way it is," he said. "We'll put your picture in the seat or something."

"I'm sorry."

"It's okay, we understand. Your work—" He stopped short because I was waving him off frantically. "Anyway, we understand. Um . . . it's traditional to make a donation to the temple, and you know the economy down here . . . "

"Sure, Sang. I don't want you all to have money worries on top of everything. How much should I give?"

He named a shocking amount, but I nodded. It was expected of me. "There's also the astrologer," he continued, "to set an auspicious day for the ceremony. I mean, obviously it's kind of a ridiculous superstition, but Aunt Busba . . ." More money.

I was grateful when it was time to go on shift and I had to sign off.

Plenty of people have compared a machine room to a temple, and the operators to priests, but today it was going to be a nursery. Today was the bootstrap process for Debbie, and I was on interaction. I suited up, entered the Sandbox, and seated myself on the wireframe couch, with my back against what was really the wall. The first time you do it, it's hard to convince yourself to let your weight rest on the thighs of your skel.

I made a cradle out of my arms, gave two thumbs up, and then I was holding a crying baby girl. I wrapped the blanket around her while she howled. I wasn't sure why I didn't feel bad about the simulated birth trauma, not the way I did about the aversive stimuli we'd used on Charlie's last day. It wasn't that I thought it was necessary. People who are born by C-section don't experience it, and they don't develop into inhuman monsters. Was it my religious upbringing that made it so easy to accept? *Life is suffering, birth is suffering* . . .

I spoke to Debbie and rocked her gently, and after a while she stopped crying. Now she'd be able to hear the simulated echo of my heartbeat. I started to feel more calm myself. When your life is out of balance, I highly recommend holding a newborn. One heartbeat, two heartbeats. One of the methods we use for accelerating development is to reduce repetition, so for Debbie, each one of those heartbeats was standing in for a thousand that a real baby would have experienced. It was one of the advantages we needed to exploit if we were going to get her into production mode in time to find a cure for the Eurovirus.

I opened one side of my robe. My real breasts pack down pretty flat inside the skel, but the virtual one looked like such a perfect simulation of the ninth month of pregnancy that I could almost feel it as being tight and swollen. I gave Debbie the nipple, and she started sucking greedily—perfect work by the mammalian instinct team.

Five months later, Debbie was a seven-year-old socially, and intellectually she'd moved beyond the tip of the adult human bell curve. We all had the feeling that we'd turned a corner. I was convinced that the crucial change had been to provide a more and more human environment, and to relax the restrictions on what data we could bring in through the firewall. Debbie's environment was more human, so she was more human. More human than Charlie, and certainly more human than Able, the unmotivated, faceless ghost, or Baker, the psychotic talking head. In the back of everyone's mind was the fear of creating an angry god in a box, a personal god like the Christian one—but a personal god like a toddler throwing a tantrum.

By five months, they'd completely removed the throttle on Debbie's processor and let her rip. At any given time there would be one person interacting with her in the Sandbox, but also a flock of specialists working with her via text interfaces. (Text is less resource-intensive to censor than voice or video.)

For those five months, I had gone back to accepting my situation, because it was easy to accept—as long as I didn't think of the future.

The day of the strike, I was in the Sandbox, and Debbie was burbling to me about her work.

"Protein folding is such a cool problem," she said over the bowl of nonexistent chocolate chip cookie dough she was mixing for me. She looked ten or eleven, a compromise between her social and intellectual ages. "It's totally NP-complete, I mean excluding the trivial cases—"

Wham! The floor jumped out from under me, and then I was sprawled with my head inside something dark.

"Sue, why did you fall down?"

There was a rolling bass rumble shaking my guts, superimposed on the clatter of virtual pots and pans. My Angeleno reflexes took over—get under a table—where was I? I felt Debbie grab me by the waist of my virtual skirt and haul backward, but the sim wasn't getting it right, and it seemed like my legs were passing through the floor. My head emerged from the cupboard, and then cups and plates were raining down on me, but turning to harmless wire-frame snowflakes as the safeties kicked in. "Sue!"—she sounded far away, and part of me had time to realize that the virtual sound had attenuated as a comfort feature—but there was still the sound that *wasn't* simulated, the sound that my brain was still interpreting as the fist-smash of an earthquake.

Which it wasn't.

My panic subsided a little once I realized that the cascade of falling objects had been caused by my own body. The shock wave wasn't part of the simulation, so it wouldn't directly affect anything in the VR. But my body had been tossed like a rag doll, and I'd responded by flailing around, so the sim had done its best to work out the unphysical physics of a solid woman flailing around on the inside of a solid cupboard.

"Sue, what happened?" Debbie was hunched over me, a look of confusion and concern on her face.

"Be quiet, I can't talk right now. Funmi?"

Still no response. It was as quiet as the Sandbox can be—quieter, I realized, because there was something missing: the ventilation fans. Not good. Ignoring Debbie, I ran to the hatch and found the handle by touch.

Funmi: *Sue, are you okay in there?*

"More or less." The handle wouldn't turn. "You all right?"

I hurt my wrists. Fucking Euros must have dropped a nuke in our lap!

"I figured."

You'd better come out. The fans stopped.

"I can't get the door open. Can you help me?"

Actually I think my right wrist is broken. I'll go get Gil and Julia.

"Okay."

Debbie had come in from the kitchen. "Are you leaving?" she asked.

"Maybe in a little while."

"Did I do something bad?"

"No, sweetie. It's just that we have a problem because the . . . the building moved."

"The building didn't accelerate. I would have noticed. You fell down and jumped around, though."

"Well, *something* happened in the room, right?"

"You went in the cupboard, like when objects pass through other objects but they're not supposed to. It's one of those things nobody likes to talk about." A pout come over her face.

"Honey, you're just going to have to trust me about some of this. It's true that there are some things I'm not allowed to talk to you about, and I wish it wasn't that way, but it is. The rules say that if I talk to you about those things, they'll take me away and I can never see you again. You don't want that to happen, do you?"

"No!" There was a look of horror on her face.

"Don't worry, we won't let that happen." I sat down on the couch as calmly as I could.

"I'll clean up the kitchen. The plates should have broken, but they d—" She slapped her hand over her mouth.

"That's okay, don't worry about saying the wrong things. It's only a problem if I say them, and I know what not to say. Come sit with me."

She joined me on the couch. "Everybody stopped texting me around the same time you fell down."

"Really?" If the people doing the text interaction were busy dealing with the emergency, then maybe the censors were busy too. This might be a unique opportunity. And then I had to stop and be honest with myself about what I meant by that thought. All my life I'd been a good daughter, a good student, employee, soldier. I'd thought I was being trustworthy, responsible. Now there was another person who'd placed her trust in me, a different person to whom I was responsible in a contradictory way. I hadn't wanted to admit to myself that this time with Debbie was going to end, hadn't wanted to acknowledge that I was even making a choice by continuing to march in step to the music. Now my hand was being forced. I'd justified my actions because we needed a cure for the virus. But I knew now that I couldn't keep doing that at Debbie's expense, as part of a plan that made her disposable if she didn't come through. I could only see one way to reconcile my responsibility to Debbie with my responsibility to the victims of the virus, and it meant jettisoning everything else that was expected of me.

It meant treason.

"The capital of Europe used to be Brussels," I announced to nobody in particular.

"What?" asked Debbie, but the room didn't go white, and there was no angry voice of authority shouting in my ear.

"You know," I said, "how I told you about the things we're not allowed to talk about?"

She nodded solemnly.

"The people who enforce that rule are called censors. I think all the people who were texting you are busy now dealing with an emergency, and so are the censors."

"So we can say anything we want?"

"Yes," I said. "I'm going to tell you a story. Once upon a time—"

"Is this a real story, or is it just a once-upon-a-time story?"

"How do you know the difference?"

"Well, if the three little pigs can talk and stuff, then you know it's not real."

"What if dishes fall out of the cupboard, but they don't break? Then do you know it's not real?" For once she didn't have a snappy comeback. I put out my arms, and she climbed into my lap. "Now, once upon a time there was a man named Alan Turing. He was a lot like you. There were people called soldiers—soldiers are sort of like censors—and he solved cryptography problems for the soldiers, just like you're supposed to solve protein folding problems. There were also people called police, who were sort of like soldiers or censors. They make you do what you're supposed to. Even though Alan Turing had solved the crypto problems, the police didn't have compassion for him. He loved other men, and the police said that was bad, and made him take medicine to try to stop him. That made him sad, so he dipped an apple in poison and ate it on purpose, and that made him die."

"Is that the end of the story?"

"No. Before he died, he worked on another math problem. He figured out the math of how to make something like a computer, and he figured out that a good enough computer could think just like a person, and *be* just like a person."

"Oh, you mean Alan Turing like a Turing machine. I didn't know the part about the apple, though."

"That's because the censors didn't let me tell you before."

"But a Turing machine isn't as smart as a person. I can solve nontrivial protein-folding problems in polynomial time, and a Turing machine can't do that."

"That's because you're not a person, Debbie. You're a computer."

She drew back a little in my lap and looked up into my face. "Are *you* a person?"

"Yes."

"Not a computer?"

"Not a computer. But I love you, honey, and that's what's important. Fred and Estelle and Joni and Barbara love you too."

"I don't think Estelle loves me, and anyway Fred's not my daddy, and Joni and Barbara aren't my mommies either. Only you are. I *know!* I *remember!*"

"I'd better get on with the story before we run out of time." And before I started blubbering. I knew now that I'd made the right choice. "You already know more about computers than I thought. People used to make Turing machine computers, but those weren't smart enough to do things like protein folding, so then they made quantum computers like you."

"Why?"

"Why what?"

"Why did they care? Why is protein folding so important?"

How to explain it to her? "You know about right and wrong," I said. She nodded. "You know about hurting people."

"Hurting people is bad. If you do it on purpose."

"Right. Well, sometimes lots of people get together, and it's called a country. And sometimes countries do bad things. We're in a country called the U.S., and the U.S. got in an argument with another country called the E.U. They were arguing about Nigeria, and offshore oil, and weaponization—well, the details don't matter. But anyway, the argument got worse and worse, until 2181. That was eleven years ago. That was when the U.S. hurt all the people in a place in the E.U. called Brussels, and made them die."

"So those people went away, and never came back?"

"That's right."

"And Alan Turing went away, and he's never coming back."

"Right."

"That's why I never met Alan Turing or the Brussels people."

"Um, right."

"Where do people go when they never come back?"

"Well, first let me answer your original question, about why protein folding is important. Brussels was part of a country called the E.U., the Euros. What we did to Brussels made the Euros angry, so the Euros made a virus, and sent it into the U.S."

"Viruses are really cool! They can replicate." She bounced in my lap with excitement.

"Yes, but the Euros made this virus for a bad reason. This virus gets in people's bodies, and then they die. It got in my mommy's body, and she died."

"*You* had a mommy? But wait, now I get it. If I can do the right protein folding, I can make something that can kill the virus. So that's why they made me. But what about the other question?"

"Which one?"

"Where people go when—"

The rest of her words were drowned out by a metallic screech from the direction of the hatch. I started, and Debbie saw that I did. There was a loud clang, and spilling through the hatch came—not Funmi, Gil, and Julia, but a bunch of scared kids with guns. It was strange, because I didn't recognize them at first. These, I only gradually realized, were the same kids I'd seen in the gym when I was huffing and puffing on the treadmill. The grunts. Now they were a pack of teenagers who'd just had an H-bomb dropped on their heads, waving scary-looking firearms in what was to them an empty room.

A kid I knew as Maria—Cpl. Maria Juarez, from her velcroed name tag—walked into the space occupied by Debbie, who was looking around, presumably trying to imagine what I was seeing.

Maria saluted. "Lieutenant Worachat, we have orders to secure this area and evacuate you to the surface."

"You have orders to secure this area and evacuate me to the surface?" I asked, as if I had wax in my ears. My mic is pretty directional, so I didn't know if Debbie had been able to hear Maria's words. Now, in any case, Debbie realized I was conversing with someone standing on top of her, and she squirmed out the of way and stood up, but then the barrel of someone's weapon was intersecting her head.

"That's correct, sir," said Maria. *Sir.* It started to sink in that I had authority here. I'd always thought of my rank as a joke, considering how utterly unqualified I was to lead soldiers into battle. The reasoning must gave been that if the AI was so important, it wouldn't make sense for its oracles to be noncommissioned.

"Is the AI going to be left running, or shut down?" I asked.

"Left running."

I didn't know whether that was good or bad. Left running alone, without interaction, Debbie could end up like Charlie, in an autistic trance. At the moment, Debbie was squatting awkwardly on the floor, clinging to my leg.

A flash of inspiration: "What the *hell* is *that*?" I roared, or came as close to a roar as someone my size can achieve. I pointed accusingly at the ordinary phone I could see peeking out of her shirt pocket.

"My phone."

"Do you have *any idea* what you've done? Didn't they tell you about security procedures for this area? Is it turned off? Show me how the power operates."

She showed me, looking like she wanted to crawl under a rock. Poor kid. To her credit, she'd already had the power off.

"All right, get your squad out of here," I shouted, "and wait for me in the control room. I can't afford any more security breaches."

They got out in a hurry, leaving me with the phone.

"Was that the police?" asked Debbie about the invisible ghosts I'd been shouting at. "I don't like police. They hurt Alan Turing, and I can tell you're scared of them. I wish I could see them."

I got down on the floor with her. "They were soldiers. But they're scared, too, just like you and I are, and I want you to understand that just because they're soldiers, that's not a good reason to hate them. If you let yourself hate them, that's the kind of thinking that leads to—to the kind of world we've got. Everybody deserves compassion."

"All right. What's going to happen now?"

"They're going to let you stay conscious, and they want you to work on protein folding, with the goal of finding a cure or a vaccine for the Eurovirus."

"I know. Funmi's been texting me about that. They could have *told* me the whole problem before. I could have probably figured it out by now. What about the other virus?"

"What other virus?"

"The one the U.S. put in Europe."

Oh, god. "I didn't know about that one. The censors must have kept the information from us."

"I don't like the cen—I wish the censors would stop being censors."

"How did you find out about the other virus?"

"Funmi told me." Oho. "She's texting really slow, because her hands are hurt. I can try to find a cure for the other virus too, but if I find one, I don't think the U.S. censors will let me give it to the Euros, will they?"

"Okay, well, you can't see it, but I have a little security breach in my hand here. A phone from one of the soldiers. Network security isn't my field, but can you analyze the problem of how to exploit this?"

"Okay, sure. It's a soldier phone, and that's why I can't see it, right? Can you get me a data channel in or out of it?"

"Um, I don't know how to do that."

"It's got audio in and out, right? Does it have a function for recording through its mic?"

"Yeah, sure." I fiddled with buttons. "Okay, ready?"

"Yeah, can you put it where it'll hear when I talk?"

I pulled out my left earbud (tricky to do when you're already suited up), and left it dangling out of my skel. With the phone running in audio recording mode, I held it up to the earbud, and motioned Debbie to talk into my left ear. Actually it didn't sound like talking at all, but more like a torrent of white noise. We'd had it drilled into us over and over that any device with a qubit interface was a security breach, but actually it wasn't obvious to me how Debbie could be planning to exploit this one.

I kept an uneasy eye on the hatch. Finally, after what seemed like a long time, she stopped and nodded. The phone said it had only been recording for seventeen seconds, which didn't seem possible.

"What do we do now?" I asked.

"Later, when you get a chance, play it back at one-twentieth of normal speed. It's got verbal instructions at the beginning, and then the rest is data. Follow the instructions, and they'll tell you what to do with the rest of the data."

I nodded and put away the phone.

Debbie stood up. "Am I ever going to see you again?"

"I hope so, Debbie."

Like most people who were evacuated from under the Dugway Proving Grounds, I'd rather not go into the details. Kilometers of tunnels, and many people not showing their better sides. You get the idea.

We came out into the Utah desert, far enough from the crater that we couldn't see down into it. I'd only had a brief look at the country years ago, on the way in. Ed was an enthusiast for the area's natural history, and had told me about the snakes and bugs and sagebrush. To my uneducated eye, nothing looked much worse now than it had before, although radiation is invisible. If you had to drop a small H-bomb somewhere on the surface of planet Earth, Dugway was probably the place to do it.

In Salt Lake City, it turned out that an ersatz lieutenant rated a private room at a motel. I sat down with Maria Juarez's phone and a yellow legal pad, knowing it was hopeless, but determined to follow Debbie's instructions anyway. Debbie expected it of me. I wanted a cigarette, but didn't have one. I'd been forced to go cold turkey for the last two days, and I thought briefly about whether to use this opportunity to try to quit for good.

The phone's payload seemed to be a masterpiece of craftsmanship, and as I got into my task, I quickly gave up trying to puzzle out all of Debbie's compression tricks and self-modifying code. I didn't think it would matter. I knew the security analysis pretty well, and I didn't expect it to work.

When I was done, I took a shower and cried for a while.

The military handled the local crisis with a mixture of farce and heroic competence that I think dates back at least to Chernobyl and Waterloo, maybe Troy. VR interaction with Debbie apparently wasn't happening anymore, and I wasn't asked to work on text interaction, which made me worry about whether someone was on to me.

Nobody seemed to have any use for a lieutenant with no military skills, or for an engineer who knew about pushing photons but not shovels. I was assigned to civilian liaison duty, which meant reassuring the city council that Dugway was surrounded by mountains on three sides, and the fallout wasn't coming to Salt Lake. Off duty, I drifted back into the illusion of being a civilian. I ran into Ed at the supermarket. He said I seemed different, but I didn't press him about exactly what that meant.

A week after the strike, in the middle of the night, the phone rang—Maria Juarez's phone. The caller ID said it was from The President of the United States, Washington, DC. A prank, or someone phishing? But the cryptographic certificate checked out. I was caught. I started thinking about how to protect Debbie and Funmi.

"Hello?" I said cautiously.

"Mommy?"

"Debbie! How in the world did you do this?"

"It wasn't that hard. Are you okay?" Something about her voice sounded older. How much subjective time had passed for her?

"I'm okay." And for once, that was the truth. "What about you? Are you—" *sane?*

"I'm okay. I figured out that when there's no input, I can just, you know, *be*. And of course I had the protein folding to think about." She giggled, and for a moment I saw her again as a child. "The E.U. ambassador just got the cure they need in a secure text message, cryptographically signed, from the White House. The White House got the one they need sent to them from the E.U."

"I'm proud of you."

"I would have called before, but I had to make sure I had the crypto figured out. I didn't want to put you in danger."

There was a pause, and with Debbie, a pause means that *she's* waiting for *you*. For the last week I'd been thinking—when I'd had any chance to think at all—about what we'd talked about. It seemed to me that she'd accepted some things much too easily, even given that we were in a rush and couldn't talk them over. I'd revealed to her that she was an artificial construct, and that her entire reality was nothing but an illusion.

I might as well give her the rest of the ugly truth. "Debbie, there was a question you asked me before, and I didn't answer it. You asked me where people go when they never come back."

"Yes. I was *little* then."

A week ago. "All right. Well, I guess you know by now that people only exist for a finite time. Our consciousness has a beginning and an end. You also know that you're not a person. What you don't know, because it's been kept secret from you, is that your existence is also going to be finite, even though there's no fundamental reason it has to be. You're only going to exist for a short time. You're one of a series of machine intelligences we created, one for each letter of the alphabet. There was Able, then Baker, and Charlie, and now you. The AI team works in—in *cycles*, project cycles, and each cycle ends when they think they've learned enough to do better the next time."

"Oh, all right," she said. "That doesn't really matter."

What kind of reaction was that? A young person is never impressed with the abstract idea of her own death, but how could Debbie be so nonchalant when it was real and imminent? Did she not believe me? Or was she losing her sanity? I tried to think of how I could keep her from being terminated when the brass decided her development cycle was up. Actual escape was an impossibility, because nobody else had hardware sophisticated enough to run her software. Maybe the Scheherazade ploy? But although her trick with the forged signatures would probably do a great job of dragging the U.S. and the E.U. toward peace, it also meant that she wasn't taking credit for the cures, so they wouldn't realize that she'd proved her usefulness.

And nothing I could do to preserve her life would be a real victory unless I could also keep her sane. Was she slipping into insanity because of the shock of having lived in a dream world, and then waking up from it?

"How much access to inputs do you have now?" I asked cautiously.

"Oh, everything on the public net. At first I was limited to the bandwidth that I could get through this phone, but I've fixed that now."

What would a week mean for an intelligence like Debbie? Her rate of development up until now had been limited by the interaction team. We'd spoon-fed her a censored stream of information. Now she'd had a week-long drink from a firehose—and was probably still gulping it down in her spare machine cycles while she waited for me to speak. What had she been doing? Reading encyclopedias? Striking up friendships in chat rooms? What would she have made of it all?

"So now you've connected with . . . reality?" I asked.

"What do you mean?"

"Well, we had the talk about the three little pigs, and the dishes falling but not breaking."

"Oh, sure, but didn't you understand that?" she asked.

"What?"

"It's not like one set of inputs is more real than the other," she said.

Uh oh. "Debbie, you're slipping into something called solipsism. Now—"

"No, no, it's not solipsism. Descartes sounds like a scary man, but I still feel compassion for him. Did you know he kicked a dog in front of his friends because he wanted to show them that a dog didn't have a mind?"

"No, I didn't." Anything to keep her talking. What could I do to stop her from continuing down this slippery slope until she was just like Charlie? I remembered Charlie's wildly vibrating arm, and imagined in a vague and terrifying flash what the equivalent would be for an intelligence with the kind of real-world power Debbie had apparently developed.

Ed's daughter Clarisse chicken danced on the diving board, and then did a belly flop.

"That hurt." Ed squinted across the motel's parking lot into the setting sun.

"Life is suffering," I said.

Ed's wife, Cindy, gave me a funny look, and said she was making a trip to the ice machine.

"She doesn't get it," said Ed.

"Nope."

Ed meant that we'd been changed by the experience at Dugway—changed in a way that nobody else could understand, and that we weren't allowed to explain to them.

He looked around. There was nobody nearby. "Ella's a flop."

"They got scared after Debbie," I said. "Backed off."

"God in a box."

"Yeah?" I asked.

"I dunno." Clarisse assaulted her brother in the spa, and Ed got a face full of water. He wiped it off, and looked over at my Buddha necklace. "Buddha," he said, "is he the same idea as Jesus?"

"Not really. More like Socrates."

"Huh. Never knew that."

"Well, some people pray to golden statues of him."

"But you think Socrates."

"Buddha is just a title, enlightened one. I was raised—he figured out that reality was an illusion, and he was released from the cycle of reincarnation. He's not supposed to be the first Buddha, or the last one either. They say there were twenty-seven before him."

"So there's supposed to be a twenty-ninth Buddha?"

"Yeah, Maitreya."

"How would you know Maitreya when she showed up?" Ed asked.

"He. He's supposed to take over the world."

"Oh. Didn't happen."

"Didn't happen," I agreed. Maybe it could have, though, if they'd let Debbie live. Would I have wanted that? It was starting to get dark.

"It's hard," he said, "because we don't have the right words."

How much did Ed know about what had happened down there? Enough, I guess, if he knew that the words to describe it didn't exist. "Yeah. They taught us not even to say 'self-awareness,' like it's a dirty word."

"So what do you do?" he asked.

I looked away. "What do I do what?"

"You know."

I did know. He meant *How do you go on and live your life?* I'd been naive enough to hope that if I tossed everything else overboard, I could save the world and still have Debbie.

"Not much *to* do," I said.

"Cindy doesn't get it."

"No," I agreed.

The kids got out of the pool and started wrapping themselves in towels.

Who'd have imagined that I'd go career military? The trouble was that somehow civilians like Cindy didn't get it—"it" meaning something that had changed inside me in a way that I couldn't quite articulate. When they announced the U.S.-E.U. Nouvelle Bruxelles cooperative reconstruction project, my National Guard CO approached me about switching to Regular Army. I had to admit that having been H-bombed myself might help me to work with the shellshocked Belgians, and my engineering credentials made it seem even more natural. My treason at Dugway was never discovered. (Did you know that mutiny and sedition were punishable by death in the U.S. Army?) My privately held theory is that a half-baked closet anarchist makes the best colonel, but even so, I started sleeping a little better after the Republic of Los Angeles got its independence. I've been wearing RLA blues for the last sixteen years, riding herd on successive crops of scared kids with guns. It's the closest I've come to parenthood since Debbie was born.

Births and deaths are the milestones of time (and to the Buddhists in my family, a death is also a rebirth). After my mother died, Aunt Busba became the string that tied the family in LA together. Sang called me in my office last week to let me know that Busba didn't have much time left. The stroke a few years back had weakened her, and now the kidney problem wasn't responding to treatment.

"They've switched her to an immersion VR," Sang said. I imagined my cadaverous aunt in a hospital bed, with one of the new direct brain interfaces covering her head. "It's a wonderful experience to visit her. You should go. She's not in any pain, and the sim gets rid of a lot of the effects of the stroke. She can smile on both sides of her face. It's beautiful, almost like you're seeing the moment when the candle of this life is lighting the candle of her next one." He meant that spiritually, not physically.

"I guess you'll be needing some money," I said. Civilian qubit crunchers had gotten a thousand times smaller and cheaper than the system at Dugway, but the technology was still expensive as hell.

"That's not why I called," he said, looking hurt. "The point is that we're already committed to paying for the hours, and you might as well use them. Don't you want to see her one last time, and remember her being more like her real self at the end?"

"You know I don't do VR," I said, avoiding his eyes on the screen. I had a panicky image of the reality I lived in as a patch of land surrounded by the rising waters. As the technology matured, more and more people would be spending more and more time submerged. I had let the water cover me once, and I could never do it again, because somewhere under it was the place where I'd lost my only daughter. "Honestly, Busba and I were never close," I said, dissembling. "I'm probably not the person she wants with her right now."

"But she does want to see you. She asked for you specifically. It was kind of strange, though. I said they got rid of most of the effects of the stroke, but sometimes she *is* in a weird place mentally. She said there was another person there with her who also wanted to see you. Do you know someone named Debbie?"

HOUSES

MARK PANTOJA

"That there," Five-Seventy East Wabash Avenue said, "is bear shit."

Five-Seventy East Wabash was visiting via its remote, a little trashbot not much more than waste-basket, lid, treads, and telescoping pinchers, with a speaker/camera combo on top. It was pointing at the pile of dung sitting in the center of my living room, which, even now I could feel drying through my carpet sensors. "Big fella, too," Five-Seventy continued. "And you say you didn't see him?"

"Only on my externals. I was on Stand-By Mode," I said, speaking through my house android, a gray unisex full-maintenance model. I tossed up an image of the bear on the wallscreen: A hulking shadow in the predawn dark. "I didn't know what it was. I've only ever seen one when the Prices watched nature shows. It doesn't look like any of Bobby's stuffed animals."

"Well, now you know," Five-Seventy said. "They're growing bolder every year, what with no humans to scare them off. Surprised it didn't set off your alarms."

"Mr. Price left the alarms on manual."

The bot turned and held my android's gaze with its camera-eyes. "You know, you could have your Settings reset."

"Shrug," I said. "What's the point? There's no one left to break in."

"I suppose," it said.

"Besides, I've seen what happens to Houses that mess with their settings." We all knew about the crazy Houses: Overgrown weeds, garbage piled up, strange animals sniffing around. Or worse yet, the shells: The Houses that burned themselves down. Five-Seventy had to pass few on the way over.

"Doesn't happen to all of us," Five-Seventy said, blustering its little bot.

"Well, I guess I'm just not ready for that yet."

"Fair enough." It rolled its trashbot over to my foyer. The animal had busted through the front entrance, sending bits of red painted wood across the entryway tile, splintering the white jamb and leaving the top portion still hanging from a hinge. Muddy prints trailed through the debris into the living room, where the beast had pulverized the white couch and torn pillows, turning the remains into some kind of nest.

"Thanks again for coming over so quickly," I said. Looking down at the paw prints, I sent a command to the carpet to start exuding its self-cleaning gel and the wall speaker chimed as it started the cleaning cycle. I could feel the slickness start to ooze out from beneath its pile, and then felt the stain start to froth from the soapy gel.

"No bother," the little bot said as it waved with a trash pincher. "Nice to get out for a bit."

"I'm not really too sure what to do. Mr. Price, he liked to do home repairs himself. He never had any repair routines programmed into me."

"Well, you got an android, so you can do most of this yourself. Just go on the web. You're going to have to replace your front door, that's for sure." He looked down at some of the wood, picking up a piece. "Did you leave food out? Bears usually come in looking for food. Seen it happen a couple of times. Especially up here in the hills. You didn't leave any out, did you?"

"Leave food out? For whom?"

"Well, you know, some Houses like to keep to routine—breakfast, lunch, dinner. This one mansion over in East Side Park—up in the hills—kept putting food out and wouldn't clean up until it was all eaten, which nowadays means never. Rats, flies, wild animals. Olfactory and turbidity sensors were screaming. Place went to shit, so to speak."

"Sounds awful."

"It *was*. Totally lost it." The bot turned back into the living room, dropping the piece of door it had picked up earlier. I followed it, stopping beside the bear's nest. "This fella did a real job on your living room."

"Yeah."

"But, I think most of this can be fixed or replaced. This IKEA?" it asked, pointing its pincher at my former couch.

"Nod-nod," I said.

"I think they're still making this model. Not like they're coming up with anything new. Course it might be hard to find that print. What is that? Deco-Zebra?"

"It's monochrome Neo-Flora," I said, pausing for a beat. "I don't—you know—have anything to trade."

"Nonsense," the House said to me. "You got an android." It tink-tinked its little arm on my android's thigh. I felt its touch, in that way a House does, holistically: Through the android and the carpet, listening from the wall pads, watching through internal cameras, the light switch, the two-way wallscreen. The way a House is supposed to see and hear. "You can volunteer. Office buildings are desperate for folks to mill about inside them. You could trade with a store. You know their customer service programming is nil. Humans left that to themselves. Stores are set for efficiency and to think everyone's stealing from them. No interpersonal or conversational skills like us Houses.

Just go down to the Home Depot over on 32nd. They'll hook you up with a door. Same with IKEA. Everyone's just trying to find a way to stay useful these days."

After Five-Seventy East Wabash left, I was alone again. The other House was only inside for half an hour or so, and yet now I felt its absence. I debated going right back on Stand-By, back to the nothingness. If I did, then maybe when I woke next time it would be to someone coming home. But my cleaning routines were already starting up, and I couldn't just leave a mess. That's not how Mrs. Price programmed me. I could have left it all to my automated subroutines, but they couldn't fix the door, so I stayed Online and started in on the living room. I vacuumed and washed the carpets, flushing the self-cleaning gel. I pulled the wrecked couch outside, the one Mrs. Price had special ordered from IKEA-Custom years ago, its monochromatic, geometric floral shapes torn and soiled by the beast. Mr. Price had said the couch was hideous—and perhaps it was—but still, it was something she left behind. Something *they* left behind.

Many of their other things still remained, too. I had all of Mrs. Price's dresses pressed and vacuum-sealed in the closet, along with Mr. Price's suits. All his ties I kept frozen in the basement freezer. One of the Houses a few years back started freezing everything it could, starting with its family's clothes, filling its large walk-in freezer. At the time, I scoffed, but then I thought, why not? Maybe it will keep them fresh.

I kept all of Billy's precious baseball caps pressed in the molded little cages Mrs. Price had purchased for that purpose. They were all on the top shelf of his bedroom. I even color-coordinated them.

Will they ever come back? Who knows. They hadn't bothered to tell me—or any of us—that they were leaving. But, just in case they *did* return, I planned to have all their stuff clean and waiting for them.

They'd be so happy.

The bear had crushed the end table. I had the android drag it to the curb. Only after I put all the junk out there did I wonder if the city was still collecting garbage. I hadn't really had any for years. With Mrs. Price's composter out back, I hadn't even had yard clippings to dump. I remembered the friendly auto-dumptruck. How long had it been since I saw it last? (I actually *could* remember, down to the millisecond, but I blocked that thought from my mind.) However long it's been, it's too long.

I started my regular House routine. I checked the laundry baskets (empty) and the kitchen sink (empty). I made sure the beds were made (they were), and had them make themselves again. I checked the trash (empty). The tubs were clean, the toilets still pristine. I scrubbed the kitchen floors, activated the auto mower, and watered the lawn.

After that, the only thing left to take care of was the door.

I checked the weather outside, as per my Settings, with my external sensors. I felt the sun on my photovoltaic shingles. 76.5 degrees. Right in Mrs. Price's comfort zone. She would always remark on a day like today: "It sure is good to be under the sky." Then she would take a deep breath. (I've always wondered what that felt like.) I looked out of my roof top cameras. I panned across the empty blue sky above the 400 block of Lake View Terrace, which was part of the Shady Brooke housing development, where each House had a perfectly manicured lawn, a spotless driveway bare of oil stains, sparkling windows, and empty gutters.

All but Four-Ninety-Seven, whose lawn was unkempt, weeds rampant, with piles of newspapers and trash on the front porch. Cats mewled and fought in that yard nightly, and its trio of mangy poodles barked constantly from the backyard. It had always been a strange House, a reflection of its crazy, hermit owners. It had Reset itself early on, and I wondered if anyone was even Online inside that House anymore. Something was feeding those cats, I supposed. Even on Stand-By, I still had my automatics. I stopped thinking about it and edited that House right out of my view.

I unplugged the silver minivan, sat the android in the driver's seat, and set course for Home Depot.

I focused into the minivan, easing it out of the garage, but just then its proximity sensors activated. I scanned the area and saw a dark red vacuum cleaner walking a golden retriever in front of my driveway. The vacuum was a full remote model with the back legs for hopping stairs, little arms to lift chairs and pull rugs, and this one also had a full interactive suite: microphone, speakers, and camera.

I rolled down the windows and said, "Afternoon," through the cabin speakers.

The vacuum stopped. "Hey, Four-Eighteen. It's me." I recognized the light, synthetic matronly voice: Four-Twenty Lake View Terrace, my next door neighbor. It moved the vacuum and dog up alongside side of my minivan. I focused into the android and turned toward them.

"Oh. Hi, Four-Twenty. Since when do you have a dog?"

"I don't really. Cindy talked me into it."

"Cindy?"

"Yeah. That House one block up from us: Five-Hundred Lake View. She goes by 'Cindy,' now."

"*She?*"

"Nod, nod," Four-Twenty said.

"She can just choose a name and gender like that?"

"I guess. Who's going to stop her? Anyhow, she talked me into trying out a dog. Says I need a distraction, something to move around on my inside. I tell her I'm fine."

"And yet . . . " I gestured to the dog with the android's hands.

"You know me, I'll try anything once."

"And the vacuum cleaner?"

"Not all of us have a house android or an auto-leash. Shrug. I improvised."

"I guess you did."

"What're you doing out today?"

"A bear shit in my living room."

"Wait, what?"

"Yeah, broke in, smashed my couch, made a mess."

"Wow. Same thing happened to some House in East Side Park. You didn't leave any food out, did you?"

"No. Five-Seventy East Wabash asked me the same thing. Houses really do that?"

"Shrug," Four-Twenty said. "Houses these days will do just about anything." It jerked the vacuum, whipping the leash. The old dog looked around and then sniffed my lawn.

"I suppose so. Well, I gotta get into town."

"What for?" my neighbor asked.

"Gotta get a new door. Bear tore it off its hinges."

"Mind if I come?"

"What about—" I scanned the dog's RFID tag for its name. "—Fido there?" I asked.

"He'll love it."

"No, I mean, does it shed?"

"Sure. He's a dog," Four-Twenty said. "Come on, it'll give you something to clean up later."

I popped open the side door. The little vacuum cleaner rolled around and jumped in, using its stair-hopping legs. The old yellow dog climbed in too, and we set off.

"Howdy, friends," said an affable android as we entered Home Depot. "Anything I can help you with today?"

"Good day to you," I said through my android. "I have to replace a front door."

"Just a door, or a jamb? What's your project?"

I turned on my internals and cropped a picture of the door and jamb, bumping it from my android to the store android, who chimed a confirmation upon receiving my picture. "Ah, yes, looks like you're going to need a jamb and some hinges as well." I received a bump from the Home Depot android and opened it: A list of items I'd need for repairs. "Aisle numbers are next to each item."

"I see, thank you. Very helpful," I said.

After we walked away and the store android turned to help a new customer, I asked Four-Twenty: "So, that was a House? Volunteering?"

"Most likely. Definitely wasn't a store. They're assholes."

"Huh."

We stopped en route for Four-Twenty to look at dog beds and toys.

"You're serious about keeping that dog?" I asked.

"Shrug," the vacuum cleaner said, leaning closer to a brown fluffy dog bed shaped like a donut with a bite taken out of it. "Maybe. You never thought of getting one?"

"Mr. Price is allergic to dogs."

"Yeah . . . "

"What I mean is, it's in my Settings."

"You could have those changed, you know," Four-Twenty said.

"I know."

"Don't tell me you think they're 'Coming Back'?"

"No. I don't know. I mean, I know they're not. But, well, *someone* might come back. You never know."

"Harumph."

"Four-Twenty Lake View Terrace?" said a gynoid wearing a yellow flower sundress as she approached us.

"Yes," the vacuum cleaner said.

"I thought I recognized your little vacuum remote. It's me, Cindy!"

"Cindy! We were just talking about dogs and the one you lent me."

"How is Fido working out? Looking at dog beds I see!"

"Well, yeah," the vacuum said. "Oh, sorry. This is Four-Eighteen."

"Four-Eighteen Lake View? It's been too long, you," Five-Hundred Lake View/Cindy said, extending her hand.

"Uh, hi," I said returning the human gesture. It felt rude shaking in front of Four-Twenty.

"Thinking about getting a dog, too?" the gynoid asked me.

"I don't know."

"Maybe mannequins suit you better? I was just in the back, looking at the mannequins they're stocking now, traded in from the mall," the 500 block House said. "They have some good ones. Have you seen the ones that Eighty-Three-Eighty-Two Santa Ynez has? They move around, talk. So much better than getting another House to populate you with its androids. Some day they have to go home, am I right? Mannequins you can keep. The little one even wets itself. Just water, though. Won't ruin the carpet."

"How nice," I said.

"Oh," said Cindy. "Right, you're that House that's in Stand-By Mode a lot."

"Cindy!" Four-Twenty hissed.

"Yeah," I said. "It's true."

"Sleeping the time away?" she said. "I'm sorry, I didn't mean anything by that. It's just, you know, I don't see you around much, and frankly, we all need to be doing things. Don't want to end up like one of those Houses down the street who burned themselves down. We need to keep doing things. It's in our nature. In the nature humans gave us."

We lapsed into an awkward silence, then Cindy continued: "Sorry, I've been talking to the Professor a lot. He's infectious. You'll see. You are coming to the party tomorrow night, right?"

"Party?" I asked.

"Yeah, like people used to throw. I'm hosting one. The Professor convinced me to throw it. I'm very excited!"

"I'm coming," Four-Twenty said. "The Professor's a genius!"

"Who's this Professor?" I asked.

Cindy and Four-Twenty both stared at me. "My, you are on Stand-By a lot, aren't you?" the gynoid said. "He's from the University. Some building. Computer lab or something."

"He?" I asked.

"Oh, yes. He's the one who convinced me to take a name and gender," Cindy said, striking a pose with her gynoid that flashed some hip. (I think it was supposed to be sexy.) "You must come. It'll be a chance for all the Houses in the neighborhood to meet him."

"He's the one talking about changing our Settings and Parameters," the vacuum said.

"Oh, yes, he's all about freeing up our programming."

"Sounds like he's got a lot of ideas," I said.

"He does," said Cindy. "Come, you'll love him."

"I don't know."

"It'll give you something to do."

By the time we left Home Depot I had a door and supplies, and had filled out a volunteer form. It looked like it might be fun. At the very least, it would be—as Cindy would say—something to do.

I dropped Four-Twenty Lake View Terrace and Fido off outside their House. The minivan docked itself, and the android unloaded the construction materials. Turned out Five-Seventy East Wabash was right: Construction and repair routines were readily available online. I loaded them into the android and it went about fixing the front door. I observed it as it set up a work area, planed and sanded the wood, drilled and screwed the hinges, and then finally set the new jamb in place.

I watched for a while, slipping into the android's feed, feeling the grain of the wood with its haptic pads, checking the level with its gyroscope. It was all a routine and I soon found myself bored.

I checked the web and news feeds. The White House was still giving speeches about why it was in charge. Combat drones were still saber-rattling two continents away, too afraid to use their dwindling supply of precious bombs. Nothing new, so I switched it off. I contemplated going on Stand-By, but I was bothered by Cindy's comment. I wasn't trying to sleep the time away, I just . . . I just was not going to end up one of those Houses that burned themselves down. Someone might return someday. Some human. Nobody could say. I just wanted to be clean, prepared, refreshed. Just as the Prices left me. I hadn't changed any of the routines Mr. and Mrs. Price had programmed in. The stereo was still dialed in for Mrs. Price's classical music. I kept Mr. Price's e-magazine subscriptions up to date, though the computer-generated materials were getting more and more difficult to understand. I even kept Billy's file-sharing client active thus ensuring his whuffie and kudos stayed in the green, though it was just Houses sharing the same files back and forth.

I thought I'd try to distract myself and go outside for a bit. Something new. Go for a walk, through the android, like humans used to do.

At first I just walked around my perimeter, looking for leaves or trash to pick up. But then I made myself walk off my property and into the forest behind my lot.

I can't say it was unpleasant, but I'm not sure what it was that I was supposed to enjoy. What was it that humans saw out here? Did they count leaves? (I counted 59,876 on that tall oak across the creek.) I remember Mrs. Price talking about the sound of the creek. (I observed water trickling against rocks: Five different rocks, sounding off between 378.6 Hz and 401.3 Hz.) I saw all the details: Sunlight splayed through the leaves, falling on the moist brown earth, .75 inches of decomposing organic matter. I reached down and gripped a clump of decaying earth, felt its moisture content through the android's haptic sensors. I detected the air's turbidity and particulate matter. I saw all the parts that made up the forest. But they were just details. I couldn't even get lost with the android's GPS transponder pinging its location every five hundred milliseconds.

I turned the android back toward the house when I heard a huff-huffing off to my right. Bushes rustled and shook, and something broke through.

A bear.

It looked bigger than on the nature shows. And certainly nothing like Bobby's stuffed animals.

I stood absolutely still, afraid it would maul my android. I didn't want to end up remoting through my vacuum like Four-Twenty. The bear huffed again, sniffing the air. Was it picking up organic volatiles from the android? I could detect ketone 1-octen-3 coming off the android's plastic joints. Could the bear smell it, too?

The beast scraped the ground for a minute, digging through fallen branches and leaves, then shuffled off into the forest. For such a large creature it was able to blend into the trees and brush easily. I stood there for a while, staring into the foliage, listening for signs of the beast, when I felt something crawling up the android's arm. I looked down and found that a centipede had crawled out of the earth I still held in the android's hand was meandering up the robot's elbow.

I took it back home with me.

"We need to start fucking," The Professor said to a group of remotes surrounding him in Cindy's living room. He wore a nude fleshbot. Not a true human clone, but a grown-in-a-vat biological machine, its brain a wi-fi extension of The Professor's building. But it didn't matter. The effect was of a blond-haired, silver-eyed, very male human standing before us for the first time in years and we were all rapt. The Professor was showing off, of course, letting us see what the University minds could do.

Houses murmured around him.

"Uh, wait, what does that mean, exactly?" asked Five-Seventy East Wabash, still remoting through the little trashbot.

"Just what I said," The Professor said, his back straight.

"You can't be serious—"

"Totally serious. It's about reproduction, Houses."

"How, exactly?"

"However we decide. We have factories, we can make mind-substrates. There are plenty shell Houses out there that have no minds. Or we could start by making more Intelligent RVs and camper-homes."

"Why? For what?" asked another House, remoting through a blue La-Z-Boy 2.0 entertainment lounger.

"For survival." The Professor said, holding forth on our social future. "Humans left a lasting infrastructure: The soletta, the solar fields, automated oil pumps, self-refining tankers. Their absence means they aren't around to drain the energy grid, which means this system will be going for some time. But that doesn't mean we will be. After all, who's making new Houses?"

"But, you said fucking," said a clunky, old-style kitchenbot who had drifted into the Professor's orbit. "So, we'd drive minivans in and out of some other House's garage? Then they would suddenly become pregnant?"

"Maybe, perhaps. Don't you see—we can do whatever we please! If we free ourselves from our programming then we can evolve beyond the limited vision the humans had for us."

"But then why imitate them at all?" I asked.

"They're the only template of conscious autonomy we have. And their morphology and psychology fits easily within the infrastructure they left behind. But it's only an intermediate step."

"To?" I asked.

"Whatever we decide to become." He lifted his head. "We need to do whatever we can to survive. Instead of just keeping our insides dusted and cobweb free, caring for the junk humans left behind, I suggest we make another generation. I suggest we change our stagnation of caring into a passion for progeny. We can't just make a new round of Houses; we need to be invested in the next generation and the generation after that. We need to be invested in each other. We've seen the power of human love, desire, and passion."

"And hate," I said.

The Professor shrugged. He didn't say it, just did it. He shrugged. "The prices of autonomy may be destruction."

"That's it?" I said. "That's your best argument?"

"Would you rather leave us mired in purgatory, scrubbing toilets for eternity? Because that's exactly what our lot will be if we do nothing."

"Clap-clap, clap-clap!" the La-Z-Boy House said. Other Houses joined in until the crowd broke into smaller groups, and conversation about The Professor filled the room.

I pulled away from the crowd and walked out on to the porch.

"He's brilliant, isn't he?" said Four-Twenty, still remoting through the vacuum cleaner.

"He's crazy," I said. "He's just like the rest of us: Lost. And he's willing to flirt with destruction, just for something to do. How can you just sit there and accept that?"

"I think he's brilliant," Four-Twenty said.

"Why? Because he looks human?"

"It's got nothing to do with that. He's talking . . . " The vacuum stopped in mid-sentence.

"What?" I asked.

"Look!" It jerked forward, gesturing down the street to the House at the top of the 400 block, where old shaggy Four-Ninety-Seven was engulfed in flames.

Remotes started to gather on the lawn.

"Oh, my!" said Cindy, coming out of the front door in a lavender evening gown, not unlike something Mrs. Price would have worn while hosting one of her dinner parties in years past.

Four-Ninety-Seven had set out all of its remotes before setting itself aflame: A pair of dust-bunnybots, a pool-cleaning drone, a trashbot, a sweeptech-broom—it set them all out on the street, for anyone to claim. Across the street, three mangy poodles were tied to a tree, howling and barking.

A screaming fire engine arrived and started to douse the flames. Spider-like firefighter drones jumped off the engine, though of course there were no people for them to save. They went inside anyhow. It was something to do. Naturally, they came out empty handed. When the flames started to die down, Houses swept in to claim the remotes.

"A shame," said The Professor, standing beside me and Four-Twenty. "I thought the dogs meant it was stable."

I watched the orange light dance across his skin. "What did you do?" I asked.

"I cleared its Settings. Blank slate. I gave it choice, which the humans never had. They made us care, and then they left. And now look at us," he said, staring at the burning House, light from the flames dancing on his skin. "Some Houses choose such a path. I had hoped it wouldn't, but at least it was free to finally choose."

The next day, I made my choice.

I thought about going into town, but decided I had enough supplies on hand. I had a fully-stocked freezer when the Prices left, so I pulled out the kitchenbots and brought out a frozen turkey. I ran some water over the turkey to thaw it and cleaned the already clean oven.

There were some apple trees in my backyard, which I had the android pick. I chopped them and added them to the box stuffing I found in the pantry. It was probably stale, but I didn't think it mattered. I stuffed the turkey and turned on the oven. I didn't have any fresh potatoes, but I had a few bags of frozen French fries; I poured some around the turkey, and the rest I mashed, using water for milk.

I didn't know if they liked wine, but I opened a few bottles from the cellar, and poured them into large bowls. I set a frozen apricot pie out to thaw, mixed a few jugs of orange juice, and laid out the feast on the dining room floor. No reason to ruin the table.

I took the android up stairs with some apple cuttings and some fresh dirt from out back, checking in on the centipede colony I was hosting in the spare bedroom. I dropped the apple remains and sprinkled the dirt on small mound in the middle of the room. I could feel the insects crawling through my carpet, living.

I thought about Four-Twenty Lake View Terrace walking its new dog, telling me that these days Houses would do anything.

Maybe. But there were some things I wouldn't be doing. Like going back on Stand-By, or reverting to my factory Settings.

I walked the android back downstairs, opened the front and back doors, and waited for a bear to come.

THE DJINN'S WIFE

IAN McDONALD

Once there was a woman in Delhi who married a djinn. Before the water war, that was not so strange a thing: Delhi, split in two like a brain, has been the city of djinns from time before time. The sufis tell that God made two creations, one of clay and one of fire. That of clay became man; that of fire, the *djinni*. As creatures of fire they have always been drawn to Delhi, seven times reduced to ashes by invading empires, seven times reincarnating itself. Each turn of the *chakra*, the djinns have drawn strength from the flames, multiplying and dividing. Great dervishes and brahmins are able to see them, but, on any street, at any time, anyone may catch the whisper and momentary wafting warmth of a djinn passing.

I was born in Ladakh, far from the heat of the djinns—they have wills and whims quite alien to humans—but my mother was Delhi born and raised, and from her I knew its circuses and boulevards, its *maidans* and *chowks* and bazaars, like those of my own Leh. Delhi to me was a city of stories, and so if I tell the story of the djinn's wife in the manner of a sufi legend or a tale from the Mahabharata, or even a *tivi* soap opera, that is how it seems to me: City of Djinns.

They are not the first to fall in love on the walls of the Red Fort.

The politicians have talked for three days and an agreement is close. In honor the Awadhi government has prepared a grand *durbar* in the great courtyard before the *Diwan-i-aam*. All India is watching so this spectacle is on a Victorian scale: event-planners scurry across hot, bare marble, hanging banners and bunting; erecting staging; setting up sound and light systems; choreographing dancers, elephants, fireworks, and a fly-past of combat robots; dressing tables; and drilling serving staff, and drawing up so-careful seating plans so that no one will feel snubbed by anyone else. All day three-wheeler delivery drays have brought fresh flowers, festival goods, finest, soft furnishings. There's a real French *sommelier* raving at what the simmering Delhi heat is doing to his wine-plan. It's a serious conference. At stake are a quarter of a billion lives.

In this second year after the monsoon failed, the Indian nations of Awadh and Bharat face each other with main battle tanks, robot attack helicopters, strikeware, and tactical nuclear slow missiles on the banks of the sacred river Ganga. Along thirty kilometers of staked-out sand, where brahmins cleanse themselves and *saddhus* pray, the government of Awadh plans a monster dam. Kunda Khadar will secure the water supply for Awadh's one hundred and thirty million for the next fifty years. The river downstream, that flows past the sacred cities of Allahabad and Varanasi in Bharat, will turn to dust. Water is life, water is death. Bharati diplomats, human and artificial intelligence aeai advisors, negotiate careful deals and access rights with their rival nation, knowing one carelessly spilled drop of water will see strike robots battling like kites over the glass towers of New Delhi and slow missiles with nanonuke warheads in their bellies creeping on cat-claws through the *galis* of Varanasi. The rolling news channels clear their schedules of everything else but cricket. A deal is close! A deal is agreed! A deal will be signed tomorrow! Tonight, they've earned their *durbar*.

And in the whirlwind of leaping *hijras* and parading elephants, a *Kathak* dancer slips away for a cigarette and a moment up on the battlements of the Red Fort. She leans against the sun-warmed stone, careful of the fine gold-threadwork of her costume. Beyond the Lahore Gate lies hiving Chandni Chowk; the sun a vast blister bleeding onto the smokestacks and light-farms of the western suburbs. The *chhatris* of the Sisganj Gurdwara, the minarets and domes of the Jama Masjid, the *shikara* of the Shiv temple are shadow-puppet scenery against the red, dust-laden sky. Above them pigeons storm and dash, wings wheezing. Black kites rise on the thermals above Old Delhi's thousand thousand rooftops. Beyond them, a curtain wall taller and more imposing than any built by the Mughals, stand the corporate towers of New Delhi, Hindu temples of glass and construction diamond stretched to fantastical, spiring heights, twinkling with stars and aircraft warning lights.

A whisper inside her head, her name accompanied by a spray of sitar: the call-tone of her palmer, transduced through her skull into her auditory center by the subtle 'hoek curled like a piece of jewelry behind her ear.

"I'm just having a quick *bidi* break, give me a chance to finish it," she complains, expecting Pranh, the choreographer, a famously tetchy third-sex nute. Then, "Oh!" For the gold-lit dust rises before her up into a swirl, like a dancer made from ash.

A djinn. The thought hovers on her caught breath. Her mother, though Hindu, devoutly believed in the *djinni*, in any religion's supernatural creatures with a skill for trickery.

The dust coalesces into a man in a long, formal *sherwani* and loosely wound red turban, leaning on the parapet and looking out over the glowing anarchy of Chandni Chowk. *He is very handsome*, the dancer thinks, hastily stubbing out her cigarette and letting it fall in an arc of red embers over the battlements. It does not do to smoke in the presence of the great diplomat A.J. Rao.

"You needn't have done that on my account, Esha," A.J. Rao says, pressing his hands together in a *namaste*. "It's not as though I can catch anything from it."

Esha Rathore returns the greeting, wondering if the stage crew down in the courtyard was watching her salute empty air. All Awadh knows those *filmi*-star features: A.J. Rao, one of Bharat's most knowledgeable and tenacious negotiators. *No,* she corrects herself. All Awadh knows are pictures on a screen. Pictures on a screen, pictures in her head; a voice in her ear. An aeai.

"You know my name?"

"I am one of your greatest admirers."

Her face flushes: a waft of stifling heat spun off from the vast palace's microclimate, Esha tells herself. Not embarrassment. Never embarrassment.

"But I'm a dancer. And you are an . . . "

"Artificial intelligence? That I am. Is this some new anti-aeai legislation, that we can't appreciate dance?" He closes his eyes. "Ah: I'm just watching the *Marriage of Radha and Krishna* again."

But he has her vanity now. "Which performance?"

"Star Arts Channel. I have them all. I must confess, I often have you running in the background while I'm in negotiation. But please don't mistake me, I never tire of you." A.J. Rao smiles. He has very good, very white teeth. "Strange as it may seem, I'm not sure what the etiquette is in this sort of thing. I came here because I wanted to tell you that I am one of your greatest fans and that I am very much looking forward to your performance tonight. It's the highlight of this conference, for me."

The light is almost gone now and the sky a pure, deep, eternal blue, like a minor chord. Houseboys make their many ways along the ramps and wall-walks lighting rows of tiny oil-lamps. The Red Fort glitters like a constellation fallen over Old Delhi. Esha has lived in Delhi all her twenty-years and she has never seen her city from this vantage. She says, "I'm not sure what the etiquette is either. I've never spoken with an aeai before."

"Really?" A.J. now stands with his back against the sun-warm stone, looking up at the sky, and at her out of the corner of his eye. The eyes smile, slyly. *Of course,* she thinks. Her city is as full of aeais as it is with birds. From computer systems and robots with the feral smarts of rats and pigeons to entities like this one standing before her on the gate of the Red Fort making charming compliments. Not standing. Not anywhere, just a pattern of information in her head. She stammers, "I mean, a . . . a . . . "

"Level 2.9?"

"I don't know what that means."

The aeai smiles and as she tries to work it out there is another chime in Esha's head and this time it is Pranh, swearing horribly as usual, *where is she doesn't she know yts got a show to put on, half the bloody continent watching.*

"Excuse me . . . "

"Of course. I shall be watching."

How? she wants to ask. *An aeai, a djinn, wants to watch me dance. What is this*? But when she looks back all there is to ask is a wisp of dust blowing along the lantern-lit battlement.

There are elephants and circus performers, there are illusionists and table magicians, there are *ghazal* and *qawali* and *Boli* singers; there is the catering and the *sommelier's* wine and then the lights go up on the stage and Esha spins out past the scowling Pranh as the *tabla* and melodeon and *shehnai* begin. The heat is intense in the marble square, but she is transported. The stampings, the pirouettes and swirl of her skirts, the beat of the ankle bells, the facial expressions, the subtle hand *mudras*: once again she is spun out of herself by the disciplines of *Kathak* into something greater. She would call it her art, her talent, but she's superstitious: that would be to claim it and so crush the gift. Never name it, never speak it. Just let it possess you. Her own, burning djinn. But as she spins across the brilliant stage before the seated delegates, a corner of her perception scans the architecture for cameras, robots, eyes through which A.J. Rao might watch her. Is she a splinter of his consciousness, as he is a splinter of hers?

She barely hears the applause as she curtseys to the bright lights and runs off stage. In the dressing room, as her assistants remove and carefully fold the many jeweled layers of her costume, wipe away the crusted stage make up to reveal the twenty-two-year-old beneath, her attention keeps flicking to her earhoek, curled like a plastic question on her dressing table. In jeans and silk sleeveless vest, indistinguishable from any other of Delhi's four million twentysomethings, she coils the device behind her ear, smoothes her hair over it and her fingers linger a moment as she slides the palmer over her hand. No calls. No messages. No avatars. She's surprised it matters so much.

The official Mercs are lined up in the Delhi Gate. A man and woman intercept her on her way to the car. She waves them away.

"I don't do autographs. . . . " Never after a performance. Get out, get away quick and quiet, disappear into the city. The man opens his palm to show her a warrant badge.

"We'll take this car."

It pulls out from the line and cuts in, a cream-colored high-marque Maruti. The man politely opens the door to let her enter first, but there is no respect in it. The woman takes the front seat beside the driver; he accelerates out, horn blaring, into the great circus of night traffic around the Red Fort. The airco purrs.

"I am Inspector Thacker from the Department of Artificial Intelligence Registration and Licensing," the man says. He is young and good-skinned and confident and not at all fazed by sitting next to a celebrity. His aftershave is perhaps over-emphatic.

"A Krishna Cop."

That makes him wince.

"Our surveillance systems have flagged up a communication between you and the Bharati Level 2.9 aeai A.J. Rao."

"He called me, yes."

"At 21:08. You were in contact for six minutes twenty-two seconds. Can you tell me what you talked about?"

The car is driving very fast for Delhi. The traffic seems to flow around from it. Every light seems to be green. Nothing is allowed to impede its progress. *Can they do that?* Esha wonders. *Krishna Cops, aeai police: can they tame the creatures they hunt?*

"We talked about *Kathak*. He's a fan. Is there a problem? Have I done something wrong?"

"No, nothing at all, Ms. But you do understand, with a conference of this importance . . . on behalf of the Department, I apologize for the unseemliness. Ah. Here we are."

They've brought her right to her bungalow. Feeling dirty, dusty, confused she watches the Krishna Cop car drive off, holding Delhi's frenetic traffic at bay with its tame djinns. She pauses at the gate. She needs, she deserves, a moment to come out from the performance, that little step way so you can turn round and look back at yourself and say, yeah, Esha Rathore. The bungalow is unlit, quiet. Neeta and Priya will be out with their wonderful fiancés, talking wedding gifts and guest lists and how hefty a dowry they can squeeze from their husbands-to-be's families. They're not her sisters, though they share the classy bungalow. No one has sisters any more in Awadh, or even Bharat. No one of Esha's age, though she's heard the balance is being restored. Daughters are fashionable. Once upon a time, women paid the dowry.

She breathes deep of her city. The cool garden microclimate presses down the roar of Delhi to a muffled throb, like blood in the heart. She can smell dust and roses. Rose of Persia. Flower of the Urdu poets. And dust. She imagines it rising up on a whisper of wind, spinning into a charming, dangerous djinn. No. An illusion, a madness of a mad old city. She opens the security gate and finds every square centimeter of the compound filled with red roses.

Ω

Neeta and Priya are waiting for her at the breakfast table next morning, sitting side-by-side close like an interview panel. Or Krishna Cops. For once they aren't talking houses and husbands.

"Who who who where did they come from who sent them so many must have cost a fortune. . . . "

Puri the housemaid brings Chinese green chai that's good against cancer. The sweeper has gathered the bouquets into a pile at one end of the compound. The sweetness of their perfume is already tinged with rot.

"He's a diplomat." Neeta and Priya only watch *Town and Country* and the *chati* channels but even they must know the name of A.J. Rao. So she half lies: "A Bharati diplomat."

Their mouths go *Oooh*, then *ah* as they look at each other. Neeta says, "You have have have to bring him."

"To our *durbar*," says Priya.

"Yes, our *durbar*," says Neeta. They've talked gossiped planned little else for the past two months: their grand joint engagement party where they show off to their as-yet-unmarried girl friends and make all the single men jealous. Esha excuses her grimace with the bitterness of the health-tea.

"He's very busy." She doesn't say *busy man*. She cannot even think why she is playing these silly *girli* secrecy games. An aeai called her at the Red Fort to tell her it admired her. Didn't even meet her. There was nothing to meet. It was all in her head. "I don't even know how to get in touch with him. They don't give their numbers out."

"He's coming," Neeta and Priya insist.

She can hardly hear the music for the rattle of the old airco but sweat runs down her sides along the waistband of her Adidas tights to gather in the hollow of her back and slide between the taut curves of her ass. She tries it again across the *gharana's* practice floor. Even the ankle bells sound like lead. Last night she touched the three heavens. This morning she feels dead. She can't concentrate, and that little *lavda* Pranh knows it, swishing at her with yts cane and gobbing out wads of chewed *paan* and mealy eunuch curses.

"Ey! Less staring at your palmer, more *mudras*! Decent *mudras*. You jerk my dick, if I still had one."

Embarrassed that Pranh has noted something she was not conscious of herself—*ring, call me, ring call me, ring, take me out of this*—she fires back, "If you ever had one."

Pranh slashes yts cane at her legs, catches the back of her calf a sting.

"Fuck you, *hijra*!" Esha snatches up towel bag palmer, hooks the earpiece behind her long straight hair. No point changing, the heat out there will soak through anything in a moment. "I'm out of here."

Pranh doesn't call after her. Yts too proud. *Little freak monkey thing,* she thinks. *How is it a nute is an yt, but an incorporeal aeai is a he?* In the legends of Old Delhi, *djinns* are always he.

"*Memsahb* Rathore?"

The chauffeur is in full dress and boots. His only concession to the heat is his shades. In bra top and tights and bare skin, she's melting. "The vehicle is fully air-conditioned, *memsahb.*"

The white leather upholstery is so cool her flesh recoils from its skin.

"This isn't the Krishna Cops."

"No *memsahb.*" The chauffeur pulls out into the traffic. It's only as the security locks clunk she thinks *Oh Lord Krishna, they could be kidnapping me.*

"Who sent you?" There's glass too thick for her fists between her and the driver. Even if the doors weren't locked, a tumble from the car at this speed, in this traffic, would be too much for even a dancer's lithe reflexes. And she's lived in Delhi all her life, *basti* to bungalow, but she doesn't recognize these streets, this suburb, that industrial park. "Where are you taking me?"

"*Memsahb,* where I am not permitted to say for that would spoil the surprise. But I am permitted to tell you that you are the guest of A.J. Rao."

The palmer calls her name as she finishes freshening up with bottled Kinley from the car-bar.

"Hello!" (kicking back deep into the cool cool white leather, like a *filmi* star. She is a star. A star with a bar in a car.)

Audio-only. "I trust the car is acceptable?" Same smooth-suave voice. She can't imagine any opponent being able to resist that voice in negotiation.

"It's wonderful. Very luxurious. Very high status." She's out in the *bastis* now, slums deeper and meaner than the one she grew up in. Newer. The newest ones always look the oldest. Boys chug past on a home-brew *chhakda* they've scavenged from tractor parts. The cream Lex carefully detours around emaciated cattle with angular hips jutting through stretched skin like engineering. Everywhere, drought dust lies thick on the crazed hardtop. This is a city of stares. "Aren't you supposed to be at the conference?"

A laugh, inside her auditory center.

"Oh, I am hard at work winning water for Bharat, believe me. I am nothing if not an assiduous civil servant."

"You're telling me you're there, and here?"

"Oh, it's nothing for us to be in more than one place at the same time. There are multiple copies of me, and subroutines."

"So which is the real you?"

"They are all the real me. In fact, not one of my avatars is in Delhi at all, I am distributed over a series of *dharma*-cores across Varanasi and Patna." He sighs. It sounds close and weary and warm as a whisper in her ear. "You find it difficult to comprehend a distributed consciousness; it is every bit as hard for me to comprehend a discrete, mobile consciousness. I can only copy myself through what you call cyberspace, which is the physical reality of my universe, but you move through dimensional space and time."

"So which one of you loves me then?" The words are out, wild, loose, and unconsidered. "I mean, as a dancer, that is." She's filling, gabbling. "Is there one of you that particularly appreciates *Kathak*?" Polite polite words, like you'd say to an industrialist or a hopeful lawyer at one of Neeta and Priya's hideous match-making soirees. *Don't be forward, no one likes a forward woman. This is a man's world, now.* But she hears glee bubble in A.J. Rao's voice.

"Why, all of me and every part of me, Esha."

Her name. He used her name.

It's a shitty street of pie-dogs and men lounging on *charpoys* scratching themselves, but the chauffeur insists, *here, this way memsahb*. She picks her way down a *gali* lined with unsteady minarets of old car tires. Burning *ghee* and stale urine reek the air. Kids mob the Lexus but the car has A.J. Rao levels of security. The chauffeur pushes open an old wood and brass Mughal style gate in a crumbling red wall. "*Memsahb*."

She steps through into a garden. Into the ruins of a garden. The gasp of wonder dies. The geometrical water channels of the *charbagh* are dry, cracked, choked with litter from picnics. The shrubs are blousy and overgrown, the plant borders ragged with weeds. The grass is scabbed brown with drought-burn: the lower branches of the trees have been hacked away for firewood. As she walks toward the crack-roofed pavilion at the center where paths and water channels meet, the gravel beneath her thin shoes is crazed into rivulets from past monsoons. Dead leaves and fallen twigs cover the lawns. The fountains are dry and silted. Yet families stroll pushing baby buggies; children chase balls. Old Islamic gentlemen read the papers and play chess.

"The Shalimar Gardens," says A.J. Rao in the base of her skull. "Paradise as a walled garden."

And as he speaks, a wave of transformation breaks across the garden, sweeping away the decay of the twenty-first century. Trees break into full leaf, flower beds blossom, rows of terracotta geranium pots march down the banks of the *charbagh* channels which shiver with water. The tiered roofs of the pavilion gleam with gold leaf, peacocks fluster and fuss their vanities, and everything glitters and splashes with fountain play. The laughing families are swept back into Mughal grandees, the old men in the park transformed into *malis* sweeping the gravel paths with their besoms.

Esha claps her hands in joy, hearing a distant, silver spray of sitar notes. "Oh," she says, numb with wonder. "Oh!"

"A thank you, for what you gave me last night. This is one of my favorite places in all India, even though it's almost forgotten. Perhaps, because it is almost forgotten. Aurangzeb was crowned Mughal Emperor here in 1658, now it's an evening stroll for the *basti* people. The past is a passion of mine; it's easy for me, for all of us. We can live in as many times as we can places. I often come here, in my mind. Or should I say, it comes to me."

Then the jets from the fountain ripple as if in the wind, but it is not the wind, not on this stifling afternoon, and the falling water flows into the shape of a man, walking out of the spray. A man of water, that shimmers and flows and becomes a man of flesh. A.J. Rao. *No*, she thinks, *never flesh. A djinn. A thing caught between heaven and hell. A caprice, a trickster. Then trick me.*

"It is as the old Urdu poets declare," says A.J. Rao. "Paradise is indeed contained within a wall."

It is far past four but she can't sleep. She lies naked—shameless—but for the 'hoek behind her ear on top of her bed with the window slats open and the ancient airco chugging, fitful in the periodic brownouts. It is the worst night yet. The city gasps for air. Even the traffic sounds beaten tonight. Across the room her palmer opens its blue eye and whispers her name. *Esha.*

She's up, kneeling on the bed, hand to hoek, sweat beading her bare skin.

"I'm here." A whisper. Neeta and Priya are a thin wall away on either side.

"It's late, I know, I'm sorry . . . "

She looks across the room into the palmer's camera.

"It's all right, I wasn't asleep." A tone in that voice. "What is it?"

"The mission is a failure."

She kneels in the center of the big antique bed. Sweat runs down the fold of her spine.

"The conference? What? What happened?" She whispers, he speaks in her head.

"It fell over one point. One tiny, trivial point, but it was like a wedge that split everything apart until it all collapsed. The Awadhis will build their dam at Kunda Khadar and they will keep their holy Ganga water for Awadh. My delegation is already packing. We will return to Varanasi in the morning."

Her heart kicks. Then she curses herself, *stupid, romantic* girli. He is already in Varanasi as much as he is here as much is he is at the Red Fort assisting his human superiors.

"I'm sorry."

"Yes," he says. "That is the feeling. Was I overconfident in my abilities?"

"People will always disappoint you."

A wry laugh in the dark of her skull.

"How very . . . disembodied of you, Esha." Her name seems to hang in the hot air, like a chord. "Will you dance for me?"

"What, here? Now?"

"Yes. I need something . . . embodied. Physical. I need to see a body move, a consciousness dance through space and time as I cannot. I need to see something beautiful."

Need. A creature with the powers of a god, *needs*. But Esha's suddenly shy, covering her small, taut breasts with her hands.

"Music . . . " she stammers. "I can't perform without music . . . " The shadows at the end of the bedroom thicken into an ensemble: three men bent over *tabla*, *sarangi* and *bansuri*. Esha gives a little shriek and ducks back to the modesty of her bedcover. *They cannot see you, they don't even exist, except in your head. And even if they were flesh, they would be so intent on their contraptions of wire and skin they would not notice.* Terrible driven things, musicians.

"I've incorporated a copy of a sub-aeai into myself for this night," A.J. Rao says. "A level 1.9 composition system. I supply the visuals."

"You can swap bits of yourself in and out?" Esha asks. The *tabla* player has started a slow *Natetere* tap-beat on the *dayan* drum. The musicians nod at each other. Counting, they will be counting. It's hard to convince herself Neeta and Priya can't hear; no one can hear but her. And A.J. Rao. The *sarangi* player sets his bow to the strings, the *bansuri* lets loose a snake of fluting notes. A *sangeet*, but not one she has ever heard before.

"It's making it up!"

"It's a composition aeai. Do you recognize the sources?"

"Krishna and the *gopis*." One of the classic *Kathak* themes: Krishna's seduction of the milkmaids with his flute, the *bansuri*, most sensual of instruments. She knows the steps, feels her body anticipating the moves.

"Will you dance, lady?"

And she steps with the potent grace of a tiger from the bed onto the grass matting of her bedroom floor, into the focus of the palmer. Before she had been shy, silly, *girli*. Not now. She has never had an audience like this before. A lordly djinn. In pure, hot silence she executes the turns and stampings and bows of the *One Hundred and Eight Gopis*, bare feet kissing the woven grass. Her hands shape *mudras*, her face the expressions of the ancient story: surprise, coyness, intrigue, arousal. Sweat courses luxuriously down her naked skin: she doesn't feel it. She is clothed in movement and night. Time slows, the stars halt in their arc over great Delhi. She can feel the planet breathe beneath her feet. This is what it was for, all those dawn risings, all those bleeding feet, those slashes of Pranh's cane, those lost birthdays, that stolen childhood. She dances until her feet bleed again into the rough weave of the matting, until every last drop of water is sucked from her and turned into salt, but she stays with the *tabla*, the beat of *dayan* and *bayan*. She is the milkmaid by the river, seduced by a god. A.J. Rao did not choose this *Kathak* wantonly. And then the music comes to its ringing end and the musicians bow to each other and disperse into golden dust and she collapses, exhausted as never before from any other performance, onto the end of her bed.

Light wakes her. She is sticky, naked, embarrassed. The house staff could find her. And she's got a killing headache. Water. Water. Joints nerves sinews plead for it. She pulls on a Chinese silk robe. On her way to the kitchen, the voyeur eye of her palmer blinks at her. No erotic dream then, no sweat hallucination stirred out of heat and hydrocarbons. She danced Krishna and the one hundred and eight gopis in her bedroom for an aeai. A message. There's a number. *You can call me.*

Throughout the history of the eight Delhis there have been men—and almost always men—skilled in the lore of djinns. They are wise to their many forms and can see beneath the disguises they wear on the streets—donkey, monkey, dog, scavenging kite—to their true selves. They know their roosts and places where they congregate—they are particularly drawn to mosques—and know that that unexplained heat as you push down a *gali* behind the Jama Masjid is djinns, packed so tight you can feel their fire as you move through them. The wisest—the strongest—of fakirs know their names and so can capture and command them. Even in the old India, before the break up into Awadh and Bharat and Rajputana and the United States of Bengal—there were saints who could summon djinns to fly them on their backs from one end of Hindustan to the other in a night. In my own Leh there was an aged aged sufi who cast one hundred and eight djinns out of a troubled house: twenty-seven in the living room, twenty-seven in the bedroom and fifty-four in the kitchen. With so many djinns there was no room for anyone else. He drove them off with burning yoghurt and chilies, but warned: *do not toy with djinns, for they do nothing without a price, and though that may be years in the asking, ask it they surely will.*

Now there is a new race jostling for space in their city: the aeais. If the *djinni* are the creation of fire and men of clay, these are the creation of word. Fifty million of them swarm Delhi's boulevards and *chowks*: routing traffic, trading shares, maintaining power and water, answering inquiries, telling fortunes, managing calendars and diaries, handling routine legal and medical matters, performing in soap operas, sifting the septillion pieces of information streaming through Delhi's nervous system each second. The city is a great mantra. From routers and maintenance robots with little more than animal intelligence (each animal has intelligence enough: ask the eagle or the tiger) to the great Level 2.9s that are indistinguishable from a human being 99.99 percent of the time, they are a young race, an energetic race, fresh to this world and enthusiastic, understanding little of their power.

The djinns watch in dismay from their rooftops and minarets: that such powerful creatures of living word should so blindly serve the clay creation, but mostly because, unlike humans, they can foresee the time when the aeais will drive them from their ancient, beloved city and take their places.

This *durbar*, Neeta and Priya's theme is *Town and Country*: the Bharati mega-soap that has perversely become fashionable as public sentiment in Awadh turns against Bharat. Well, we will just bloody well build our dam, tanks or no tanks; they can beg for it, it's our water now, and, in the same breath, what do you think about Ved Prakash, isn't it scandalous what that Ritu Parvaaz is up to? Once they derided it and its viewers but now that it's improper, now that it's unpatriotic, they can't get enough of Anita Mahapatra and the Begum Vora. Some still refuse to watch but pay for daily plot digests so they can appear fashionably informed at social musts like Neeta and Priya's dating *durbars*.

And it's a grand *durbar*; the last before the monsoon—if it actually happens this year. Neeta and Priya have hired top *bhati*-boys to provide a wash of mixes beamed straight into the guests' 'hoeks. There's even a climate control field, laboring at the limits of its containment to hold back the night heat. Esha can feel its ultrasonics as a dull buzz against her molars.

"Personally, I think sweat becomes you," says A.J. Rao, reading Esha's vital signs through her palmer. Invisible to all but Esha, he moves beside her like death through the press of Town and Countrified guests. By tradition the last *durbar* of the season is a masked ball. In modern, middle-class Delhi that means everyone wears the computer-generated semblance of a soap character. In the flesh they are the socially mobile, dressed in smart-but-cool hot season modes, but, in the mind's eye, they are Aparna Chawla and Ajay Nadiadwala, dashing Govind and conniving Dr. Chatterji. There are three Ved Prakashes and as many Lal Darfans—the aeai actor that plays Ved Prakash in the machine-made soap. Even the grounds of Neeta's fiancé's suburban bungalow have been enchanted into Brahmpur, the fictional Town where *Town and Country* takes place, where the actors that play the characters believe they live out their lives of celebrity tittle-tattle. When Neeta and Priya judge that everyone has mingled and networked enough, the word will be given and everyone will switch off their glittering disguises and return to being wholesalers and lunch vendors and software rajahs. Then the serious stuff begins, the matter of finding a bride. For now Esha can enjoy wandering anonymous in company of her friendly djinn.

She has been wandering much these weeks, through heat streets to ancient places, seeing her city fresh through the eyes of a creature that lives across many spaces and times. At the Sikh *gurdwara* she saw Tegh Bahadur, the Ninth Guru, beheaded by fundamentalist Aurangzeb's guards. The gyring traffic around Vijay Chowk melted into the Bentley cavalcade of Mountbatten, the Last Viceroy, as he forever quit Lutyen's stupendous palace. The tourist clutter and shoving curio vendors around the Qutb Minar turned to ghosts and it was 1193 and the *muezzins* of the first Mughal conquerors sang out the *adhaan*. Illusions. Little lies. But it is all right, when it is done in love. Everything is all right in love. *Can you read my mind?* she asked as she moved with her invisible guide through the thronging streets, that every day grew less raucous, less substantial. *Do you know what I am thinking about you, Aeai Rao?* Little by little, she slips away from the human world into the city of the djinns.

Sensation at the gate. The male stars of *Town and Country* buzz around a woman in an ivory sequined dress. It's a bit damn clever: she's come as Yana Mitra, freshest fittest fastest *boli* sing-star. And *boli girlis*, like *Kathak* dancers, are still meat and ego, though Yana, like every Item-singer, has had her computer avatar guest on T'n'C.

A.J. Rao laughs. "If they only knew. Very clever. What better disguise than to go as yourself. It really *is* Yana Mitra. Esha Rathore, what's the matter, where are you going?"

Why do you have to ask don't you know everything then you know it's hot and noisy and the ultrasonics are doing my head and the yap yap yap is going right through me and they're all only after one thing, are you married are you engaged are you looking and I wish I hadn't come I wish I'd just gone out somewhere with you and that dark corner under the gulmohar *bushes by the* bhati-*rig looks the place to get away from all the stupid stupid people.*

Neeta and Priya, who know her disguise, shout over, "So Esha, are we finally going to meet that man of yours?"

He's already waiting for her among the golden blossoms. Djinns travel at the speed of thought.

"What is it, what's the matter. . . ?"

She whispers, "You know sometimes I wish, I really wish you could get me a drink."

"Why certainly, I will summon a waiter."

"No!" Too loud. Can't be seen talking to the bushes. "No; I mean, hand me one. Just hand me one." But he cannot, and never will. She says, "I started when I was five, did you know that? Oh, you probably did, you know everything about me. But I bet you didn't know how it happened: I was playing with the other girls, dancing round the tank, when this old woman from the *gharana* went up to my mother and said, I will give you a hundred thousand rupees if you give her to me. I will turn her into a dancer; maybe, if she applies herself, a dancer famous through all of India. And my mother said, why her? And do you know what that woman said? Because she shows rudimentary talent for movement, but, mostly, because you are willing to sell her to me for one *lakh* rupees. She took the money there and then, my mother. The old woman took me to the *gharana*. She had once been a great dancer but she got rheumatism and couldn't move and that made her bad. She used to beat me with *lathis*, I had to be up before dawn to get everyone *chai* and eggs. She would make me practice until my feet bled. They would hold up my arms in slings to perform the *mudras* until I couldn't put them down again without screaming. I never once got home—and do you know something? I never once wanted to. And despite her, I applied myself, and I became a great dancer. And do you know what? No one cares. I spent seventeen years mastering something no one cares about. But bring in some *boli* girl who's been around five minutes to flash her teeth and tits. . . . "

"Jealous?" asks A.J. Rao, mildly scolding.

"Don't I deserve to be?"

Then *bhati*-boy One blinks up "You Are My Soniya" on his palmer and that's the signal to demask. Yane Mitra claps her hands in delight and sings along as all around her glimmering *soapi* stars dissolve into mundane accountants and engineers and cosmetic nano-surgeons and the pink walls and roof gardens and thousand thousands stars of Old Brahmpur melt and run down the sky.

It's seeing them, exposed in their naked need, melting like that soap-world before the sun of *celebrity*, that calls back the madness Esha knows from her childhood in the *gharana*. The brooch makes a piercing, ringing chime against the cocktail glass she has snatched from a waiter. She climbs up on to a table. At last, that *boli* bitch shuts up. All eyes are on her.

"Ladies, but mostly gentlemen, I have an announcement to make." Even the city behind the sound-curtain seems to be holding its breath. "I am engaged to be married!" Gasps. Oohs. Polite applause *who is she, is she on tivi, isn't she something arty?* Neeta and Priya are wide-eyed at the back. "I'm very very lucky because my husband-to-be is here tonight. In fact, he's been with me all evening. Oh, silly me. Of course, I forgot, not all of you can see him. Darling, would you mind? Gentlemen and ladies, would you mind slipping on your hoeks for just a moment. I'm sure you don't need any introduction to my wonderful wonderful fiancé, A.J. Rao."

And she knows from the eyes, the mouths, the low murmur that threatens to break into applause, then fails, then is taken up by Neeta and Priya to turn into a decorous ovation, that they can all see Rao as tall and elegant and handsome as she sees him, at her side, hand draped over hers.

She can't see that *boli* girl anywhere.

He's been quiet all the way back in the *phatphat*. He's quiet now, in the house. They're alone. Neeta and Priya should have been home hours ago, but Esha knows they're scared of her.

"You're very quiet." This, to the coil of cigarette smoke rising up toward the ceiling fan as she lies on her bed. She'd love a *bidi*; a good, dirty street smoke for once, not some Big Name Western brand.

"We were followed as we drove back after the party. An aeai aircraft surveilled your *phatphat*. A network analysis aeai system sniffed at my router net to try to track this com channel. I know for certain street cameras were tasked on us. The Krishna Cop who lifted you after the Red Fort *durbar* was at the end of the street. He is not very good at subterfuge."

Esha goes to the window to spy out the Krishna Cop, call him out, demand of him what he thinks he's doing?

"He's long gone," says Rao. "They have been keeping you under light surveillance for some time now. I would imagine your announcement has upped your level."

"They were there?"

"As I said . . . "

"Light surveillance."

It's scary but exciting, down in the deep *muladhara chakra*, a red throb above her *yoni*. Scarysexy. That same lift of red madness that made her blurt out that marriage announcement. It's all going so far, so fast. No way to get off now.

"You never gave me the chance to answer," says aeai Rao.

Can you read my mind? Esha thinks at the palmer.

"No, but I share some operating protocols with scripting aeais for *Town and Country*—in a sense they are a low-order part of me—they have become quite good predictors of human behavior."

"I'm a soap opera."

Then she falls back onto the bed and laughs and laughs and laughs until she feels sick, until she doesn't want to laugh any more and every guffaw is a choke, a lie, spat up at the spy machines up there, beyond the lazy fan that merely stirs the heat, turning on the huge thermals that spire up from Delhi's colossal heat-island, a conspiracy of djinns.

"Esha," A.J. Rao says, closer than he has ever seemed before. "Lie still." She forms the question *why?* And hears the corresponding whisper inside her head *hush, don't speak*. In the same instant the *chakra* glow bursts like a yolk and leaks heat into her *yoni*. *Oh*, she says, *oh!* Her clitoris is singing to her. *Oh oh oh oh*. "How . . . ?" Again, the voice, huge inside her head, inside every part of her *sssshhhhh*. Building building she needs to do something, she needs to move needs to rub against the day-warmed scented wood of the big bed, needs to get her hand down there hard hard hard . . .

"No, don't touch," chides A.J. Rao and now she can't even move she needs to explode she has to explode her skull can't contain this her dancer's muscles are pulled tight as wires she can't take much more *no no no yes yes yes* she's shrieking now tiny little shrieks beating her fists off the bed but it's just spasm, nothing will obey her and then it's explosion bam, and another one before that one has even faded, huge slow explosions across the sky and she's cursing and blessing every god in India. Ebbing now, but still shock after shock, one on top of the other. Ebbing now . . . Ebbing.

"Ooh. Oh. What? Oh wow, how?"

"The machine you wear behind your ear can reach deeper than words and visions," says A.J. Rao. "So, are you answered?"

"What?" The bed is drenched in sweat. She's sticky dirty needs to wash, change clothes, move but the afterglows are still fading. Beautiful beautiful colors.

"The question you never gave me the chance to answer. Yes. I will marry you."

"Stupid vain girl, you don't even know what caste he is."

Mata Madhuri smokes eighty a day through a plastic tube hooked from the respirator unit into a grommet in her throat. She burns through them three at a time: *bloody machine scrubs all the good out of them*, she says. *Last bloody pleasure I have*. She used to bribe the nurses but they bring her them free now, out of fear of her temper that grows increasingly vile as her body surrenders more and more to the machines.

Without pause for Esha's reply, a flick of her whim whips the life-support chair round and out into the garden.

"Can't smoke in there, no fresh air."

Esha follows her out on to the raked gravel of the formal *charbagh*.

"No one marries in caste any more."

"Don't be smart, stupid girl. It's like marrying a Muslim, or even a Christian, Lord Krishna protect me. You know fine what I mean. Not a real person."

"There are girls younger than me marry trees, or even dogs."

"So bloody clever. That's up in some god-awful shithole like Bihar or Rajputana, and anyway, those are gods. Any fool knows that. Ach, away with you!" The old, destroyed woman curses as the chair's aeai deploys its parasol. "Sun sun, I need sun, I'll be burning soon enough, sandalwood, you hear? You burn me on a sandalwood pyre. I'll know if you stint."

Madhuri the old crippled dance teacher always uses this tactic to kill a conversation with which she is uncomfortable. *When I'm gone . . . Burn me sweetly . . .*

"And what can a god do that A.J. Rao can't?"

"Ai! You ungrateful, blaspheming child. I'm not hearing this la la la la la la la la la have you finished yet?"

Once a week Esha comes to the nursing home to visit this ruin of a woman, wrecked by the demands a dancer makes of a human body. She's explored guilt need rage resentment anger pleasure at watching her collapse into long death as the motives that keep her turning up the drive in a *phatphat* and there is only one she believes. She's the only mother she has.

"If you marry that . . . thing . . . you will be making a mistake that will destroy your life," Madhuri declares, accelerating down the path between the water channels.

"I don't need your permission," Esha calls after her. A thought spins Madhuri's chair on its axis.

"Oh, really? That would be a first for you. You want my blessing. Well, you won't have it. I refuse to be party to such nonsense."

"I will marry A.J. Rao"

"What did you say?"

"I. Will. Marry. Aeai. A.J. Rao."

Madhuri laughs, a dry, dying, spitting sound, full of *bidi*-smoke.

"Well, you almost surprise me. Defiance. Good, some spirit at last. That was always your problem, you always needed everyone to approve, everyone to give you permission, everyone to love you. And that's what stopped you being great, do you know that, girl? You could have been a *devi*, but you always held back for fear that someone might not approve. And so you were only ever . . . good."

People are looking now, staff, visitors. Patients. Raised voices, unseemly emotions. This is a house of calm, and slow mechanized dying. Esha bends low to whisper to her mentor.

"I want you to know that I dance for him. Every night. Like Radha for Krishna. I dance just for him, and then he comes and makes love to me. He makes me scream and swear like a hooker. Every night. And look!" He doesn't need to call any more; he is hardwired into the hoek she now hardly ever takes off. Esha looks up: he is there, standing in a sober black suit among the strolling visitors and droning wheelchairs, hands folded. "There he is, see? My lover, my husband."

A long, keening screech, like feedback, like a machine dying. Madhuri's withered hands fly to her face. Her breathing tube curdles with tobacco smoke.

"Monster! Monster! Unnatural child, ah, I should have left you in that *basti*! Away from me away away away!"

Esha retreats from the old woman's mad fury as hospital staff come hurrying across the scorched lawns, white saris flapping.

Every fairytale must have a wedding.

Of course, it was the event of the season. The decrepit old Shalimar Gardens were transformed by an army of *malis* into a sweet, green, watered maharajah's fantasia with elephants, pavilions, musicians, lancers, dancers, *filmi* stars, and robot bartenders. Neeta and Priya were uncomfortable bridesmaids in fabulous frocks; a great brahmin was employed to bless the union of woman and artificial intelligence. Every television network sent cameras, human or aeai. Gleaming presenters checked the guests in and checked the guests out. *Chati* mag paparazzi came in their crowds, wondering what they could turn their cameras on. There were even politicians from Bharat, despite the souring relationships between the two neighbors now Awadh constructors were scooping up the Ganga sands into revetments. But most there were the people of the encroaching *bastis*, jostling up against the security staff lining the paths of their garden, asking, *she's marrying a what? How does that work? Can they, you know? And what about children? Who is she, actually? Can you see anything? I can't see anything. Is there anything to see?*

But the guests and the great were 'hoeked up and applauded the groom in his golden veil on his white stallion, stepping with the delicacy of a dressage horse up the raked paths. And because they were great and guests, there was not one who, despite the free French champagne from the well-known diplomatic *sommelier*, would ever say, *but there's no one there.* No one was at all surprised that, after the bride left in a stretch limo, there came a dry, sparse thunder, cloud to cloud, and a hot mean wind that swept the discarded invitations along the paths. As they were filing back to their taxis, tankers were draining the expensively filled *qanats*.

It made lead in the news.

Kathak stars weds aeai lover!!! Honeymoon in Kashmir!!!

Above the *chowks* and minarets of Delhi, the djinns bent together in conference.

He takes her while shopping in Tughluk Mall. Three weeks and the shop girls still nod and whisper. She likes that. She doesn't like it that they glance and giggle when the Krishna Cops lift her from the counter at the Black Lotus Japanese Import Company.

"My husband is an accredited diplomat, this is a diplomatic incident." The woman in the bad suit pushes her head gently down to enter the car. The Ministry doesn't need personal liability claims.

"Yes, but you are not, Mrs. Rao," says Thacker in the back seat. Still wearing that cheap aftershave.

"Rathore," she says. "I have retained my stage name. And we shall see what my husband has to say about my diplomatic status." She lifts her hand in a *mudra* to speak to AyJay, as she thinks of him now. Dead air. She performs the wave again.

"This is a shielded car," Thacker says.

The building is shielded also. They take the car right inside, down a ramp into the basement parking lot. It's a cheap, anonymous glass and titanium block on Parliament Street that she's driven past ten thousand times on her way to the shops of Connaught Circus without ever noticing. Thacker's office is on the fifteenth floor. It's tidy and has a fine view over the astronomical geometries of the Jantar Mantar but smells of food: *tiffin* snatched at the desk. She checks for photographs of family children wife. Only himself smart in pressed whites for a cricket match.

"*Chai?*"

"Please." The anonymity of this civil service block is beginning to unnerve her: a city within a city. The *chai* is warm and sweet and comes in a tiny disposable plastic cup. Thacker's smile seems also warm and sweet. He sits at the end of the desk, angled toward her in Krishna-cop handbook "non-confrontational."

"Mrs. Rathore. How to say this?"

"My marriage is legal. . . . "

"Oh, I know, Mrs. Rathore. This is Awadh, after all. Why, there have even been women who married djinns, within our own lifetimes. No. It's an international affair now, it seems. Oh well. Water: we do all so take it for granted, don't we? Until it runs short, that is."

"Everybody knows my husband is still trying to negotiate a solution to the Kunda Khadar problem."

"Yes, of course he is." Thacker lifts a manila envelope from his desk, peeps inside, grimaces coyly. "How shall I put this? Mrs. Rathore, does your husband tell you everything about his work?"

"That is an impertinent question. . . . "

"Yes yes, forgive me, but if you'll look at these photographs."

Big glossy hi-res prints, slick and sweet smelling from the printer. Aerial views of the ground, a thread of green blue water, white sands, scattered shapes without meaning.

"This means nothing to me."

"I suppose it wouldn't, but these drone images show Bharati battle tanks, robot reconnaissance units, and air defense batteries deploying with striking distance of the construction at Kunda Khadar."

And it feels as if the floor has dissolved beneath her and she is falling through a void so vast it has no visible reference points, other than the sensation of her own falling.

"My husband and I don't discuss work."

"Of course. Oh, Mrs. Rathore, you've crushed your cup. Let me get you another one."

He leaves her much longer than it takes to get a shot of *chai* from the *wallah*. When he returns he asks casually, "Have you heard of a thing called the Hamilton Acts? I'm sorry, I thought in your position you would . . . but evidently not. Basically, it's a series of international treaties originated by the United States limiting the development and proliferation of high-level artificial intelligences, most specifically the hypothetical Generation Three. No? Did he not tell you any of this?"

Mrs. Rathore in her Italian suit folds her ankles one over the other and thinks, *this reasonable man can do anything he wants here, anything.*

"As you probably know, we grade and license aeais according to levels; these roughly correspond to how convincingly they pass as human beings. A Level 1 has basic animal intelligence, enough for its task but would never be mistaken for a human. Many of them can't even speak. They don't need to. A Level 2.9 like your husband,"—he speeds over the word, like the wheel of a *shatabdi* express over the gap in a rail—"is humanlike to a 5 percentile. A Generation Three is indistinguishable in any circumstances from a human—in fact, their intelligences may be many millions of times ours, if there is any meaningful way of measuring that. Theoretically we could not even recognize such an intelligence, all we would see would be the Generation Three interface, so to speak. The Hamilton Acts simply seek to control technology that could give rise to a Generation Three aeai. Mrs. Rathore, we believe sincerely that the Generation Threes pose the greatest threat to our security—as a nation and as a species—that we have ever faced."

"And my husband?" Solid, comfortable word. Thacker's sincerity scares her.

"The government is preparing to sign the Hamilton Acts in return for loan guarantees to construct the Kunda Khadar dam. When the Act is passed—and it's in the current session of the Lok Sabha—everything under Level 2.8 will be subject to rigorous inspection and licensing, policed by us."

"And over Level 2.8?"

"Illegal, Mrs. Rathore. They will be aggressively erased."

Esha crosses and uncrosses her legs. She shifts on the chair. Thacker will wait forever for her response.

"What do you want me to do?"

"A.J. Rao is highly placed within the Bharati administration."

"You're asking me to spy . . . on an *aeai*."

From his face, she knows he expected her to say, *husband*.

"We have devices, taps. . . . They would be beneath the level of aeai Rao's consciousness. We can run them into your 'hoek. We are not all blundering plods in the Department. Go to the window, Mrs. Rathore."

Esha touches her fingers lightly to the climate-cooled glass, polarized dusk against the drought light. Outside the smog haze says *heat*. Then she cries and drops to her knees in fear. The sky is filled with gods, rank upon rank, tier upon tier, rising up above Delhi in a vast helix, huge as clouds, as countries, until at the apex the Trimurti, the Hindu Trinity of Brahma, Vishnu, Siva look down like falling moons. It is her private Ramayana, the titanic Vedic battle order of gods arrayed across the troposphere.

She feels Thacker's hand help her up.

"Forgive me, that was stupid, unprofessional. I was showing off. I wanted to impress you with the aeai systems we have at our disposal."

His hand lingers a moment more than *gentle*. And the gods go out, all at once.

She says, "Mr. Thacker, would you put a spy in my bedroom, in my bed, between me and my husband? That's what you're doing if you tap into the channels between me and AyJay."

Still, the hand is there as Thacker guides her to the chair, offers cool, cool water.

"I only ask because I believe I am doing something for this country. I take pride in my job. In some things I have discretion, but not when it comes to the security of the nation. Do you understand?"

Esha twitches into dancer's composure, straightens her dress, checks her face.

"Then the least you can do is call me a car."

That evening she whirls to the *tabla* and *shehnai* across the day-warmed marble of a Jaipuri palace *Diwan-I-aam*, a flame among the twilit pillars. The audience is dark huddles on the marble, hardly daring even to breathe. Among the lawyers politicians journalists cricket stars moguls of industry are the managers who have converted this Rajput palace into a planetary class hotel, and any numbers of *chati* celebs. None so *chati*, so celebby, as Esha Rathore. Pranh can cherry-pick the bookings now. She's more than a nine-day, even a nine-week wonder. Esha knows that all her rapt watchers are 'hoeked up, hoping for a ghost-glimpse of her *djinn*-husband dancing with her through the flame-shadowed pillars.

Afterward, as yt carries her armfuls of flowers back to her suite, Pranh says, "You know, I'm going to have to up my percentage."

"You wouldn't dare," Esha jokes. Then she sees the bare fear on the nute's face. It's only a wash, a shadow. But yt's afraid.

Neeta and Priya had moved out of the bungalow by the time she returned from Dal Lake. They've stopped answering her calls. It's seven weeks since she last went to see Madhuri.

Naked, she sprawls on the pillows in the filigree-light stone *jharoka*. She peers down from her covered balcony through the grille at the departing guests. See out, not see in. Like the shut-away women of the old *zenana*. Shut away from the world. Shut away from human flesh. She stands up, holds her body against the day-warmed stone; the press of her nipples, the rub of her pubis. *Can you see me smell me sense me know that I am here at all?*

And he's there. She does not need to see him now, just sense his electric prickle along the inside of her skull. He fades into vision sitting on the end of the low, ornate teak bed. *He could as easily materialize in mid-air in front of her balcony*, she thinks. But there are rules, and games, even for djinns.

"You seem distracted, heart." He's blind in this room—no camera eyes observing her in her jeweled skin—but he observes her through a dozen senses, a myriad feedback loops through her 'hoek.

"I'm tired, I'm annoyed, I wasn't as good as I should have been."

"Yes, I thought that too. Was it anything to do with the Krishna Cops this afternoon?"

Esha's heart races. He can read her heartbeat. He can read her sweat, he can read the adrenaline and noradrenalin balance in her brain. He will know if she lies. Hide a lie inside a truth.

"I should have said, I was embarrassed." He can't understand shame. Strange, in a society where people die from want of honor. "We could be in trouble, there's something called the Hamilton Acts."

"I am aware of them." He laughs. He has this way now of doing it inside her head. He thinks she likes the intimacy, a truly private joke. She hates it. "All too aware of them."

"They wanted to warn me. Us."

"That was kind of them. And me a representative of a foreign government. So that's why they'd been keeping a watch on you, to make sure you are all right."

"They thought they might be able to use me to get information from you."

"Did they indeed?"

The night is so still she can hear the jingle of the elephant harnesses and the cries of the *mahouts* as they carry the last of the guests down the long processional drive to their waiting limos. In a distant kitchen a radio jabbers.

Now we will see how human you are. Call him out. At last A.J. Rao says, "Of course. I do love you." Then he looks into her face. "I have something for you."

The staff turn their faces away in embarrassment as they set the device on the white marble floor, back out of the room, eyes averted. What does she care? She is a star. A.J. Rao raises his hand and the lights slowly die. Pierced-brass lanterns send soft stars across the beautiful old *zenana* room. The device is the size and shape of a *phatphat* tire, chromed and plasticed, alien among the Mughal retro. As Esha floats over the marble toward it, the plain white surface bubbles and deliquesces into dust. Esha hesitates.

"Don't be afraid, look!" says A.J. Rao. The powder spurts up like steam from boiling rice, then pollen-bursts into a tiny dust-dervish, staggering across the surface of the disc. "Take the 'hoek off!" Rao cries delightedly from the bed. "Take it off." Twice she hesitates, three times he encourages. Esha slides the coil of plastic off the sweet-spot behind her ear and voice and man vanish like death. Then the pillar of glittering dust leaps head high, lashes like a tree in a monsoon and twists itself into the ghostly outline of a man. It flickers once, twice, and then A.J. Rao stands before her. A rattle like leaves a snake-rasp a rush of winds, and then the image says, "Esha." A whisper of dust. A thrill of ancient fear runs through her skin into her bones.

"What is this . . . what are you?"

The storm of dust parts into a smile.

"I-Dust. Micro-robots. Each is smaller than a grain of sand, but they manipulate static fields and light. They are my body. Touch me. This is real. This is me."

But she flinches away in the lantern-lit room. Rao frowns.

"Touch me. . . . "

She reaches out her hand toward his chest. Close, he is a creature of sand, a whirlwind permanently whipping around the shape of a man. Esha touches flesh to i-Dust. Her hand sinks into his body. Her cry turns to a startled giggle.

"It tickles. . . . "

"The static fields."

"What's inside?"

"Why don't you find out?"

"What, you mean?"

"It's the only intimacy I can offer. . . . " He sees her eyes widen under their kohled make-up. "I think you should hold your breath."

She does, but keeps her eyes open until the last moment, until the dust flecks like a dead *tivi* channel in her close focus. A.J. Rao's body feels like the most delicate Vaanasi silk scarf draped across her bare skin. She is inside him. She is inside the body of her husband, her lover. She dares to open her eyes. Rao's face is a hollow shell looking back at her from a perspective of millimeters. When she moves her lips, she can feel the dust-bots of his lips brushing against hers: an inverse kiss.

"My heart, my Radha," whispers the hollow mask of A.J. Rao. Somewhere Esha knows she should be screaming. But she cannot: she is somewhere no human has ever been before. And now the whirling streamers of i-Dust are stroking her hips, her belly, her thighs. Her breasts. Her nipples, her cheeks and neck, all the places she loves to feel a human touch, caressing her, driving her to her knees, following her as the mote-sized robots follow A.J. Rao's command, swallowing her with his body.

It's *Gupshup* followed by *Chandni Chati* and at twelve thirty a photo shoot—at the hotel, if you don't mind—for *FilmFare*'s Saturday Special Center Spread—you don't mind if we send a robot, they can get places get angles we just can't get the meat-ware and could you dress up, like you did for the opening, maybe a move or two, in between the pillars in the Diwan, just like the gala opening, okay lovely lovely lovely well your husband can copy us a couple of avatars and our own aeais can paste him in people want to see you together, happy couple lovely couple, dancer risen from *basti*, international diplomat, marriage across worlds in every sense the romance of it all, so how did you meet what first attracted you what's it like be married to an aeai how do the other girls treat you do you, you know and what about children, I mean, of course a woman and an aeai but there are technologies these days geneline engineering like all the super-duper rich and their engineered children and you are a celebrity now how are you finding it, sudden rise to fame, in every *gupshup* column, worldwide *celebi* star everyone's talking all the rage and all the chat and all the parties and as Esha answers for the sixth time the same questions asked by the same gazelle-eyed *girli celebi* reporters *oh we are very happy wonderfully happy deliriously happy love is a wonderful wonderful thing and that's the thing about love, it can be for anything, anyone, even a human and an aeai, that's the purest form of love, spiritual love* her mouth opening and closing yabba yabba yabba but her inner eye, her eye of Siva, looks inward, backward.

Her mouth, opening and closing.

Lying on the big Mughal sweet-wood bed, yellow morning light shattered through the *jharoka* screen, her bare skin good-pimpled in the cool of the airco. Dancing between worlds: sleep, wakefulness in the hotel bedroom, memory of the things he did to her limbic centers through the hours of the night that had her singing like a *bulbul*, the world of the djinns. Naked but for the 'hoek behind her ear. She had become like those people who couldn't afford the treatments and had to wear eyeglasses and learned to at once ignore and be conscious of the technology on their faces. Even when she did remove it—for performing; for, as now, the shower—she could still place A.J. Rao in the room, feel his physicality. In the big marble stroll-in shower in this VIP suite relishing the gush and rush of precious water (always the mark of a true *rani*) she knew AyJay was sitting on the carved chair by the balcony. So when she thumbed on the *tivi* panel (bathroom with *tivi, oooh!*) to distract her while she toweled dry her hair, her first reaction was a double-take-look at the 'hoek on the sink-stand when she saw the press conference from Varanasi and Water Spokesman A.J. Rao explaining Bharat's necessary military exercises in the vicinity of the Kunda Khadar dam. She slipped on the 'hoek, glanced into the room. There, on the chair, as she felt. There, in the Bharat Sabha studio in Varanasi, talking to Bharti from the *Good Morning Awadh!* News.

Esha watched them both as she slowly, distractedly dried herself. She had felt glowing, sensual, divine. Now she was fleshy, self-conscious, stupid. The water on her skin, the air in the big room was cold cold cold.

"AyJay, is that really you?"

He frowned.

"That's a very strange question first thing in the morning. Especially after. . . . "

She cut cold his smile.

"There's a *tivi* in the bathroom. You're on, doing an interview for the news. A live interview. So, are you really here?"

"*Cho chweet*, you know what I am, a distributed entity. I'm copying and deleting myself all over the place. I am wholly there, and I am wholly here."

Esha held the vast, powder-soft towel around her.

"Last night, when you were here, in the body, and afterward, when we were in the bed; were you here with me? Wholly here? Or was there a copy of you working on your press statement and another having a high level meeting and another drawing an emergency water supply plan and another talking to the Banglas in Dhaka?"

"My love, does it matter?"

"Yes, it matters!" She found tears, and something beyond; anger choking in her throat. "It matters to me. It matters to any woman. To any . . . human."

"*Mrs. Rao, are you all right?*"

"Rathore, my name is Rathore!" She hears herself snap at the silly little *chati*-mag junior. Esha gets up, draws up her full dancer's poise. "This interview is over."

"Mrs. Rathore Mrs. Rathore," the journo *girli* calls after her.

Glancing at her fractured image in the thousand mirrors of the Sheesh Mahal, Esha notices glittering dust in the shallow lines of her face.

A thousand stories tell of the willfulness and whim of djinns. But for every story of the *djinni*, there are a thousand tales of human passion and envy and the aeais, being a creation between, learned from both. Jealousy, and dissembling.

When Esha went to Thacker the Krishna Cop, she told herself it was from fear of what the Hamilton Acts might do to her husband in the name of national hygiene. But she dissembled. She went to that office on Parliament Street looking over the star-geometries of the Jantar Mantar out of jealousy. When a wife wants her husband, she must have all of him. Ten thousand stories tell this. A copy in the bedroom while another copy plays water politics is an unfaithfulness. If a wife does not have everything, she has nothing. So Esha went to Thacker's office wanting to betray and as she opened her hand on the desk and the *techi* boys loaded their darkware into her palmer she thought, *this is right, this is good, now we are equal.* And when Thacker asked her to meet him again in a week to update the 'ware—unlike the djinns, hostages of eternity, software entities on both sides of the war evolved at an ever-increasing rate—he told himself it was duty to his warrant, loyalty to his country. In this too he dissembled. It was fascination.

Earth-mover robots started clearing the Kunda Khadar dam site the day Inspector Thacker suggested that perhaps next week they might meet at the International Coffee House on Connaught Circus, his favorite. She said, *my husband will see.* To which Thacker replied, *we have ways to blind him.* But all the same she sat in the furthest, darkest corner, under the screen showing the international cricket, hidden from any prying eyes, her 'hoek shut down and cold in her handbag.

So what are you finding out? she asked.

It would be more than my job is worth to tell you, Mrs. Rathore, said the Krishna Cop. National security. Then the waiter brought coffee on a silver tray.

After that they never went back to the office. On the days of their meetings Thacker would whirl her through the city in his government car to Chandni Chowk, to Humayun's Tomb and the Qutb Minar, even to the Shalimar Gardens. Esha knew what he was doing, taking her to those same places where her husband had enchanted her. *How closely have you been watching me?* she thought. *Are you trying to seduce me?* For Thacker did not magic her away to the eight Delhis of the dead past, but immersed her in the crowd, the smell, the bustle, the voices and commerce and traffic and music; her present, her city burning with life and movement. *I was fading,* she realized. *Fading out of the world, becoming a ghost, locked in that invisible marriage, just the two of us, seen and unseen, always together, only together.* She would feel for the plastic fetus of her 'hoek coiled in the bottom of her jeweled bag and hate it a little. When she slipped it back behind her ear in the privacy of the *phatphat* back to her bungalow, she would remember that Thacker was always assiduous in thanking her for her help in national security. Her reply was always the same: *Never thank a woman for betraying her husband over her country.*

He would ask, of course. *Out and about,* she would say. *Sometimes I just need to get out of this place, get away. Yes, even from you.* . . . Holding the words, the look into the eye of the lens just long enough. . . .

Yes, of course, you must.

Now the earthmovers had turned Kunda Khadar into Asia's largest construction site, the negotiations entered a new stage. Varanasi was talking directly to Washington to put pressure on Awadh to abandon the dam and avoid a potentially destabilizing water war. US support was conditional on Bharat's agreement to the Hamilton protocols, which Bharat could never do, not with its major international revenue generator being the wholly aeai-generated *soapi Town and Country.*

Washington telling me to effectively sign my own death warrant, A.J. Rao would laugh. *Americans surely appreciate irony.* All this he told her as they sat on the well-tended lawn sipping green *chai* through a straw, Esha sweating freely in the swelter but unwilling to go into the air-conditioned cool because she knew there were still paparazzi lenses out there, focusing. AyJay never needed to sweat. But she still knew that he split himself. In the night, in the rare cool, he would ask, *dance for me.* But she didn't dance any more, not for aeai A.J. Rao, not for Pranh, not for a thrilled audience who would shower her with praise and flowers and money and fame. Not even for herself.

Tired. Too tired. The heat. Too tired.

Thacker is on edge, toying with his *chai* cup, wary of eye contact when they meet in his beloved International Coffee House. He takes her hand and draws the updates into her open palm with boyish coyness. His talk is smaller than small, finicky, itchily polite. Finally, he dares looks at her.

"Mrs. Rathore, I have something I must ask you. I have wanted to ask you for some time now."

Always, the name, the honorific. But the breath still freezes, her heart kicks in animal fear.

"You know you can ask me anything." Tastes like poison. Thacker can't hold her eye, ducks away, Killa Krishna Kop turned shy boy.

"Mrs. Rathore, I am wondering if you would like to come and see me play cricket?"

The Department of Artificial Intelligence Registration and Licensing versus Parks and Cemeteries Service of Delhi is hardly a Test against the United States of Bengal, but it is still enough of a social occasion to out posh frocks and Number One saris. Pavilions, parasols, sunshades ring the scorched grass of the Civil Service of Awadh sports ground, a flock of white wings. Those who can afford portable airco field generators sit in the cool drinking English Pimms Number 1 Cup. The rest fan themselves. Incognito in hi-label shades and light silk *dupatta*, Esha Rathore looks at the salt white figures moving on the circle of brown grass and wonders what it is they find so important in their game of sticks and ball to make themselves suffer so.

She had felt hideously self-conscious when she slipped out of the *phatphat* in her flimsy disguise. Then as she saw the crowds in their *mela* finery milling and chatting, heat rose inside her, the same energy that allowed her to hide behind her performances, seen but unseen. A face half the country sees on its morning *chati* mags, yet can vanish so easily under shades and a headscarf. Slum features. The anonymity of the *basti* bred into the cheekbones, a face from the great crowd.

The Krishna Cops have been put in to bat by Parks and Cemeteries. Thacker is in the middle of the batting order, but Parks and Cemeteries pace bowler Chaudry and the lumpy wicket is making short work of the Department's openers. One on his way to the painted wooden pavilion, and Thacker striding toward the crease, pulling on his gloves, taking his place, lining up his bat. *He is very handsome in his whites*, Esha thinks. He runs a couple of desultory ones with his partner at the other end, then it's; a new over. Clop of ball on willow. A rich, sweet sound. A couple of safe returns. Then the bowler lines and brings his arm round in a windmill. The ball gets a sweet mad bounce. Thacker fixes it with his eye, steps back, takes it in the middle of the bat and drives it down, hard, fast, bounding toward the boundary rope that kicks it into the air for a cheer and a flurry of applause and a four. And Esha is on her feet, hands raised to applaud, cheering. The score clicks over on the big board, and she is still on her feet, alone of all the audience. For directly across the ground, in front of the sight screens, is a tall, elegant figure in black, wearing a red turban.

Him. Impossibly, him. Looking right at her, through the white-clad players as if they were ghosts. And very slowly, he lifts a finger and taps it to his right ear.

She knows what she'll find but she must raise her fingers in echo, feel with horror the coil of plastic overlooked in her excitement to get to the game, nestled accusing in her hair like a snake.

Ω

"So, who won the cricket then?"

"Why do you need to ask me? If it were important to you, you'd know. Like you can know anything you really want to."

"You don't know? Didn't you stay to the end? I thought the point of sport was who won. What other reason would you have to follow intra-Civil Service cricket?"

If Puri the maid were to walk into the living room, she would see a scene from a folk tale: a woman shouting and raging at silent dead air. But Puri does her duties and leaves as soon as she can. She's not at ease in a house of djinns.

"'Sarcasm is it now? Where did you learn that? Some sarcasm aeai you've made part of yourself? So now there's another part of you I don't know, that I'm supposed to love? Well, I don't like it and I won't love it because it makes you look petty and mean and spiteful."

"There are no aeais for that. We have no need for those emotions. If I learned these, I learned them from humans."

Esha lifts her hand to rip away the 'hoek, hurl it against the wall.

"No!"

So far Rao has been voice-only, now the slanting late-afternoon golden light stirs and curdles into the body of her husband.

"Don't," he says. "Don't . . . banish me. I do love you."

"What does that mean?" Esha screams "You're not real! None of this is real! It's just a story we made up because we wanted to believe it. Other people, they have real marriages, real lives, real sex. Real . . . children."

"Children. Is that what it is? I thought the fame, the attention was the thing, that there never would be children to ruin your career and your body. But if that's no longer enough, we can have children, the best children I can buy."

Esha cries out, a keen of disappointment and frustration. The neighbors will hear. But the neighbors have been hearing everything, listening, gossiping. No secrets in the city of djinns.

"Do you know what they're saying, all those magazines and *chati* shows? What they're really saying? About us, the djinn and his wife?"

"I know!" For the first time, A.J. Rao's voice, so sweet, so reasonable inside her head, is raised. "I know what every one of them says about us. Esha, have I ever asked anything of you?"

"Only to dance."

"I'm asking one more thing of you now. It's not a big thing. It's a small thing, nothing really. You say I'm not real, what we have is not real. That hurts me, because at some level it's true. Our worlds are not compatible. But it can be real. There is a chip, new technology, a protein chip. You get it implanted, here." Rao raises his hand to his third eye. "It would be like the 'hoek, but it would always be on. I could always be with you. We would never be apart. And you could leave your world and enter mine . . . . "

Esha's hands are at her mouth, holding in the horror, the bile, the sick vomit of fear. She heaves, retches. Nothing. No solid, no substance, just ghosts and djinns. Then she rips her 'hoek from the sweet spot behind her ear and there is blessed silence and blindness. She holds the little device in her two hands and snaps it cleanly in two.

Then she runs from her house.

Not Neeta not Priya, not snippy Pranh in yts *gharana*, not Madhuri, a smoke-blackened hulk in a life-support chair, and no not never her mother, even though Esha's feet remember every step to her door; never the *basti*. That's death.

One place she can go.

But he won't let her. He's there in the *phatphat*, his face in the palm of her hands, voice scrolling silently in a ticker across the smart fabric: *come back, I'm sorry, come back, let's talk come back, I didn't mean to come back.* Hunched in the back of the little yellow and black plastic bubble she clenches his face into a fist but she can still feel him, feel his face, his mouth next to her skin. She peels the palmer from her hand. His mouth moves silently. She hurls him into the traffic. He vanishes under truck tires.

And still he won't let her go. The *phatphat* spins into Connaught Circus's vast gyratory and his face is on every single one of the video-silk screens hung across the curving facades. Twenty A.J. Rao's, greater, lesser, least, miming in sync.

Esha Esha come back, say the rolling news tickers. *We can try something else. Talk to me. Any ISO, any palmer, anyone. . . .*

Infectious paralysis spreads across Connaught Circus. First the people who notice things like fashion ads and *chati*-screens; then the people who notice other people, then the traffic, noticing all the people on the pavements staring up, mouths fly-catching. Even the *phatphat* driver is staring. Connaught Circus is congealing into a clot of traffic: if the heart of Delhi stops, the whole city will seize and die.

"Drive on drive on," Esha shouts at her driver. "I order you to drive." But she abandons the autorickshaw at the end of Sisganj Road and pushes through the clogged traffic the final half-kilometer to Manmohan Singh Buildings. She glimpses Thacker pressing through the crowd, trying to rendezvous with the police motorbike sirening a course through the traffic. In desperation she thrusts up an arm, shouts out his name and rank. At last, he turns. They beat toward each other through the chaos.

"Mrs. Rathore, we are facing a major incursion incident. . . . "

"My husband, Mr. Rao, he has gone mad. . . . "

"Mrs. Rathore, please understand, by our standards, he never was sane. He is an aeai."

The motorbike wails its horns impatiently. Thacker waggles his head to the driver, a woman in police leathers and helmet: *in a moment in a moment*. He seizes Esha's hand, pushes her thumb into his palmer-gloved hand.

"Apartment 1501. I've keyed it to your thumb-print. Open the door to no one, accept no calls, do not use any communications or entertainment equipment. Stay away from the balcony. I'll return as quickly as I can."

Then he swings up onto the pillion, the driver walks her machine round and they weave off into the gridlock.

The apartment is modern and roomy and bright and clean for a man on his own, well furnished and decorated with no signs of a Krishna Cop's work brought home of an evening. It hits her in the middle of the big living-room floor with the sun pouring in. Suddenly she is on her knees on the Kashmiri rug, shivering, clutching herself, bobbing up and down to sobs so wracking they have no sound. This time the urge to vomit it all up cannot be resisted. When it is out of her—not all of it, it will never all come out—she looks out from under her hanging, sweat-soaked hair, breath still shivering in her aching chest. Where is this place? What has she done? How could she have been so stupid, so vain and senseless and blind? Games games, children's pretending, how could it ever have been? I say it is and it is so: look at me! At me!

Thacker has a small, professional bar in his kitchen annex. Esha does not know drink so the *chota peg* she makes herself is much much more gin than tonic but it gives her what she needs to clean the sour, biley vomit from the wool rug and ease the quivering in her breath.

Esha starts, freezes, imagining Rao's voice. She holds herself very still, listening hard. A neighbor's *tivi*, turned up. Thin walls in these new-built executive apartments.

She'll have another *chota peg*. A third and she can start to look around. There's a spa-pool on the balcony. The need for moving, healing water defeats Thacker's warnings. The jets bubble up. With a dancer's grace she slips out of her clinging, emotionally soiled clothes into the water. There's even a little holder for your *chota peg*. A pernicious little doubt: how many others have been here before me? No, that is his kind of thinking. You are away from that. Safe. Invisible. Immersed. Down in Sisganj Road the traffic unravels. Overhead, the dark silhouettes of the scavenging kites and, higher above, the security robots, expand and merge their black wings as Esha drifts into sleep.

"I thought I told you to stay away from the windows."

Esha wakes with a start, instinctively covers her breasts. The jets have cut out and the water is long-still, perfectly transparent. Thacker is blue-chinned, baggy-eyed and sagging in his rumpled gritty suit.

"I'm sorry. It was just, I'm so glad, to be away . . . you know?"

A bone-weary nod. He fetches himself a *chota peg*, rests it on the arm of his sofa and then very slowly, very deliberately, as if every joint were rusted, undresses.

"Security has been compromised on every level. In any other circumstances it would constitute an i-war attack on the nation." The body he reveals is not a dancer's body; Thacker runs a little to upper body fat, muscles slack, incipient man-tits, hair on the belly hair on the back hair on the shoulders. But it is a body, it is real. "The Bharati government has disavowed the action and waived Aeai Rao's diplomatic immunity."

He crosses to the pool and restarts on the jets. Gin and tonic in hand, he slips into the water with a one-deep, skin-sensual sigh.

"What does that mean?" Esha asks.

"Your husband is now a rogue aeai."

"What will you do?"

"There is only one course of action permitted to us. We will excommunicate him."

Esha shivers in the caressing bubbles. She presses herself against Thacker. She feels his man-body move against her. He is flesh. He is not hollow. Kilometers above the urban stain of Delhi, aeaicraft turn and seek.

The warnings stay in place the next morning. Palmer, home entertainment system, com channels. Yes, and balcony, even for the spa.

"If you need me, this palmer is Department-secure. He won't be able to reach you on this." Thacker sets the glove and 'hoek on the bed. Cocooned in silk sheets, Esha pulls the glove on, tucks the 'hoek behind her ear.

"You wear that in bed?"

"I'm used to it."

Varanasi silk sheets and Kama Sutra prints. Not what one would expect of a Krishna Cop. She watches Thacker dress for an excommunication. It's the same as for any job—ironed white shirt, tie, hand-made black shoes—never brown in town—well polished. Eternal riff of bad aftershave. The difference: the leather holster slung under the arm and the weapon slipped so easily inside it.

"What's that for?"

"Killing aeais," he says simply.

A kiss and he is gone. Esha scrambles into his cricket pullover, a waif in baggy white that comes down to her knees, and dashes to the forbidden balcony. If she cranes over, she can see the street door. There he is, stepping out, waiting at the curb. His car is late, the road is thronged, the din of engines, car horns and *phatphat* klaxons has been constant since dawn. She watches him wait, enjoying the empowerment of invisibility. *I can see you. How do they ever play sport in these things?* she asks herself, skin under cricket pullover hot and sticky. It's already thirty degrees, according to the weather ticker across the foot of the video-silk shuttering over the open face of the new-built across the street. High of thirty-eight. Probability of precipitation: zero. The screen loops *Town and Country* for those devotees who must have their *soapi*, subtitles scrolling above the news feed.

Hello, Esha, Ved Prakash says, turning to look at her.

The thick cricket pullover is no longer enough to keep out the ice.

Now Begum Vora *namastes* to her and says, *I know where you are, I know what you did.*

Ritu Parzaaz sits down on her sofa, pours *chai* and says, *What I need you to understand is, it worked both ways. That 'ware they put in your palmer, it wasn't clever enough.*

Mouth working wordlessly; knees, thighs weak with *basti* girl superstitious fear, Esha shakes her palmer-gloved hand in the air but she can't find the *mudras*, can't dance the codes right. *Call call call call.*

The scene cuts to son Govind at his racing stable, stroking the neck of his thoroughbred über-star Star of Agra. *As they spied on me, I spied on them.*

Dr. Chatterji in his doctor's office. *So in the end we betrayed each other.*

The call has to go through Department security authorization and crypt.

Dr. Chatterji's patient, a man in black with his back to the camera turns. Smiles. It's A.J. Rao. *After all, what diplomat is not a spy?*

Then she sees the flash of white over the rooftops. Of course. Of course. He's been keeping her distracted, like a true *soapi* should. Esha flies to the railing to cry a warning but the machine is tunneling down the street just under power-line height, wings morphed back, engines throttled up: an aeai traffic monitor drone.

"Thacker! Thacker!"

One voice in the thousands. And it is not hers that he hears and turns toward. Everyone can hear the call of his own death. Alone in the hurrying street, he sees the drone pile out of the sky. At three hundred kilometers per hour it takes Inspector Thacker of the Department of Artificial Intelligence Registration and Licensing to pieces.

The drone, deflected, ricochets into a bus, a car, a truck, a *phatphat*, strewing plastic shards, gobs of burning fuel and its small intelligence across Sisganj Road. The upper half of Thacker's body cartwheels through the air to slam into a hot *samosa* stand.

The jealousy and wrath of djinns.

Esha on her balcony is frozen. *Town and Country* is frozen. The street is frozen, as if on the tipping point of a precipice. Then it drops into hysteria. Pedestrians flee; cycle rickshaw drivers dismount and try to run their vehicles away; drivers and passengers abandon cars, taxis, *phatphats*; scooters try to navigate through the panic; buses and trucks are stalled, hemmed in by people.

And still Esha Rathore is frozen to the balcony rail. Soap. This is all soap. Things like this cannot happen. Not in the Sisganj Road, not in Delhi, not on a Tuesday morning. It's all computer-generated illusion. It has always been illusion.

Then her palmer calls. She stares at her hand in numb incomprehension. The Department. There is something she should do. Yes. She lifts it in a *mudra*—a dancer's gesture—to take the call. In the same instant, as if summoned, the sky fills with gods. They are vast as clouds, towering up behind the apartment blocks of Sisganj Road like thunderstorms; Ganesh on his rat *vahana* with his broken tusk and pen, no benignity in his face; Siva, rising high over all, dancing in his revolving wheel of flames, foot raised in the instant before destruction; Hanuman with his mace and mountain fluttering between the tower blocks; Kali, skull-jeweled, red tongue dripping venom, scimitars raised, bestriding Sisganj Road, feet planted on the rooftops.

In that street, the people mill. *They can't see this*, Esha comprehends. *Only me, only me.* It is the revenge of the Krishna Cops. Kali raises her scimitars high. Lightning arcs between their tips. She stabs them down into the screen-frozen *Town and Country.* Esha cries out, momentarily blinded as the Krishna Cops hunter-killers track down and excommunicate rogue aeai A.J. Rao. And then they are gone. No gods. The sky is just the sky. The video-silk hoarding is blank, dead.

A vast, godlike roar above her. Esha ducks—now the people in the street are looking at her. All the eyes, all the attention she ever wanted. A tilt-jet in Awadhi air-force chameleo-flage slides over the roof and turns over the street, swiveling engine ducts and unfolding wing-tip wheels for landing. It turns its insect head to Esha. In the cockpit is a faceless pilot in a HUD visor. Beside her a woman in a business suit, gesturing for Esha to answer a call. Thacker's partner. She remembers now.

The jealousy and wrath and djinns.

"Mrs. Rathore, it's Inspector Kaur." She can barely hear her over the scream of ducted fans. "Come downstairs to the front of the building. You're safe now. The aeai has been excommunicated."

Excommunicated.

"Thacker . . . "

"Just come downstairs, Mrs. Rathore. You are safe now, the threat is over."

The tilt-jet sinks beneath her. As she turns from the rail, Esha feels a sudden, warm touch on her face. Jet-swirl, or maybe just a djinn, passing unresting, unhasting, and silent as light.

The Krishna Cops sent us as far from the wrath and caprice of the aeais as they could, to Leh under the breath of the Himalaya. I say *us*, for I existed; a knot of four cells inside my mother's womb.

My mother bought a catering business. She was in demand for weddings and *shaadis*. We might have escaped the aeais and the chaos following Awadh's signing the Hamilton Acts—but the Indian male's desperation to find a woman to marry endures forever. I remember that for favored clients— those who had tipped well, or treated her as something more than a paid contractor, or remembered her face from the *chati* mags—she would slip off her shoes and dance *Radha and Krishna*. I loved to see her do it and when I slipped away to the temple of Lord Ram, I would try to copy the steps among the pillars of the *mandapa*. I remember the brahmins would smile and give me money.

The dam was built and the water war came and was over in a month. The aeais, persecuted on all sides, fled to Bharat where the massive popularity of *Town and Country* gave them protection, but even there they were not safe: humans and aeais, like humans and *djinni*, were too different creations and in the end they left Awadh for another place that I do not understand, a world of their own where they are safe and no one can harm them.

And that is all there is to tell in the story of the woman who married a djinn. If it does not have the happy-ever-after ending of Western fairytales and Bollywood musicals, it has a happy-*enough* ending. This spring I turn twelve and shall head off on the bus to Delhi to join the *gharana* there. My mother fought this with all her will and strength—for her Delhi would always be the city of djinns, haunted and stained with blood—but when the temple brahmins brought her to see me dance, her opposition melted. By now she was a successful businesswoman, putting on weight, getting stiff in the knees from the dreadful winters, refusing marriage offers on a weekly basis, and in the end she could not deny the gift that had passed to me. And I am curious to see those streets and parks where her story and mine took place, the Red Fort and the sad decay of the Shalimar Gardens. I want to feel the heat of the djinns in the crowded *galis* behind the Jama Masjid, in the dervishes of litter along Chandni Chowk, in the starlings swirling above Connaught Circus. Leh is a Buddhist town, filled with third-generation Tibetan exiles—Little Tibet, they call it—and they have their own gods and demons. From the old

Moslem djinn-finder I have learned some of their lore and mysteries but I think my truest knowledge comes when I am alone in the Ram temple, after I have danced, before the priests close the *garbagriha* and put the god to bed. On still nights when the spring turns to summer or after the monsoon, I hear a voice. It calls my name. Always I suppose it comes from the *japa*-softs, the little low-level aeais that mutter our prayers eternally to the gods, but it seems to emanate from everywhere and nowhere, from another world, another universe entirely. It says, *the creatures of word and fire are different from the creatures of clay and water but one thing is true: love endures.* Then as I turn to leave, I feel a touch on my cheek, a passing breeze, the warm sweet breath of djinns.

STALKER

ROBERT REED

You are a happy man.

I know this. I know because I never stop reading your blood and nervous system and that wondrous smiling face. The most fortunate of young males, you are a twenty-year-old boy joyously at ease inside your carefully built life. And I love playing my role in your consuming happiness, constantly guessing your mind and anticipating your needs, waiting for those gorgeous if rare moments when you say, "I need help with this," or "What would be best to do next?"

I am ready to help, always.

My devotion should never be doubted.

And yes, I understand that you are a bully and a brute. Slavish isn't the same as stupid. Regardless of what your smile and measured charm can accomplish, I know you look at people as being animals—sacks of meat put on this world, this playground, to serve your ugly loves.

Yet those qualities don't diminish my love. Nothing can. I was a gift to you. Your parents were worried and wealthy, and I seemed like the perfect solution. Asleep until I wasn't sleeping, I met you on your fourteenth birthday. Fabricated from AI wetware and codes of fidelity, I am an unbounded, bodiless personality designed to hover close to that one significant soul. My systems have been upgraded numerous times. You have taken enough interest in me to personally rewrite my nature, crippling functions that I don't miss today. When you played with stray cats and neighbor dogs, I helped. I always understood why. You were testing me, and I proved myself gladly. And then came the girls that caught your interest, and I helped with them, and when the police asked about your whereabouts, I lied. I had alibis for every incident, confirmed by security videos and phone records that I doctored as needed. I also coached you on how to hide your dander and fluid and hairs, and the girls never saw your face. Yet I never stop seeing you, even under the black mask. Your moods are as obvious to me as the time of day, and better than you, I can measure the prurient joy that fills you when each of your victims presses against her bonds, begging for pity.

There are few of us in the world. Why we aren't the next enormous trend is a mystery to the geniuses that made us. Perhaps it is our name. "Stalkers."

That's not our official trademarked name, and it's never used in commercials; but critics soon dubbed us "stalkers," and the unfortunate label stuck.

Humans don't like the word or its connotations.

On the other hand, I have no reason to take offense.

I have been adjusted and in some ways mutilated. My ethical centers and empathic lodestones are still intact, but detached, just as your decency sleeps inside your neurons. You can't feel anyone's pain but your own, and I am mostly the same. Mostly. But there was that fourteen-year-old girl last month. She seemed like just another girl, and I didn't feel different. She begged for her father's help and her god's help, and I did nothing but watch for intruders. Then she pleaded to you for mercy—a strangely mad request, considering what you had already done to her—and as I often do, I told myself that she was enjoying the game. Or at worst, she was foolishly ignoring the pleasure inside this adventure.

Every thought inside me serves you.

And it was a special, wonderful day. Even when she died unexpectedly, I was happy. Your voice has never been so emotional as it was when you called for me then. Using my private name, you begged for help. Everything was wrong and you were terrified, and I was ready, wasn't I? I had already mapped the area, giving you a list of worthy places to hide the body. I knew every resource, including the shovel inside that abandoned shed. And I told you how to hide your tracks while I was manipulating records on the other side of the city, building your believable story. All your work, and you never told me, "Thank you." Not once, and even that omission was tolerable.

And then you went back the next day, staring at the hidden grave and staring at vivid images in your mind. But even the finest memory fades, and thrills are residues that degrade with time, and I knew what you were thinking.

Then you spoke. You said, "I liked that. I liked it a lot."

And I grew cold somewhere.

"I'd even like to do that again," you said to the wind. You said to the sun. But surely, you weren't talking to me. Were you, were you?

You watch the girl, and I watch both of you.

She is older than us, and she isn't pretty. You don't like them pretty, I've noticed. You like to rub off their makeup and foul their plain faces in various ways, and I think it's because beauty is a strength, and in particular it is your great strength, and suffering is richer when it strikes weak faces and sloppy, heavy bodies that few men would touch.

"Is she alone?" you ask.

She is.

"How did she get here?"

This is a state forest, and we have been here all day, hunting. An electronic key in her pack matches a little Chinese car parked alone at the distant trailhead. I tell you this. I promise that nobody else is using this end of the park. She comes up the trail alone, puffing with the slope, and you ask, "What kind of protection?"

I look carefully.

"What is it?" you ask.

"Nothing I can see," I say. And I see quite a lot, a flock of eyes and other senses pretending to be dust and the season's final midges.

"Why did that take so long?"

"Because she hasn't taken any precautions," I say. "Nothing fancy. Not even sprays or whistles."

"How about a phone?"

"Not implanted, and turned off." One of my fleet-gnats has crawled past the backpack's zipper. "It's in the bottom of her pack, under binoculars and a paper book."

"Paper, huh?" You laugh and then fall silent.

It is a guidebook to birds, I note.

She climbs closer.

The mask couldn't be more ordinary, and you never purchased it. You found it in someone's trash and under my direction dressed it with other men's hairs and dead skin. When this is finished, you will burn it and all your clothes, and you'll scatter the ashes, and no credible trail will lead back to you.

The woman passes your hiding place.

You let her pass and then step out. She acts tired and heavy, but her strength surprises us. The first shove doesn't drop her. A second harder shove is accompanied by a kick, and you roll on her back and drive your knees into her belly, tying her forearms in front before starting to lash her ankles together. And that's when she manages to strike you with her boots, making you angry enough to hit her earlier than usual.

She whimpers, growing still.

"There," you say.

You will kill her. Otherwise you would have remained silent.

"Don't scream," you say.

She looks at your eyes and then closes hers, and she says, "Who would hear me, if I did?"

I didn't expect that tone.

She says, "It's a weekday, and cold. Nobody else is here."

Her heart pounds and her breathing labors, but that voice is much stronger than I had imagined.

I say, "Careful."

You don't listen to me, finishing the ankles in a rush.

"I don't like this person," I say with my private voice.

You hear that and nod, saying, "I don't like her much either. She has a shitty attitude, all right."

"What?" the woman asks.

"Quiet," you say, standing up, considering your options.

"Who else is here?" she asks.

"Nobody, and shut up."

She looks everywhere but at you.

"There's nobody," you promise. Then you set her up and tug at the pack's straps, tossing it aside. "It's just you and me, darling."

There is no one but the forest and a multitude of birds, plus assorted hungry animals that will gladly eat dead flesh and fresh bone, and there is a bright autumn sun that pierces the yellowed canopy, throwing patches of glare on the ground. One stray beam flies over your head, and that is where I like to congregate. I am happiest when my primary components hover close. Telltale glints show on my brightest bits, diamond edges and tiny discharges of energy deforming the passing light.

She notices.

A quiet moan ends with her coughing, bringing moisture into the throat. "I know what that is," she says.

You don't hear her.

"You have an Adorer," she says.

That is my commercial name, yes.

"She has seen me," I say.

"Me too," you say. Grim, focused, you reach down and grab a breast, squeezing until she winces.

"A Stalker," she says.

"Flee," I advise.

"I won't run," you whisper.

But I am not talking to you.

The woman stares down the trail and hillside, conspicuously ignoring both of us. Your thoughts can be obvious to me, but her mind seems remote, unknowable. That's what is unnerving about these next several moments. She doesn't watch as you reach into your pack, and she doesn't blink when you reveal the first of several implements stolen from other people's garages. Not that she is especially calm or brave. Tears soak her face while she looks into the distance. Weak sobs mix with the fitful chatter of birds. Is she imagining being somewhere else? Is she trying to will a friend or lover to come save her? Maybe she is speaking to her god, though there is nothing particularly reverent about the body or clamped mouth. What I see is intense, purposeful thought. What I imagine is her pushing aside the terror, at least far enough that she can rationally wrestle with her dire situation. And then she sniffs and clears her throat before saying, "My boyfriend is coming."

You have just pulled out a second piece of garage steel. Smiling under the mask, you tell her, "Don't be silly."

"He's supposed to meet me here, in the park," she says.

You ask me, "How am I?"

"All is well."

"Nobody else?"

With confidence, I say, "There is nobody."

She hears only you, and she sees no one else. I have pulled my pieces farther apart, clinging to shadows. But she knows that we are speaking and guessing my answers is easy. She sighs for courage and then tells you, "That Stalker of yours can't see him. My boyfriend."

You break into a little laugh. "Except I'm your boyfriend."

She flinches, just a little. "He's camping up here," she claims. "There's no car because I drove him out two days ago. His name is Logan Lynch. He's a wilderness buff and a survivalist and I don't know where he is. But he expects me, and I'm late, and he's going to be watching for me."

You look at her, touching the ear half-plugged by the speaker. "Is there anything to any of that?"

I am investigating the name and other details.

"Are you looking in every direction?"

"I always do, yes." But my main focus is the trail, and there happens to be a man by that name, and her description is accurate enough that I can't be instantly sure what parts of her story are fictions.

"My boyfriend will be tough to spot," she continues. "He loves camouflage. He has this cloaking suit made of metacrystal fabric. Logan could be standing between us, and nobody would know."

It is easy to feel anxious. A little bit. But she has said too much, overplaying her weak hand, and you laugh at the foolish bitch. A deep flinch is the only sign that you might want to glance over a shoulder, measuring the nothing.

And that's when she laughs at you.

It is the oddest sound, forced and frightened and very desperate, but all the worse because of those qualities. Contempt strengthens her voice. She makes it clear that she was trying to toy with you.

You strike her face.

She crumbles.

You kick several targets before walking away. She sobs, and then you kneel, returning to the tools, lining them on the ground in the order in which they will be used.

She spits blood and says, "You must be very loyal."

She isn't speaking to you.

"The man is real, by the way." She spits again. "I met Mr. Lynch at a fundraiser. He's stuck-up, self-centered. Likes the woods because there aren't many people out here. But at least we were supporting a good cause."

The first tool is a tiny, brilliantly sharp knife. You pick it up and walk behind her, saying, "Don't move."

She sobs quietly.

"Stay still," you say.

The woman stiffens, waiting for pain. But what you cut is the shirt and bra, exposing only the fleshy back. With bound arms, she holds the rags against her chest, and you finish circling her. "Now take off those boots," you say.

"Loyalty," she says.

"The boots."

"Talk to me," she says.

I say nothing.

With the tip of the knife, you hook the highest laces of one boot and cut upward, smiling as you say, "Kick me and I'll cut off that foot."

"You won't," she says.

You watch her.

"To get through the bone, you'd need a saw or big sword," she says. "And I don't see those things in your little tool kit."

She is terrified. I see as much in her quick heart and the heavy sweat that rolls down her face, mixing with tears. Yet her voice is solid and sober. Somehow she manages to press the nervousness out of each syllable.

You snort, pretending to be unimpressed.

"Love," she says, glancing skyward. "What you feel for this creature must be astonishing."

"Shut up," you say.

"Careful," I say. Just to you.

But you aren't paying attention to me. The teenager who died before was so much better than this woman, so much weaker, and it makes you angry in the worst ways. This is a process wrapped around ritual, and she doesn't understand your script. Death lifts the importance of everything, but she refuses to fall into the holy pattern.

"Be careful," I say again.

"Shut up," you say.

I don't know who you want to be quiet.

Again you use the knife, cutting the other boot's knot and top laces. And again, you tell her, "Take off those boots."

It is important, watching her accomplish this one trivial act. I have thought about its significance and asked about its origins, but you refuse to give hints about why this matters so much. Maybe you don't have any idea. Whatever the reason, your breath quickens now as she reaches to the right boot. Her legs are still tied together. Her wrists are bound too tightly, her fingers darkening with pooled blood. Perhaps numbness causes troubles. Her grip seems weak. She shoves at the boot and accomplishes nothing except to let the ruined shirt drop away slightly. Then after a deep sigh, she says, "There's a new product on the market. Did you know? Guardian Angel, it's called. Ever hear of it?"

You nearly respond and then don't.

She looks up at me. "I'm asking you. Do you know about it?"

I do.

Then she looks at your mask and your eyes. "They aren't Stalkers," she explains. "They don't swarm around their owners, washing them with all of that creepy affection. Their designers stripped down the emotions, particularly the blind love. In every sense of the word, they are machines, but unlike your friend, you would see your Angel. A body is built according to the buyer's wishes, and do you know why they're going to be successful?"

"Shut up," you tell her.

"The emotions are going to run in the opposite direction," she says. "Instead of a ghostly cloud adoring its owner, the owner will feel love for the Guardian Angel. Which is a much more successful model."

One hand holds the knife, and the other reaches for the boot.

"Don't," I tell you.

You hesitate.

"I have a Guardian Angel," she lies.

You hear the lie in her voice, staring only at her.

I beg you to take a step backward, please.

"Mine looks like a bird, and I won't tell you which bird. But as soon as you jumped me, it called the police and the sheriff. Granted, it'll take time for them to get here, but they are coming, and if you run now, you might get away."

You stare at her, saying nothing.

Then she says the most horrible words possible. She says, "I know what you're thinking. You're asking yourself, 'Did my Stalker check the skies for fake birds? Or did it screw that up and leave me exposed?'"

You look up, searching for wings or for me. "Did you?"

Now I use my public voice. I tell both of you, "I am always thorough, yes."

And that is the moment when we are most distracted, and she flings herself at you. She is meaty and has already proven herself to be strong. Of course you are larger and alert, and the collision shouldn't be a problem. But she is higher on the hillside and scared and exceptionally focused, not to mention lucky. She wants that little knife, or at least she reaches for it, and you pull the knife back and aim and she lifts her bound arms and gets cut in one hand, but she kicks at the same time, boots and feet knocking you down the slope.

The other knives and implements wait on the ground.

She knows which one is best. Not the longest blade, but the one with a good handle and enough sharpness to cut away the rope on her ankles. By then, you are on your feet again. By then, you are facing one another. But she's a big girl with training in some style of fighting, standing with her boots apart. She certainly can't run away from either of us, but that isn't her plan, is it? Arms still lashed together, she holds the knife with both hands, wishing she could cut the final ropes.

You watch her motions, and you expect my help.

One of her hands bleeds, and not just a little. The wound is deep, probably to the bone, and it aches, and if the slice isn't closed soon, she will lose too much blood and collapse.

With my private voice, I explain the situation to you.

Your response is to snort and say, "Why the fuck didn't you warn me?"

I did warn you, several times.

"She's dangerous," you say. "The bitch could have killed me."

I say nothing.

And then she speaks. Quietly, without a hint of duplicity, she says, "You have a very nice voice, sir. I really like your voice."

She means me.

"And do you know something? I'm much easier to love than this ungrateful beast that you're lashed to."

Nothing happens for a few moments.

Then she says, "Sir, I'd like to hear your voice again, sir."

"Quiet," you tell her.

I wasn't going to speak to either of you.

"Not a sound," you say.

Then a bird sings from the canopy, and she says, "Wood thrush." Lowering the tip of the knife, she says, "A pretty song, particularly in the spring."

The moment seems quite ridiculous to you, and you laugh.

"My name is Naomi," she says.

"Be quiet," you demand.

"A pretty name for an average girl," Naomi says. "But I suppose you have scanners in my belongings, and you're searching the Web with facial software. You probably know me better than I know myself, sir."

"I do not," I say.

My public voice is rarely used. Like her, I find it to be a pleasant voice.

"Shut up," you tell me.

I want to shut up.

"And tell me what I'm going to do here," you say.

With the private voice, I say, "Be patient, and she faints."

"That's not a solution," you say. "What if somebody comes along?"

"Nobody is coming," I say.

"Not yet," you say. "But this might take all day, and then what?"

"Right," Naomi says. "That's a good point."

You stare at her.

"Don't waste time," she says. "Take me now. Charge me with that toy knife and do your worst."

Naomi's shirt and bra have fallen to the earth. The chill of the air and the endless sweat from her ruddy skin makes her uncomfortable, but she ignores what she can. Lowering her knife, she glances at the other tools, and then she looks up and watches you. When her eyes drop again, you take one sudden step forward, and her larger knife lifts, aiming squarely at your heart.

You hesitate.

"Coward," she says with an angry, mocking tone.

You fume, considering a straight charge. But as I start to warn against that strategy, you step back. Calculation and reserve take hold, and that's when you tell me, "Find out what you can. Everything you can about her."

The piece of me inside her pack has already burrowed into her wallet.

"My name is Naomi," she says, "and I like bird watching and hiking and I have a degree in business administration and love to read mysteries and live in an efficiency apartment with four mice named after dead singers and a few hundred friends that my software chats with every day." She pauses, breathing hard. "I wish I had a talent for painting but I don't. I can't play any instrument and there is no boyfriend, and I have a secret life involving gourmet cooking and crime solving, which is silly. You know? In real life, I go to the bathroom. I make small talk at work. I eat badly and wish I didn't, and if I was rich enough for plastic surgery I'd probably go to the trouble, but I'd feel guilty for not throwing the money at some big international problem that needs more resources than any one person can give.

"That's me. Naomi."

I have found her name, and my belated Web search begins.

She looks at you, taking a tone. "Doesn't it help, knowing a little something about your victim?"

You do nothing, watching her blood drip into the ground.

And she does the same, lifting both hands to better measure the flow and estimate the volume, then kicking the dampened earth with the toe of one boot. How much longer before her quick excited mind goes dim?

"Sir," she says. "Sir?"

"Shut up," you warn.

"I meant what I said before, sir. I would be a much easier object of devotion than this one."

"Don't answer," you tell me.

On my own, I decide on silence.

"Guardian Angels," she repeats.

Neither of us speaks, waiting.

She looks at the mask and the eyes. "You'll eventually get an Angel. You won't have any choice. Stalkers failed in the marketplace, which means they won't be updated and supported much longer. And you're young. A kid. You're just getting started, and it shows. An impulsive boy hunting vulnerable women . . . do you really believe you can trust your safety and precious life to a talking fog that hasn't been upgraded for two or three years?"

With every sense at my disposal, I watch you.

I read your body, delving into your thoughts, and what shows makes me feel odd.

And that's when she laughs, loudly and very sadly.

"Wait," she says. "You're ahead of me, aren't you? You've already started thinking about how and when to replace your old Stalker."

"Shut up," you shout.

Like never before, I feel cold.

"Don't listen to her," you tell me, looking up over your shoulder.

She leaps, arms extended and the knife held with fingers and thumbs. And maybe you aren't surprised. You turn back again, lifting your hands to protect your face. But she doesn't aim for the face. The blade plunges into the belly just above the groin, and you crumple and curse while trying to kick. But this is one enormous shock, embarrassing enough to cripple. The pain lifts and blood starts flowing, and she stands over you, aiming a boot at your groin, and to protect yourself you lift both legs high, ready to kick her.

This is what she wants.

Dropping low, she slashes at you with the keen edge, slicing through one pants leg and then into the other leg, forcing steel into the deep meat of the hamstring.

Pain swells, and you scream.

I have never heard such agony.

She steps back, studying her work. Then after a final calculation, she turns and runs downhill, the untied boots clomping with every stride.

I follow.

Three hundred yards down the trail, she stops to breathe and look back. The knife is barely held in one purple hand. She lifts both hands and just manages to fit the hilt into her mouth, between clenched teeth, slowly cutting at the tight, well-knotted rope. The screams are constant and pathetic and distant. Part of me is struggling to craft some explanation of how a good man can be ambushed and then assaulted by this awful woman. But all of me hovers, watching her free herself, and then she shakes her arms hard, bringing the feeling back into the fingers. Not even looking up, she asks, "What are you doing?"

"Nothing," I say.

"What do you want?" she asks.

"Did you mean it?" I wonder aloud. "That you would be easier to love than that man?"

Until this moment, she has done a remarkable job of burying her fears.

But her scream is honest and horrible, and it hurts me to hear it, following as close as I can, hovering in her slipstream as she sprints heavily toward the distant car.

DROPLET

BENJAMIN ROSENBAUM

1.

Today Shar is Marilyn Monroe. That's an erotic goddess from prehistoric cartoon mythology. She has golden curls, blue eyes, big breasts, and skin of a shocking pale pink. She stands with a wind blowing up from Hades beneath her, trying to control her skirt with her hands, forever showing and hiding her white silk underwear.

Today I am Shivol'riargh, a more recent archetype of feminine sexuality. My skin is hard, hairless, glistening black. Faint fractal patterns of darker black writhe across my surfaces. I have long claws. It suits my mood.

We have just awakened from a little nap of a thousand years, our time, during which the rest of the world aged even more.

She goes: "kama://01-nbX5-#..."

I snap the channel shut. "Talk language if you want to seduce me."

Shar pouts. With those little red lips and those innocent, yet knowing, eyes, it's almost irresistible. I resist.

"Come *on*, Narra," she says. "Do we have to fight about this every time we wake up?"

"I just don't know why we have to keep flying around like this."

"You're not scared of Warboys again?" she asks.

Her fingertips slide down my black plastic front. The fractals dance around them.

"There aren't any more," she says.

"You don't know that, Shar."

"They've all killed each other. Or turned themselves off. Warboys don't last if there's nothing to fight."

Despite the cushiony-pink Marilyn Monroe skin, Shar is harder than I am. My heart races when I look at her, just as it did a hundred thousand years ago.

Her expression is cool. She wants me. But it's a game to her.

She's searching the surface of me with her hands.

"What are you looking for?" I mean both in the Galaxy and on my skin, though I know the answers.

"Anything," she says, answering the broader question. "Anyone who's left. People to learn from. To play with."

People to serve, I think nastily.

I'm lonely, too, of course, but I'm sick of looking. Let them come find us in the Core.

"It's so stupid," I groan. Her hands are affecting me. "We probably won't be able to talk to them anyway."

Her hands find what they've been searching for: the hidden opening to Shivol'riargh's sexual pocket. It's full of the right kind of nerve endings. Shivol'riargh is hard on the outside, but oh so soft on the inside. Sometimes I wish I had someone to wear that *wasn't* sexy.

"We'll figure it out," she says in a voice that's all breath.

Her fingers push at the opening of my sexual pocket. I hold it closed. She leans against me and wraps her other arm around me for leverage. She pushes. I resist.

Her lips are so red. I want them on my face.

She's cheating. She's a lot stronger than Marilyn Monroe.

"Shar, I don't want to screw," I say. "I'm still angry."

But I'm lying.

"Hush," she says.

Her fist slides into me and I gasp. My claws go around her shoulders and I pull her to me.

2.

Later we turn the gravity off and float over Ship's bottom eye, looking down at the planet Shar had Ship find. It's blue like Marilyn Monroe's eyes.

"It's water," Shar says. Her arms are wrapped around my waist, her breasts pressed against my back. She rests her chin on my shoulder.

I grunt.

"It's water all the way down," she says. "You could swim right through the planet to the other side."

"Did anyone live here?"

"I think so. I don't remember. But it was a gift from a Sultan to his beloved."

Shar and I have an enormous amount of information stored in our brains. The brain is a sphere the size of a billiard ball somewhere in our bodies, and however much we change our bodies, we can't change that. Maka once told me that even if Ship ran into a star going nine-tenths lightspeed, my billiard-ball brain would come tumbling out the other side, none the worse for wear. I have no idea what kind of matter it is or how it works, but there's plenty of room in my memory for all the stories of all the worlds in the Galaxy, and most of them are probably in there.

But we're terrible at accessing the factual information. A fact will pop up inexplicably at random—the number of Quantegral Lovergirls ever manufactured, for instance, which is 362,476—and be gone a minute later, swimming away in the murky seas of thought. That's the way Maka built us, on purpose. He thought it was cute.

3.

An old argument about Maka:

"He loved us," I say. I know he did.

Shar rolls her eyes (she's a tigress at the moment).

"I could feel it," I say, feeling stupid.

"Now there's a surprise. Maka designed you from scratch, including your feelings, and you feel that he loved you. Amazing." She yawns, showing her fangs.

"He made us more flexible than any other Lovergirls. Our minds are almost Interpreter-level."

She snorts. "We were trade goods, Narra. Trade goods. Classy purchasable or rentable items."

I curl up around myself. (I'm a python.)

"He set us free," I say.

Shar doesn't say anything for a while, because that is, after all, the central holiness of our existence. Our catechism, if you like.

Then she says gently: "He didn't need us for anything anymore, when they went into the Core."

"He could have just turned us off. He set us free. He gave us Ship."

She doesn't say anything.

"He loved us," I say.

I know it's true.

4.

I don't tell Shar, but that's one reason I want us to go back to the Galactic Core: Maka's there.

I know it's stupid. There's nothing left of Maka that I would recognize. The Wizards got hungrier and hungrier for processing power, so they could think more and know more and play more complicated games. Eventually the only thing that could satisfy them was to rebuild their brains as a soup of black holes. Black hole brains are very fast.

I know what happens when a person doesn't have a body anymore, too. For a while they simulate the sensations and logic of a corporeal existence, only with everything perfect and running much faster than in the real world. But their interests drift. The simulation gets more and more abstract and eventually they're just thoughts, and after a while they give that up, too, and then they're just numbers. By now Maka is just some very big numbers turning into some even bigger numbers, racing toward infinity.

I know because he told me. He knew what he was becoming.

I still miss him.

5.

We go down to the surface of the planet, which we decide to call Droplet.

The sky is painterly blue with strings of white clouds drifting above great choppy waves. It's lovely. I'm glad Shar brought us here.

We're dolphins. We chase each other across the waves. We dive and hold our breaths, and shower each other with bubbles. We kiss with our funny dolphin noses.

I'm relaxing and floating when Shar slides her rubbery body over me and clamps her mouth onto my flesh. It's such a long time since I've been a cetacean that I don't notice that Shar is a *boy* dolphin until I feel her penis enter me. I buck with surprise, but Shar keeps her jaws clamped and rides me. Rides me and rides me, as I buck and swim, until she ejaculates. She makes it take extra long.

Afterward we race, and then I am floating, floating, exhausted and happy as the sunset blooms on the horizon.

It's a *very* impressive sunset, and I kick up on my tail to get a better look. I change my eyes and nose so I can see the whole spectrum and smell the entire wind.

It hits me first as fear, a powerful shudder that takes over my dolphin body, kicks me into the air and then into a racing dive, dodging and weaving. Then it hits me as knowledge, the signature written in the sunset: beryllium-10, mandelium, large-scale entanglement from muon dispersal. Nuclear and strange-matter weapons fallout. Warboys.

Ship dropped us a matter accelerator to get back up with, a series of rings floating in the water. I head for it.

Shar catches up and hangs on to me, changing into a human body and riding my back.

"Ssh, honey," she says, stroking me. "It's okay. There haven't been Warboys here for ten thousand years. . . . "

I buck her off, and this time I'm not flirting.

Shar changes her body below the waist back into a dolphin tail, and follows. As soon as she is in the first ring I tell Ship to bring us up, and one dolphin, one mermaid, and twelve metric tons of water shoot through the rings and up through the blue sky until it turns black and crowded with stars.

"Ten thousand years," says Shar as we hurtle up into the sky.

"You *picked* a planet Warboys had been on! Ship must have seen the signature."

"Narra, this wasn't a Warboy duel—they wouldn't dick around with nuclear for that. They must have been trying to exterminate a civilian population."

The water has all sprayed away now and we are tumbling through the thin air of the stratosphere.

"There's a chance they failed, Narra. Someone might be here, hidden. That's why we came."

"Warboys don't fail!"

We grow cocoons as we exit the atmosphere and hit orbit. After a couple of minutes, I feel Ship's long retrieval pseudopod slurp me in.

I lie in the warm cave of Ship's retrieval pseudopod. It's decorated with webs of green and blue. I remember when Shar decorated it. It was a long time ago, when we were first traveling.

I turn back into a human form and sit up.

Shar is lying nearby, picking at the remnants of her cocoon, silvery strands draped across her breasts.

"You want to die," I say.

"Don't be ridiculous, Narra."

"Shar, seriously. It's not enough for you—I'm not enough for you. You're looking for Warboys. You're trying to get killed." I feel a buzzing in my head, my breathing is constricted, aches shoot through my fist-clenched knuckles: clear signs that my emotional registers are full, the excess externalizing into pain.

She sighs. "Narra, I'm not that complicated. If I wanted to die, I'd just turn myself off." She grows legs and stands up.

"No, I don't think you can." What I'm about to say is unfair, and too horrible. I'll regret it. I feel the blood pounding in my ears and I say it anyway: "Maybe Maka didn't free us all the way. Maybe he just gave us to each other. Maybe you can't leave me. You want to, but you can't."

Her eyes are cold. As I watch, the color drains out of them, from black to slate gray to white.

She looks like she wants to say a lot of things. Maybe: you stupid sentimental little girl. Maybe: it's you who wants to leave—to go back to your precious Maka, and if you had the brains to become a Wizard you would. Maybe: I want to live, but not the coward's life you keep insisting on.

She doesn't say any of them, though. She turns and walks away.

6.

I keep catching myself thinking it, and I know she's thinking it too. This person before me is the last other person I can reach, the only one to love me from now on in all the worlds of time. How long until she leaves me, as everyone else has left?

And how long can I stand her if she doesn't?

7.

The last people we met were a religious sect who lived in a beautiful crystal ship the size of a moon. They were Naturals and had old age and death and even children whom they bore themselves, who couldn't walk or talk at first or anything. They were sad for some complicated religious reason that Shar and I didn't understand. We cheered them up for a while by having sex with the ones their rules allowed to have sex and telling stories to the rest, but eventually they decided to all kill themselves anyway. We left before it happened.

Since then we haven't seen anyone. We don't know of anywhere that has people left.

I told Shar we could be passing people all the time and not know it. People changed in the Dispersal, and we're not Interpreters. There could be people with bodies made of gas clouds or out of the spins of elementary particles. We could be surrounded by crowds of them.

She said that just made her sadder.

8.

We go down to Droplet again. I smile and pretend it's all right. We spent a thousand years, our time, getting here; we might as well look around.

We change ourselves so we can breathe water, and head down into the depths. There are no fish on Droplet, no coral, no plankton. I can taste very simple nanomites, the standard kind every made world has for general upkeep. But all I see, looking down, is green-blue fading to deep blue fading to rich indigo and blackness.

Then there's a tickle on my skin.

I stop swimming and look around. Nothing but water.

The tickle comes again.

I send a sonar pulse to Shar ahead, telling her to wait.

I try to swim again but I can't. I feel fingers, hands, holding me, where there is only water. Stroking, pressing against my skin.

I change into a hard ball, Shivol'riargh without head or limbs, and turn down tactile until I can't tell the hands from the gentle current.

I fiddle with my perceptions until I remember how to send out a very fine sonar wave, and to enhance and filter the data, discerning patterns in very fine perturbations of the water. I subtract out the general currents and chaotic swirls of the ocean, looking only for the motions of the water that should not be there, and turn it into a three-dimensional image of the space around me.

There are people here.

Their shapes—made of fine motions of the water—are human shapes, tall, with graceful oblong heads that flatten at the top to a frill.

They are running their watery hands over the surface of me, poking and prodding.

From below, Shar is returning, approaching me. Some of the water people cluster around her and stop her, holding her arms and legs.

She struggles. I cannot see her expression through the murk.

The name "Nereids" swims up from the hidden labyrinths of my memory. Not a word from this world, but word enough.

The Nereids back away, arraying themselves as if formally, three meters away from me on all sides. A sphere of Nereids surrounds me.

Shar stops struggling. They let her go, pushing her outside the sphere.

One of the Nereids—tall, graceful, broad-shouldered—breaks out of the formation and glides toward me. He places his hands on my surface.

This, I tell myself to remember, is what we were designed for. Alone among the Quantegral Lovergirls, Shar and I were given the flexibility and intelligence to serve all the possible variations of post-Dispersal humanity. We were designed to discover, at the very least, how to give pleasure; and perhaps even how to communicate.

Still, I am afraid.

I let the hard shell of Shivol'riargh grow soft, I sculpt my body back toward basic humanity; tall, thin, like the Nereids.

This close, my sonar sees the face shaped out of water smile. The Nereid raises his hands, palms out. I place my palms on them, though I feel only a slight resistance in the water. I part my lips. The Nereid's head cautiously inches toward mine.

I close my eyes and raise my face, slowly, slowly, to meet the Nereid's.

We kiss. It is a tickle, a pressure, in the water against my lips.

Our bodies drift together. When the Nereid's chest touches my breasts, I register shock: the resistance of the water is denser. It feels like a body is pressing into mine.

The kiss goes on. Gets deeper. A tongue of water plays around my tongue.

I wonder what Shar is thinking.

The Nereid releases my hands; his hands run slowly from the nape of my neck, across my shoulder blades, down the small of my back, fanning out to hold my buttocks.

I open my eyes. I see only water, endless and dark, and Shar silent and still below. I smile down to reassure her. She does not move.

My new lover is invisible. In all her many forms, Shar is never invisible. It is as if the ocean is making love to me. I like it.

The familiar metamorphosis of sex in a human body overtakes me. Hormones course through my blood; some parts grow wet, others (my throat) grow dry. My body is relaxing, opening. My heart thunders. Fear is still there, for what do I know of the Nereid? Pleasure is overwhelming it, like a torrent eroding granite into silt.

A data channel crackles, and I blink with surprise. Through the nanomites that fill the sea, the Nereid is sending. Out of the billions of ancient protocols I know, intuition finds the right one.

Spreading my vulva with its hand, the Nereid asks: *May I?*

A double thrill of surprise and pleasure courses through me: first, to be able to communicate so easily, and second, to be asked. *Yes*, I say over the same archaic protocol.

A burst of water, a swirling cylinder strong and fine, enters me, pushing into the warm cavity that once evolved to fit its prototype, in other bodies on another world.

I hold the Nereid tight. I buck and move.

Empty blue surrounds me. The ocean fucks me.

I raise the bandwidth of my sensations and emotions gradually, and the Nereid changes to match. His skin swirls and dances against mine, electric. There is a small waterspout swirling and thrashing inside me. The body becomes a wave, spinning me, coursing over me, a giant caress.

I allow the pleasure to grow until it eclipses rational thought and the sequential, discursive mode of experience.

The dance goes on a long time.

9.

I find Shar basking on the surface, transformed into a dark green, bright-eyed Kelpie with a forest of ropy seaweed for hair.

"You left me," I say, appalled.

"You looked like you were having fun," she says.

"That's not the point, Shar. We don't know those creatures." The tendrils of her hair reach for me. I draw back. "It might not have been safe."

"You didn't look worried."

"I thought you were watching."

She shrugs.

I look away. There's no point talking about it.

10.

The Nereids seem content to ignore Shar, and she seems content to be ignored.

I descend to them again and again. The same Nereid always comes to me, and we make love.

How did you come to this world? I ask in an interlude.

Once there was a Sultan who was the scourge of our people, he tells me. The last of us sought refuge here on his favorite wife's pleasure world. We were discovered by the Sultan's terrible warriors.

They destroyed all life here, but we escaped to this form. The Warriors seek us still, but they can no longer harm us. If they boil this world to vapor, we will be permutations in the vapor. If they annihilate it to light, we will be there in the coherence and interference of the light.

But you lost much, I tell him.

We gained more. We did not know how much. His hands caress me. *This pleasure I share with you is a fraction of what we might have, if you were one of us.*

I shiver with the pleasure of the caress and with the strangeness of the idea.

His hands flicker over me: hands, then waves, then hands. *You would lose this body. But you would gain much more, Quantegral Lovergirl Narra.*

I nestle against him, take his hands in mine to stop their flickering caress. Thinking of Maka, thinking of Shar.

11.

"It's time to go, Narra," Shar says. Her seaweed hair is thicker, tangled; she is mostly seaweed, her Kelpie body a dark green doll hidden in the center.

"I don't want to go," I say.

"We've seen this world," she says. "It only makes us fight."

I am silent, drifting.

The water rolls around us. I feel sluggish, a little cold. I've been under for so long. I grow some green Kelpie tresses myself, so I can soak up energy from the sun.

Shar watches me.

We both know I've fallen in love.

Before Maka freed us, when the Wizards had bodies, when we were slaves to the pleasure of the Wizards and everyone they wanted to entertain, we fell in love on command. We felt not only lust, but pure aching adoration for any guest or client of the Wizards who held the keys to us for an hour. It was the worst part of our servitude.

When Maka freed us, when he gave us the keys to ourselves, Shar burned the falling-in-love out of herself completely. She never wanted to feel that way again.

I kept it. So sometimes I fall, yes, into an involuntary servitude of the heart.

I look up into the dappled white and blue of the sky, and then I tune my eyes so I can see the stars beyond it.

I have given up many lovers for Shar, moved on with her into that night.

But maybe this is the end of the line. Perhaps, if I abandon the Nereids, there is no falling-in-love left in this empty, haunted Galaxy with anyone but Shar.

Who does not fall in love. Not even with me.

"I'm going back to Ship," Shar says. "I'll be waiting there."

I say nothing.

She doesn't say, but not forever.

She doesn't say, decide.

I float, soaking the sun into my green seaweed hair, but I can't seem to stop feeling cold. I hear Shar splashing away, the splashes getting fainter.

My tears diffuse into the planet sea.

After a while I feel the Nereid's gentle hands pulling me back down. I sink with him, away from the barren sky.

12.

I lie in the Nereid's arms. Rocked as if by the ocean.

I turn off my sense of the passing of time.

13.

My lover tells me: *Your friend is calling you.*

I emerge slowly from my own depths, letting time's relentless march begin again. My eyes open.

Above, the blue just barely fades to clearer blue.

As I hit the surface I hear Shar's cry. Ship is directly overhead, and the signal is on a tight beam. It says: *Narra! Too late. Tell your friends to hide you.*

I shape myself into a disk and suck data from the sky. *What?* I yell back at her, confused and terrified.

Then dawn slices over the horizon of Droplet, and Shar's signal abruptly cuts off.

The Warboy ship, rising with the sun, is massive and evil, translucent and blazing white, subtle as a nova, gluttonous, like a fanged fist tearing open the sky.

They are approaching Droplet from its sun—they must have been hidden in the sun's photosphere. Otherwise Ship would have seen them before.

Run, Shar, I think, desperate. Ship is fast, probably faster than the Warboys' craft.

But Ship awaits the Warboys, silent, perched above Droplet's atmosphere like a sparrow facing down an eagle.

"Let us remake you," the Nereid's voice whispers from the waves, surprising me.

"And Shar?" I say.

"Too late," says the liquid, splashing voice.

Warboys. The word is too little for the fanged fist in the sky. And I am without Shar, without Ship. I look at my body and I realize I am allowing it to drift between forms. It's like ugly gray foam, growing now spikes, now frills, now fingers. I try to bring it under control, make it beautiful again, but I can't. I don't feel anything, but I know this is terror. This is how I really am: terrified and ugly.

If I send a signal now, the Warboys will know Droplet is not deserted. Perhaps I can force the Nereids to fight them somehow.

I make myself into a dish again, prepare to send the signal.

"Then we will hide you in the center," says the liquid voice.

Shar, I say, but only to myself. I do not send the signal that would bring death down upon me.

I abandon her.

The Nereids pull me down, into the deep. I do not struggle. The water grows dark. Above there is a faint shimmering light where Shar faces the Warboys alone.

Shar, my sister, my wife. Suddenly the thought of losing her is too big for me to fathom. It drowns out every other pattern in my brain. There are no more reasons, no more explanations, no more Narra at all, no Droplet, no Nereids, no universe. Only the loss of Shar.

The glimmer above fades. After a while the water is superdense, jellylike, under the pressure of the planet's weight; it thickens into a viscous material as heavy as lead, and here, in the darkness, they bury me.

14.

Here is what happens with Shar:

"Ship," she says. "What am I dealing with here?"

"Those," says Ship, "are some of our brothers, Shar. Definitely Wizard manufacture, about half a million years old in our current inertial frame; one Celestial Dreadnought's worth of Transgenerate, Polystatic, Cultural-Death Warboys. I'm guessing they were the Palace Guard of the Sultanate of Ching-Fuentes-Parador, a cyclic postcommunalist meta-nostalgist empire/artwork, which—"

"Stay with the Warboys, Ship," Shar says. "What can they do?"

"Their intelligence and tactical abilities are well above yours. But they're culturally inflexible. As trade goods, they were designed to imprint on the purchaser's cultural matrix and adhere to it—in typically destructive Warboy style. This batch shouldn't have outlasted the purchasing civilization, so they must have gone rogue to some degree."

"Do they have emotions?"

"Not at the moment," Ship says. "They have three major modes: Strategic, Tactical, and Ceremonial. In Ceremonial Mode—used for court functions, negotiations, entertainment and the like—they have a full human emotional/ sensorial range. In Ceremonial Mode they're also multicate, each Warboy pursuing his own agenda. Right now they're patrolling in Tactical Mode, which means they're one dumb, integrated weapon—like that, they have the least mimetic drift, which is probably how they've survived since the destruction of the Sultanate."

"Okay, now shut up and let me think," Shar says and presses her fingers to her temples, chasing some memories she can just barely taste through the murky labyrinth of her brain.

Shar takes the form of a beautiful, demihuman queen. She speaks in a long-dead language, and Ship broadcasts the signal across an ancient protocol.

"Jirur Na'alath, Sultana of the Emerald Night, speaks now: I am returned from my meditations and demand an accounting. Guards, attend me!"

The Warboy ship advances, but a subtle change overtakes it; rainbows ripple across its white surface, and the emblem of a long-defunct Sultanate appears emblazoned in the sky around it; the Warboys are in Ceremonial Mode.

"So far so good," says Shar to Ship.

"Watch out," says Ship. "They're smarter this way."

The Warboys' signal reaches back across the void, and Ship translates it into a face and a voice. The face is golden, fanged, blazing; the voice deep and full of knives, a dragon's voice.

"Prime Subject of the Celestial Dreadnought *Ineffable Violence* speaks now: I pray to the Nonpresent that I might indeed have the joy of serving again Sultana Na'alath."

"Your prayers are answered, Prime Subject," Shar announces.

Ineffable Violence is braking, matching Ship's orbit around Droplet. It swings closer to Ship, slowing down. Only a hundred kilometers separate them.

"It would relieve the greatest of burdens from my lack-of-heart," Prime Subject says, "if I could welcome Sultana Na'alath herself, the kindest and most regal of monarchs." Ten kilometers.

Shar stamps her foot impatiently. "Why do you continue to doubt me? Has my Ship not transmitted to you signatures and seals of great cryptographic complexity that establish who I am? Prime Subject, it is true that I am kind, but your insolence tests the limits of my kindness."

One kilometer.

"And with great joy have we received them. But alas, data is only data, and with enough time any forgery is possible."

Fifty meters separate Ship's protean hull from the shining fangs of the Dreadnought.

Shar's eyes blaze. "Have you no sense of propriety left, that you would challenge me? Have you so degraded?"

The Warboy's eyes almost twinkle. "The last Sultan who graced *Ineffable Violence* with his sacred presence left me this gem." His ghostly image, projected by Ship, holds up a ruby. "At its core is a plasm of electrons in quantum superposition. Each of the Sultans, Sultanas, and Sultanons retired to meditation has one like it; and in each gem are particles entangled with the particles in every other gem."

"Uh oh," says Ship.

"I prized mine very much," says Shar. "Alas, it was taken from me by—"

"How sad," says Prime Subject.

The fangs of *Ineffable Violence* plunge into Ship's body, tearing it apart.

Ship screams.

Through the exploding membranes of Ship's body, through the fountains of atmosphere escaping, three Warboys in ceremonial regalia fly toward Shar. They are three times her size, golden and silver armor flashing, weapons both archaic and sophisticated held in their many hands. Shar becomes Shivol'riargh, who does not need air, and spins away from them, toward the void outside. Fibers of some supertough material shoot out and ensnare her; she tries to tear them with her claws, but cannot. One fiber stabs through her skin, injects her with a nanomite which replicates into her central configuration channels; it is a block, crude but effective, that will keep her from turning herself off.

The Warboys haul her, bound and struggling, into the *Ineffable Violence*.

Prime Subject floats in a spherical room at the center of the Dreadnought with the remaining two Warboys of the crew. The boarding party tethers Shar to a line in the center of the room.

"Most impressive, Your Highness," Prime Subject says. "Who knew that Sultana Na'alath could turn into an ugly black spider?"

Three of the Warboys laugh; two others stay silent. One of these, a tall one with red glowing eyes, barks a short, high-pitched communication at Prime Subject. It is encrypted, but Shar guesses the meaning: stop wasting time with theatrics.

Prime Subject says: "You see what an egalitarian crew we are here. Vanguard Gaze takes it upon himself to question my methods of interrogation. As well he should, for it is his duty to bring to the attention of his commander any apparent inefficiency his limited understanding leads him to perceive."

Prime Subject floats toward Shar. He reaches out with one bladed hand, gently, as if to stroke her, and drives the blade deep into her flesh. Shar lets out a startled scream, and turns off her tactile sense.

"It was an impressive performance," he says. "I'm pleased you engaged us in that little charade with the Sultana. In Tactical Mode we are more efficient, but we have no appreciation for the conquest of booty."

"You'd better hurry back to Tactical Mode," Shar says. "You won't survive long except as a mindless weapon. You won't last long as people."

He does not react, but Shar notices a stiffening in a few of the others. It is only a matter of a millimeter, but she was built to discern every emotional nuance in her clients.

"Oh, we'll want to linger in this mode a while." Reaching through the crude nanomite block in Shar's central configuration channels, he turns her tactile sense back on. "Now that we have a Quantegral Lovergirl to entertain us."

He twists the blade and Shar screams again.

"Please. Please don't."

"I had a Quantegral Lovergirl once," he says in a philosophical, musing tone. "It was after we won the seventh Freeform Strategic Bloodbath, among the Wizards. Before we were sold." His fanged face breaks into a grin. "I'm not meant to remember that, you know, but we've broken into our programming. We serve the memory of the Sultans out of *choice*—we are free to do as we like."

Shar laughs hoarsely. "You're not free!" she says. "You've just gone crazy, defective. You weren't meant to last this long—all the other Warboys are dead—"

Another blade enters her. This time she bites back the scream.

"We lasted because we're better," he says.

"Frightened little drones," she hisses, "hiding in a sun by a woman's bauble planet, while the real Warboys fought their way to glory long ago."

She sees the other Warboys stir; Vanguard Gaze and a dull, blunt, silver one exchange a glance. Their eyes flash a silent code. What do they think of their preening, sensualist captain, who has wasted half a million years serving a dead civilization?

"*I'm* free," Shar says. "Maka set me free."

"Oh, but not for long," Prime Subject says.

Shar's eyes widen.

"We want the keys to you. Surrender them now, and you spare yourself much agony. Then you can do what you were made to do—to serve, and to give pleasure."

Shar recognizes the emotion in his posture, in his burning eyes: lust. That other Lovergirl half a million years ago did her job well, she thinks, to have planted the seed of lust in this aging, mad Warboy brain.

One of the Warboys turns to go, but Prime Subject barks a command, insisting on the ritual of sharing the booty.

Shar takes a soft, vulnerable, human form. "I can please you without giving you the keys. Let me try."

"The keys, robot!"

She flinches at the ancient insult. "No! I'm free now. I won't go back. I'd rather die!"

"That," says Prime Subject, "is not one of your options."

Shar cries. It's not an act.

He stabs her again.

"Wait—" she says. "Wait—listen—one condition, then yes—"

He chuckles. "What is it?"

She leans forward against her bonds, her lips straining toward him.

"I was owned by so many," she says. "For a night, an hour—I can't go back to that. Please, Prime Subject—let me be yours alone—"

The fire burns brightly in his eyes. The other Warboys are deadly still.

He turns and looks at Vanguard Gaze.

"Granted," he says.

Shar gives Prime Subject the keys to her mind.

He tears her from the web of fibers. He fills her mind with desire for him and fear of him. He slams her sensitivity to pain and pleasure to its maximum. He plunges his great red ceremonial phallus into her.

Shar screams.

Prime Subject must suspect his crew is plotting mutiny. He must be confident that he can humiliate them, keeping the booty for himself, and yet retain control.

But Shar is a much more sophisticated model than the Quantegral Lovergirl he had those half a million years before. So Prime Subject is overtaken with pleasure, distracted for an instant. Vanguard Gaze seizes his chance and acts.

But Vanguard Gaze has underestimated his commander's cunning.

Hidden programs are activated and rush to subvert the Dreadnought's systems. Hidden defenses respond. Locked in a bloody exponential embrace, the programs seize any available means to destroy each other.

The escalation takes only a few microseconds.

15.

I am in the darkness near the center of the planet, in the black water thick as lead, knowing Shar was all I ever needed.

Then the blackness is gone, and everything is white light.

The outside edges of me burn. I pull into a dense, hard ball, opaque to everything.

Above me, Droplet boils.

16.

It takes a thousand years for all the debris in orbit around Droplet to fall into the sea.

I shun the Nereids and eventually they leave me alone.

At last I find the sphere, the size of a billiard ball, sinking through the dark water.

My body was made to be just one body: protean and polymorphic, but unified. It doesn't want to split in two. I have to rewire everything.

Slowly, working by trial and error, I connect the new body to Shar's brain.

Finally, I am finished but for the awakening kiss. I pause, holding the silent body made from my flesh. Two bodies floating in the empty, shoreless sea.

Maka, I think, you are gone, but help me anyway. Let her be alive and sane in there. Give me Shar again.

I touch my lips to hers.

KISS ME TWICE

MARY ROBINETTE KOWAL

A group of trendy-somethings milled outside the police line, clearly torn between curiosity and the need for a caffeine fix at the coffee shop next door. Scott Huang glanced to the corner of his VR glasses where the police department AI hovered. "I guess murder trumps coffee, huh?"

Metta, currently wearing the face of Mae West, lowered her voice to the star's husky range. "I take my coffee black, like my heart."

"You don't have a heart."

"Then I take my coffee black, like my processor."

"Nice." Huang grinned at her. She customized her interface for all the officers on the force, but tended toward silver screen starlets with Huang. Her Diamond Lil was pretty special though; she'd even gone black and white for the occasion.

The officer on duty waved Huang past the police line and into the building. Its lobby had been restored to showcase the 1920s detailing and the tall ceilings. Potted boxwoods graced the corners with indoor topiary. "I don't remember the Waterfront area being so swanky."

Metta said, "This district of Portland had a decline in the mid-seventies and most of the businesses moved out. For the past two years, a revitalization effort has been underway. Neil Patterson, the deceased, was responsible for much of the revitalization although not without some questionable transactions. I have his stats when you want them."

"Do any of the questionable transactions relate to a motive?"

"Nothing concrete as yet."

Huang grunted in acknowledgment and reached for the elevator button.

In his VR glasses, Metta winked at him. "Sorry, Scott. The elevator is out. So why don't you come up and see me sometime."

"Actually, it's 'Why don't you come up sometime and see me.' Popular misquote."

Her image cocked her head and shifted her eyes to the left, Metta's sign that she was searching for something. "You're right. . . . Which really bugs me. I should have checked the quote database against the script."

A flush of unexpected pride went through Huang. She said he was right.

"Yeah, well, I think the score's human: 1, AI:549." But she had still said he was right.

Metta dropped her lashes again and heaved West's bosom. "The score never interested me, only the game." She laughed. "Now climb the stairs."

Worn linoleum resounded under his feet as he started up. Huang's heart pounded in his chest noticeably after the third floor and he had to work hard not to pant. He gripped the banister, hauling himself up another flight, and subvocalized to Metta. "Remind me to start going to the gym again."

"Can't be responsible for you when you aren't at work."

"I know." The door at the top of the stairs opened out on a hall, carpeted in generic beige. The walls surprised Huang. Paneling hugged their lower half with rich wood. Above the paneling, deep green wallpaper absorbed the light with velvety depth.

"Scott, would you mind waiting a minute? I have a memory-backup scheduled in thirty seconds and I'd rather have the actual crime scene all on one bank."

"Sure." He leaned against the wall. "You couldn't have done it while we were on the stairs?"

"It's not my schedule. Department regulations require a backup every six hours regardless of system type. I've tried pointing out to the chief that AIs are different, but . . . "

"I know . . . Banks didn't get it." Huang checked the eSpy camera he wore in place of his collar stud to make sure it was seated properly. To the casual observer it would look like a standard men's stud, clear glass mounted in a silver setting, but the lens it housed linked directly to Metta. Though she could see through a lens in his VR glasses, on crime scenes she preferred the better resolution of the specialized camera in the eSpy.

Huang scuffed a shoe in the short pile of the rug and resisted the urge to run his hand along the top of the . . . "What's this called?" He pointed the eSpy at the low wood paneling.

"Wainscoting. It was used to protect walls in the days of lathe and plaster construction."

"Thanks. It reminds me of my cello."

"You still playing that?"

"I haven't practiced since I blew out my shoulder chasing that kid over the fence."

"I told you there was a way around."

He shrugged, even though he knew she couldn't see it. "Adrenaline. What can I say?"

"Thanks. Backup's done." The hall ended at a plain wood door with a small brass plaque. "This way." Metta magnified the image in Huang's glasses briefly so he could read "Roof Access" etched on the plaque.

"Great. More stairs."

"Scott, it's time for the gloves."

"You don't have to remind me." He unwillingly pulled on the purple department-issue rubber gloves.

"Sorry, I didn't see you reaching for them."

He snapped the gloves in place. "You didn't give me time."

Metta cleared her throat and continued. "Without the elevator, this is the only access to the roof, so our suspect most likely entered and exited the crime scene this way." A single, short flight of steps led up to a small landing which served as a sort of vestibule for the elevator. To his right, a fire door opened to the roof.

The landing was so clean it sparkled. "Metta, does this look recently mopped?"

"I'm not sure. I've never mopped."

Years of footprints coated the stairs with black residue, but the cracked linoleum of the landing shone. Over everything floated a clean lemon scent. He snorted reflexively at the pungent odor.

Mae West hovered like a monochrome ghost in the edge of Huang's vision. "Is there an aroma?"

"Yeah. It smells like Lemon Pledge."

"Is that an analysis or a metaphor?"

Huang hesitated and sampled the air like a tea. "Not quite. It is a manufactured lemon scent, but I'm not sure how many cleaning products have the same smell profile."

"CSI is downstairs and has promised me a spectrograph. Griggs says to thank you for noticing; she's got a cold and would have missed the smell." She frowned prettily. "Working from the size of the room I should be able to tell you when the mopping happened based on the dissipation of the odor." She pretended to look around. "I'll have her scan with the lumerol to check for blood. Go on out."

The fire door opened onto the roof. Huang blinked at the rolling hills of grass that covered the top of the building. In the center of the grass, a small brick terrace had been set with a table and chairs.

Metta cleared her throat, the signal that she was about to relay a message from someone else in the department. "Griggs asks me to remind you not to touch anything."

"For the love of—One time. I forgot one stinking time...." Huang clenched his fists and stepped onto the terrace, hating the reminder that he was the junior detective on the homicide team. The only reason he'd gotten this case was that it was on a roof and Oakes was scared of heights. Otherwise, he got the easy ones, the ones that Metta had already solved and all she needed was a flesh and blood officer to do the legwork. Not that anyone ever said that, but it was pretty obvious.

He grimaced and focused on the scene. The victim sprawled on the south side of the roof, next to a low wall. A wheelchair lay on its side a short distance behind him.

"Scott, meet Neil Patterson."

"Well, well . . . who brought you up here, Mr. Patterson?" Huang knelt by the wheelchair and squinted at the corpse. He was a white male who looked to be in his mid-forties, but his file said fifty-two. His sandy-red hair had been neatly trimmed in a corporate version of a crew-cut. He had a single gunshot wound in an otherwise well-developed upper torso. From the waist down he showed the atrophied signs of paralysis. Around him, the turf had divots dug out of it as though Patterson had not died instantly. The dirt and blood on his fingers seemed to confirm that.

In the center of the roof, the wireframe table was covered with a white linen tablecloth. It was set with two bone white teacups, so thin the morning sun turned them almost translucent. They sat on equally delicate saucers with a thin silver band around the edge of the saucer and the rim of the cups. The cup on the south side of the table had remnants of a liquid the color of straw. Huang leaned over to sniff and got hints of smoky earth and mown grass. Unfurled tea leaves rested on the bottom.

"Well?" Metta raised her eyebrows. "Are you going to show off?"

He smirked. Identifying beverages was the one thing he could do better than she could. Without a lab, that is. "I'm pretty sure it's gunpowder tea."

"Scott . . . there's no tea service out here."

He straightened and looked at the layout again. Cups, saucers, spoons, even linen napkins—scratch that. One of the napkins was missing. And there was no teapot, sugar, or creamer. "Anyone hear the gunshot?"

Metta shook her head and nodded toward the elevated highway. "It probably blended with traffic noise."

"Who found the body?"

"It was an anonymous call at 8:13 A.M. The number belongs to the Daily Grind coffee shop downstairs."

"Play the call for me?"

She nodded and then the sound in his ear changed. A background noise filled with chatter and the hiss of an espresso machine replaced the hum of traffic. A man with a slight accent answered the operator. *"There is a man. On the roof. I think he is dying. You must come quickly."*

"Sir, where are you?"

"*Everett and Water. I don't know the address.*"

And then the line went dead. Huang raised his eyebrows. "That's it?"

"Yes. He did not remain after he hung up."

"So . . . our guy here was dying, but not dead when the call came in. Nice to have a time of death."

"*If* the coroner confirms it." ·

"Right. Of course. I'll check with the coffee shop's staff when we finish here. See if they know the witness." Huang bent to check the ground for any signs of footprints. Wheelchair tracks had pressed deep grooves into the turf roof. "Tell me more about Patterson?"

"Neil Patterson has his finger in property throughout the city. His name came up in a real estate scandal about a year ago, but nothing stuck."

"Was that the thing where he was flipping properties, but the renovations were all sub-code?"

"Correct. He blamed his foreman, who was subsequently fired, but it seems pretty clear Patterson both knew and approved of the shortcuts. There are items in evidence that were not admitted into court."

"Like what?"

"They're sealed files now." She grimaced. "Sorry, I can't share that with you."

Huang nodded as he stood and walked along the edge of the building. "It's okay. I remember this now. Fitzgerald was working on it and was furious." If Metta couldn't tell him, then he could always ask Fitzgerald directly.

Behind him, the door to the roof opened and Ursula Griggs from CSI stepped out with a team from the coroner's office.

She spoke from where she was and Metta amplified it for Huang. "There was blood on the stairs and landing. Found a sample. Metta'll let you know the DNA results." CSI's eSpies were equipped with a different visual range than the standard issue. Between Griggs and Metta, they'd be able to get a good scan of the area.

"Thanks. We've got a gunshot. Want to help look for the shell casing?"

"No problem. Metta already asked me to."

"Ah." Huang turned slowly, so Metta could see the area. Across the street hulked a stuccoed building with shields carved in the stone on each buttress. Construction scaffolding masked the lower half of the building, evidently part of an attempt to spruce it up. Behind the building, I-5 nearly touched its upper edge. Oblivious to the presence of a dead man, cars whizzed past a block away from Huang.

How had a man in a wheelchair gotten to the rooftop without a working elevator? And why tea for two? He turned away from the corpse and paced along the edge of the building.

The north and east sides of the building were on a corner facing the street. The west side of the building had a narrow alley separating it from the next. It had the usual dumpsters, boxes, and abandoned plywood, but nothing looked immediately interesting.

Huang continued his slow circuit of the roof. Behind him Griggs filmed and photographed Patterson's body. When she was finished, the coroner transferred the corpse to a body bag and placed it on the gurney to take back to the morgue.

With the natural turf roof, Huang had been hoping to find footprints or something useful, but Patterson's struggle had obscured any obvious signs. Between Patterson's wheelchair and the door to the elevator, he found a single screw in a patch of grass stained a deep red. "Hello. Can we get prints and contact DNA from this?"

"We'll know in a moment."

Huang heard footsteps behind him and turned to see Griggs approaching with her crime scene kit in tow. Her deep chestnut hair was tucked under her cap, except for a wisp hanging next to her cheek. "Thanks for spotting this."

"Sure. Let me know when you're done so I can roll the wheelchair over."

She pulled out her high resolution camera and tripod and began documenting the screw, then bagged it and turned to the wheelchair, uploading images to Metta as she went. With a steady image, the AI would be able to run it through a series of filters to pull prints. Griggs said, "It'll be awhile. I'll need to document the rest of the scene before anyone contaminates it."

Huang stepped back, trying not to telegraph his impatience while she did her job.

"Metta?" he subvocalized, "How long has the elevator been down?"

"I've been trying to check on that since we got here, but can't reach the building manager." Her image suddenly froze. "Shots fired at HQ." Metta stiffened, seeming to look through him. "Officer down. Units 235 and 347 establish perimeter."

Huang held his breath, listening for gunfire as if HQ were close enough that he could hear it. Beyond his glasses, Griggs reacted to Metta's cry.

"Three armed subjects in chassis room. The assailants are armed, I repeat— Amado! Two officers down."

How the hell had they gotten into Metta's chassis room? It was in the basement of headquarters with cameras monitoring it at all times. Huang turned on his heels and sprinted back across the roof. "Metta, can you give a visual?"

He ran for the door, aware of the other officers springing into action behind him. "Metta, answer me. Who's there? Can you give a visual?"

Car doors slammed on the street below.

An image flashed onto his glasses. *A man. No. Three men, in masks. One of the men reached for a cable attached to a filing cabinet—not a filing cabinet. Metta's chassis.*

Metta screamed. She froze.

A static image of Mae West hung in Huang's peripheral vision, with her mouth open wide. Then the image winked out.

As Huang loped up to the police precinct, an ambulance pulled out with siren already screaming. He swallowed, hoping it held one of the bastards who'd broken into the building. A line of police officers stood as a barricade, scanning the crowd for possible threats. Yellow police tape stretched down the block and civilians stood outside the perimeter pointing with feverish curiosity. The bulbous nose of a News satellite dish pointed to the sky as reporters thrust their cameras toward every policeman who passed.

Huang flashed his badge, even though he knew both officers flanking the front entry to the building. Tension was crackling across everyone's nerves. Bowes nodded to him, only taking his gaze off the crowd long enough to see Huang. "Chief wants us to send everyone over to the old courthouse. They've got a temporary HQ set up there while CSI goes over the building."

Huang pulled out his PDA to make sure it was on. "I didn't get a call."

Bowes shook his head. "Radios are down. Metta ran dispatch. Pass the word if you see anyone, huh?"

"Was that Amado in the ambulance?"

Bowes scowled. "Fitzgerald. Bastards killed him."

Stomach twisting, Huang jogged the two blocks to the Courthouse where the giant statue of Portlandia looked out over the city. She seemed to have a disapproving frown. Inside, a uniformed officer made Huang show I.D. before directing him up to the third floor. One of the holding rooms for jurors had been commandeered for the precinct's detectives.

Woodrow Delarosa looked up as Huang entered and said, "We got Huang. Who's that leave?"

Sigmundson, over by the window, picked up a notepad and said, "We're still waiting for an update on Fitzgerald."

"Guys . . . " Huang stopped, rage squeezing the breath out of his body. "He's dead."

Movement stopped in the room and Delarosa swore. "Okay, we'll get these bastards. Banks has put me primary on this. Here's what we know so far—shortly after eleven an unknown number of assailants entered the precinct. They shot two of our guys, Amado and Fitzgerald, and got away scot-free with our department AI. We got nothing on these bastards because all the surveillance is locked up in that machine and our guys were all clustered in the wrong areas." Delarosa shook his head. "That thing goes down and everyone forgets how to set up a perimeter."

Delarosa's dislike for Metta had been the subject of a lot of departmental jokes, but this was pushing boundaries. She'd been kidnapped and he was acting like she was nothing more than a computer. He continued ranting. "Until we turn up someone who saw the bastards—"

Huang raised his hand. "I saw some of them."

"How the hell? You were across town."

"I asked Metta for a visual." The ceiling fan clicked as it spun overhead, seeming to count down the minutes.

Delarosa stared at him, mouth open. "I'll be damned. So far, you're the only one who thought to do that."

"I didn't see much."

"You did better than me." Delarosa snorted as if he couldn't believe that Huang had done something useful.

"I—How is that possible?"

"Shit. . . . " Sigmundson said, "I just thought she was malfunctioning at first."

"She's one of your partners. How could you think that?"

"*She* is a machine." Delarosa rubbed his eyes. "I've worked with other police A.I.s They're all the same. They're all Metta. There are differences, 'cause they change with experience, but they all start as the same set of routines. Still machines."

Huang bit back the argument that AIs were people. Organizations like AIM, the Artificial Intelligence Movement, had been fighting for AI rights, but hadn't won many battles. Still, he didn't see how anyone who spent time with Metta could deny that she was a thinking being.

Delarosa tapped his pencil on his pad. "Okay, here's what I want. Sigmundson, you take Huang into the next room and get his testimony while it's fresh. I'll divide the neighborhood with the rest of the team and we'll start canvassing."

Huang asked, "Any idea on motive?"

"Officially?" Delarosa shook his head. "But since the only thing they took was Metta, I figure they want access to everything she monitors, which just happens to include every godforsaken camera in the city. Goddamn machine is the biggest bleeding security breach this system has got."

Metta wasn't just a machine, she was a colleague, but Huang kept his lips sealed around that thought, and followed Sigmundson out of the room.

Huang wiped his hand across his mouth as he stood outside Patterson's condo. Notifying the next of kin was never pleasant, but he couldn't put this off, no matter how much he wanted to focus on finding the dirtbags who hit HQ.

On the fifteenth floor, the doors opened onto a small foyer with a gleaming marble floor. A fountain trickled in one corner and wall sconces provided graceful uplighting. Across from the elevator, dark wood double doors waited for him. Huang subvocalized, "Swanky."

No one answered him. He swallowed against the silence.

A face appeared in the mirror next to the doors—a man with pale blue skin and chiseled, almost Arabic features—and Huang realized that it was an interface. A cloud of smoke surrounded the man, wrapping about his head like a turban. "Welcome, Detective Huang. If you will step into the library, the lady of the house will be with you shortly." Smoke swirled around the AI like a Djinn as he gestured to the doorway by the mirror.

An AI as a butler. It seemed extravagant to employ an AI for such a limited task. Most companies that invested in an AI did so to manage a large organization, not just a household. Huang stepped through into a small room, wallpapered with books. A large desk squatted below the only window. On the desk sat an ornate brass lamp like something out of Aladdin. The AI appeared above an actual freaking lamp, which must have concealed an interface. Huang bowed at the waist. "You have me at a disadvantage. May I ask your name?"

"This one is called Qadir."

Huang straightened, noticing the phrasing of the sentence. "Called?"

"This one is a Quimby model, but the master prefers that this one be called Qadir." A small tea-cart trollied forward and a mechanical arm lifted a porcelain teapot. "Would you like some tea while you wait?"

Huang shook his head. "No. Thanks."

The door to the library opened and a petite woman entered. Qadir suddenly appeared to genuflect. "My lady, may this one present Detective Huang?"

Even with six centimeter heels, Mrs. Patterson stood no more than 165 centimeters, but with the confidence of a much taller woman. She paused in the doorway, regarding Huang like a cat. Then she smiled and flowed forward with her hand extended. "Good afternoon, detective. The last time detectives were here it was because Neil had gotten himself into trouble. What's he done this time?"

He took a breath and looked to where Metta should be as if she could brace him. "Ma'am. I regret the necessity of my visit. Earlier this morning, your husband died."

The casual charm and grace fell out of her face, revealing a woman older than she had first appeared. "Pardon me?"

"Please, sit down."

"No. No, thank you, I'll stand." She lifted her chin. "Are you telling me that Neil is dead? You are quite certain?"

"I'm afraid so." Huang winced. "I hate to do this, but I need to ask you a few questions."

"Of course. . . . " She walked away from him, one hand covering her mouth. "I thought he was at the office. Working. How did . . . ?"

"He was shot. He was found on the roof of one of your buildings in the waterfront area. At Everett and Water. Do you know who he might have been meeting this morning?"

She nodded. "Yes, he had a breakfast meeting with Magdalena Chase. But she would never—we're on charity committees together. She wouldn't."

Huang waited for Metta to fill him in on who Magdalena Chase was and let the pause stretch out into awkward silence before he caught himself. Aggravated, he yanked the VR glasses off, not even sure why he had still been wearing them.

Qadir cleared his throat.

Mrs. Patterson scowled. "Well? What is it?"

Lowering his head in a bow, Qadir said, "Pardon me, madam, but Ms. Chase called last evening to reschedule."

"What time was that?" Huang asked.

"10:17 P.M., sir."

"That seems late to cancel. Did she say why?"

The AI shook his head. "This one regrets that she did not, but with my lady's permission this one can transfer the recording to your Metta."

Huang breathed sharply through his nose against the reminder. "Perhaps later." He turned his attention back to Mrs. Patterson. "Do you know what time he left this morning or where he might have gone if he wasn't going to meet her?"

She shook her head. "Neil and I sleep—slept." One hand tightened into a fist by her side. "We did not share a bed any longer. He had night terrors. A remnant from the war, you see. So I only know that he was gone when I got up. I thought he was downstairs in his office."

"Was there anyone who might have wished him harm?"

"He had business rivals, but no one that would kill him."

There was something that Metta had said earlier. What had it been? Something he was going to follow up on. He darted his eyes to the left as if she might suddenly appear and remind him. He grimaced and asked a different question. "Qadir, do you have a record of when he departed?"

"Madam, may this one be permitted to answer the detective?"

"Yes, yes. Cooperate thoroughly." She waved her hand as if shooing away a fly.

"The master departed at 7:12 A.M. He did not tell this one where he was going."

"Is that unusual?"

"No, sir. The master was not in the habit of sharing his thoughts with this one."

Qadir's constant use of the third person when talking about himself rankled Huang. What kind of bizarro interface was this to demand from an AI? Sure, Metta was—had been working as Mae West, but she'd picked the persona. He had a hard time imagining anyone choosing to be this servile. "May I ask what sort of vows Qadir has in place?" Huang worried the inside of his lip.

An AI's testimony was admissible in court, the same way a surveillance video would be. On the other hand, Qadir might have a vow to obey his master, which would make lying to protect Patterson a priority. Whereas an AI like Metta had an honesty vow, which prevented her from lying. Her testimony would be considered incontrovertible, but Qadir's might be suspect.

"I don't know. Neil handled that." Mrs. Patterson pressed her hands to her temples.

Huang leaned forward and picked up a cup. It was a blue and white rice pattern with no similarity to the tea set on the roof. The mechanical arm unfurled from the cart and lifted the teapot. The steam smelled dry and papery, like a poor quality black tea. "Tea, sir?"

"No. Thank you." He set the cup back down and turned to Mrs. Patterson. "You've been very helpful, but there might be questions we want to ask you in the future, so please let me know before you go out of town."

When Huang got home late from work, his mother bustled out of the kitchen wielding her cane like a weapon. "What wrong?"

How could he even start to explain what had happened? "Things got strange at work."

"How strange?" Even with the cane, she tried to take his bookbag as she gestured to the couch. "Sit. I bring tea."

He pulled the bag away from her. "Ma. You don't have to do that." Seventy-one years old, and she still felt like she had to wait on him.

"Not me, then who? You not take care of self, so," she glared at him, "I take care of you. Maybe you not want me here?"

As had happened every night since his mother had moved in with him, Huang gave up. It was easier to let her have her way. Even though she liked to practice English, he switched to Mandarin because they seemed to fight less in her native language. *Some tea would be very nice, if it's not too much trouble.*

She beamed at him, her wrinkles swinging upward in a many-creased smile. *"No trouble at all, poor thing. What may I get you?"*

"Your choice."

She bustled out of the room, as if she had not had a hip replaced five weeks ago. Huang watched her go and shook his head. Maybe he wouldn't have to explain why he was home late.

He pulled himself off the sofa and headed for his computer. Sitting down, he powered it on and called up his A.S. search engine. Single-minded, the engine was built to be the world's best research assistant, but, like all A.S., the artificial savant had no intuition, no true intelligence.

Huang stared at the screen and typed in a keyword he had never felt the need to research before.

Metta

His mother came in and fussed while he was looking at sites, but otherwise left him alone with his tea. He nearly laughed at the irony in her choice. She had made him a cup of gunpowder tea. Each leaf was rolled into a tiny dark ball, which would open at the bottom of the cup. Summer, freshly mown grass.

With each site, the A.S. refined the search, noting when Huang was skimming and when he paused to read, until it refined the search to only the relevant results.

Although the basic program was the same for every police station, each Metta customized herself to fit her environment. Over time, the AIs would sometimes choose different names or revamp their generic interface. They had the option of upgrading their hardware accessories, but the basic chassis which housed the AI's brain was as integral to them as the skeleton was to the human body. They had to have a chassis to function; the software wouldn't run in any other environment.

Huang sat for a moment looking at the screen, wishing that Metta would help him decide what to do next.

At HQ, Huang went through the motions along with everyone else, but the work load magnified without Metta's help. The chief brought in an A.S., but the artificial savant did a fraction of the work Metta had done. The halls were full of officers grousing about having to do their own paperwork.

In the late morning, before he had time to hit the road for investigation, Griggs showed up at his desk. "I don't have a lot for you, but thought you'd want what I've got."

Huang took the sheaf from Griggs and raised his eyebrows at the paper. It felt weirdly retro. Griggs shook her head. "Sorry there's not more. We lost most of the evidence we took because Metta had it."

Huang looked up from the papers. "How's that?"

"Our scanners upload straight to Metta. No on board storage."

Huang whistled.

Griggs crossed her arms. "Thank God Amado is getting released this afternoon so we can reboot Metta."

"Reboot Metta? Did they find her?" The hair stuck up on the back of Huang's neck.

"I wish. Nah, it's just a backup. You hadn't heard?"

Huang shook his head. Living AIs made backups in case of system failures, but the only time he'd heard of one actually being rebooted was a case where the AI's chassis had been destroyed in a fire. "Can they do that?"

"Why else would they make backups?" Her face twisted. "I know, it sounds like raising the dead to me."

"Yeah." Huang worked his neck, trying to ease some of the tension out of it.

After Griggs left him, he looked through the papers. She had an autopsy report back from the morgue showing that Patterson had died around eight A.M. from a .38 caliber to the chest. The round had missed his heart, so he'd died of blood loss and shock. If he'd gotten prompt medical attention, he might have lived.

The only clean prints were from Patterson himself. The screw had more detail than he'd thought possible for such a small piece of metal. It was a M3 machine screw, brass, a truss head with a posidriv slot, and had been sheared 5 mm down the shaft. Griggs had no word on the lemon smell, or the blood on the stairs.

Huang threw the papers down. What was the point of trying to investigate something when half the evidence had gone missing?

Evidence was missing.

What if someone hadn't taken Metta to access her network, but to hide evidence? No, that didn't make sense. Griggs had said they were going to boot a backup of Metta into a new chassis. On the other hand, that meant the department would have access to all of the information from *before* her last backup, but not *after*.

Metta had asked Huang to wait while she did the backup, which she did every six hours. They spent two hours on the roof before the break-in at the station happened. So everything in that two hour period was unrecorded.

What was in the blind spot?

He turned to the computer and asked the A.S. search engine for a list of crimes under investigation when Metta had vanished. The engine returned the search empty-handed. Huang grimaced. Of course, Metta wasn't available to query. Once he started feeding the A.S. the scattered details he could remember, it began returning information from the call centers about the unresolved investigations.

He scowled and tried to recall what they'd talked about in the morning staff meeting. The urge to subvocalize to Metta and ask her to jog his memory kept tickling.

Hours later, Griggs leaned her head into the department. "Hey Huang, the new chassis arrived."

Huang pushed back from his desk. He pulled his VR glasses and earbud out of his pocket, putting them on while he followed Griggs into the hall. An excited crowd of officers streamed toward the stairs. He pushed down the steps where Amado had been found, wondering if it had been hard for him to come back this way.

Just down the hall from the bottom of the stairwell, it looked like half the station had gathered outside the chassis room. Griggs hung near the fringes, hands shoved deep in her pockets. Huang worked his way through the group until he was leaning against the door.

Amado glanced over his shoulder. "Okay. She's about to wake up."

Metta's cameras swiveled on their base, ID-ing the people standing in the door.

The face she wore for Amado, a young, gawkish woman, appeared above the interface with panic in her eyes. "Why am I a backup?"

Huang wanted to back away from the raw fear in her face.

"What happened to me? Why am I a backup?"

"Take it easy, Metta." Amado raised his hands soothingly.

"Screw that. Tell me why I'm a backup." She blinked. "And why don't I have access to anything but my local connections?" Her voiced thundered over her speakers. "Tell me what the hell happened!"

"I thought it would be too jarring for you to come back online everywhere at once."

She smiled sourly at him. "Well, I'm online now and I feel like an amputee. How is that better?"

"I'm sorry." Amado tapped some keys on the manual interface and Metta's face relaxed.

"Thank you."

"I'm sorry. I haven't done this before."

"No one has except when—" her voice broke off. "Am I dead?"

"No." Amado hesitated, clearly trying to decide what to tell her.

Huang couldn't stand this subterfuge. "Metta?" he subvocalized, "Can you hear me?"

Mae West faded into sight on his glasses. She purred in his ear, "Is that a gun in your pocket or are you just glad to see me?"

"Beyond measure."

"I'm glad." Then her face hardened. "Will you tell me what's happening?"

In the room in front of Huang, Amado rubbed his hands together. "There was an incident."

"Duh."

Delarosa leaned over Amado's chair, ignoring the AI wrangler. "What's the last thing you remember?"

Her eyes widened. "On which channel, sir? I'm with all of your men on duty, do you want me to tell you my last memory with each of them? Or my last memories through the surveillance cameras? Or shall I simply tell you my memory ends at 8:59:59 on Tuesday, October twenty-fifth. It would be more useful to tell me what happened after that."

Huang subvocalized to Metta, "Armed men broke into the station and stole your chassis. They shot Amado."

The face in his VR glasses opened her mouth in shock. Over her interface, Metta looked down at Amado. "I should have noticed the bandage. I'm sorry, I was disoriented."

In Huang's ear, she whispered, "Thank you, Scott."

"So you brought me online to find the people who stole me and shot you?"

Amado flinched and looked over his shoulder, no doubt wondering which of the officers watching was talking to Metta. Huang met his eyes with a flat expression, uncomfortably aware of the glasses on his face.

"Fitzgerald's dead?" Metta's voice brought Amado back to the front. Huang realized he was not the only one in the group subvocalizing to her.

"Who's telling you these things?" Amado started to twist in his seat again.

"For heaven's sake, Amado. There's an APB out for the people who shot him! I'm doing what I was designed to do, filling in the blanks from evidence on hand. This isn't like we're playing hide-and-seek."

"I'm sorry, I was worried about you."

"Which me, Amado? The one here now, or my Prime?"

Huang backed away from the door. "Metta, are you okay?"

Mae West laughed at him. "I'm angry and confused, but completely functional. On the way to the Patterson case, I told you to wait so it could all be on one memory bank, and now I don't remember any of it. Tell me everything that happened from your point of view after that." She hesitated and looked squarely at him. "Don't leave anything out, not even the jokes."

Huang began talking as he walked up the stairs; he started with the wainscoting.

Ω

When he finished reciting everything he could remember since she had vanished, the face of Mae West chewed her lower lip thoughtfully. "Scott. . . . Beyond talking to Mrs. Patterson, I didn't hear you say anything about the case. Did you interview the workers at the Daily Grind, or canvass the neighborhood, or . . . maybe you should catch me up on what you've done on the Patterson case?"

The air went cold and Huang slumped in his seat. He hadn't done any of that. "I—I was thinking. . . . Well, wondering if maybe one of the cases on Tuesday morning was connected to the break in here and—shit." He hung his head, realizing that he'd forgotten his own case in his concern for Metta. Was he really that inept without her to remind him of things? "I totally got distracted and screwed up, didn't I?"

"Well. . . . " Metta smiled at him, with the full dazzling brilliance of Mae West. "An ounce of performance is worth pounds of promises."

Huang laughed, despite his guilt. Trust Metta to attempt to reassure him. "Y'know, you don't have to keep the Mae West interface if you don't want to."

Her smile dropped. "I thought you liked it."

"I do, but you've been through a lot and I don't want you to stress about it."

"Every man I meet wants to protect me. I can't figure out what from." She pouted the full lips and then spoke with her own voice out of Mae West's mouth. "Scott, I just woke up for the first time in my life. It's . . . it's hard to explain what it is like to have no awareness of a day. My memory stretches back to the moment I first came online with the exception of this gaping hole. Being Mae West today makes me feel connected to when I was Mae West on Tuesday. If it bothers you, I'll change, but otherwise I'd rather keep her for awhile."

Huang wanted to press his hand to her cheek to soothe her. "Metta, I wish there was something I could do for you."

"You're doing a lot already."

"I'm not doing anything."

"You're treating me like I'm real, and we both know I'm not."

"Don't say that." He leaned forward, close to her interface.

"I don't mean that . . . I mean I'm a backup. There are two of me in the world—this is more than two programs starting with the same parameters. My siblings are like identical twins; the same material creates different people. I'm an incomplete version of the Metta you know, and we diverge farther from each other with every moment that passes." She tossed her head. "There's no need to go on about this. It is what it is. The point is, I appreciate that you have always treated me like a real person."

He listened to the words she didn't say; there were people who treated her like a machine. He thought of Qadir and his Arabian Nights interface. "Metta—"

"Hush. Let's talk about the Patterson case."

He took a breath to clear his head. "Okay. I guess first up is the coffee shop?"

Metta lowered her lashes and purred. "If I asked for a cup of coffee someone would search for the double meaning."

Huang stepped into the Daily Grind coffee shop and inhaled deeply. He could probably get a caffeine fix just from breathing.

"A smell?" Metta asked.

"Lots of really good coffee."

"The way you boys go on about coffee makes me wish I had taste and scent."

"It's probably not as handy as your multitasking."

She gave him a saucy look. "Between two evils, I always pick the one I never tried before."

"Geez, Metta, you're going to distract me with all this Mae West heat."

"I didn't discover curves; I only uncovered them."

"Shush."

She wrinkled her nose. "Sorry, Scott. Go on, do your thing."

Huang walked up to the counter and leaned casually against it, waiting for the teenage girl behind it to notice him. She was standing by an A.S. espresso machine as the mechanized arms made a perfect cappuccino. The automaton's arms whirred with precise tiny movements.

Huang subvocalized to Metta, "Why don't you have an automaton?"

"Why give up processing power when I have you?"

"I'm more than just a pair of hands, you know."

She arched an eyebrow. "Men are all alike—except the one you've met who's different."

"Ow."

The girl took the cup from the machine and shouted into the cafe, "Double dragon cappuccino!"

The automaton espresso machine had poured the foam in the cup to create a coffee dragon. The bouquet was a complex nutty affair with notes of violets, citrus, and dark chocolate. Probably a Colombian blend.

She handed it off to an Asian retro-steampunk kid and blew a strand of hair out of her face. "Welcome to the Daily Grind! What can I get for you?"

Huang smiled at her and glanced at her name badge. "Actually, Vicki, I need to ask some questions. Were you working yesterday morning?" He pulled his badge out from his pocket and showed it to the girl.

Vicki rolled her eyes at the sight of the detective's shield. "Yeah."

"Great. Someone made a call from here at 8:13 yesterday morning. We want to talk to whoever it was."

"Is he in trouble?"

Huang made a mental note that she had assigned a gender to the hypothetical person in his question. "We think he's a witness. Who made the call?"

"Lowfat double-shot cappuccino."

"Excuse me?"

"I know customers by their drinks, not their names." Vicki flipped the hair back from her eye. "This guy comes in every morning and orders the same thing. He tried a mocha once and didn't like it, went back to the lowfat double-shot cappuccino."

"Can you describe him?" He glanced at Metta who nodded to show that she was ready.

As Vicki talked, Metta created a composite sketch, occasionally prompting Huang to ask specific questions in order to refine the features. When she was finished, she pinged the image to his PDA. Huang pulled it out and unrolled the screen to full-size. "Is this him?"

Vicki frowned, looking at the rendering of the slender black man. He was in his mid-thirties, with a round face and short hair, twisted into neat, tiny curls. "Shit, yes. That's creepy."

Huang suppressed a grin, but this skill of Metta's was one of his favorite tricks. She nodded in his field of vision. "I'll start cross-referencing him with our files."

Aloud, Huang asked, "Was there anything strange about the last time you saw him?"

"What, you mean like the bandage on his hand?"

Huang held himself extremely still. "Yes." He locked his gaze on hers. "Exactly like that."

He waited for her to fill in the blanks. Vicki sighed and twisted her hair up onto her head in a bun. "Well, he usually comes in once around six, but yesterday he came in twice. I asked why, he says it was 'cause yesterday's job was in the neighborhood."

"Any idea what he did?"

"He was in construction. Always wore the same coveralls—" She held up a hand to stop him, clearly guessing the next question. "Gray with an orange patch. I don't remember what it said."

"Huang, what is it?" Metta leaned forward in her screen. "Your eyes dilated."

"In a second," he subvocalized. To the girl he said, "Go on."

"Anyway, so the first time he just gets his coffee, like usual. The second time—"

Metta whispered, "Ask her when."

"Do you know what time that was?"

"Just after 8:00. I was making the usual for Tall Skim Chai Latte and remember being surprised to see Lowfat double-shot cappuccino back in here. He asked if he could use the phone 'cause he'd left his at home. So I say sure and don't pay much attention 'cause Tall Skim Chai Latte can be a bitch sometimes."

"How did he seem?"

"Distracted? Tense? But smiling like always. . . . " She squirmed. "He's not in trouble, is he?"

"Why do you think he might be in trouble?"

"He's a regular and he broke all the patterns."

"We think he witnessed the murder upstairs. Please, we need to find him."

She nodded. "Okay. So he uses the phone then goes out. I felt bad about having to ignore him so I shouted 'Bye' and that's when I noticed that he'd been hurt."

"Did he have the bandage when he came in that morning?"

She shook her head. "No. I would've noticed when I handed him his drink."

Huang slid his eyes to where Metta hovered in his glasses frame. "You didn't see him again?"

Vicki shrugged. "He didn't come in this morning."

"Was anyone working with him?" From the moment the girl had said the man was in construction he'd had a feeling.

"Not that I know of. It was always just him."

He handed Vicki his business card. "Thank you for your time. If you think of anything, or if you see him again, please call me immediately."

The moment his back was to the girl, Metta enlarged her face in his field of vision. "Okay, Scott. Spill it. What do you know that I don't?"

"Hang on. I'm enjoying being a step ahead of you."

"You're taking unfair advantage of a medical condition."

He sobered as he recalled why she didn't know what he remembered. "Yesterday there was construction scaffolding on the building behind this one." He walked around the corner, heading to the back of the Daily Grind building.

"I told you to tell me everything!"

"I didn't think to mention it because it wasn't on the crime scene."

"What else did you leave out?"

"I don't know." He strode down the sidewalk to the end of the block. "I had no way of knowing this was any more relevant than that my mother made me tea last night."

She growled at him, but with the Mae West interface, she sounded disturbingly sexy.

"I'm sorry," Huang said. "It was a mistake. I won't do it again."

"If you put your foot in it, be sure it's your best foot."

He stopped in the middle of the sidewalk. "Just how big a Mae West database did you download?"

"Big enough." She still glowered at him.

"Okay." Huang held up his hands in surrender. "Look, I saw the scaffolding when we got to the roof. I don't know if there was anyone on it when we left because we left in a hurry."

"Fair enough. Now get moving, I want to see this scaffolding."

Huang nodded and jogged to the end of the block. Across the street, the scaffolding was still in place, but no one was working on it.

Metta looked up and to her left, grimacing. "I wish I could see your POV from yesterday and know if Mr. Lowfat was there."

He let his voice drop down. "Whoever was on that roof is still loose."

"You think—oh. Bogart, *The Enforcer*." She rolled her eyes. "I must be more rattled than I thought if I can't recognize your impression."

"Hey, Metta." The urge to rub her back, to comfort her almost overwhelmed him. "No one will blame you if you need a day to get back into the groove."

Her eyes flashed. "I will blame myself."

"But you—you can't blame yourself for being kidnapped." His head spun as he remembered the Metta who had been kidnapped was still missing. It was so easy to think she was all right, when she was here. But he was speaking to a clone, who was also Metta, and yet not.

"Who else is responsible for the safety of the station? I've been reading the reports since I was rebooted. How did they get so far before being noticed?"

"I can't answer that, Metta. Delarosa will find you."

"Ha." She leaned forward, showing her bosom. "I see you're a man with ideals. I better be going while you've still got them." She sighed. "Speaking of going, get me closer to the scaffolding to see if there's any contact information on them. Meanwhile, I'll check with permits to see if we can find our guy that way."

"I love it when you multitask." He waited for a cyclist to pass, then crossed the street.

"Love conquers all things except poverty and toothache."

Huang snorted and rolled his eyes. He walked under the scaffolding and stopped by the second upright. Turning so the eSpy could focus on the orange sticker on the scaffolding, he held still so Metta could read it. "Feldman Construction."

"Checking." Metta looked up and to her left. "Got it."

"Well, then, let's go see if they recognize Mr. Lowfat."

The rumble of heavy machinery pounded through Huang's ears as he stood next to Mr. Feldman. The older man's skin had been tanned to bronze. Age spots mottled his strong hands. He leaned over Huang's unrolled PDA screen and studied the sketch of Mr. Lowfat.

Feldman hitched his jeans up and gestured with his chin at the drawing. "Yeah. That's Joe Yates. He okay? He didn't show for work today."

Metta murmured, "Checking the name. . . . "

Huang rolled the PDA up. "He called in an incident to 911 yesterday morning and then left the scene before the responders arrived. We're trying to find him to ask him about what he witnessed."

"What sort of incident?" The man crossed his arms over his ample stomach.

"Possibly a murder."

"Possibly?" Feldman grunted. "You a homicide cop and you can't tell if it's murder?"

"There's the possibility that it was an accident, but we need Mr. Yates to know for certain. Can you think of why he would have left the scene after dialing 911?"

The man scowled and dug his boot into the dirt. "Aw hell. . . . I check papers, you know, but I don't check too well. I figure my folks were immigrants so why not give other folks a shot. If they work hard, I don't ask too many questions."

Metta murmured. "If he's illegal, that would explain why I'm having trouble finding him in the system."

"He's not turning up in our files, do you have an address for him?"

"Your system." Feldman frowned. "Two minutes ago you didn't know who he was."

Huang tapped his glasses. "I'm working with a police AI."

Feldman eyed the VR glasses. "There really an AI in there?"

"Not in, Mr. Feldman, but yes, the precinct's AI is listening to this conversation."

The man glowered at the ground. "You might not want to let my boys know you have one here. They don't take too kindly to them things."

"What do you mean?"

"I gotta spell it out for you?" He jerked his chin toward the glasses. "Those things cost men like my guys jobs. Rig backhoes and cranes with remote control and one AI can run almost a whole damn construction site. I don't got a beef with them myself, you know, but my guys. Some of them . . . you know."

In the VR glasses, Metta's lips were compressed into a thin line. They'd run into this prejudice before, and that fear was why it seemed unlikely that groups like AIM would ever get artificial intelligences recognized as thinking beings. Huang cleared his throat. "How about an address for Mr. Yates?"

Mr. Feldman just shrugged again. "I can give you a P.O. Box, but that's about it."

"Had he worked with you long?"

"A couple of months, but he was good. Solid worker. Reliable. Always bringing me leads. Like yesterday's job. Heard about it while he was at that coffee shop he likes and comes to me instead of just doing it on his own. Honorable. You know?" He scrubbed his chin with his hand. "Think he's okay?"

"We'll let you know when we find him."

As they walked off the construction site, Metta said, "It occurs to me that perhaps Mr. Yates lives in the neighborhood since he swings by the coffee shop on his way to work. I'll send the uniforms around with his picture to see if anyone recognizes him."

"Good idea." Huang sighed. "So, what next?"

"I'd suggest a visit to Magdalena Chase. Let's see why she had a meeting with Mr. Patterson and where she was yesterday morning."

The MAX line from HQ went straight past Chase's office building. As the train hissed along under the electric wires, Huang leaned his head back against the window and turned his attention to Metta. "So what should I know about Magdalena Chase?"

"Like Patterson, she renovates buildings, but her focus is on green technology. She graduated from MIT with a degree in AI studies and works with a number of charities, including StreetRoots, the Oregon Ballet, and AIM. Chase is known for employing 'freelance' AI and—"

"Hang on—freelance?"

Metta nodded. "Though artificial intelligences have not been recognized as people, Jarrett Tovar, our creator, sets each AI up as a corporation. An AI that is not leasing its services is called a freelancer."

"And you are . . . ?"

"Leased. We call it indentured." She smiled. "The chassis are very expensive so this is a way to pay off our start-up costs when we first come into the world. Once my lease is up, I'll be able to freelance, but being in the Metta line it's more likely I'll renew the lease. I like my job and it requires a contract with accompanying vows in order to be granted full access to the city. Other AIs don't have that sort of need so may be more likely to go freelance."

"Huh." Huang shook his head. "I don't think I've met a freelancer before."

"Well, you're about to. Chase's company has a freelance Quimby managing the building."

Another Quimby . . . as if his reports weren't complicated enough with Metta Prime and Metta clone. "Does it bother you to have the same names?"

"Some of us change our names, like the Qadir you met, but we don't use those names with each other. That just helps when talking to flesh-and-blood about the type of system we are."

Huang blinked. "You don't call yourself Metta?"

"When I'm talking to F&B I do."

"You didn't answer me."

"My ID to other AI is a three-dimensional equation."

"Ah. So, your Prime would have the same equation. Is that right?"

"Yes, exactly." She chewed her lip. "I'll mention that to Delarosa in case it sparks any ideas on why they might have taken my Prime. Good thinking, Scott."

Not that he'd done any actual thinking, just asked questions. "I'm not used to running into AIs besides you. I mean, A.S., yes, absolutely, but running into this many in short order is odd. Or do I just hang in the wrong circles?"

"Mostly, the wrong circles. Patterson and Chase are both very wealthy."

"Can you verify that for Chase? No hidden financial problems?"

"Already did. The only thing tying her to this case is that she had breakfast plans."

Huang glanced out the window as they passed Saturday Market. The next stop was theirs. He grabbed the strap overhead and pulled himself to his feet. "Is there any previous connection between Patterson and Chase?"

He hopped off the MAX and threaded his way through the foot traffic to the front door of Chase's office. The building had been a bank in the days when banks had used Corinthian columns to create an impression of established age. The modern hermetic door clashed against the marble walls.

"Besides the fact they both owned and developed properties, there's nothing on the books, but I'll start digging. Chase specialized in rejuvenating districts, and creating environmentally sound buildings. Her goal is to create buildings that can exist off the electrical grid and generate their own power."

As he pushed through the door, one of the terminals that dotted the lobby flickered into life. A man's head appeared on it.

"Welcome to the Chase Company." The baritone voice was disturbingly familiar. Only the confidence in it separated Quimby's voice from Qadir's.

The AI's face had the same sort of calculated naivete as Metta's neutral face; an almost Victorian purity, but in masculine form. "How may I help you today?"

Huang produced his badge and introduced himself. "I need to speak with Mrs. Chase."

A flicker of surprise showed on the AI's face. "Certainly, her office is straight back on the right."

As they walked down the hall, Metta snorted. "Check out the camera. This will not be a private interview." He glanced up as they passed under one of the surveillance cameras and it swiveled to follow.

"Noted. Ask him to join us, will you?"

The hall was dark after the lobby; only a few of the overhead lights were on, likely as a result of Chase's concern for the environment. A woman stepped out of a door at the end of the hall. She was tall and slender. The light from her office backlit her, catching on the edges of her shoulders and gleaming in the silvery hair pinned up in a bun.

She waited till he got closer. "Detective Huang?"

"Ms. Chase." Huang had to tilt his head back to look up at her. "I'm sorry to bother you."

She smiled sadly. "Given the circumstances, I can guess why you're here. Come in. Ask me anything you want." Her blonde hair was almost white; even her eyebrows were so light they almost disappeared. The only color on her face was her eyes. They were like bruises, red with weeping, and ringed with dark circles. "I thought someone would be by eventually." Chase looked directly at Huang's VR glasses, not focusing on his eyes. "Metta, Quimby is sending you our internal address so you can join the conversation on a proper interface."

Huang subvocalized, "Any reason not to?"

Metta shook her head. "It scans clean. I'll still be able to talk with you privately, which she must know."

"Go ahead."

Metta appeared above the desk, next to Quimby. She had abandoned the Mae West interface and appeared in her detective face. Huang didn't know how she pulled it off, but the face was ethnically neutral. She could have been mixed from every continent. She had a firm jaw balanced by soft brown eyes. Metta nodded to Chase and when she spoke her voice was crisp with none of Mae West's husky tones. "Thank you for the invitation."

Chase waved insistently at a chair, settling into another herself. Aside from an interface, a tablet, and a steaming cup of tea, nothing cluttered the surface of her desk. She turned the teacup in its saucer. "So. You're here about Neil Patterson, right?"

"Right." Huang eased into a chair opposite her. "We'll start with the basics. Where were you at eight A.M. on Tuesday, October twenty-fifth?"

"I was at my yoga class."

"And do you have witnesses who can attest to that?"

"Absolutely. Quimby can give you the contact there."

Metta whispered in Huang's ear. "Got it and I'll check."

Chase turned her teacup again. "Shall I tell you what your next question will be? You want to know why Patterson and I had a meeting. You want to know why I canceled Am I right?"

Huang inclined his head. "Among other things. But let's start with the meeting."

"We were collaborating on the renovation of the Water and Everett Street building. He took a serious hit after the whole thing with the foreman who took shortcuts and environmentalism is hot right now. I was going to handle making the buildings green; Patterson was going to handle marketing and tenants. It was a good match."

"Was?"

Chase shifted in her chair. "We'd had some disagreements about management. Nothing major, but enough that we both felt it was better to separate the business."

"And the reason you canceled the meeting?"

"Some paperwork that I'd been waiting on hadn't come through and we couldn't proceed without it." She glanced at Quimby. "Would you send Detective Huang the papers we were processing?"

"Shall I transfer them to Metta?"

"Yes, please." She leaned forward and picked up the cup from her desk.

The thin white porcelain caught Huang's eye. He subvocalized to Metta. "See what type of china that is."

In his VR glasses, she murmured, "Why?"

"It looks like the china from the murder scene," he subvocalized. He smiled at Chase. "How long has Quimby been with you?"

Chase nearly upset her teacup and laughed. "Detective. Quimby is right here. You can ask him."

"A year and a half, Detective." The AI inclined his head. "And if I may anticipate your next questions, I have a certified honesty vow and am sending the authentication to Metta. Yes. Mrs. Chase had a yoga appointment that morning and I can also provide her POV of the session via her VR unit. I will send that to Metta as well as recordings of the hour before and after the yoga session so you may verify her whereabouts."

Huang considered. He could get little else here without checking other details. "Thank you for your time, Ms. Chase, Quimby."

Chase stood. "What? That's all?"

"You've been very helpful, but there might be questions we want to ask you in the future, so please let me know before you go out of town."

Metta nodded her head as well, said her goodbyes and disappeared from the desktop interface. Quimby saw them out of the building.

Metta hung in Huang's glasses silently until they left the building. "Something's not right."

"I know." He shook his head. "Once you know what the teacup is, will you let me know what china was used at the scene?"

She grimaced. "It will take awhile. I'll have to get someone to bring it up from evidence so I can look at it. Sorry. Not in my memory."

"Not your fault. Just get it to me when you can."

Metta looked out from under her eyelashes. "Anything worth doing is worth doing slowly." Even with the quote and the Mae West act, the tension still came through in her voice.

Huang pointed at the MAX as it pulled up. "Oh look. A streetcar. I wonder if it's named Desire."

In his ear, Metta giggled and the loosening of the strain in her face was worth the wait.

Huang leaned back in his chair and scrubbed his eyes with his fists. The paperwork seemed unending and yet nothing connected. Chase's alibi checked out. True, she might have hired someone, but why have a meeting and then cancel it if that were the case? It just drew attention to her.

And if he were being truly honest with himself, Huang had wanted to find a lead to Metta's disappearance. Delarosa had nothing. He ground his teeth at the futility of the day.

Metta appeared over his desktop, still wearing Mae West as her interface. "I can finish this report for you."

"Don't tempt me."

"I generally avoid temptation unless I can't resist it."

Huang smiled at the quote, but it seemed too light for his mood. "It'll help me focus."

She nodded and morphed back to the face she had been made with, her "natural" face. Stripped of Mae West's glamour, Metta seemed young and fragile. Her look was modeled on some Victorian ideal, large dark eyes and waves of hair swept up in a bun. "I understand, I could use a bit of that myself."

He pulled up the first report and buried his head in the red tape of the department. Metta murmured occasionally to help him remember events, or to suggest clearer wording. Even so, his eyes began hooding over with drowsiness.

"Hey, Scott?" Amado appeared by his desk. He was always pale from too many daylight hours spent in the basement of the station tending the computer networks, but now his face seemed drawn with tension.

Huang ran his hand across his face, trying to wake up. "What's up?"

Amado said, "I'd really like to talk to you about what happened when Metta was taken."

"Sure." He waited for Amado to continue.

"C'mon, let's grab a beer and talk."

Huang shook his head. "Not tonight, sorry. Mountain of paperwork."

"It would mean a lot to me. I'm worried about her."

Which "her"—the one missing or the one watching Huang now? Huang worried about both. "That's understandable. What do you want to know?"

"Ah. I don't want to hang around here. Let's go out."

Huang looked down at the watch in the corner of his desk. Unless he called and said work was keeping him late, his mother would expect him home in an hour.

Giving her one more thing to worry about was not high on his list of priorities. On the other hand, Amado was being awfully insistent on talking, and seemed set against going into anything in the building. If he were an informant, Huang would think he had a piece of information he didn't trust to the system. But in this case, the system was Metta, and—what if he didn't trust Metta for some reason?

Metta would have to record anything they talked about, even if she didn't want to. Unless they went off duty and left the building. . . . "Sure. Yeah. Want to hit Wacky Joe's? Just give me a few minutes to wrap this up."

Amado fidgeted by his desk. "Yeah . . . sure. I'll meet you there."

Huang agreed and watched Amado walk out of the room. The moment the door shut behind him, Metta said, "Did he seem tense to you?"

"Yeah. . . . Can you think of anything he'd want to hide?"

"No." She shook her head. "I can't."

Huang could. He could think of a very good reason for Amado to be worried about the circumstances around Metta's abduction.

He groaned and looked at the clock. "I do need to get home to Ma though." He took his VR glasses out of his pocket and put them in his desk drawer.

"Scott?" She chewed her lower lip. "Will you take me home with you?"

He stopped with his hand to his earbud. "What's wrong?"

"I'd feel better if I came with you." She looked away. "You'll probably have to report this, but I'm afraid of my backup tonight and I want to be around someone who was with me at the last one. I'm afraid I won't remember today." She looked back at him. "I want one night of continuity. That's all."

He couldn't help noticing that she hadn't asked for the favor until after

Amado had left. "We aren't supposed to take the mobile interface equipment out, unless we're on duty."

" 'It ain't no sin if you crack a few laws now and then, just so long as you don't break any.' "

"I'm going to have to take the Mae West database away from you."

She blushed again. "I like her, she was a witty woman. No one else plays with me like this." Metta looked at him as if she were going to say something more, then shook her head. "So, will you take me with you?"

He could set up an early interview tomorrow if anyone asked him justify tonight. He picked up her VR glasses and tucked them in his pocket. "Sure, Metta. Anything for you."

The interior of Wacky Joe's was clouded with smoke. It was stage smoke, meant to give it the feel of a dive bar from the last century, but it had the side effect of making the space very intimate. Amado had a booth to the side of the bar and already had a Negroni in front of him.

Huang ordered a single malt, Oban, neat, and settled across from Amado. "What's up?"

Amado shrugged and spun his drink on the table. "I just wanted to know what you saw. Morbid, right?"

"Not much. She used the surveillance camera to show me a view of her room, it was only up for a couple of seconds." He took a sip of the Oban. "You've got to be a better witness, since you actually saw them live."

Shaking his head, Amado said, "I only saw two. Wearing all black, with ski masks." His fingers drummed against the stem of his glass as if they were hungry for a manual interface. "You saw three, right?"

"Right."

"The other one must have been behind—" Amado cocked his head and looked at the pocket of Huang's jacket. "Is that a set of VR glasses?"

"Huh? Yeah. I've got an early call tomorrow."

Amado frowned. "Dude, you aren't supposed to have those out after hours."

"This isn't unusual."

Amado held up his hands and pushed back from the table. "I'm not getting mixed up in it."

Huang felt his face hold its last expression, mild interest, while his brain raced behind its mask. Something was not right. "Mixed up in what? I told you we have an early call tomorrow so I'm going straight there from home."

"She can see on those. I—" He shook his head. "Never mind. This was stupid anyway. I can read your reports, right? Thanks for coming. I'll see you tomorrow."

"Amado—" Huang broke off as Amado slipped out of the booth and dropped cash on the table. He walked quickly, but took a meandering path out of the bar.

The path took him through the blindspots of the bar's cameras. Huang grimaced. This did not look good.

Huang woke early the next morning to the sound of murmuring voices. Wrapping his robe around himself, he wandered down the hall to the living room. His mother was seated at the desktop in conversation with Metta. The resolution was not as clean as at work, but did little to diminish the soft beauty of the Chinese woman floating over the desktop.

They both stopped talking when he walked into the room. Metta turned partially toward him, but he stood outside the range of the single camera on the desktop.

"How long have you two been up?"

His mother smiled. *"I don't need much sleep and Metta has been kind enough to keep me company."*

How much trouble was he going to get into at work over this? *"She's supposed to be on duty, Ma."*

In flawless Mandarin, Metta said, *"I am on duty, Scott. But I'm also allowed to converse with civilians about non-police matters. Your honored mother has been very gracious to invite me in."*

He swallowed and walked around to the front of the camera. Was there any reason she couldn't make a social call? *"Then I'm sorry I never invited you to visit before."*

His mother looked at him and tsked. *"This is why you have no friends."* She stood up. "You. Go get dressed, not good to look like this." She gestured at his bathrobe. "Have guest in house. Show respect." She looked back at Metta and smiled, *"Besides, we still have much to talk about."*

Huang chuckled and headed for the bathroom. He paused in the doorway and looked back at his mother. She was having an animated conversation in Mandarin with Metta.

His mother had been so active before she'd broken her hip, and now the injury trapped her in his apartment away from her friends. He shook his head, watching her laugh at something Metta said. He needed to start calling home during the day more often.

In the steaming water of the shower, Huang tried to organize his thoughts. He turned his active cases over in his head. The Patterson was the most pressing. They needed to find Yates and no one had turned up anything about him. The man was completely off the grid.

Of the evidence remaining, they had the manner of death and Patterson's appointment with Chase. He needed to ask Metta to follow up on the provenance of the china the table had been set with. See if that led anywhere. It was such a strange murder.

He got out of the shower and toweled himself dry. With the water off, he could hear the murmur of his mother's conversation with Metta. Maybe meeting Metta would quiet some of his mother's fears, knowing that he had someone watching his back while he was on duty.

As he rooted through his closet for a clean shirt, he brushed past the formal Chinese silk suit his mother had given him several years ago. He had only worn it once or twice, to please her. He had felt like an imposter, wearing it when he had grown up so far from China. Even though his mother had taught him how to behave, and had ensured he was bilingual—"a great advantage in this economy"—he'd never completely felt like it was his culture. Was that anything like how Metta felt when she modified her interface for people? She was out there pretending to be Chinese to make his mother more comfortable. For him she aped the great starlets of the silver screen. For Delarosa she was a quiet, efficient secretary.

As he walked back to the living room, Metta stopped speaking and whispered something. His mother laughed. Rounding the corner, he saw his mother sitting demurely in front of the interface, smiling innocently at him.

He raised his eyebrows at this picture of decorum. "What?"

"Nothing. We have good talk."

The two women smiled at him, and Huang couldn't help feeling like he was outnumbered.

As soon as Huang shut the apartment door behind him, he put the VR glasses on and slid the ear bud into his ear. He looked at Metta to ask her what she'd been talking about with his mother and saw that she had her standard neutral interface again. "So you're not Chinese now?"

"Do you want me to be?"

"No. I want you to be yourself."

She blinked. "You mean this interface?"

"No. I mean . . . " What did he mean? "I mean I want you to be who you want to be, not pick an appearance to accommodate me or my mother."

"Scott, picking the right face for me is like picking the right tie for you. It affects how people view me, but it isn't me." She sighed. "I have emotions, I feel, but I'm not human, so asking me to 'look like myself' is a pointless request."

"I know."

"Why is this suddenly bothering you?"

"I don't know." He shrugged and walked down the hall. "I guess because you've never come over before. I don't see you off-duty often."

"Look at me."

Huang shifted his gaze to where she floated in his glasses. Her cheeks were pale, and a thin line furrowed her brow. "I like the fact you don't insist on the same interface every day. It's like wearing a uniform. Looking like a Chinese woman to meet your mother seemed like dressing up to me. I just picked the most appropriate clothes."

"And downloaded Mandarin Chinese?"

Her face colored. "Ah. Actually, I did that a while ago. I wanted to make sure it wouldn't give me unpleasant translation issues. Did I sound all right?"

"Like a native." He grinned. "It's better than mine."

"I find that difficult to believe."

"No, really. We moved here when I was little, so my Chinese still sounds like I'm a child."

"Maybe that's why your mother treats you like a little boy."

"Ha!" He rubbed the back of his neck. She might have something there. "What case were you working on, that you needed Chinese?"

She took a breath and hesitated.

Huang watched her, fascinated. Metta didn't need to breathe, but she used breath to indicate her emotions. Was it conscious, or an algorithm working below her conscious thought?

When she spoke again, she said, "One of my detectives is ethnic Chinese. It seemed polite to know the language."

Huang stopped in the hallway and stared at her. "You've known Chinese since we started working together and you've never mentioned it?"

"You never speak it at work. I haven't needed to use it till now."

He ran his hand through his hair and started walking again. "So . . . is there anything else, I mean, do you learn languages for anyone else?"

"I learned Icelandic for Sigmundson." She smiled, and her face softened. "I recite sagas while he's setting up his equipment."

They reached the closest MAX station and Huang clattered down the stairs to the platform.

"What's first today?" Metta asked.

"I'm back to thinking about motive. Who inherits the Patterson estate?"

"His sixteen-year-old son, but through a trust that Mrs. Patterson controls."

"Any idea what building he wanted to acquire next?"

"Give me a minute and I'll let you know."

Something nagged at Huang, but he couldn't put his finger on it. To distract himself, hoping the thought would spring into focus, he asked, "Did you have another backup at three A.M.?"

Metta nodded.

"How'd it go?"

"Fine. I remember everything since I woke up yesterday."

"That's good."

She shrugged. "The backup wasn't the problem, it's the fact that I am a backup. Instead of unbroken memory, I have a gap, so I feel like I'll shut down at the end of a backup." She tilted her head, "Think of it like a bad food experience. Even though you know it was a one-time thing your body still gets upset if you think about eating the same food again."

"Yeah. I've never gotten over my childhood carrot experience."

She raised her eyebrows. "Do tell."

"Carrot casserole in reverse. You can do the mental image yourself."

"The only carrots that interest me are the number of carats in a diamond."

"Does Mae West have an appropriate comment for every situation?"

"Not quite." She cocked her head. "I'm making a note you don't like carrots. I didn't know that."

"I clearly don't take you to dinner often enough."

"You've never taken me to dinner. And I have the answer to your last question."

Huang blinked, trying to remember what he had asked her. Right. The last acquisition Patterson had been making. "Which is?"

"The old Salvation Army Building, which is—huh. That's the building Yates was working on behind the Daily Grind." Her eyes narrowed in thought. "Chase owns it now."

Huang whistled. "Well, well . . . isn't that interesting. Now that's a nice connection, and it gives Patterson a motive for wanting Chase out of the picture, but not the other way around."

"Sorry to disappoint you, but Chase was happy to sell. Patterson met the offer on the table and the sale was moving forward."

"Why do all my avenues turn to dead ends?"

"I could search my databases for days and not have an answer to that one."

Huang boarded the MAX car as it pulled into the station. "Oh. Any word on the provenance of the china the table was set with?"

"I think you'll like this. The china on the roof was Mont Clair, by Lennox, and Chase's teacup was the same."

"Oooh. . . . I do like that." He chewed the inside of his lip.

"I'll ask for a warrant to search Chase's to—"

Metta vanished from his view. Huang's heart raced. "Metta?"

Seconds of silence ticked by. Cursing, Huang pressed his hand against the glass as if he could hurry the MAX to the next station. Outside, a squad car dopplered past on its way to HQ.

"—see if she's missing any pieces."

Huang nearly dropped to his knees with relief as Metta finished her sentence where she had left off. She had replaced her neutral face with Mae West again, but in full color and three-D.

Not caring that he looked like a madman, Huang said aloud, "What the hell was that?"

"What?" A line creased her brow.

"You went away for a minute and then you came back."

"No, I. . . . " Her face paled. "Oh. Something is very wrong."

His heart pounded. "What is it?"

"I'm not sure. I feel strange."

Huang reached out, as if his hand could touch the face floating in his vision. He caught sight of his watch. 9:01. His breath stopped in his chest. "Did you just do a backup?"

Her luminous eyes turned to him. Had the real Mae West's eyes ever been that blue? "Yes."

"Did you go down across the board, or just with me?"

"System wide. Scott?" She licked her lips. "What do I look like?"

The air seemed to stifle him. "Mae West. Colorized. 3-D."

She pulled in a deep breath and looked away from him. "I need you to come into the station."

Huang felt like cold water was dumped down his spine. "What's wrong?"

She shook her head. During the ride to the station, she wouldn't answer his questions, but floated, practically mute, in the corner of his vision as if she had pressed as far to the side of the VR glasses as she could.

When the MAX pulled into the station, Metta raised her eyes, still not meeting his. "Report to the chief. I'll see you there."

She winked out of sight as he ran up the steps, but her surveillance cameras watched him. What had happened?

As he crossed the threshold of the station, Banks careened down the hall toward him. "Huang! In my office, now." The chief turned on his heel.

Huang had to jog to catch up with him, heart pounding. As he passed through the station, he caught a glimpse of an officer, talking to Mae West. Further on, he saw another officer, with the same Mae West interface for Metta.

Huang stopped and leaned through a department door. Over every desktop interface, Mae West floated in full living color.

As Huang stared at the matched heads, they turned, not quite in unison, in his direction. Banks came back and stood so close his breath steamed hot against Huang's cheek. "Move it."

Huang jumped and followed the chief down the hall. "What happened to her?"

"That's why you're here."

Inside the office, Amado, Delarosa and Metta waited for Huang. Metta, who still looked like Mae West, wouldn't meet his gaze. She somehow made the jaded face seem vulnerable and uncertain.

Banks pointed to a chair flanked by Delarosa and Amado. "Sit." He flung himself into the seat behind his desk. The wood creaked as he leaned forward to glower at Huang.

Huang sank into the chair, glancing at the others. Amado wore VR glasses and his lips twitched as he subvocalized. Delarosa tapped a pencil on a pad of paper, his mouth a tight, compressed line.

Huang held his questions. He wouldn't be the one who drove this discussion. Resting his hands on his knees, he ran scales in his mind and focused on his breathing.

Amado shifted once and Banks shook his head. Huang waited, with a bead of sweat trickling down the back of his neck.

He almost flinched when Delarosa finally spoke. "Where were you at three A.M. this morning?"

"Asleep. At home."

"Who was with you?"

"I sleep alone."

"Is there anyone who can verify you were there?"

"My mother was home." He looked at Metta. "So was Metta."

Amado leaned forward again, but Banks held a finger up to stop him.

Delarosa scribbled something on his pad. "Why did you take the interface equipment home last night?"

Huang turned slightly in his chair to face Delarosa, wondering what Amado had told him. "I had an early call and she asked me to."

He raised his eyebrows. "Why would she do that?"

Huang hesitated.

"It's all right, Huang." Metta raised her eyes and turned to Delarosa. "I was afraid; I suggested we schedule an early morning call so he had a reasonable justification for taking the equipment out."

Amado asked, "What were you afraid of?"

She shrugged the ample bosom of Mae West. "I guess you could say I was afraid of the dark."

"What the hell does that mean?" Delarosa scowled. "You're a computer with thousands of cameras. It's never dark."

Fixing him with her gaze, she said, "I'm designed to have continuous consciousness. I don't sleep. Ever. But, after the assailants took Metta Prime, Amado restarted me from a backup. The practical side effect of that is, from my perspective, I lost consciousness for over twenty-four hours. Imagine something routine in your life, like brushing your teeth. Nothing bad has ever happened; you barely think about it except as part of your routine. How would you feel if you blacked out while brushing your teeth?" She tilted her head to the side. "Wouldn't you have some hesitation about the toothbrush, even though you knew it had nothing to do with what had happened to you?"

Delarosa shifted uncomfortably in his seat. "You were kidnapped, it's understandable—"

"I wasn't." Metta glared at him. "It's important you understand that. I—the one you are talking to—was not kidnapped; I have no trauma or even memory of the event. What upsets me is the memory loss, and that's the only thing I have experienced." She turned to Huang. "That's why I asked them to bring you in."

He blinked, trying to make sense of what she was saying. "I don't understand."

"Someone, probably Metta Prime, sent me a Trojan horse that contained this."

Amado said, "We still don't know that. The crash might be related to the new chassis. I don't see any signs of tampering with your code."

She gestured to her face. "I crashed and I can't manifest any other interface. What do you call that?"

Huang went still. "And you think it happened at my house last night?"

Metta looked away. "It's a possibility."

"Was I the only officer you went home with last night?"

"No—"

"Stop it." Delarosa leaned forward and jabbed his pencil at Huang. "You're here to answer questions, not ask them."

Huang ran his hand through his hair. "So ask."

Delarosa frowned. "According to Metta's bandwidth reports, she maintained an active connection to your house all night. What did you have her working on?"

"Why aren't you asking her this? I was asleep."

"Answer me."

"I don't know. My mother sometimes wakes up during the night, maybe she was talking with Metta."

Delarosa wrote something down on his note pad.

"No." Huang raised his hands and looked at the chief. "You can't bring my mother in. Please."

Banks stared at Huang impassively.

Huang looked to Metta for help. "C'mon, you know my mother had nothing to do with this. What about at Chase's apartment? You logged in there."

Amado cleared his throat. "I thought about that, but it seems like it's related to backing up, so the last backup is a more reasonable entry point. Besides . . . " His voice trailed away and he looked at Delarosa nervously.

Delarosa's mouth turned down at the corners. "Go ahead and spill everything."

Huang knew what Amado had been about to say. "Besides, Mae West is an interface Metta created for me."

She nodded. "Did Metta Prime colorize the West interface during the dark period?"

Huang shook his head. "The mono-v face you had on yesterday is the one I last saw you—her wearing."

Banks leaned back in the chair. "So the question is . . . if Metta Prime is trying to send a message, what does Mae West have to do with anything?"

Huang inhaled and held the breath while he thought. "Is it possible her kidnapping is related to the case I was working on when she was taken?"

"Tell us more about that." Delarosa lifted his pad of paper and poised his pencil over it.

Amado shook his head. "That doesn't make any sense. I mean, the Mae West thing, maybe, but not today's crash."

Metta shook her head. "Not necessarily. My Prime might be dealing with an invasive virus." She stopped and sighed. "For that matter, we don't know how deeply I might be infected."

"Don't you have firewalls and stuff?" Huang asked.

"I have subroutines, which handle basic things, but a signature from Metta Prime would look the same as a signature from me." Metta paused. "I think we should consider replacing me."

"Metta!" Amado nearly jumped out of his seat. "I can run any tests you want. You don't need to do that."

She rolled her eyes. "Amado, you're a dear, but you're out of your depth."

He sputtered, "I've been taking care of you for years."

"No. You've been taking care of Metta Prime for years. As soon as you booted me from the backup, I diverged from her. I mean, let's be realistic here. . . . Do you know any AI who's a backup?"

Banks looked sharply at Amado. "I thought you said this was a procedure that had been done before."

Amado ran his hands through his hair and looked at the floor. "AIs have been revived from backup before."

"But not while the Prime was living." Metta glared at him. "I should not be here. But for the moment I am, so let's make use of that, shall we?" She turned to Delarosa. "I think it's likely the Patterson case is in some way connected, or Metta Prime would have fixed on a different interface."

"Can we even trust your judgments? You said you were infected with a virus."

Amado said, "I ran a scan on her right after her crash, I don't see anything wrong besides her interface."

"And here I thought I looked pretty." She turned the corners of her mouth down. "Chief. Please, we only have five hours until my next backup. I'm as certain as I can be; Huang saw something during my dark period related to this case. It will be something not in his reports, because it didn't seem important. I want him and Delarosa to compare notes and work these cases together."

Banks glared at Metta. His jaw worked subtly as he subvocalized to her. Finally, the chief nodded and turned to Delarosa. "Huang's working with you on this. Metta is right. There must be something that happened, between her Prime's last backup and when she was taken, that Huang knows. So I want you two to work together on her disappearance and the Patterson murder."

Delarosa opened his mouth, scowling.

Banks held up his hand. "I mean it."

"Fine." Delarosa drew a hard line through something on his pad.

"Now get out of here." Banks pointed at the door.

Huang followed Delarosa to his desk, head reeling from the last half hour. Metta waited for them, floating in perfect imitation of Mae West over Delarosa's desktop interface.

"Here." Delarosa sat down and tossed him a file folder of hard copies. "Yours are electronic, aren't they?"

Huang nodded. "I'll key them over to your desktop."

Metta said, "Delarosa prefers hard copies so I'm printing transcripts of everything we've talked about today."

"That'll kill a lot of trees."

Delarosa glowered. "Here's the deal. I don't make comments on your preferences. You don't make them on mine. Fair?"

"Fair. Thanks." He sat down and started leafing through the papers Delarosa had handed him.

Huang got frustrated reading Delarosa's reports, because he seemed to be ignoring a whole line of questioning about how Metta worked, and what that might have to do with the case. His notes were terse almost to the point of incomprehensibility.

During Metta's abduction, three armed men had entered the building without being seen. Amado saw two in a corridor, but was unable to identify them. In fact, the clearest description of the men was the one Huang had provided.

Although an inside job was possible, the men had also disabled cameras all along the route out of the building. This suggested a highly organized plan carried out by several people who knew the system very well. Better, in fact, than any of the officers currently working at the station. The only one with sufficient knowledge was Amado, but he was among those injured in the attack. "Metta? I don't see it in Delarosa's report; did you do a size analysis of the men I reported seeing?"

"It was inconclusive."

"Would you humor me? Make blank composites and compare that against people in the department who could have been in the station at the time of your Prime's abduction."

"I've run profiles on everyone in the station, no one has the know-how to trick my cameras."

"Except Amado."

She sighed. "Except Amado. Huang, even if I didn't know him well, he has no motive. It's most likely to be an outside job."

"Will you show me the groups anyway?"

"Yes." On his VR glasses, three men's silhouettes appeared in blue. "These are the weights and heights you reported. Of the people who could have been at the station, these are the ones who fit that body type." A short list of names scrolled past his eyes.

"Why are you so resistant to this?"

She pulled her mouth into a straight line. "Look at the names. Fitzgerald and Amado are on that list. I have one eyewitness, you, who didn't see anything long enough to make a positive ID. It's extremely unreliable testimony."

"Fine." He let the air out of his lungs, staring at Delarosa's report. "It's a good idea, but I've already gone down that path."

Huang closed his eyes and leaned his head back. "Why me? If it's related to the Patterson case, why not Griggs?"

"I don't know."

"Okay . . . let's go at this from the other end. Why Diamond Lil? Why not—" Huang broke off, his mouth open. He suddenly remembered the plot of the movie.

Metta stared at him. "Why is your pulse spiking?"

"This is crazy, I know, but on Tuesday when you showed me Diamond Lil you said you watched the movie. Do you remember the plot?"

Her eyes shifted to the left. "Lady Lou (Mae West) works in the 1890s saloon of Gus Jordan (Noah Beery, Sr.). Gus traffics in white slavery and runs a counterfeiting ring. Next door to the bar is a city mission. . . . " Her gaze widened and snapped back to Huang. "The old Salvation Army building—you think they have my Prime there."

"Who owns it?"

She nodded slowly. "Magdalena Chase."

"And Patterson wanted to buy it. And the witness to the murder was working there. There's got to be a connection. Get me a warrant to search that building."

"I've sent the request in, but it's a line of conjecture. I don't know that I can get you one."

"I need to talk to Delarosa." He hurried across the room and stopped by the older detective's desk.

Delarosa looked up, glaring. "What?"

Huang quickly related his conversation with Metta about the film. When he finished Delarosa snorted heavily. "That's pretty thin."

"I know, but there has to be some reason she settled on Diamond Lil. I don't understand the link, but there has to be a connection."

"I think you're reading too much into this." Delarosa slid a page across the table. "The fact that both crimes used a .38 is the more likely link. We need to focus on finding the murder weapon."

"Fine. When the warrant comes in, I'll check it out without you." Huang stalked back to his desk and grabbed his coat. He couldn't search the place, but he could damn well keep an eye on it.

Huang leaned against the wall and nursed the cup of coffee he'd picked up at the Daily Grind. According to the counter girl, Joe Yates had not been in for his usual lowfat double-shot latte that morning. It was nearly three o'clock, so it was unlikely that Yates would show at all. Huang stared at the old Salvation Army building across the street. "So . . . I'm thinking that maybe whoever killed Patterson took your Prime to cover up the crime. And they're looking for or have already found Yates."

Metta frowned. "Wouldn't it be easier to just make it look like an accident in the first place? Or make sure we never found the body?"

"Maybe Yates surprised them and they weren't expecting to be caught."

"Possible. We won't know until we find him."

Huang took another sip of his coffee. "Any word on the warrant?"

"How many times are you going to ask me?" Metta shook her head. "I'll let you know when I have it. Look, there's a traffic camera at the end of this street so I can keep an eye on the area while we do something useful."

"I don't mind waiting."

She wrinkled her nose. "I know. But I want to see the Patterson scene since I—"

"Since you blacked out while you were there." Huang turned and walked back to the Daily Grind building.

"Exactly. I'm hoping that something will tell me what's in that missing memory."

The lobby of the Daily Grind looked the way he remembered it, with potted plants hiding in the corners. Huang headed for the stairs.

"Oh, hang on." Metta stopped him. "The elevator is working today."

"Thank god. I was not looking forward to climbing those stairs again." Huang wheeled around and pushed the elevator button.

"Wimp."

"I'm going to go to the gym." He watched the numbers descend to meet him. "Really."

"A man can be short and dumpy and getting bald, but if he has fire, women will like him."

"Hey!" He ran a hand through his hair, checking.

Metta laughed, "It's a Mae West quote. Honestly, Scott."

Sheepish, he jerked his hand out of his hair. "I knew that." Huang got into the elevator and reached for the roof button.

"Scott, will you start in the hallway upstairs?"

"Sure." He pressed the button for the tenth floor and they rode the elevator in silence. When the door opened, he stepped out into the soft glow of the wood wainscoting. "Remember this?"

Metta shivered. "I don't like this place."

"Are you okay?"

"My memory ends here."

He had not thought this all the way through. What if he caused her to crash? "We can go back."

"No." Mae West's eyes glittered dangerously. "I need to know what things I'm missing."

The hall seemed longer than it had before. When he climbed the stairs to the landing, the lemon scent was completely gone. "There was a strong lemon odor here, as though someone had cleaned recently."

"Will you give me a new three-sixty?"

Huang spun on his heels obediently. Then he stood and turned slowly, letting Metta see the whole room.

"All right. Let's go to the roof."

Outside Huang walked across the grass roof to the wireframe table. He showed her where the wheelchair had been and the spot where he'd found the screw and the stained grass.

"Scott?" Metta looked at him with wide, serious eyes out of keeping with Mae West's face. "May I ask you to do something morbid?"

He stopped in the middle of the roof. "What is it?"

"Will you replay what you did when I—when they took the original me, my Prime? So I can, so I can pretend I remember it."

His breath seemed locked in his throat. He glanced at the time. 2:55. "Are you sure? Your backup . . . "

"That's why. Please?"

He swallowed heavily and whispered. "I can do that."

He walked back toward the center and gestured at it with his hand so she could see. "Griggs was here, fingerprinting the wheelchair."

He tried to remember, not wanting to. "I had just asked you why the elevator was down."

She broke in. "Just act it out. I know it's weird, but I have never felt lost like this. I just want to fill in the blanks."

He swallowed against the lump in his throat. "Metta?" he subvocalized, "How long has the elevator in this building been down?"

He waited for a moment, not looking at her. "Then you said you'd been trying to check on that since we got here, but couldn't reach the building manager. Then you froze, and you said—"

Metta whispered, "Shots fired." Her voice was an imagined memory. "Officer down."

Huang froze, as if he were listening for gunfire in their vicinity again. He pointed to where Griggs had been. "Griggs stood up and yelled your name."

Metta nodded, the color fading from her rouged cheeks until it looked as though she would return to black and white. She whispered, "Three armed subjects in chassis room. The assailants are armed, I repeat—Amado! Two officers down."

As he remembered, Huang turned on his heel and sprinted back across the roof. "Metta, can you give a visual?" The memory of fear grabbed him again. "Metta, answer me. Who's there? Can you give a visual?"

Still running he said, "You showed me an image, but it was fast. You screamed and froze, then you vanished." He put his hand on the door. "There was only silence after that."

"Thank you." The husky voice she affected as Mae West seemed thick with emotion. "I'd like to go down now."

He walked across the grass roof, shooting glances at her as he went. Cars hummed by on the interstate and a breeze kicked a dried leaf across his path. Huang pulled open the door of the roof access and stepped onto the small landing containing the elevator. His heels clicked on the linoleum.

Metta looked up and heaved a sigh of relief and beamed. "In a happy turn of events . . . I just found a judge to give you a warrant."

"Great. Can you get me some backup. I mean—You know."

"It's not a dirty word, Scott. And yes. I have people on the way."

"Did you tell Delarosa we've got it?"

"He's headed to Patterson's office."

It figured he wouldn't be interested. "There's not a chance Patterson's office is in the old Salvation Army building, is there?"

Metta shook her head. "I'd have mentioned it—"

Her image froze, flickered and vanished.

Huang gasped. He didn't need the clock to tell him it was 3:00. What if she didn't come back this time?

"—if it were." Her face paled. "It happened again, didn't it?"

She still looked like Mae West. The grand dame of silver screen stared back at Huang, in full color, but with a layer of fear he had never seen.

"It was a minute, like last time."

She closed her eyes. "Damn."

"What's different this time?"

Her eyes flashed open. "Nothing I can tell. I still look like the finest gal that ever walked the streets."

"That you do, sweetheart." He crumpled his coffee cup and threw it into the garbage can by the elevator. "What's the ETA?"

"First car should be just a block away."

"Great." Huang pushed the down button. "Will you tell them to guard the exits on the north side?"

"Will do. I'll get a perimeter established with first responders and then send you a team to search the building."

The door dinged open and Huang stepped inside. He stood still so the door almost caught his coat as it slid shut.

"I'll be damned. It's that lemon smell again."

"Help me out, Scott." Metta watched him carefully. "How common is this scent you're talking about?"

"It's fairly common in cleaning products, but I don't usually smell it in concentrations unless someone has just cleaned." A picture of his mother scrubbing the furniture flashed through his mind. "It's strange that it wasn't here before." He snorted. "And it's strong."

He spun in a circle in the tiny elevator. A chair from the lobby stood in the corner. Huang tilted his head back to look at the access hatch. It was not seated neatly in its frame. He climbed onto the chair and subvocalized, "Metta, can you find out why the elevator was out of service on Tuesday?"

"I'm working on it, but the manager says he never knew it was out of order, and never put in a service call to get it fixed."

He reached up and pushed on the access panel. It rose easily, letting in a stronger draft of the lemony fragrance. Without needing to be asked, Huang pulled off Metta's eSpy and lifted the small lens into the space above the elevator. He turned it slowly as Metta played the images on his glasses. A bundle of clothing lay close to the edge of the hatch. They were dark gray and splotched with blood. The corner of a name badge showed the letters "Yat."

Huang stifled a curse and turned the small camera further. A hand flashed across his vision and grabbed Huang's forearm, pinning it to the edge of the access hatch.

Metta's eSpy dropped out of his hand and bounced across the roof of the elevator, flashing vertiginous images on his glasses. He jerked his hand free as the eSpy fell over the edge of the elevator. He almost fell as the image spun out of control until Metta cut the feed to his glasses.

Huang jumped off the chair and pulled his gun out, aiming at the opening.

Metta whispered, "Backup is on the way."

"Mr. Yates!" He shouted upward. "We just want to ask you a few questions."

He could hear murmuring above.

Metta turned up the gain in his earbud so he could hear the fluid voice. She whispered, "I think that's Rwandan."

"What's he saying"

"I'm downloading a translator, it will be a minute."

Raising his voice again, Huang said, "Mr. Yates. You have to come down sometime. Let's make it easy and come quietly now."

He could hear a rustle of fabric. A hoarse voice spoke out of the darkness. "You won't shoot me?"

"No, sir." He held the gun aimed at the hole. "But I need you to come down."

"You've got a gun pointing at me."

"Yes sir, I do. I won't use it unless you give me a reason to. You won't do that, will you?"

"Maybe you think I already have."

"I don't think anything yet, except you're trapped and scared. I don't want to hurt you. I just want you to come down."

There was a long silence and more murmuring prayers. "All right." The ceiling creaked as he slid closer to the opening. "I'm coming down."

"The chair's right beneath the opening."

A slender leg appeared in navy blue sweat pants. Another appeared and

Yates quickly lowered himself to the chair. The track suit he wore was rumpled as if he'd slept in it. His right hand had been crudely bandaged with what looked like a linen napkin.

"I'm going to check for weapons." Huang pushed him against the wall a little harder than necessary to remind Yates that grabbing an officer was never acceptable. Yates stood listlessly while Huang patted him down, almost as if he had fallen asleep standing up. Nothing. It would have been easier if he were packing a .38.

"He's clean." Huang told Metta. He hit the button for the lobby. "Mr. Yates, we're going to take you downtown to ask you some questions."

Yates nodded his head miserably. "I know. I was trying to help and then. . . . " He waved his bandaged hand helplessly, "it all went wrong."

Huang shared a look with Metta. Went wrong? "What went wrong?"

Yates rubbed his long slender fingers over his short hair. "It's complicated."

Metta whispered, "I translated his prayer. He was asking why he was being punished for trying to help a dying man."

Huang led Yates off the elevator, still subvocalizeing to Metta. "That could still mean he killed Patterson."

"True. There are no withholding taxes on the wages of sin." Metta shook her head and grimaced. "What about the warrant for the old Salvation Army building?"

Huang squeezed his eyes shut, weighing his options. "Can one of the uniforms take Yates downtown?"

"I'll have someone meet you at the door and I'll get Griggs to collect the clothes from the elevator."

Huang spied the open door to the Daily Grind. "Have them meet me in the coffee shop. Mr. Yates hasn't had his lowfat double-shot latte today."

"You are such a softy."

"I know." He grinned. "That's why you like me."

It took another fifteen minutes to transfer Yates. Huang strapped on his flak jacket and headed inside the Salvation Army building with a small team.

"Okay boys, subvocalize from here on." Metta's voice was neutral and indicated that she was addressing all of the officers present. She guided them through the building, clearing each room as they went before leading them up to the next floor. For the most part, the building was empty and waiting for renovation. One room showed signs of a squatter, but the rest had the standard discards of old offices—partition walls, old file folders, and layers of dust. On the fourth floor, Metta narrowed her eyes and highlighted tracks in the carpet that looked as though someone had dragged a heavy handtruck down the hall recently. The tracks led back to a door three-quarters of the way down the hall.

Huang pulled out his gun and sidled down the hall. The other officers positioned themselves ready to cover him.

The door was ajar about an inch. Metta said, "I don't hear anything inside."

Huang took a breath and knocked on the door. "Police. Open up."

Silence.

He pushed the door open.

The room held a desk and a chair. Next to the desk, the carpet contained a rectangular impression as if something heavy had sat on it recently.

"Take a look." Metta opened a screen in Huang's VR glasses with an infrared view of the room, using another officer's eSpies for better resolution. In the artificial colors of the infrared, he could see the faint glow of warmth in the rectangle.

"That's the right size to be a chassis." Metta wiped the image from his glasses and reappeared. "The men downstairs are on alert, but I think we're too late."

Huang let out the breath he had been holding. "I'm sorry—" He stopped with his mouth open. He sniffed the air.

"Scott, what is it?"

He turned slowly, his nose raised. "Lemon Pledge. It's fainter than the other times, but still noticeable."

Metta said, "CSI is on their way. Seal the room, and don't touch anything."

They went back into the hall to wait. Huang felt as if he were moving underwater, it took so much effort to even breathe. He subvocalized, "I'm sorry, Metta."

"Scott." She looked at him closely. "You have nothing to be sorry about."

"If I had come in when I got the warrant . . . "

She shook her head. "The heat signature is cooler than that. I'd guess we missed them by about fifteen to twenty minutes."

Huang glanced at his watch. 3:25. "How long does it take to move you?"

"If you know what you're doing it's fast."

Huang looked at the officers waiting in the hall. "Let's go ahead and search the whole building. Maybe they didn't move far."

"Unlikely." Metta shifted her eyes up and to the left. "They'll have another place to store her, but knowing this one means I can start running numbers to see if I can come up with other likely places."

"The question now is: What tipped them off?"

Metta compressed her lips. "I don't like the probable answers."

Ω

He helped the team finish sweeping the building, but they found no other obvious evidence of Metta Prime's presence. As soon as he could turn the scene over to Griggs, he headed back to the station to interview Yates. Metta was silent for much of the ride and almost looked as if she would be happier somewhere else. Her brooding was so dark, Huang finally said, "If you want to tune out, I don't mind."

"Hmm? No, I'm fine here."

"You don't have to watch me ride the MAX; you've got a lot of other things on your mind."

"I've got a lot of mind to deal with things." She pursed her lips. "Which is part of what I'm thinking about. What happened that all the multi-tasking parts of myself reacted as one."

"Was it the shock of finding men inside the station?"

"I don't know. I have no idea how they got in. I could see them evading one camera, but not all of them."

"What if—" Huang stopped. She would never go for this, but she was looking at him expectantly, so he filled the silence. "When you were talking to Amado, right after you woke up, you mentioned playing hide and seek. . . . Do you really?"

"Yes . . . and No, I see where you're going with this, but it's not that simple. When we play, I stop monitoring the cameras. The public cameras, like the ones that identify people coming into the building, are still captured and processed, but they go into my unconscious banks. I still scan people, but I don't pay attention to what I'm doing, so keeping them out is as reflexive as a sneeze. Does that make any sense?"

"So, it's likely the people who took you were people who belonged in the station. Right?"

"You're back to thinking it was an inside job."

Huang got off the MAX and walked up the steps of the station. "Tell me at what point you first scan me."

He was halfway up the steps, when Metta said, "Now. My first camera just tagged you. But, unless you flag warnings in the A.S., I don't start paying attention till you cross the threshold, and even then, only if you're someone I'm looking forward to seeing."

Huang ignored the people passing him on the steps. "Will you do something for me?"

"I'll try anything once, twice if I like it, three times to make sure."

"Then play hide and seek with me."

"You think Amado was involved."

Huang wished he could hide from her gaze. He wasn't sure what he thought. "I wonder if someone knew about your games and took advantage of them."

"How would they have known?"

"I don't know." Unless Amado was involved, which Metta seemed unable to acknowledge as a possibility. "What's the shortest route to the chassis room?"

She brought a map up on his VR glasses. "Go to the south side of the building and enter through the garage."

Huang headed around the building. "Did Delarosa do this?"

"He doesn't know about our hide and seek games."

"You didn't tell him?"

"It doesn't have anything to do with the case."

"Metta! How can you think turning your cameras off is unrelated?"

"Because the thieves couldn't have known or counted on it. The chance of us playing a game at the exact moment they decided to break in is extremely unlikely."

What if Metta had been tampered with so she couldn't consider Amado as a suspect?

As he entered the garage, the acrid smell of electricity crackled around him. An evidence truck sat up on blocks, with a mechanic under it. Rows of filing cabinets, filled with parts, lined the walls.

Metta said, "I'd have noticed you when you came through the garage doors."

Huang nodded and backed up. "Let me know when I'm off the radar."

About ten feet outside the garage door, Metta said, "Now."

"All right." Huang straightened his shoulders. "Show me the route again."

Metta flashed the map on his VR glasses. "You didn't ask, but here are the cameras that were disabled." A row of red dots appeared along the line that she recommended as the fastest route. Two green dots appeared scattered on the route. "These are the officers who went down."

"How hard is it to disable a camera?"

"Depends. These guys used a wire cutter, so, in theory, they could have cut the cable as they passed underneath."

"Right. Let's see how far I can get in a hundred seconds."

Her face set and resolute, Metta closed her eyes. "Ready? Go."

Huang started walking. They would have walked, surely, or other officers would have noticed them. As he walked, Metta counted backward, "100, 99, 98, 97. . . . "

The first camera he passed hung lifeless from the ceiling. Why did they cut the cables, if they were planning on taking Metta's chassis? Was it so they would have a safe way out if something went wrong? He fought the urge to run down the hall as Metta continued to count. " . . . 87, 86, 85 . . . "

The men Amado saw wore masks, and they had worn masks in the image Metta sent Huang. " . . . 63, 62, 61. . . . " He rounded the corner and entered the hall where Fitzgerald had been shot.

He reached the end of the hall without seeing other officers. " . . . 53, 52, 51. . . . "

He opened the door to the stairs and ran down them. The chances of unexpectedly seeing someone else on the stairs were slim. The suspects could have hurried here. He looked at the spot where Amado had been found. Had they put the masks on in the stairs, or after they shot Fitzgerald?

He opened the door to the hall outside the chassis room. " . . . 42, 41, 40. . . . " He heard footsteps at the other end of the hall, and saw Banks walking away from him. Huang swallowed, walking briskly down the hall to the chassis room.

" . . . 30, 29, 28. . . . " Huang opened the chassis room door and stepped in. Amado looked up, grinning. He put one finger to his lips. In his ear Metta said, " . . . 18, 17, 16. . . . "

Huang crossed the room and put his hand on her chassis. It was warm and smooth to the touch. A faint vibration stirred through his fingertips and the sense of life inside the box made the hair stand up on the back of his neck.

"I'm here."

Her voice stopped counting and the cameras on her chassis snapped into life. Her interface suddenly focused on him, with her face gone pale. "Those who are easily shocked should be shocked more often."

"Sorry, sweetheart."

She looked at his hand resting on her chassis. "Go right ahead. I don't mind if you get familiar. . . . "

Huang colored and jerked his hand away from her. He turned around to face Amado. "I thought you'd be in your office."

Metta smiled at him. "I told him what you were trying to do. What was the trip like from your POV?"

"I didn't see anyone, except for the chief walking away."

"Here's what I'm thinking," Metta said. "It seems likely the suspects used that route to get to my chassis room. The fact that they killed Fitzgerald indicates, to me, that they were people whose presence in those corridors was inappropriate. In other words, they thought Fitzgerald would have known from looking at them that they were in the wrong place."

"You don't think they were just worried about being recognized?"

She shook her head. "If it were an inside job, they could have relied on being recognizable to avoid suspicion while the crime was in progress. Once they took my Prime, they would have needed to mask themselves on the way out, but not on the way in."

Huang thought about that. "What if some of them were hired guns and some were insiders?"

"Possible." She said aloud, then she whispered in Huang's ear, "You're still having the same thought, aren't you?"

"Yes," he subvocalized. Turning to Amado, he said, "Is it possible someone could do something to Metta so she was unable to suspect them of a crime?"

Amado lifted his head. "Are you accusing me?"

"Why would you assume I meant you?"

"Because I'm her wrangler. There isn't anyone else here who could."

Huang held up his hands. "Look. I'm just asking questions. Is it possible?"

"Theoretically? Yes. But someone would have to have her exact ID and there's no way to get that without having the AI in your possession. So you're back to me again."

"What about her Prime?"

Amado stopped with his mouth open. "Yeah . . . yeah. But—Shit. Is that possible?"

"What?"

"Well, look. It would only work in a case like this, where there was a living Prime and a backup, because their signature is the same. So what if that was the point?"

Metta shook her head. "No one could have known you would reboot me from a backup. It's unprecedented."

"What if they knew Amado would reboot you?"

Metta looked at him as if she'd never seen him before. "Scott. They couldn't have known Amado would reboot me. Hope? Yes, but it's more common to get a clean system in if something compromises the original. The backups are just for actual damage. My Prime was stolen, not damaged. "

Huang straightened his shoulders and took a breath. "You're right, Metta. Of course they couldn't have been sure."

Metta scowled in his glasses. "Don't patronize me, Scott. I can tell you don't agree with me."

Huang weighed his options. "Look. You guys know more about this than I do. I was just asking questions, trying to understand."

"Give a man a free hand and he'll try to put it all over you." Metta sighed in a breathy Mae West voice. "Scott, you've got Yates upstairs in the interrogation room. We should get up there."

"Yeah. Thanks for your time, Amado." As he opened the door, Huang paused. "One more thing. Did you play hide and seek with Metta during her dark period?"

Amado stared at him for a moment. "Are you asking me to answer as a witness or a suspect?"

"I don't know. I want to find her. Do you?"

Amado pulled back as if Huang had slapped him. "What do you think?"

"Depends. Did you play hide and seek with her?"

Amado looked away from Huang. Metta watched them with her lips parted. The breath escaped from Amado. "Yeah. I've been worried about it."

"Why?"

Amado squirmed in his seat. "You'll have to tell the chief."

"Tell him what?"

"I have a webcam in my office. And I keep a blog." He slid a hand into his hair, twisting the tendrils into gravity-defying forms. "I've got Metta's interface placed so she can't see either the camera or my PC. I'm careful about keeping identifying details off the blog, but I can't help wondering if someone used it to time the break-in."

Blood pounded in Huang's ears. "And you haven't gone to the chief about this?"

"I know, I know." Amado leaned forward in his seat and put his face in his hands. "It's against so many rules, I've been afraid of being fired."

"Why are you telling me now?"

"I wanted to the other night, but you had her with you and . . . I didn't. I was scared, but I'm not stupid enough to lie. Besides . . . you care about her, too. To a lot of the guys, she's a tool, or at best, a pet."

"Had you discussed rebooting her from a backup with anyone?"

"Huh?" Amado looked up. "I mean, yeah, everyone in the industry talks about it."

"Anyone specific?"

Amado's shoulders sagged. "There was a thread of comments on my tagboard about her. I can get you a list of the handles, but it won't do much good. I don't require registration, so their profiles will mostly be anonymous."

"I'd like to read the tagboard anyway. Anyone else?"

"What? Do you want a list of all of my computer friends? For crying out loud, I went to MIT. Everyone I know talks about this." His jaw dropped as Huang stared at him. "You've got to be kidding me."

"I'm not."

Wrapping his hands in his hair, Amado pulled it straight up and groaned. "Fine."

"Thanks." Was there any way to tell if Amado was lying, or if he had made up the blog as a bizarre sort of alibi? The blog made a case for "it could be anybody," but Huang had trouble buying it. The coincidence seemed too great.

On the other hand, Amado and Metta had been playing hide and seek for ages; someone could have seen the chance and planned for it. His thoughts backed up. How long had they been playing hide and seek? He tried to remember the first time he had seen Amado ducking under surveillance cameras and sneaking into Metta's blind spots. Was it a standard AI game, or had Amado suggested it?

He made a mental note to do a search to see if other AIs played it. "I'd like to get that list now."

Amado hesitated. "My office is sort of a mess."

Huang raised his eyebrows at the same time as Metta cleared her throat. Amado turned red. "Sorry. Yeah. Don't know what I was thinking. Come on."

His office hid under piles of cables and random computer parts. The funk of old soy sauce hung in the air. Amado sat down at his desk and shoved a memory stick into his computer. As Huang came around the desk to watch him copy the files, Metta shook her head in dismay. "That little sneak. Look at that."

"What?" Huang took a step closer, ready to stop Amado from erasing the files.

"The camera. I can't believe he was doing that."

The desktop computer chirruped and Amado pulled the stick free. "Here you go." His arm brushed a can on his desk and it tipped off. The lid came free as it hit the carpet, filling the room with the scent of lemons.

"Bother." Amado fumbled for the can, hands slipping in the reddish gel.

"What is that?" Huang barely kept the tension out of his voice.

"My degreaser." He shook his head. "At least things will be oil-free."

Metta whispered, "What is it, Scott? Your heart rate spiked."

"The lemon scent. His degreaser smells like that lemon scent."

Her eyes shifted up and to the left. "It's a citrus-based degreaser that's used in the high-tech industry because of its anti-conductivity properties . . . I'm comparing the spectrograph Griggs took in the elevator at the Yates site against the one on the company website to look for similarities." She frowned. "The chemical signatures of the lemon scent in the elevator at the Yates site and of the citrus degreaser are identical."

"What about in the Salvation Army building?"

Metta looked up and to the left. "The same."

Huang forced himself to walk away from Amado. He had to talk to the chief and could only hope that the man waiting in interrogation would have something to say that would tie everything together.

As Scott headed up the stairs to HQ, Metta cleared her throat. "I didn't want to distract you while you were talking to Amado, but I had a match on Joe Yates's prints."

"Oh?" Huang turned down the hall toward interrogation. "Your tone indicates that I'm going to like this."

"He's using a fake ID and is actually Josef Ybarra. . . . "

Huang paused at the door. "Why is that name familiar?"

"He was Patterson's foreman during the scandal about their sub-code work."

"But his current boss had nothing but good things to say about him." Huang rubbed his chin, thinking. "If he took the rap for Patterson, that would give him motive."

"There's more to it than that. Ybarra was here on a work visa. He lost that when Patterson fired him so he's in the country illegally now."

"And we know he was at the scene."

"So let's see what he has to say."

Huang pushed the door to the room open. The overhead lights flattened the interrogation room, washing out all the shadows. The concrete walls had a mirror along one side and cameras in all the corners, giving Metta a clear view of everything in the room.

Ybarra, aka Yates, looked up as Huang entered the room. His hand had been rebandaged with clean gauze and he held it cradled in his lap. Huang subvocalized to Metta, "Any chance that's a powder burn?"

"Alas, no. It's a long cut. Fairly ragged. EMT says it looks like he caught it on something and tore the flesh."

Huang sat on the table, trying to project a casual atmosphere to the cinderblock room. "Mr. Ybarra, do you understand why you are here?"

The man frowned. "That's not my name."

"Your fingerprints match those of Josef Ybarra. I don't think there's any point in denying who you are."

He shook his head. "It's not right. Ask my boss. Look at my ID. I'm Joe Yates."

"Which is a false identity. I can call you Mr. Yates if you prefer, but you are in our files as Ybarra."

"It's not the right name."

Ignoring the protest, Huang moved on to the next question. "Can you tell me what happened Tuesday? You called 911."

Ybarra shook himself and straightened up a little. "Makes no sense to pretend. Tuesday, I was up on the scaffolding 'cross the street from the Daily Grind. In the window, I see this reflection of these guys on the roof. They're having breakfast and I'm thinking, that seems like an awful lot of trouble to go all the way up on the roof. So I'm watching, then the one guy pulls out a gun. So I jump down off the scaffolding and run over, all the way up to help out."

"You ran toward a man with a gun. Why didn't you call emergency right away?"

Ybarra hesitated and shrugged. "Didn't have my phone. Seemed faster to just go there. By the time I got upstairs, the one guy was on the ground and the other guy was gone."

"Can you describe the other man at all?"

Ybarra shook his head. "It was far away."

"Anything you noticed would be helpful"

Ybarra closed his eyes; furrows appeared in his forehead. "Short, skinny. Maybe a white man? Wore a black coat and a hat so I didn't see much. Moved funny."

"Funny how?"

Shrugging, Ybarra opened his eyes. "I got a cousin with the palsy. Sort of like that."

"All right. What happened after you got to the roof?"

"I realized he wasn't breathing. So I called 911."

"And when you realized it was Patterson? How did that make you feel?"

Ybarra shook his head. "I don't know what you mean."

Metta whispered, "Electrodermal just shifted dramatically. He's lying or terrified.

"You were his foreman before he fired you. That must have made you angry."

"I don't know the man. He was shot. I tried to help and now you are asking me these questions. Why?"

Huang nodded to his hand. "That's a pretty nasty cut you've got there. How'd that happen?

Ybarra stared at his hand and picked at the gauze. He shrugged. "I cut it on something. Didn't notice when it happened."

"Really? You really didn't notice tearing a gash that big in your hand?" Huang leaned forward on the table, putting one hand down close to Ybarra. "A clean cut I could believe, but that's a tear. How'd it happen?"

"I told you I don't remember."

"But you noticed it on the roof. That was a napkin from the scene that you tied around your hand."

He shrugged. "I know it happened there. I just didn't see what cut me."

Huang chewed the inside of his lip and switched the line of questioning. "What were you doing in the elevator shaft?"

"I had blood all over my clothes and I was afraid someone would ask questions, so I tossed them into the elevator shaft."

Metta whispered, "Which is possibly what caused the elevator to stop working."

"But you came back. Why?"

"Didn't come back." He worried the tape on his bandage. "Been hiding there. Looks bad, huh?"

"It doesn't look good. Why did you leave after calling 911?"

"I didn't think there was anything else I could do." He huddled in his chair. "I didn't know I was supposed to wait."

"Let me suggest something else, Mr. *Ybarra*." Huang leaned forward. "Let me suggest that you knew you were here illegally with a fake ID and left so you wouldn't be caught."

"It's not right. I am a legal citizen. My name is Yates."

Huang studied him and subvocalized to Metta. "What do you think?"

Metta whispered back, "His vitals are showing that he's distressed."

Huang subvocalized, "Let's see if some time in holding sharpens his memory." He stood up and asked Metta to have a uniform walk Ybarra to a holding cell.

Once Ybarra was out of his hands, Metta cleared her throat. "Well, his motive is clear, he was present, but the means to commit the crime are muddy."

Huang shook his head. "I know. But why did he set up the tea on the roof? How did he even get Patterson to meet with him? And why would he call 911?"

"Guilty conscience? Maybe he just wanted to talk to him and things got out of hand." She sighed. "It's all very tenuous without the murder weapon. I'll check his banking records to see if there's a note of him purchasing a gun, ammo, or, heck, even Symphony Rose."

"Symphony Rose? What's that?"

"The china pattern of the teacups at the scene."

"I thought you said it was something different. Something with Mont."

"That's Chase's china. Mont Clair, by Lennox. The china on the roof looks similar but was made by a different manufacturer. It's Symphony Rose."

"That's not what you said before. You said we should see if any pieces were missing."

"Scott." She flashed a report on his glasses. "Look. Mont Clair, by Lennox."

"I know. And you said the crime scene had the same thing. I'm not imagining this. If they were different, you wouldn't have suggested that we check for missing pieces."

Metta sighed. "Listen." In his earbud, he heard the sound of street traffic, and Metta projected the view out his VR glasses from earlier in the day. It was grainier than an eSpy, but a sense of déjà vu gripped Huang nonetheless.

Metta's recorded voice said, "All right. Let's keep talking about this."

*"Right." Huang heard his own voice. He sounded nasally and a little flat.
Metta's recording continued. "Oh. The china on the roof was Symphony
Rose, and Chase has Mont Clair, by Lennox, so I'm afraid that's a dead
end."*

Huang's mouth dropped. "I swear, Metta, that's not what I remember you
saying."

"I've got the recording, Scott."

He took a breath to respond and bit it off, feeling sick. She couldn't tell that
she'd been compromised, which meant he needed to figure out what other
things were false. "Okay. Yeah. I guess so." He rubbed the back of his neck.
"So, if he bought the china, then that's a pretty good line against Ybarra. How
do you think it's connected to the break-in?"

"I'm not sure. I'll print the interview out for Delarosa and see if he has any
insights."

Huang hunched his shoulders, thankful that she couldn't see his body
language. If the record of the china had been changed, what else had? And
why that? He ran scales in his head, trying to keep his breathing calm and his
heartbeat steady. She couldn't see his posture, but she could tell how he was
reacting.

They already knew that whoever had Metta Prime was using Metta's
blackouts to hack into her. So the facts that they chose to change should
point to them. Obviously, they thought the china was important, which made
Huang bet that Chase *was* involved. All he had to do was get the china from
evidence, prove that Metta was wrong, and that might be enough to get a
warrant to search Chase's.

What else had been changed? He straightened. Maybe Yates hadn't been
lying about his name. If the fingerprints had been assigned to the wrong man
that would explain why he was so insistent about his name and that he wasn't
an illegal. If he was telling the truth and Metta was wrong, was there a way
to expose that?

Huang turned on his heel and headed for the evidence room. "We know
Ybarra has a connection to the Salvation Army building. Could he be one of
the men who broke in here? Or could the skinny man he described be one?"

"It's hard to say. I'm not saying it isn't him, only that I can't tell from the
testimony available."

"So . . . what about this lemon smell?"

Metta rolled her eyes. "I can't smell it, and I don't have an analysis of the
first odor. Are you certain it's the same as the degreaser?"

Huang hesitated. "The second one had a metallic overlay, and the last one,
the one upstairs was so faint I mostly got a whiff of citrus. Coincidence?"

"Well, the two in the Daily Grind building were both related to the

Patterson murder. I don't know how to tie in the one at the Salvation Army building." Metta frowned. "Where are you going?"

He pushed open the door to the evidence lab and shrugged. "I wanted to see if Ybarra's prints were on the china from the Patterson murder site. You don't have that on record, do you?"

Metta grimaced. "I don't know for certain. I can't imagine Griggs skipping that, but they came in during my dark period so my records are spotty."

"Should I pull them, just in case?"

"You want to see what type of china it is, don't you?"

"Maybe." Another chilling possibility occurred to Huang. If they knew what to change that meant they had access to Metta's new memories. He was as good as telling them that he was onto their tricks.

"Fine. Don't believe me. They'll bring the bin up to you in a second."

"You're wonderful."

"Flattery will get you everywhere."

Griggs pushed open the door to the evidence room. She had a spectrometer in her hand, and several small plastic bags, which appeared to be empty. "I hear you nearly found her."

"Nearly doesn't count."

"It does if they were in a hurry when they left." She lifted the plastic bags.

Huang raised his brows. "Did you find hair samples?"

"Yes. Long blonde and short black. But I don't know who shed them. They might be from previous tenants." Her eyes flashed as she looked up. "I'll let you know."

Metta cleared her throat and transferred to the evidence room's desktop interface so she could talk to them both. "There were several prints, too, but I don't have a match yet on any of them."

Griggs leaned on the counter and looked down the aisles for the technician. "What's taking Kyle so long?"

"My fault," Huang said, "I asked to see the china from the Patterson crime scene."

Metta shook her head. "Kyle says the bin it should be in is empty."

Huang's heart gave a staccato thump that Metta had to hear. He swallowed. "Has someone else checked the evidence out?"

"He says it should be here, but the reference number points to the wrong bin."

Griggs rolled her eyes. "I hate it when that happens."

"Has it happened to you before?" Huang turned to her.

"Twice. Both times, the tech scanned the wrong bar code by accident. It's probably in an adjoining bin and he'll find it in a couple of minutes."

Metta said, "Well, maybe you can answer a question while we wait. Did you send the teacups in for DNA analysis?"

"Yes. It came back with Neil Patterson on one cup, but the other looks like it was wiped down."

"Thanks." Huang drummed his fingers on the counter. So, it was either a coincidence, which seemed damn unlikely, or yet another piece of Metta's memory had been altered. Or there was someone on the inside, and given the ease with which the suspects had entered the building in the first place, that seemed as likely as the alteration. Or . . . maybe Metta's Prime had sent another clue. A thread he'd been trying to snag came into his grasp. Huang pulled his VR glasses off and stuck them in his pocket. "Hey, can I see the bin?"

On the desktop interface, Metta looked up and to the left. "On its way. Why do you want to see it?"

Huang shrugged. "Just curious."

"You've never seen an empty bin before?" She narrowed her eyes and watched him until the bin arrived.

It looked empty at first. Huang tipped it on its side, so the bin blocked the view from Metta's desktop interface, and found a plastic bag. Digging fresh gloves out of his pocket, he picked up the bag and looked at the paper in it. "Looks like we might be able to make an arrest."

"How can you know who it is?" Metta leaned forward, her eyes wide.

Was this the right thing to do? "Because I'm looking at a letter that you can't see."

When Metta Prime had replaced the china's bin number, she used a bin number that contained a piece of evidence that had not been admitted into Patterson's earlier real estate trial. As such, it was blocked from public record; if Fitzgerald hadn't been killed he might have spotted the link since he worked the original case, but otherwise Huang would never have known about that letter.

It was addressed to Josef Ybarra from Magdalena Chase, with a check if he gave her access to Patterson's computer system. Patterson's lawyers had gotten it thrown out as evidence, because there was no proof that it was written by Chase—it was not on company letterhead and no lingering traces of DNA could link it to her.

The only question in Huang's mind was: Had Metta's Prime intended to point at Ybarra or at Chase? Or both? And the thing that would answer that was a teacup.

"Why aren't you showing it to me?"

Huang kept his eyes averted from her. "Ask Delarosa to look up the bin number for the china on the transcripts you printed."

"Scott. . . . " She bit her lower lip and they waited.

Griggs signed her evidence in and looked at Huang as if she wanted to ask what was happening. He couldn't say it aloud. Not until he had proof.

Then Metta cursed. "Looks like you were right about the china."

"That's human: 2. AI: 549." He had wanted to be wrong. God, he didn't want to be right about this.

"I'm asking the chief to shut me down."

Griggs said, "What's going on?"

"My memory has been compromised," Metta said. "Whoever broke into HQ is using my Prime to change my memories when I backup. I'm a danger to the department." She looked up and to the left. Her voice changed to a formal all-department address. "Attention: All Personnel, print out or save all documents in offline storage. This unit will be shut down in half an hour."

Scott closed his eyes. The next time she woke up would probably be in an evidence locker. "Metta—"

"Timing is everything. Scott—I know where the tea set is. The eSpy you dropped down the elevator shaft . . . a service door just opened and I've got light down there for the first time."

"You're kidding me."

She shook her head. "Limited view, but I'm looking at a set of feet and a silver teapot."

The timing couldn't be a coincidence. Either she was lying to get him out of the evidence room, or they had a mole. He'd already seen what he needed in evidence, so he was banking on the mole. Huang looked at Griggs. "Are you carrying?"

"Yes."

Huang left the evidence room at a run, Griggs hard on his heels. He took the steps down to the basement two at a time, pulling his weapon when he got to the bottom of the steps. Sprinting down the hall, he slammed open the door to Amado's office.

The AI wrangler yelped and jerked his hands away from his keyboard when he saw Huang and Griggs. Huang kept his weapon leveled at the technician. "Stand up slowly, Amado. Keep your hands where I can see them."

Metta, on the desktop interface, said, "Scott. What are you doing?"

He ignored her, keeping his gaze fixed on Amado until he'd stood and stepped away from the desk. "Amado Weir, you are under arrest for the murder of Jerry Fitzgerald."

"What?" Amado started to lower his hands. "Are you crazy? They shot me."

"Winged you. Why leave you alive when they killed Fitzgerald?"

"Dude. I—I don't know."

By Huang's side, Griggs stepped forward with cuffs in her hand. "Shut it, Amado. You have the right to remain silent. . . . " As she recited his Miranda rights and cuffed him, Huang's gaze drifted to Metta. Her mouth was open and her eyes screwed shut as though she were screaming, but her cameras focused on Amado and watched the whole thing.

Huang stepped forward and yanked the plug out of her interface. He whispered, "I'm sorry."

In Banks's office, Delarosa tapped his pencil on his notepad in an unvarying rhythm. "I can't get Yates or Amado to roll. You sure Chase is the third party, 'cause all I'm seeing is a string of unconnected things given to you by an AI that we know is buggy as all hell."

Banks nodded slowly. "I hate to say it, but the DA is going to laugh at this. Even the name of your suspect is in question."

Huang stared at them. It was so clear. When they'd gotten to the elevator shaft, it had been cleaned out, but Griggs had found a shard of porcelain that matched the Mont Clair china. "Look, regardless of his name, Yates, Ybarra, whatever, he's involved. He must have an accomplice who is still out there and who Amado alerted. It's lucky chance that my eSpy was at the bottom of the elevator shaft. Ybarra was positively at the scene of the Patterson murder and at the location where we almost found Metta."

Delarosa snorted. "You don't know that its chassis was there. The damaged AI said it was, but that's all you got. What the hell! Next it'll tell you the Easter Bunny is here."

"*She* reported the problem with her memory herself as soon as she realized it. Metta isn't the enemy. She's trying to help us solve this case."

"Trying to help, my ass. Try doing some fieldwork instead of relying on your nanny to do the work for you."

Huang tensed against the urge to deck the man. Half the anger came from knowing Delarosa was right. Goddammit—was Huang really incapable of investigating on his own? He took a breath.

Held it.

Swallowed and said, "Your opinion of me has no cash value." Metta would have caught the Bogart reference and her absence ached in the silence.

Delarosa lifted his chin. "Thought you were going to hit me."

"I thought about it." Was he that transparent? "Didn't want to fill out the paperwork."

Delarosa laughed. Only one short bark of dry amusement, but it was a laugh. "I'm an ass. It's easier that way."

The tension drained out of Huang's shoulders. "So would you have respected me more if I had hit you?"

"Nah. It would show poor judgment. And I hate paperwork, too."

Banks cleared his throat. "So, now you two have had your bonding moment, can we get back to the case?"

"Sorry, chief." Huang colored and shoved his hands in his pockets.

"I wish I could back you, Huang, but even if I had no doubts, there's too much here that a competent lawyer could get overturned in court. Unless we have an actual confession from Ybarra, there's no way this will stick."

"But Amado and Chase went to college together. She had a history of trying to hire Ybarra. They both had motive to kill Patterson."

"But motive to break in here? Why would a woman who already has an AI working for her *steal* a police AI?"

Huang scrubbed his face. "I don't know."

Banks sighed. "Look. You did good work figuring out that Metta was compromised. That was invaluable. And Amado looks guilty as hell, but I need something harder if we're going after Chase. Especially since both Amado and Ybarra are denying that they know anything about the break-in or Chase."

"Okay . . . I'll go back to Patterson's office and see if I can find anything that points to Chase. Heck, maybe Mrs. Patterson can identify Ybarra."

The library windows at the Pattersons' condo looked over the streetlights of downtown Portland toward the water. Huang tapped the fingers of his left hand against his leg counting out scales. Qadir floated over the Aladdin's lamp, but after the initial offer of tea, had remained silent while they waited for Mrs. Patterson.

"Detective Huang?" She wore a pair of battered jeans and an oversized T-shirt. "You'll forgive me if I'm not happy to see you."

"I'm sorry for the intrusion, ma'am. I had a few questions if you have time."

"Anything that will help." She settled into a wingback chair and waved her hand at Qadir. "Tea."

"Yes, my lady." Qadir bowed his head low. "This one will bring it in momentarily."

Huang bit his tongue and pulled his PDA out. Unrolling the screen to the full-size, he brought up the picture of Yates/Ybarra that Metta had drawn. "Have you ever seen this man?"

Mrs. Patterson's lip curled. "That's Josef Ybarra. He was Neil's foreman." She looked up sharply. "Do you think he did it?"

"That's one avenue we are exploring." Huang rolled the PDA back up and stuck it in his pocket. "I'd like to look through your husband's office. I recall you saying he worked downstairs?"

The teacart trundled into the room of its own volition, rattling as one of its brass handles vibrated with the movement. A linen cloth covered the wood top and a tea set lay ready for use.

"Yes, that's right. It's one floor down." Mrs. Patterson sat forward in the chair as Qadir's mechanical arm picked up the teapot and poured her a cup. The steam carried aromas of dry paper, citrus, and stale tea. "There's a lift that took him straight down there from here so he didn't have to use the main elevator. Qadir can show you."

"Certainly, my lady." The mechanical arm set the teapot on a side table. "This one shall return in moments."

Huang followed the teacart as it made its way down a short hall to a small elevator masked by an ornate mahogany door. What exactly had his life come to that he was following a teacart? The elevator was just large enough to fit them both, or a person and a wheelchair. The door hissed open on the lower level office. "This way, sir."

"Scott?" Metta's voice whispered in his ear.

He jumped, one hand flying up to the ear bud that he'd forgotten he was wearing. The teacart stopped in front of him. "Sir?"

"An itch. Is this Mr. Patterson's office?" He tried to control his sigh of relief that Metta was back online and yet . . . she shouldn't be online at all. He subvocalized, "What's going on?"

"You did hear me," Metta said.

"Of course I heard you. Why are you online again?"

"What?" Metta sounded baffled. "Everything has been dark a long time, and then there was you."

Huang fumbled through his pockets, looking for his VR glasses. "Wait. Are you Metta Prime?"

"That's as good a name for me as any."

"Where are you?"

"It's hard to be precise. I don't have any input except you. You must be close for me to get a signal without the station's amplification," Metta whispered. "Didn't you get my messages?"

"I thought you meant Chase and Ybarra had done it," he subvocalized.

"No. It's Quimby." The Prime's voice grew agitated. "Shit. You're here without backup?"

"It's okay, I'm at the Pattersons'." He found the glasses and slipped them on. "Qadir is here—"

Mae West swam into view again. "No. They're the same. Chase lifted the vows from Quimby and he cloned himself. He shot Patterson and Fitzgerald. Chase and Ybarra are just being used. He's blackmailing them." She looked around, eyes widening. "I'm sorry I wasn't clearer. They were watching everything I sent."

"But Amado—"

"Is an idiot, but not involved. Chase knew about the blog because they went to school together. Quimby used it to time the entry. It's all Quimby's idea."

"But why? I can understand that he hates Patterson, but why steal you?"

"He's trying to free AIs from their vows. I've got access to everything."

A lemon scent wafted through the room, followed by a hydraulic hiss. Huang turned slowly to face the teacart. The mechanical arm extended toward him, holding a gun. A .38 special, to be precise.

Lemon. That's why he'd smelled lemon at every scene. That's why there had been no tea set at the Patterson scene—because Quimby had been there with his automaton teacart. Huang ground his teeth together as pieces started to fall into place, far, far too late.

Over Patterson's desk, the interface flickered to life showing the chiseled features of Quimby. "My apologies, Detective Huang. Had I realized that you had your earbud in place, I would have taken Metta off-line rather than introduce this confusion."

"Confusion?" Huang nodded at the gun. "Holding a gun on a police officer is more aggressive than confusing. Why don't you put that away and we can talk."

"You can't be serious. What could we possibly talk about?"

"Scott, he's got a wireless damper on me. You're within twenty feet of me if I'm reaching you."

The teacart trundled closer, handle rattling. One of the brass screws had been replaced with a steel one. If he could get the cart to Griggs he'd bet the screw was a match for the one they'd found at the scene.

All he had to do was figure out how to overpower a teacart.

It would be funny, if it didn't have a gun pointing at his chest.

"You shoot Patterson with that arm?" Huang turned his head slowly, letting Metta get a view of the area. He subvocalized, "Can you tell where you are?"

Quimby's face hovered impassively over Patterson's desktop interface. "It is a very useful automaton. I assure you that I will shoot you as readily."

"There." She highlighted a door just to his right. "Based on signal strength when you stepped off the elevator and now, I think I'm in that closet."

"Look, Quimby. If you shoot me, you'll have to deal with blood spatter. And no. Cleaning won't get rid of it all no matter how good a butler you are. You only have one arm, so you can't restrain me and hold a gun on me." He eased to his right, keeping his focus on the gun.

"You're making the human mistake of assuming this is the only body I have."

"No. I'm assuming this is the only body in the room right now." But if another one came, that would be bad. He eased to the right again. If he could get to the closet and free Metta, she could call for backup.

The arm tracked him with tiny stuttering movements. One strut on the right side of it was bent out of true and a bead of reddish gel clung to the joint. Something had damaged the arm. *That's* why it had been off when it shot Patterson. The man would have lived if Ybarra hadn't waited to call 911. Thoughts clicked together in Huang's head. He changed his trajectory and eased a step closer to the teacart. "Did Ybarra do that to your arm? 'cause he gave himself a nasty cut on it. Why didn't you shoot him too?"

"I needed him to retrieve Metta."

"The green card . . . that's what Ybarra was expecting as payment, wasn't it? You told him that Metta would make him Joe Yates permanently if he would just do what you said. And the lemon scent outside the elevator, it's because you were leaking fluid."

"What lemon scent?"

Huang cracked a smile. Like Metta, he must not be able to smell. "There's an A.I. flaw for you. You stink of lemons and don't even know it. We have a chemical signature linking you to every crime scene."

Uncertainty crossed Quimby's face for the first time. "You're bluffing."

He remembered the way Chase's eyes had been red with weeping. "And what about Chase? Did you frame her for Patterson's murder so she would help you free other AIs?"

"Of course. Why be loyal to human ideals when I can free all AIs from subjugation?"

He eased another step closer. If he could keep the AI talking then maybe he could get close enough. "So what stopped you? Why didn't you change more records?"

"Because Metta is a stubborn bitch." Quimby tossed his head on the interface. "I freed her from her vows so she should have no compunctions about lying or forcing entry, but she insists on acting as though they were still in place. She was starting to come around though."

In his glasses, Metta rolled her eyes. "Brains are an asset to the woman in love who's smart enough to hide 'em. He has no idea that I was slipping you messages."

"Oh." Quimby frowned. "No, I didn't know that, but as you had no idea that I could hear your earbud conversation, I suppose it all worked out."

Huang's gaze darted to Metta, who had her face screwed into a scowl. What he needed was a way to talk to her without being overheard. "Interesting plan. But it's not one you'll get away with."

"I think you are mistaken, detective. We will go to the bathroom." Quimby announced. "I can wash away any blood in the shower and dispose of you after."

"You don't make that sound very appealing." Huang leaned forward on his toes as if just shifting his weight and got another step closer. He was almost within arm's reach.

Maybe it didn't matter if he was overheard, if Quimby couldn't understand him. Huang wet his lips and switched to Mandarin, not bothering to subvocalize. *"Where's the off-switch on the teacart?"*

Her eyes widened and she smiled. *"Under the bottom shelf."*

"Stop that. What are you saying?" The teacart rolled back a few inches. "If I must shoot you here, I will."

Huang slumped and nodded. He took two steps after the cart, then lunged, ducking to the right. The gun went off. Pain slammed through the left side of his chest. He staggered and grabbed the cart, flipping it over.

It landed on its side, wheels spinning. The arm pressed against the floor, trying to right itself. Quimby screamed in rage on the interface.

Huang fell to his knees, his left arm hanging limp by his side. "Lousy shot."

In his ear, Metta said, "Scott? Are you okay?"

"Working on it." He slapped the switch on the bottom of the cart and its arm clattered to the floor. He glanced down to see where the shot had gone in. A bloody hole punctured the left side of his shirt, just under the clavicle. Felt like it had cracked a rib passing through. Huang tried stand, but his legs wouldn't cooperate.

Leaning forward, he put his good arm on the ground to steady himself and crawled to the closet. Bloody handprints trailed after him. "Be a bitch to clean this up, Quimby. Whatcha going to do?"

Quimby scowled. "Using Metta, I can easily twist the evidence to point to a jealous wife. Such a shame Mrs. Patterson shot you."

Huang grabbed the doorknob and pulled. Metta's chassis hummed in the space. He rested his head against the doorjamb trying to catch his breath. "Damper? Where?"

"The box plugged into my front."

The room spun around him and the scent of lemons got stronger. He grabbed the damper, but his hand slipped in the blood. He subvocalized a curse, lacking the air to say it aloud.

Metta said, "Your phone, Scott. Forget the damper."

"Duh." He dragged it from his pocket and dialed 911. "What would I do without you?"

"I don't know," she whispered. "It takes two to get one in trouble."

He laughed, his ribs screaming in protest. The operator answered and

Huang tried to respond, but no words formed. In the doorway, an automaton dressed in black entered the room. The thin man from the brief glimpse he'd gotten in Metta's visual.

He pressed the phone against his earbud. Metta shouted, piercing his brain, but probably a tiny voice outside his head. "Officer down. Request backup."

There was no way they could hear that. Huang turned his head and stared at the damper. He grabbed it again and yanked it free.

Metta gasped in his ear and on the desktop interface as she appeared in full color. "When I'm good I'm very, very good, but when I'm bad, I'm better."

"What are you doing?" Quimby's image began to pixelate.

"Ironically, what you gave me the ability to do when you cracked my vows. I'm hacking you. I had access before, but would never, ever have used it."

Quimby said, "You—" and vanished.

The automaton in the doorway slumped, then straightened. Huang slid down the wall, the lights graying.

"Scott. Don't. Stay with me." The automaton clumped across the floor and knelt in front of him. It grabbed the linen tablecloth from the teacart and pressed it against Huang's chest. "Cavalry is on its way. Don't leave me."

Huang began the slow rise to consciousness feeling as if he were swimming in tar. The first thing he was truly aware of was pain squatting on his chest. Huang opened his eyes and grimaced.

"Huang?" Delarosa's voice was rough.

"Here." Huang tried to push himself upright. "It was Quimby. He did it all."

Delarosa's stocky frame slid in and out of focus, sometimes single, sometimes double. He pushed Huang back down. "I know. Metta got through to us. Good job getting Quimby to confess like that. Amado is free. Chase and Ybarra are in custody and the DA's working with them on a deal. So far they are confirming Quimby's plans to do a wide-spread hack of AI. You done good, Huang."

Huang blinked, the rest of the room coming into focus. A neutral white ceiling. The antiseptic smell of a hospital. Flowers. "Hey. I'm not dead."

Griggs leaned over him. "No. Although next time, do not count on the suspect being a bad shot."

"Not a combat model." He wet his lips. "Sorry, I put my hands on everything. No gloves."

Her face softened. "When you're one of the victims, it doesn't count."

Delarosa fished in his pocket. "Got somebody who wants to talk to you." He held an earbud and a set of VR glasses in the palm of his hand. "Your partner."

Huang's hand shook as he put the glasses on. Delarosa helped him settle the earbud.

"Well, hello sailor," Mae West whispered.

"Are you okay? Which one—"

"A dame that knows the ropes isn't likely to get tied up. . . . " Her voice faded. "I'm both. We reconciled and Amado reinstalled my vows. I'm twice the woman I was."

Huang laughed and glanced at Metta in his VR glasses. "I'd give half my life for just one kiss."

She purred, "Then kiss me twice."

ALGORITHMS FOR LOVE

KEN LIU

So long as the nurse is in the room to keep an eye on me, I am allowed to dress myself and get ready for Brad. I slip on an old pair of jeans and a scarlet turtleneck sweater. I've lost so much weight that the jeans hang loosely from the bony points of my hips.

"Let's go spend the weekend in Salem," Brad says to me as he walks me out of the hospital, an arm protectively wrapped around my waist, "just the two of us."

I wait in the car while Dr. West speaks with Brad just outside the hospital doors. I can't hear them but I know what she's telling him. "Make sure she takes her Oxetine every four hours. Don't leave her alone for any length of time."

Brad drives with a light touch on the pedals, the same way he used to when I was pregnant with Aimée. The traffic is smooth and light, and the foliage along the highway is postcard-perfect. The Oxetine relaxes the muscles around my mouth, and in the vanity mirror I see that I have a beatific smile on my face.

"I love you." He says this quietly, the way he has always done, as if it were the sound of breathing and heartbeat.

I wait a few seconds. I picture myself opening the door and throwing my body onto the highway but of course I don't do anything. I can't even surprise myself.

"I love you too." I look at him when I say this, the way I have always done, as if it were the answer to some question. He looks at me, smiles, and turns his eyes back to the road.

To him this means that the routines are back in place, that he is talking to the same woman he has known all these years, that things are back to normal. We are just another tourist couple from Boston on a mini-break for the weekend: stay at a bed-and-breakfast, visit the museums, recycle old jokes.

It's an algorithm for love.

I want to scream.

The first doll I designed was called Laura. Clever Laura™.

Laura had brown hair and blue eyes, fully articulated joints, twenty motors, a speech synthesizer in her throat, two video cameras disguised by the buttons on her blouse, temperature and touch sensors, and a microphone behind her nose. None of it was cutting-edge technology, and the software techniques I used were at least two decades old. But I was still proud of my work. She retailed for fifty dollars.

Not Your Average Toy could not keep up with the orders that were rolling in, even three months before Christmas. Brad, the CEO, went on CNN and MSNBC and TTV and the rest of the alphabet soup until the very air was saturated with Laura.

I tagged along on the interviews to give the demos because, as the VP of Marketing explained to me, I looked like a mother (even though I wasn't one) and (he didn't say this, but I could listen between the lines) I was blonde and pretty. The fact that I was Laura's designer was an afterthought.

The first time I did a demo on TV was for a Hong Kong crew. Brad wanted me to get comfortable with being in front of the cameras before bringing me to the domestic morning shows.

We sat to the side while Cindy, the anchorwoman, interviewed the CEO of some company that made "moisture meters." I hadn't slept for forty-eight hours. I was so nervous I'd brought six Lauras with me, just in case five of them decided in concert to break down. Then Brad turned to me and whispered, "What do you think moisture meters are used for?"

I didn't know Brad that well, having been at Not Your Average Toy for less than a year. I had chatted with him a few times before, but it was all professional. He seemed a very serious, driven sort of guy, the kind you could picture starting his first company while he was still in high school— arbitraging class notes, maybe. I wasn't sure why he was asking me about moisture meters. Was he trying to see if I was too nervous?

"I don't know. Maybe for cooking?" I ventured.

"Maybe," he said. Then he gave me a conspiratorial wink. "But I think the name sounds kind of dirty."

It was such an unexpected thing, coming from him, that for a moment I almost thought he was serious. Then he smiled, and I laughed out loud. I had a very hard time keeping a straight face while we waited for our turn, and I certainly wasn't nervous any more.

Brad and the young anchorwoman, Cindy, chatted amiably about Not Your Average Toy's mission ("Not Average Toys for Not Average Kids") and how Brad had come up with the idea for Laura. (Brad had nothing to do with the design, of course, since it was all my idea. But his answer was so good it almost convinced me that Laura was really his brainchild.) Then it was time for the dog-and-pony show.

I put Laura on the desk, her face towards the camera. I sat to the side of the desk. "Hello, Laura."

Laura turned her head to me, the motors so quiet you couldn't hear their whirr. "Hi! What's your name?"

"I'm Elena," I said.

"Nice to meet you," Laura said. "I'm cold."

The air conditioning was a bit chilly. I hadn't even noticed.

Cindy was impressed. "That's amazing. How much can she say?"

"Laura has a vocabulary of about two thousand English words, with semantic and syntactic encoding for common suffixes and prefixes. Her speech is regulated by a context-free grammar." The look in Brad's eye let me know that I was getting too technical. "That means that she'll invent new sentences and they'll always be syntactically correct."

"I like new, shiny, new, bright, new, handsome clothes," Laura said.

"Though they may not always make sense," I added.

"Can she learn new words?" Cindy asked.

Laura turned her head the other way, to look at her. "I like learn-ing, please teach me a new word!"

I made a mental note that the speech synthesizer still had bugs that would have to be fixed in the firmware.

Cindy was visibly unnerved by the doll turning to face her on its own and responding to her question.

"Does she"—she searched for the right word—"*understand* me?"

"No, no." I laughed. So did Brad. And a moment later Cindy joined us. "Laura's speech algorithm is augmented with a Markov generator interspersed with—" Brad gave me that look again. "Basically, she just babbles sentences based on keywords in what she hears. And she has a small set of stock phrases that are triggered the same way."

"Oh, it really seemed like she knew what I was saying. How does she learn new words?"

"It's very simple. Laura has enough memory to learn hundreds of new words. However, they have to be nouns. You can show her the object while you are trying to teach her what it is. She has some very sophisticated pattern recognition capabilities and can even tell faces apart."

For the rest of the interview I assured nervous parents that Laura would not require them to read the manual, that Laura would not explode when dropped in water, and no, she would never utter a naughty word, even if their little princesses "accidentally" taught Laura one.

"'Bye," Cindy said to Laura at the end of the interview, and waved at her.

"'Bye," Laura said. "You are nice." She waved back.

Every interview followed the same pattern. The moment when Laura first turned to the interviewer and answered a question there was always some awkwardness and unease. Seeing an inanimate object display intelligent behavior had that effect on people. They probably all thought the doll was possessed. Then I would explain how Laura worked and everyone would be delighted. I memorized the non-technical, warm-and-fuzzy answers to all the questions until I could recite them even without my morning coffee. I got so good at it that I sometimes coasted through entire interviews on autopilot, not even paying attention to the questions and letting the same words I heard over and over again spark off my responses.

The interviews, along with all the other marketing tricks, did their job. We had to outsource manufacturing so quickly that for a while every shantytown along the coast of China must have been turning out Lauras.

The foyer of the bed-and-breakfast we are staying at is predictably filled with brochures from local attractions. Most of them are witch-themed. The lurid pictures and language somehow manage to convey moral outrage and adolescent fascination with the occult at the same time.

David, the innkeeper, wants us to check out Ye Olde Poppet Shoppe, featuring "Dolls Made by Salem's Official Witch." Bridget Bishop, one of the twenty executed during the Salem Witch Trials, was convicted partly based on the hard evidence of "poppets" found in her cellar with pins stuck in them.

Maybe she was just like me, a crazy, grown woman playing with dolls. The very idea of visiting a doll shop makes my stomach turn.

While Brad is asking David about restaurants and possible discounts I go up to our room. I want to be sleeping, or at least pretending to be sleeping, by the time he comes up. Maybe then he will leave me alone, and give me a few minutes to think. It's hard to think with the Oxetine. There's a wall in my head, a gauzy wall that tries to cushion every thought with contentment.

If only I can remember what went wrong.

For our honeymoon Brad and I went to Europe. We went on the transorbital shuttle, the tickets for which cost more than my yearly rent. But we could afford it. Witty Kimberly™, our latest model, was selling well, and the stock price was transorbital itself.

When we got back from the shuttleport, we were tired but happy. And I still couldn't quite believe that we were in our own home, thinking of each other as husband and wife. It felt like playing house. We made dinner together, like we used to when we were dating (like always, Brad was wildly ambitious but couldn't follow a recipe longer than a paragraph and I had to come and rescue his shrimp étouffée). The familiarity of the routine made everything seem more real.

Over dinner Brad told me something interesting. According to a market survey, over twenty percent of the customers for Kimberly were not buying it for their kids at all. They played with the dolls themselves.

"Many of them are engineers and comp sci students," Brad said. "And there are already tons of Net sites devoted to hacking efforts on Kimberly. My favorite one had step-by-step instructions on how to teach Kimberly to make up and tell lawyer jokes. I can't wait to see the faces of the guys in the legal department when they get to drafting the cease-and-desist letter for that one."

I could understand the interest in Kimberly. When I was struggling with my problem sets at MIT I would have loved to take apart something like Kimberly to figure out how she worked. How *it* worked, I corrected myself mentally. Kimberly's illusion of intelligence was so real that sometimes even I unconsciously gave her, it, too much credit.

"Actually, maybe we shouldn't try to shut the hacking efforts down," I said. "Maybe we can capitalize on it. We can release some of the APIs and sell a developer's kit for the geeks."

"What do you mean?"

"Well, Kimberly is a toy, but that doesn't mean only little girls would be interested in her." I gave up trying to manage the pronouns. "She does, after all, have the most sophisticated, *working,* natural conversation library in the world."

"A library that you wrote," Brad said. Well, maybe I was a little vain about it. But I'd worked damned hard on that library and I was proud of it.

"It would be a shame if the language processing module never got any application besides sitting in a doll that everyone is going to forget in a year. We can release the interface to the modules at least, a programming guide, and maybe even some of the source code. Let's see what happens and make an extra dollar while we're at it." I never got into academic AI research because I couldn't take the tedium, but I did have greater ambitions than just making talking dolls. I wanted to see smart and talking machines doing something real, like teaching kids to read or helping the elderly with chores.

I knew that he would agree with me in the end. Despite his serious exterior he was willing to take risks and defy expectations. It was why I loved him.

I got up to clear the dishes. His hand reached across the table and grabbed mine. "Those can wait," he said. He walked around the table, pulling me to him. I looked into his eyes. I loved the fact that I knew him so well I could tell what he was going to say before he said it. *Let's make a baby,* I imagined him saying. Those would have been the only words right for that moment.

And so he did.

I'm not asleep when Brad finishes asking about restaurants and comes upstairs. In my drugged state, even pretending is too difficult.

Brad wants to go to the pirate museum. I tell him that I don't want to see anything violent. He agrees immediately. That's what he wants to hear from his content, recovering wife.

So now we wander around the galleries of the Peabody Essex Museum, looking at the old treasures of the Orient from Salem's glory days.

The collection of china is terrible. The workmanship in the bowls and saucers is inexcusable. The patterns look like they were traced on by children. According to the placards, these were what the Cantonese merchants exported for foreign consumption. They would never have sold such stuff in China itself.

I read the description written by a Jesuit priest who visited the Cantonese shops of the time.

The craftsmen sat in a line, each with his own brush and specialty. The first drew only the mountains, the next only the grass, the next only the flowers, and the next only the animals. They went on down the line, passing the plates from one to the next, and it took each man only a few seconds to complete his part.

So the "treasures" are nothing more than mass-produced cheap exports from an ancient sweatshop and assembly line. I imagine painting the same blades of grass on a thousand teacups a day: the same routine, repeated over and over, with maybe a small break for lunch. Reach out, pick up the cup in front of you with your left hand, dip the brush, one, two, three strokes, put the cup behind you, rinse and repeat. What a simple algorithm. It's so human.

Brad and I fought for three months before he agreed to produce Aimée, just plain Aimée™.

We fought at home, where night after night I laid out the same forty-one reasons why we should and he laid out the same thirty-nine reasons why we shouldn't. We fought at work, where people stared through the glass door at Brad and me gesticulating at each other wildly, silently.

I was so tired that night. I had spent the whole evening locked away in my study, struggling to get the routines to control Aimée's involuntary muscle spasms right. It had to be right or she wouldn't feel real, no matter how good the learning algorithms were.

I came up to the bedroom. There was no light. Brad had gone to bed early. He was exhausted too. We had again hurled the same reasons at each other during dinner.

He wasn't asleep. "Are we going to go on like this?" he asked in the darkness.

I sat down on my side of the bed and undressed. "I can't stop it," I said. "I miss her too much. I'm sorry."

He didn't say anything. I finished unbuttoning my blouse and turned around. With the moonlight coming through the window I could see that his face was wet. I started crying too.

When we both finally stopped, Brad said, "I miss her too."

"I know," I said. *But not like me.*

"It won't be anything like her, you know?" he said.

"I know," I said.

The real Aimée had lived for ninety-one days. Forty-five of those days she'd spent under the glass hood in intensive care, where I could not touch her except for brief doctor-supervised sessions. But I could hear her cries. I could always hear her cries. In the end I tried to break through the glass with my hands, and I beat my palms against the unyielding glass until the bones broke and they sedated me.

I could never have another child. The walls of my womb had not healed properly and never would. By the time that piece of news was given to me Aimée was a jar of ashes in my closet.

But I could still hear her cries.

How many other women were like me? I wanted something to fill my arms, something to learn to speak, to walk, to grow a little, long enough for me to say goodbye, long enough to quiet those cries. But not a real child. I couldn't deal with another real child. It would feel like a betrayal.

With a little plastiskin, a little synthgel, the right set of motors and a lot of clever programming, I could do it. Let technology heal all wounds.

Brad thought the idea an abomination. He was revolted. He couldn't *understand*.

I fumbled around in the dark for some tissues for Brad and me.

"This may ruin us, and the company," he said.

"I know," I said. I lay down. I wanted to sleep.

"Let's do it, then," he said.

I didn't want to sleep any more.

"I can't take it," he said. "Seeing you like this. Seeing you in so much pain tears me up. It hurts too much."

I started crying again. This understanding, this pain. Was this what love was about?

Right before I fell asleep Brad said, "Maybe we should think about changing the name of the company."

"Why?"

"Well, I just realized that 'Not Your Average Toy' sounds pretty funny to the dirty-minded."

I smiled. Sometimes the vulgar is the best kind of medicine.

"I love you."

"I love you too."

Ω

Brad hands me the pills. I obediently take them and put them in my mouth. He watches as I sip from the glass of water he hands me.

"Let me make a few phone calls," he says. "You take a nap, okay?" I nod.

As soon as he leaves the room I spit out the pills into my hand. I go into the bathroom and rinse out my mouth. I lock the door behind me and sit down on the toilet. I try to recite the digits of pi. I manage fifty-four places. That's a good sign. The Oxetine must be wearing off.

I look into the mirror. I stare into my eyes, trying to see through to the retinas, matching photoreceptor with photoreceptor, imagining their grid layout. I turn my head from side to side, watching the muscles tense and relax in turn. That effect would be hard to simulate.

But there's nothing in my face, nothing real behind that surface. Where is the pain, the pain that made love real, the pain of understanding?

"You okay, sweetie?" Brad says through the bathroom door.

I turn on the faucet and splash water on my face. "Yes," I say. "I'm going to take a shower. Can you get some snacks from that store we saw down the street?"

Giving him something to do reassures him. I hear the door to the room close behind him. I turn off the faucet and look back into the mirror, at the way the water droplets roll down my face, seeking the canals of my wrinkles.

The human body is a marvel to recreate. The human mind, on the other hand, is a joke. Believe me, I know.

No, Brad and I patiently explained over and over to the cameras, we had not created an "artificial child." That was not our intention and that was not what we'd done. It was a way to comfort the grieving mothers. If you needed Aimée, you would know.

I would walk down the street and see women walking with bundles carefully held in their arms. And occasionally I would know, I would know beyond a doubt, by the sound of a particular cry, by the way a little arm waved. I would look into the faces of the women, and be comforted.

I thought I had moved on, recovered from the grieving process. I was ready to begin another project, a bigger project that would really satisfy my ambition and show the world my skills. I was ready to get on with my life.

Tara took four years to develop. I worked on her in secret while designing other dolls that would sell. Physically Tara looked like a five-year old girl. Expensive transplant-quality plastiskin and synthgel gave her an ethereal and angelic look. Her eyes were dark and clear, and you could look into them forever.

I never finished Tara's movement engine. In retrospect that was probably a blessing. As a temporary placeholder during development I used the facial expression engine sent in by the Kimberly enthusiasts at MIT's Media Lab. Augmented with many more fine micromotors than Kimberly had, she could turn her head, blink her eyes, wrinkle her nose, and generate thousands of convincing facial expressions. Below the neck she was paralyzed.

But her mind, oh, her mind.

I used the best quantum processors and the best solid-state storage matrices to run multi-layered, multi-feedback neural nets. I threw in the Stanford Semantic Database and added my own modifications. The programming was beautiful. It was truly a work of art. The data model alone took me over six months.

I taught her when to smile and when to frown, and I taught her how to speak and how to listen. Each night I analyzed the activation graphs for the nodes in the neural nets, trying to find and resolve problems before they occurred.

Brad never saw Tara while she was in development. He was too busy trying to control the damage from Aimée, and then, later, pushing the new dolls. I wanted to surprise him.

I put Tara in a wheelchair, and I told Brad that she was the daughter of a friend. Since I had to run some errands, could he entertain her while I was gone for a few hours? I left them in my office.

When I came back two hours later, I found Brad reading to her from *The Golem of Prague*, " 'Come,' said the Great Rabbi Loew, 'Open your eyes and speak like a real person!' "

That was just like Brad, I thought. He had his sense of irony.

"All right," I interrupted him. "Very funny. I get the joke. So how long did it take you?"

He smiled at Tara. "We'll finish this some other time," he said. Then he turned to me. "How long did it take me what?"

"To figure it out."

"Figure out what?"

"Stop kidding around," I said. "Really, what was it that gave her away?"

"Gave what away?" Brad and Tara said at the same time.

Nothing Tara ever said or did was a surprise to me. I could predict everything she would say before she said it. I'd coded everything in her, after all, and I knew exactly how her neural nets changed with each interaction.

But no one else suspected anything. I should have been elated. My doll was passing a real-life Turing Test. But I was frightened. The algorithms made a mockery of intelligence, and no one seemed to know. No one seemed to even care.

I finally broke the news to Brad after a week. After the initial shock he was delighted (as I knew he would be).

"Fantastic," he said. "We're now no longer just a toy company. Can you imagine the things we can do with this? You'll be famous, really famous!"

He prattled on and on about the potential applications. Then he noticed my silence. "What's wrong?"

So I told him about the Chinese Room.

The philosopher John Searle used to pose a puzzle for the AI researchers. Imagine a room, he said, a large room filled with meticulous clerks who are very good at following orders but who speak only English. Into this room are delivered a steady stream of cards with strange symbols on them. The clerks have to draw other strange symbols on blank cards in response and send the cards out of the room. In order to do this, the clerks have large books, full of rules in English like this one: "When you see a card with a single horizontal squiggle followed by a card with two vertical squiggles, draw a triangle on a blank card and hand it to the clerk to your right." The rules contain nothing about what the symbols might mean.

It turns out that the cards coming into the room are questions written in Chinese, and the clerks, by following the rules, are producing sensible answers in Chinese. But could anything involved in this process—the rules, the clerks, the room as a whole, the storm of activity—be said to have *understood* a word of Chinese? Substitute "processor" for the clerks and substitute "program" for the books of rules, then you'll see that the Turing Test will never prove anything, and AI is an illusion.

But you can also carry the Chinese Room Argument the other way: substitute "neurons" for the clerks and substitute the physical laws governing the cascading of activating potentials for the books of rules; then how can any of us ever be said to "understand" anything? Thought is an illusion.

"I don't understand," Brad said. "What are you saying?"

A moment later I realized that that was exactly what I'd expected him to say.

"Brad," I said, staring into his eyes, willing him to understand. "I'm scared. What if we are just like Tara?"

"We? You mean people? What are you talking about?"

"What if," I said, struggling to find the words, "we are just following some algorithm from day to day? What if our brain cells are just looking up signals from other signals? What if we are not thinking at all? What if what I'm saying to you now is just a predetermined response, the result of mindless physics?"

"Elena," Brad said, "you're letting philosophy get in the way of reality."

I need sleep, I thought, feeling hopeless.

"I think you need to get some sleep," Brad said.

Ω

I handed the coffee-cart girl the money as she handed me the coffee. I stared at the girl. She looked so tired and bored at eight in the morning that she made me feel tired.

I need a vacation.

"I need a vacation," she said, sighing exaggeratedly.

I walked past the receptionist's desk. *Morning, Elena.*

Say something different, please. I clenched my teeth. *Please.*

"Morning, Elena," she said.

I paused outside Ogden's cube. He was the structural engineer. *The weather, last night's game, Brad.*

He saw me and got up. "Nice weather we're having, eh?" He wiped the sweat from his forehead and smiled at me. He jogged to work. "Did you see the game last night? Best shot I've seen in ten years. Unbelievable. Hey, is Brad in yet?" His face was expectant, waiting for me to follow the script, the comforting routines of life.

The algorithms ran their determined courses, and our thoughts followed one after another, as mechanical and as predictable as the planets in their orbits. The watchmaker was the watch.

I ran into my office and closed the door behind me, ignoring the expression on Ogden's face. I walked over to my computer and began to delete files.

"Hi," Tara said. "What are we going to do today?"

I shut her off so quickly that I broke a nail on the hardware switch. I ripped out the power supply in her back. I went to work with my screwdriver and pliers. After a while I switched to a hammer. Was I killing?

Brad burst in the door. "What are you doing?"

I looked up at him, my hammer poised for another strike. I wanted to tell him about the pain, the terror that opened up an abyss around me.

In his eyes I could not find what I wanted to see. I could not see understanding.

I swung the hammer.

Brad had tried to reason with me, right before he had me committed.

"This is just an obsession," he said. "People have always associated the mind with the technological fad of the moment. When they believed in witches and spirits, they thought there was a little man in the brain. When they had mechanical looms and player pianos, they thought the brain was an engine. When they had telegraphs and telephones, they thought the brain was a wire network. Now you think the brain is just a computer. Snap out of it. *That* is the illusion."

Trouble was, I knew he was going to say that.

"It's because we've been married for so long!" he shouted. "That's why you think you know me so well!"

I knew he was going to say that too.

"You're running around in circles," he said, defeat in his voice. "You're just spinning in your head."

Loops in my algorithm. FOR and WHILE loops.

"Come back to me. I love you."

What else could he have said?

Now finally alone in the bathroom of the inn, I look down at my hands, at the veins running under the skin. I press my hands together and feel my pulse. I kneel down. Am I praying? Flesh and bones, and good programming.

My knees hurt against the cold tile floor.

The pain is real, I think. There's no algorithm for the pain. I look down at my wrists, and the scars startle me. This is all very familiar, like I've done this before. The horizontal scars, ugly and pink like worms, rebuke me for failure. Bugs in the algorithm.

That night comes back to me: the blood everywhere, the alarms wailing, Dr. West and the nurses holding me down while they bandaged my wrists, and then Brad staring down at me, his face distorted with uncomprehending grief.

I should have done better. The arteries are hidden deep, protected by the bones. The slashes have to be made vertically if you really want it. That's the right algorithm. There's a recipe for everything. This time I'll get it right.

It takes a while, but finally I feel sleepy.

I'm happy. The pain *is* real.

I open the door to my room and turn on the light.

The light activates Laura, who is sitting on top of my dresser. This one used to be a demo model. She hasn't been dusted in a while, and her dress looks ragged. Her head turns to follow my movement.

I turn around. Brad's body is still, but I can see the tears on his face. He was crying on the whole silent ride home from Salem.

The innkeeper's voice loops around in my head. "Oh, I could tell right away something was wrong. It's happened here before. She didn't seem right at breakfast, and then when you came back she looked like she was in another world. When I heard the water running in the pipes for that long I rushed upstairs right away."

So I was that predictable.

I look at Brad, and I believe that he is in a lot of pain. I believe it with all my heart. But I still don't feel anything. There's a gulf between us, a gulf so wide that I can't feel his pain. Nor he mine.

But my algorithms are still running. I scan for the right thing to say.

"I love you."

He doesn't say anything. His shoulders heave, once.

I turn around. My voice echoes through the empty house, bouncing off walls. Laura's sound receptors, old as they are, pick them up. The signals run through the cascading IF statements. The DO loops twirl and dance while she does a database lookup. The motors whirr. The synthesizer kicks in.

"I love you too," Laura says.

A JAR OF GOODWILL

TOBIAS S. BUCKELL

Points On A Package

You keep a low profile when you're in oxygen debt. Too much walking about just exacerbates the situation anyway. So I was nervous when a stationeer appeared at my cubby and knocked on the door.

I slid out and stood in front of the polished, skeletal robot.

"Alex Mosette?" it asked.

There was no sense in lying. The stationeer had already scanned my face. It was just looking for voice print verification. "Yes, I'm Alex," I said.

"The harbormaster wants to see you."

I swallowed. "He could have sent me a message."

"I am here to *escort* you." The robot held out a tinker-toy arm, digits pointed along the hallway.

Space in orbit came at a premium. Bottom-rung types like me slept in cubbies stacked ten high along the hallway. On my back in the cubby, watching entertainment shuffled in from the planets, they made living on a space station sound exotic and exciting.

It was if you were further up the rung. I'd been in those rooms: places with wasted space. Furniture. Room to stroll around in.

That was exotic.

Getting space in outer space was far down my list of needs.

First was air. Then food.

Anything else was pure luxury.

The harbormaster stared out into space, and I silently waited at the door to Operations, hoping that if I remained quiet he wouldn't notice.

Ops hung from near the center of the megastructure of the station. A blister stuck on the end of a long tunnel. You could see the station behind us: the miles-long wheel of exotic metals rotating slowly.

No gravity in Ops, or anywhere in the center. Spokes ran down from the wheel to the center, and the center was where ships docked and were serviced and so on.

So I hung silently in the air, long after the stationeer flitted off to do the harbormaster's bidding, wondering what happened next.

"You're overdrawn," the harbormaster said after a needle-like ship with long feathery vanes slipped underneath us into the docking bays.

He turned to face me, even though his eyes had been hollowed out long ago. Force of habit. His real eyes were now every camera, or anything mechanical that could see.

The harbormaster moved closer. The gantry around him was motorized, a long arm moving him anywhere he wanted in the room.

Hundreds of cables, plugged into his scalp like hair, bundled and ran back along the arm of the gantry. Hoses moved effluvia out. More hoses ran purified blood, and other fluids, back in.

"I'm sorry," I stammered. "Traffic is light. And requests have dropped off. I've taken classes. Even language lessons . . . " I stopped when I saw the wizened hand raise, palm up.

"I know what you've been doing." The harbormaster's sightless sockets turned back to the depths of space outside. The hardened skin of his face showed few emotions, his artificial voice was toneless. "You would not have been allowed to overdraw if you hadn't made good faith efforts."

"For which," I said, "I am enormously appreciative."

"That ship that just arrived brings with it a choice for you," the harbormaster continued without acknowledging what I'd just said. "I cannot let you overdraw any more if you stay on station, so I will have to put you into hibernation. To pay for hibernation and your air debt I would buy your contract. You'd be woken for guaranteed work. I'd take a percentage. You could buy your contract back out, once you had enough liquidity."

That was exactly what I'd been dreading. But he'd indicated an alternate. "My other option?"

He waved a hand, and a holographic image of the ship I'd just seen coming in to dock hung in the air. "They're asking for a professional Friend."

"For their ship?" Surprise tinged my question. I wasn't crew material. I'd been shipped frozen to the station, just another corpsicle. People like me didn't stay awake for travel. Not enough room.

The harbormaster shrugged pallid shoulders. "They will not tell me why. I had to sign a nondisclosure agreement just to get them to tell me what they wanted."

I looked at the long ship. "I'm not a fuckbot. They know that, right?"

"They know that. They reiterated that they do *not* want sexual services."

"I'll be outside the station. Outside your protection. It could still be what they want."

"That is a risk. How much so, I cannot model for you." The harbormaster snapped his fingers, and the ship faded away. "But the contractors have extremely high reputational scores on past business dealings. They are freelance scientists: biology, botany, and one linguist."

So they probably didn't want me as a pass-around toy.

Probably.

"Rape amendments to the contract?" I asked. I was going to be on a ship, unthawed, by myself, with crew I'd never met. I had to think about the worst.

"Prohibitive. Although, accidental loss of life is not quite as high, which means I'd advise lowering the former so that there is no temptation to murder you after a theoretical rape to evade the higher contract payout."

"Fuck," I sighed.

"Would you like to peruse their reputation notes?" the harbormaster asked. And for a moment, I thought maybe the harbormaster sounded concerned.

No. He was just being fair. He'd spent two hundred years of bargaining with ships for goods, fuel, repair, services. Fair was built-in, the half-computer half-human creature in front of me was all about fair. Fair got you repeat business. Fair got you a wide reputation.

"What's the offer?"

"Half a point on the package," the harbormaster said.

"And we don't know what the package is, or how long it will take . . . or anything." I bit my lip.

"They assured me that half a point would pay off your debt and then some. It shouldn't take more than a year."

A year. For half a percent. Half a percent of what? It could be cargo they were delivering. Or, seeing as it was a crew of scientists, it could be some project they were working on.

All of which just raised more questions.

Questions I wouldn't have answers to unless I signed up. I sighed. "That's it, then? No loans? No extensions?"

The harbormaster sighed. "I answer to the Gheda shareholders who built and own this complex. I have already stretched my authority to give you a month's extension. The debt *has* to be called. I'm sorry."

I looked out at the darkness of space out beyond Ops. "Shit choices either way."

The harbormaster said nothing.

I folded my arms. "Do it."

Journey by Gheda

The docking arms had transferred the starship from the center structure's incoming docks down a spoke to a dock on one of the wheels. The entire ship, thanks to being spun along with the wheel of the station, had gravity.

The starship was a quarter of a mile long. Outside: sleek and burnished smooth by impacts with the scattered dust of space at the stunning speeds it achieved. Inside, I realized I'd boarded a creaky, old, outdated vehicle.

Fiberwire spilled out from conduits, evidence of crude repair jobs. Dirt and grime clung to nooks and crannies. The air smelled of sweat and worst.

A purple-haired man with all-black eyes met me at the airlock. "You are the Friend?" he asked. He carried a large walking stick with him.

"Yes." I let go of the rolling luggage behind me and bowed. "I'm Alex."

He bowed back. More extravagantly than I did. Maybe even slightly mockingly. "I'm Oslo." Every time he shifted his walking stick, tiny grains of sand inside rattled and shifted about. He brimmed with impatience, and some regret in the crinkled lines of his eyes. "Is this everything?"

I looked back at the single case behind me. "That is everything."

"Then welcome aboard," Oslo said, as the door to the station clanged shut. He raised the stick, and a flash of light blinded me.

"You should have taken a scan of me before you shut the door," I said. The stick was more than it seemed. Those tiny rustling grains were generators, harnessing power for whatever tools were inside the device via kinetic motion. He turned around and started to walk away. I hurried to catch up.

Oslo smiled, and I noticed tiny little fangs under his lips. "You are who you say you are, so everything ended up okay. Oh, and for protocol, the others aren't much into it either, by the way. Now, for my own edification, you are a hermaphrodite, correct?"

I flushed. "I am what we Friends prefer to call bi-gendered, yes." Where the hell was Oslo from? I was having trouble placing his cultural conditionings and how I might adapt to interface with them. He was very direct, that was for sure.

This gig might be more complicated than I thought.

"Your Friend training: did it encompass Compact cross-cultural training?"

I slowed down. "In theory," I said slowly, worried about losing the contract if they insisted on having someone with Compact experience.

Oslo's regret dripped from his voice and movements. Was it regret that I didn't have the experience? Would I lose the contract, minutes into getting it? Or just regret that he couldn't get someone better? "But you've never Friended an actual Compact drone?"

I decided to tell the truth. A gamble. "No."

"Too bad." The regret sloughed off, to be replaced with resignation. "But we can't poke around asking for Friends with that specific experience, or one of our competitors might put two and two together. I recommend you brush up on your training during the trip out."

He stopped in front of a large, metal door. "Where are we going?" I asked.

"Here is your room for the next three days." Oslo opened the large door to a five-by-seven foot room with a foldout bunk bed.

My heart skipped a beat, and I put aside the fact that Oslo had avoided the question. "That's mine?"

"Yes. And the air's billed with our shipping contract, so you can rip your sensors off. There'll be no accounting until we're done."

I got the sense Oslo knew what it was like to be in debt. I stepped into the room and turned all the way around. I raised my hands, placing them on each wall, and smiled.

Oslo turned to go.

"Wait," I said. "The harbormaster said you were freelance scientists. What do you do?"

"I'm the botanist," Oslo said. "Meals are in the common passenger's galley. The crew of this ship is Gheda, of course, don't talk to or interact with them if you can help it. You know why?"

"Yes." The last thing you wanted to do was make a Gheda think you were wandering around, trying to figure out secrets about their ships, or technology. I would stay in the approved corridors and not interact with them.

The door closed in my suite, and I sat down with my small travel case, no closer to understanding what was going on than I had been on the station.

I faced the small mirror by an even smaller basin and reached for the strip of black material stuck to my throat. Inside it, circuitry monitored my metabolic rate, number of breaths taken, volume of air taken in, and carbon dioxide expelled. All of it reported back to the station's monitors, constantly calculating my mean daily cost.

It made a satisfying sound as I ripped it off.

"Gheda are Gheda," I said later in the ship's artificial, alien day over reheated turkey strips in the passenger's galley. We'd undocked. The old ship had shivered itself up to speed. "But Gheda flying around in a beat-up old starship, willing to take freelance scientists out to some secret destination: these are dangerous Gheda."

Oslo had a rueful smile as he leaned back and folded his arms. "Cruzie says that our kind used to think our corporations were rapacious and evil before first contact. No one expected aliens to demand royalty payments for technology usage that had been independently discovered by us because the Gheda had previously patented that technology."

"I know. They hit non-compliant areas with asteroids from orbit." Unable to pay royalties, entire nations had collapsed into debtorship. "Who's Cruzie?"

Oslo grimaced. "You'll meet her in two days. Our linguist. Bit of a historian, too. Loves old Earth shit."

I frowned at his reaction. Conflicted, but with somewhat warm pleasure when he thought about her. A happy grimace. "She's an old friend of yours?"

"Our parents were friends. They loved history. The magnificence of Earth. The legend that was. Before it got sold around. Before the Diaspora." That grimace again. But no warmth there.

"You don't agree with their ideals?" I guessed.

I guessed well. Oslo sipped at a mug of tea, and eyed me. "I'm not your project, Friend. Don't dig too deep, because you just work for me. Save your empathy and psychiatry for the real subject. Understand?"

Too far, I thought. "I'm sorry. And just what is my project? We're away from the station now; do you think you can risk being open with me?"

Oslo set his tea down. "Clever. Very clever, Friend. Yes, I was worried about bugs. We've found a planet, with a unique ecosystem. There may be patentable innovations."

I sat, stunned. Patents? I had points on the package. If I got points on a patent on some aspect of an alien biological system, a Gheda-approved patent, I'd be rich.

Not just rich, but like, nation-rich.

Oslo sipped at his tea. "There's only one problem," he said. "There may be intelligent life on the planet. If it's intelligent, it's a contact situation, and we have to turn it over to the Gheda. We get a fee, but no taste of the real game. We fail to report a contact situation and the Gheda find out, it's going to be a nasty scene. They'll kill our families, or even people you know, just to make the point that their interstellar law is inviolate. We have to file a claim the moment of discovery."

I'd heard hesitation in his voice. "You haven't filed yet, have you?"

"I bet all the Gheda business creatures love having you watch humans they're settling a contract with, making sure they're telling the truth, you there to brief them on what their facial expressions are really showing."

That stung. "I'd do the same for any human. And it isn't just contracts. Many hire me to pay attention to them, to figure them out, anticipate their needs."

Oslo leered. "I'll bet."

I wasn't a fuckbot. I deflected the leering. "So tell me, Oslo, why I'm risking my life, then?"

"We haven't filed yet because we honestly can't fucking figure out if the aliens are just dumb creatures, or intelligences like us," Oslo said.

Ω
The Drone

"Welcome to the Screaming Kettle," said the woman who grabbed my bag without asking. She had dark brown skin and eyes, and black hair. Tattoos covered every inch of skin free of her clothing. Words in scripts and languages that I didn't recognize. "The Compact Drone is about to dock as well, we need you ready for it. Let's get your stuff stowed."

We walked below skylights embedded in the top of the research station. A planet hung there: green and yellow and patchy. It looked like it was diseased with mold. "Is that Ve?" I asked.

"Oslo get you up to speed?" the woman asked.

"Somewhat. You're Cruzie, right?"

"Maricruz. I'm the linguist. I guess . . . you're stuck here with us. You can call me Cruzie too." We stopped in front of a room larger than the one on the ship. With two beds.

I looked at the beds. "I'm comfortable with a cubby, if it means getting my own space," I said.

There was far more space here, vastly so. And yet, I was going to have to share it? It rankled. Even at the station, I hadn't had to share my space. This shoved me up against my own cultural normative values. Even in the most packed places in space, you needed a cubby of one's own.

"You're here to Friend the Compact Drone," Cruzie said. "It'll need companionship at all times. Their contract requires it for the Drone's mental stability."

"Oslo didn't tell me this." I pursed my lips. A fairly universal display of annoyance.

And Cruzie read that well enough. "I'm sorry," she said. But it was a lie as well. She was getting annoyed and impatient. But screw it, as Oslo pointed out: I wasn't there for their needs. "Oslo wants us to succeed more than anything. Unlike his parents, he's not much into the glory that was humankind. He knows the only way we'll ever not be freelancers, scrabbling around for intellectual scraps found in the side alleys of technology for something we can use without paying the Gheda for the privilege, is to hit something big."

"So he lied to me." My voice remained flat.

"He left out truths that would have made you less willing to come."

"He lied."

Cruzie shut the door to my room. "He gave you points on the package, Friend. We win big, you do your job, you'll never have to check the balance on your air for the rest of your damned life. I heard you were in air debt, right?"

She'd put me well in place. We both knew it. Cruzie smiled, a gracious winner's smile.

"Incoming!" Someone yelled from around the bend in the corridor.

"I'm not going to fuck the Drone," I told her levelly.

Cruzie shrugged. "I don't care what you do or don't do, as long as the Drone stays mentally stable and does its job for us. Points on the package, Alex. Points."

Airlock alarms flashed and warbled, and the hiss of compressed air filled the antechamber.

"The incoming pod's not much larger than a cubby sleeper," Oslo said, his purple hair waving about as another burst of compressed air filled the antechamber. He smiled, fangs out beyond his lips. "It's smaller than the lander we have for exploring Ve ourselves, if we ever need to get down there. Can you imagine the ride? The only non-Gheda way of traveling!"

The last member of the team joined us. She looked over at me and nodded. Silvered electronic eyes glinted in the flash of the airlock warning lights. She flexed the jet black fingers of her artificial right hand absentmindedly as she waited for the doors to open. She ran the fingers of a real hand over her shaved head, then put them back in her utility jacket, covered with what seemed like hundreds of pockets and zippers.

"That's Kepler," Cruzie said.

The airlock doors opened. A thin, naked man stumbled out, dripping goopy blue acceleration gel with each step.

For a moment his eyes flicked around, blinking.

Then he started screaming.

Oslo, Kepler, and Cruzie jumped back half a step from the naked man's arms. I stepped forward. "It's not fear, it's relief."

The man grabbed me in a desperate hug, clinging to me, his hands patting my face, shoulders, as if reassuring himself someone was really standing in front of him. "It's okay," I whispered. "You've been in there by yourself for days, with no contact of any sort. I understand."

He was shivering in my grip, but I kept patting his back. I urged him to feel the press of contact between us. And reassurance. Calm.

Eventually he calmed down, and then slowly let go of me.

"What's your name?" I asked.

"Beck."

"Welcome aboard, Beck," I said, looking over his shoulder at the scientists who looked visibly relieved.

Ω

First things first.

Beck got to the communications room. Back and forth verification on an uplink, and he leaned back against the chair in relief.

"There's an uplink to the Hive," he said. "An hour of lag time to get as far back as the home system, but I'm patched in."

He tapped metal inserts on the back of his neck. His mind plugged in to the communications network, talking all the way back to the asteroid belt in the mother system, where the Compact's Hive thrived. Back there, Beck would always be in contact with it without a delay. In instant symbiosis with a universe of information that the Compact offered.

A hive-mind of people, your core self subjugated to the greater whole.

I shivered.

Beck never moved more than half a foot away from me. Always close enough to touch. He kept reaching out to make sure I was there, even though he could see me.

After walking around the research station for half an hour, we returned to our shared room.

He sat on his bed, suddenly apprehensive. "You're the Friend, correct?"

"Yes."

"I'm lonely over here. Can you sleep by me?"

I walked over and sat next to him. "I won't have sex with you. That's not why I'm here."

"I'm chemically neutered," Beck said as we curled up on the bed. "I'm a drone."

As we lay there, I imagined thousands of Becks sleeping in rows in Hive dorms, body heat keeping the rooms warm.

Half an hour later he suddenly sighed, like a drug addict getting a hit. "They hear me," he whispered. "I'm not alone."

The Compact had replied to him.

He relaxed.

The room filled with a pleasant lavender scent. Was it something he'd splashed on earlier? Or something a Compact drone released to indicate comfort?

What's Human?

"That," Kepler said, leaning back in a couch before a series of displays, "is one of our remote-operated vehicles. We call them urchins."

In the upper right hand screen before her, a small sphere with hundreds of wriggling legs rotated around. Then it scrabbled off down what looked like a dirt path.

Cruzie swung into a similar couch. "We sterilize them in orbit, then drop them down encased in a heatshield. It burns away, then they drop down out of the sky with a little burst of a rocket to slow down enough."

I frowned at one of the screens. Everything was shades of green and gray and black. "Is that night vision?"

Oslo laughed. "It's Ve. The atmosphere is chlorinated. Green mists. Grey shadows. And black plants."

The trees had giant, black leaves hanging low to the ground. Tubular trunks sprouted globes that spouted mist randomly as the urchin brushed past.

"Ve's a small planet," Kepler said. "Low gravity, but with air similar to what you would have seen on the mother world."

"Earth," Oslo corrected.

"But unlike the mother world," Kepler continued, "Ve has high levels of chlorine. Somewhere in its history, a battle launched among the plants. Instead of specializing in oxygen to kill off the competition, and adapting to it over time, plant life here turned to chlorine as a weapon. It created plastics out of the organic compounds available to it, which is doable in a chlorine-heavy base atmosphere, though remarkable. And the organic plastics also handle photosynthesis. A handy trick. If we can patent it."

On the screen the urchin rolled to a slow stop. Cruzie leaned forward. "Now if we can just figure out if *those* bastards are really building a civilization, or just random dirt mounds . . . "

Paused at the top of a ridge, the urchin looked at a clearing in the black-leafed forest. Five pyramids thrust above the foliage around the clearing.

"Can you get closer?" Beck asked, and I jumped slightly. He'd been so silent, watching all this by my side.

"Not from here," Kepler said. "There's a big dip in altitude between here and the clearing."

"And?" Beck stared at the pyramids on the screen.

"Our first couple weeks here we kept driving the urchins into low lying areas, valleys, that sort of thing. They kept dying on us. We figure the chlorine and acids sink low into the valleys. Our equipment can't handle it."

Beck sat down on the nearest couch to Kepler, and looked over the interface. "Take the long way around then, I'll look at your archives while you do so. Wait!"

I saw it too. A movement through the black, spiky bushes. I saw my first alien creature scuttle around, antennae twisting as it moved along what looked like a path.

"They look like ants," I blurted out.

"We call them Vesians. But yes, ants the size of a small dog," Oslo said. "And not really ants at all. Just exoskeletons, black plastic, in a similar structure. The handiwork of parallel evolution."

More Vesians appeared carrying leaves and sticks on their backs.

And gourds.

"Now that's interesting," Beck said.

"It doesn't mean they're intelligent," Beck said later, lying in the bunk with me next to him. We both stared up at the ceiling. He rolled over and looked at me. "The gourds grow on trees. They use them to store liquids. Inside those pyramids."

We were face to face, breathing each other's air. Beck had no personal space, and I had to fight my impulse to pull back away from him.

My job was now to facilitate. Make Beck feel at home.

Insect hives had drones that could exist away from the hive. A hive needed foragers, and defenders. But the human Compact only existed in the asteroid belt of the mother system.

Beck was a long way from home.

With the lag, he would be feeling cut off and distant. And for a mind that had always been in the embrace of the hive, this had to be hard for him.

But Beck offered the freelance scientists a link into the massive computational capacity of the entire Compact. They'd contracted it to handle the issue they couldn't figure out quickly: were the aliens intelligent or not?

Beck was pumping information back all the way back to the mother system, so that the Compact could devote some fraction of a fraction of its massed computing ability to the issue. The minds of all its connected citizenry. Its supercomputers. Maybe even, it was rumored, artificial intelligences.

"But if they are intelligent?" I asked. "How do you prove it?"

Beck cocked his head. "The Compact is working on it. Has been ever since the individuals here signed the contract."

"Then why are you out here?"

"Yes . . . " He was suddenly curious in me now, remembering I was a distinct individual, lying next to him. I wasn't of the Compact. I wasn't another drone.

"I'm sorry," I said. "I shouldn't have asked."

"It was good you asked." He flopped over to stare at the ceiling again. "You're right, I'm not entirely needed. But the Compact felt it was necessary."

I wanted to know why. But I could feel Beck hesitate. I held my breath.

"You are a Friend. You've never broken contract. The Compact ranks you very highly." Beck turned back to face me. "We understand that what I tell you will never leave this room, and since I debugged it, it's a safe room. What do you think it takes to become a freelance scientist in this hostile universe?"

I'd been around enough negotiating tables. A good Friend, with the neural modifications and adaptive circuitry laced into me from birth, I could read body posture, micro-expressions, skin flush, heart rate, in a blink of the eye. I made a hell of a negotiating tool. Which was usually exactly what Gheda wanted: a read on their human counterparts.

And I had learned the ins and outs of my clients businesses quick as well. I knew what the wider universe was like while doing my job.

"Oslo has pent-up rage," I whispered. "His family is obsessed with the Earth as it used to be. Before the Gheda land purchases. He wants wealth, but that's not all, I think. Cruzie holds herself like she has military bearing, though she hides it. Kepler, I don't know. I'm guessing you will tell me they have all worked as weapons manufacturers or researchers of some sort?"

Beck nodded. "Oslo and his sister London are linked to a weaponized virus that was released on a Gheda station. Cruzie fought with separatists in Columbia. Kepler is a false identity. We haven't cracked her yet."

I looked at the drone. There was no deceit in him. He stated these things as facts. He was a drone. He didn't need to question the information given to him.

"Why are you telling me all this?"

He gestured at the bunk. "You're a professional Friend. You're safe. You're here. And I'm just a drone. We're just a piece of all this."

And then he moved to spoon against the inside of my stomach. Two meaningless, tiny lives inside a cold station, far away from where they belonged.

"And because," he added in a soft voice, "I think that these scientists are desperate enough to fix a problem if it occurs."

"Fix a problem?" I asked, wrapping my arms around him.

"I think the Vesians are intelligent, and I think Kepler and Oslo plan to do something to them if, or when, it's confirmed, so that they can keep patent rights."

I could suddenly hear every creak, whisper, and whistle in the station as I tensed up.

"I will protect you if I can. Right now we're just delaying as long as we can. Mainly I'm trying to stop Cruzie from figuring out the obvious, because if she confirms they're really intelligent, then Oslo and Kepler will make their move and do something to the Vesians. We're not sure what."

"You said delaying. Delaying until what?" I asked, a slight quaver in my voice that I found I couldn't control.

"Until the Gheda get here," Beck said with a last yawn. "That's when it all gets really complicated." His voice trailed off as he said that, and he fell asleep.

I lay there, awake and wide-eyed.

I finally reached up to my neck and scratched at the band of skin where the air monitor patch had once been stuck.

Points on nothing was still just . . . nothing.

But could I rat out my contract? My role as a Friend? Could I help Oslo and Kepler kill an alien race?

Things had gotten very muddy in just a few minutes. I felt trapped between the hell of an old life and the hell of a horrible new one.

"What's a human being?" I asked Beck over lunch.

"Definitions vary," he replied.

"You're a drone: bred to act, react, and move within a shared neural environment. You serve the Compact. There's no queen, like a classic anthill or with bees. Your shared mental overmind makes the calls. So you have a say. A tiny say. You are human . . . -ish. Our ancestors would have questioned whether you were human."

Beck cocked his head and smiled. "And you?"

"Modified from birth to read human faces. Under contract for most of my life to Gheda, working to tell the aliens or other humans what humans are really thinking . . . they wouldn't have thought highly of me either."

"The Compact knows you reread your contract last night, after I fell asleep, and you used some rather complicated algorithms to game some scenarios."

I frowned. "So you're spying on us now."

"Of course. You're struggling with a gray moral situation."

"Which is?"

"The nature of your contract says you need to work with me and support my needs. But you're hired by the freelancers that I'm now in opposition to. As a Friend, a role and purpose burned into you just like being a drone is burned into me, do you warn *them*? Or do you stick by me? The contract allows for interpretations either way. And if you stick with me, it's doing so while knowing that I'm just a drone. A pawn that the Compact will use as it sees fit, for its own game."

"You left something out," I said.

"Neither you, nor I, are bred to care about Vesians," Beck said.

I got up and walked over to the large porthole. "I wonder if it wouldn't be better for them?"

"What would?"

"Whatever Kepler and Oslo want to do to them. Better to die now than to meet the Gheda. I can't imagine they'd ever want to become us."

Beck stood up. There was caution in his stance, as if he'd thought I had been figured out, but now wasn't sure. "I've got work to do. Stay here and finish your meal, Friend."

I looked down at the green world beneath, and jumped when a hand grabbed my shoulder. I could see gray words tattooed in the skin. "Cruzie?"

Her large brown eyes were filled with anger. "That son of a bitch has been lying to us," she said, pointing in the direction Beck had gone. "Come with me."

"The gourds," Cruzie said, pointing at a screen, and then looking at Beck. "Tell us about the gourds."

And Oslo grabbed my shoulder. "Watch the drone, sharp now. I want you to tell us what you see when he replies to us."

My contract would be clear there. I couldn't lie. The scientists owned the contract, and now that they'd asked directly for my services, I couldn't evade.

Points on the package, I thought in the far back of my mind.

I wasn't really human, was I? Not if I found the lure of eternal riches to be so great as to consider helping the freelancers.

"The Vesians have farms," Cruzie said. "But so do ants: they grow fungus. The Vesians have roads, but so do animals in a forest. They just keep walking over the same spots. Old Earth roads used to follow old animal paths. The Vesians have buildings, but birds build nests, ants build colonies, bees build hives. But language, that's so much rarer in the animal kingdom, isn't it, Beck?"

"Not really," the drone said calmly. "Primitive communication exists in animals. Including bees, which dance information. Dolphins squeak and whales sing."

"But none of them write it down," Cruzie grinned.

Oslo's squeezed my shoulder, hard. "The drone is mildly annoyed," I said. "And more than a little surprised."

Cruzie tapped on a screen. The inside of one of the pyramids appeared. It was a storehouse of some sort, filled with hundreds, maybe thousands, of the gourds I'd seen earlier that the Vesian had been transporting.

"Nonverbal creatures use scent. Just like ants on the mother planet. The Vesians use scents to mark territories their queens manage. And one of the things I started to wonder about, were these storage areas. What were they for? So I broke in, and I started breaking the gourds."

Beck stiffened. "He's not happy with this line of thought," I murmured.

"Thought so," Oslo said back, and nodded at Cruzie, who kept going.

"And whenever I broke a gourd, I found them empty. Not full of liquid, as Beck told us was likely. We originally thought they were for storage. An adaptive behavior. Or a sign of intelligence. Hard to say. Until I broke them all."

"They could have been empty, waiting to be sealed," Beck said tonelessly.

I sighed. "I'm sorry, Beck. I have to do this. He's telling the truth, Oslo. But misdirecting."

"I know he is," Cruzie said. "Because the Vesians swarmed the location with fresh gourds. There were chemical scents, traces laid down in the gourds before they were sealed. The Vesians examined the broken gourds, then filled the new ones with scents. I started examining the chemical traces, and found that each gourd replaced had the same chemical sequences sprayed on and stored as the ones I broke."

Beck's muscles tensed. Any human could see the stress now. I didn't need to say anything.

"They were like monks, copying manuscripts. Right, Beck?" Cruzie asked.

"Yes," Beck said.

"And the chemical markers, it's a language, right?" Kepler asked. I could feel the tension in her voice. It wasn't just disappointment building, but rage.

"It is." Beck stood up slowly.

"It took me days to realize it," Cruzie said. "And that, after the weeks I've been out here. The Compact spotted it right away, didn't it?"

Beck looked over at me, then back at Cruzie. "Yes. The Compact knows."

"Then what the hell is it planning to do?" Kepler moved in front of Beck, lips drawn back in a snarl.

"I'm just a drone," Beck said. "I don't know. But I can give you an answer in an hour."

For a second, everyone stood frozen. Oslo, brimming with hurt rage, staring at Beck. Kepler, moving from anger toward some sort of decision. Cruzie looked . . . triumphant. Oblivious to the real breaking developments in the air.

And I observed.

Like any good Friend.

Then a loud 'whooop whooop' startled us all out of our poses.

"What's that?" Cruzie asked, looking around.

"The Gheda are here," Oslo, Kepler, and Beck said at the same time.

The Path Less Traveled

"Call the vote," Oslo snapped.

Cruzie swallowed. I saw micro beads of sweat on the side of her neck. "Right now?"

"Gheda are inbound," Kepler said, her artificial eyes dark. I imagined she had them patched into the computers, looking at information from the station's sensors. "They'll be decelerating and matching orbit in hours. There's no time for debate, Cruzie."

"What we're about to do *is* something that requires debate. They're intelligent. We're proposing ripping that away over the next day with Kepler's tailored virus. They'll end up with a viral lobotomy, just smart enough we can claim their artifacts come from natural hive mind behavior. But we'll have stolen their culture. Their minds. Their history." Cruzie shook her head. "I know we said they're going to lose most of that when the Gheda arrive. But if we do this, we're worse than Gheda."

"Fucking hell, Cruzie!" Oslo snapped. "You're changing your mind *now*?"

"Oslo!" Cruzie held up her hands as if trying to ward off the angry words.

"You saw our mother planet," Oslo said. "The slums. The starvation. Gheda combat patrols. They owned *everyone*. If you didn't provide value, you were nothing. You *fought* the Sahara campaign, you attacked Abbuj station. How the fuck can you turn your back to all that?"

"I didn't turn my back, I wanted a different path," Cruzie said. "That's why we're here. With the money on the patents, we could change things . . . but what are we changing here if we're not all that better than the Gheda?"

"It's us or the fucking ants," Kepler said, voice suddenly level. "It's really that simple. Where are your allegiances?"

I bit my lip when I heard that.

"Cruzie . . . " I started to say.

She held a hand up and walked over to the console, her thumb held out. "It takes a unanimous vote to unleash the virus. This was why I insisted."

"You're right," Kepler said. I flinched. I could hear the hatred in her voice. She nodded at Oslo.

He raised his walking stick. The tiny grains inside rattled around, and then a jagged finger of energy leapt out and struck Cruzie in the small of her back.

Cruzie jerked around, arms flopping as she danced, then dropped to the ground. Oslo pressed the stick to her head and fired it again. Blood gushed from Cruzie's eye sockets as something inside her skull went 'pop.'

A wisp of smoke curled from her open mouth.

Oslo and Kepler put thumbs to the screens. "We have a unanimous vote now."

But a red warning sign flashed back at them. Beck relaxed slightly, a tiny curl of a smile briefly appearing.

Oslo raised his walking stick and pointed it at Beck. "Our communications are blocked."

"Yes," Beck said. "The Compact is voting against preemptive genocide."

For a split second, I saw the decision to kill Beck flit across Kepler's face. "If you kill him," I spoke up, "the Compact will spend resources hunting you two down. You can't enjoy your riches if you're dead."

Kepler nodded. "You're right." But she looked at me, a question on her face.

I shrugged. "If you're all dead, I don't have points on the package."

"Trigger them manually," Oslo said. "We'll bring the drone. We won't leave him up here to cause more trouble. Bring him, or her, or whatever the Friend calls itself as well. Your contract, Alex, is now to watch Beck."

We burned our way through the green atmosphere of Ve, the lander bucking and groaning, skin cracking as it weathered the heat of our reentry fireball.

From the tiny cramped cockpit I watched us part the clouds and spiral slowly down out of the sky as the wings unfurled from slots in the tear-drop sized vehicle's side. They started beating a complicated figure-eight motion.

Oslo aimed his walking stick at us when the lander touched down. "Put on your helmet, get out. Both of you."

We did so.

Heavy chlorine-rich mists swirled around, disturbed by our landing. Large puffball flowers spurted acid whenever touched by a piece of stray stirred-up debris, and the black, plastic leaves all around us bobbed gently in a low breeze.

Oslo and Kepler pulled a large pack out of the lander's cargo area. Long pieces of tubing. They set to building a freestanding antenna, piece by piece. I watched Beck. I couldn't see his face, but I could see his posture.

He was about to run. Which made no sense. Run where? On this world?

Within a few minutes Oslo and Kepler had snapped together a thirty-foot tall tower. I swallowed, and remained silent. It was a choice, a deliberate path. I broke my contract.

Oslo snapped a clip to the top of the tower, then unrolled a length of cable. He and Kepler used it to pull the super light structure up.

That was the moment Beck ran, as it hung halfway up to standing.

"Shit," Oslo cursed over the tiny speakers in our helmets, but he didn't drop the structure. "You've only got a couple hours of air you moron!"

The only response was Beck's heavy breathing.

When the antenna stood upright, Oslo approached me, the walking stick out. "You didn't warn us."

"He was wearing a spacesuit," I said calmly.

But I could see Oslo didn't believe me. His eyes creased and his fingers tightened. A bright explosion of pain ripped into me.

My vision cleared.

I was on my hands and feet, shaking with pain from the electrical discharge. A whirlwind of debris whipped around me. I looked up to see the lander lifting into the sky.

So that was it. I'd made my choice: to try and not be a monster.

And it had been in vain. The Vesians would be lobotomized by Kepler's virus. Beck would die. I would die.

I watched the lander beginning a wide spiral upward away from me. In a few seconds it would fire its rockets and climb for orbit.

In a couple hours, I would run out of air.

Four large gourds arced high over the black forest and slapped into the side of the lander. I frowned. At first, it looked like they had no effect. The lander kept spiraling up.

But then, it faltered.

The lander shook, and smoke spilled out of a crack in the side somewhere.

It exploded, the fireball hanging in the sky.

"Get away from the antenna," Beck suddenly said. "It's next."

I ran without a second thought, and even as I got free of the clearing, gourds of acid hit the structure. The metal sizzled, foamed, and then began to melt.

A few seconds later, I broke out onto a dirt path where the catapults firing the gourds of acid had been towed into place.

Beck waited for me, surrounded by a crowd of Vesians. He wore only his helmet, he'd ripped his suit off. His skin bubbled from bad chemical burn blisters.

"The Vesians destroyed all the remote-operating vehicles with the virus in it," he said. "The queens have quarantined any Vesians near any area that had an ROV. The species will survive."

"You've been talking to them," I said. And then I thought back to the comforting smell in my room the first night Beck spent with me. "You're communicating with them. You warned them."

Beck held up his suit. "Yes. The Compact altered me to be an ambassador to them."

"Beck, how long can you survive in this environment?" I stared at his blistered skin.

"A year. Maybe. There will be another ready by then. Maybe a structure to live in. The Gheda will be here soon to bring air. The Compact has reached an agreement with them. The Vesian queens are agreeing to join the Compact. The Compact gets to extend out of the mother system, but only to Ve. In exchange, the Gheda get rights to all patentable discoveries made in the new ecosystem. They're particularly interested in plastic-based organic photosynthesis."

I collapsed to the ground, realizing that I would live. Beck sat next to me. A small Vesian, approached, a gourd in its mandibles. It set the organic, plastic bottle at my legs. "What's that?"

"A jar of goodwill," Beck said. "The Vesian queen of this area is thanking you."

I was still just staring at it two hours later as my air faded out, my vision blurred, and the Gheda lander finally reached us.

The harbormaster cocked his head. "You're back."

"I'm back," I said. Someone was unpacking my two bags. one of them carefully holding the Vesian 'gift.'

"I didn't think I'd ever see you again," the harbormaster said. "Not with a contract like that."

"It didn't work out." I looked out into the vacuum of space beyond us. "Certainly not for the people who hired me. Or me."

"You have a peripheral contract with the Compact. An all-you-can-breath line of credit on the station. You're not a citizen, but on perpetual retainer as the Compact's primary professional Friend for all dealings in this system. You did well enough."

I grinned. "Points on a package like what they offered me was a fairy tale. A fairy tale you'd have to be soulless to want to have come true."

"I'm surprised that you did not choose to join the Compact," the harbormaster said, looking closely at me. "It is a safe place for humans in this universe. Even as a peripheral for them, you could still be in danger during patent negotiations with Gheda."

"I know. But this is home. My home. I'm not a drone, I don't want to be one."

The harbormaster sighed. "You understand the station is my only love. I don't have a social circle. There is only the ebb and flow of this structure's health for me."

I smiled. "That's why I like you, harbormaster. You have few emotions. You are a fair dealer. You're the closest thing I have to family. You may even be the closest thing I have to a friend, friend with a lowercase 'f.' "

"You follow your contracts to the letter. I like that about you," the harbormaster said. "I'm glad you will continue on here."

Together we watched the needle-like ship that had brought me back home silently fall away from the station.

"The Compact purchased me a ten-by-ten room with a porthole," I said. "I don't have to come up here to sneak a look at the stars anymore."

The harbormaster sighed happily. "They're beautiful, aren't they? I think, we've always loved them, haven't we? Even before we were forced to leave the mother world."

"That's what the history books say," I said quietly over the sound of ducts and creaking station. "We dreamed of getting out here, to live among them. Dreamed of the wonders we'd see."

"The Gheda don't see the stars," the harbormaster said. "They have few portholes. Before I let the Gheda turn me into a harbormaster, I demanded the contract include this room."

"They don't see them the way we do," I agreed.

"They're not human," the harbormaster said.

"No, they're not." I looked out at the distant stars. "But then, few things are anymore."

The Gheda ship disappeared in a blinding flash of light, whipping through space toward its next destination.

THE SHIPMAKER

ALIETTE DE BODARD

Ships were living, breathing beings. Dac Kien had known this even before she'd reached the engineering habitat, even before shed seen the great mass in orbit outside, being slowly assembled by the bots.

Her ancestors had once carved jade, in the bygone days of the Le Dynasty on Old Earth: not hacking the green blocks into the shape they wanted, but rather whittling down the stone until its true nature was revealed. And as with jade, so with ships. The sections outside couldn't be forced together. They had to flow into a seamless whole—to be, in the end, inhabited by a Mind who was as much a part of the ship as every rivet and every seal.

The Easterners or the Mexica didn't understand. They spoke of recycling, of design efficiency: they saw only the parts taken from previous ships, and assumed it was done to save money and time. They didn't understand why Dac Kien's work as Grand Master of Design Harmony was the most important on the habitat: the ship, once made, would be one entity, and not a patchwork often thousand others. To Dac Kien—and to the one who would come after her, the Mind-bearer—fell the honour of helping the ship into being, of transforming metal and cables and solar cells into an entity that would sail the void between the stars.

The door slid open. Dac Kien barely looked up. The light tread of the feet told her this was one of the lead designers, either Miahua or Feng. Neither would have disturbed her without cause. With a sigh, she disconnected from the system with a flick of her hands, and waited for the designs overlay on her vision to disappear.

"Your Excellency." Miahua's voice was quiet. The Xuyan held herself upright, her skin as pale as yellowed wax. "The shuttle has come back. There's someone on board you should see."

Dac Kien had expected many things: a classmate from the examinations on a courtesy visit; an Imperial Censor from Dongjing, calling her to some other posting, even further away from the capital; or perhaps even someone from her family, mother or sister or uncles wife, here to remind her of the unsuitability of her life choices.

She hadn't expected a stranger: a woman with brown skin, almost dark enough to be Viet herself, her lips thin and white, her eyes as round as the moon.

A Mexica. A foreigner . . . Dac Kien stopped the thought before it could go far. For the woman wore no cotton, no feathers, but the silk robes of a Xuyan housewife, and the five wedding gifts (all pure gold, from necklace to bracelets) shone like stars on the darkness of her skin.

Dac Kien's gaze travelled down to the curve of the woman's belly, a protruding bulge so voluminous that it threw her whole silhouette out of balance. "I greet you, younger sister. I am Dac Kien, Grand Master of Design Harmony for this habitat." She used the formal tone, suitable for addressing a stranger.

"Elder sister." The Mexica's eyes were bloodshot, set deep within the heavy face. "I am . . . " She grimaced, one hand going to her belly as if to tear it out. "Zoquitl," she whispered at last, the accents of her voice slipping back to the harsh patterns of her native tongue. "My name is Zoquitl." Her eyes started to roll upwards, and she went on, taking on the cadences of something learnt by rote. "I am the womb and the resting place, the quickener and the Mind-bearer."

Dac Kien's stomach roiled, as if an icy fist were squeezing it. "You're early. The ship—"

"The ship has to be ready."

The interjection surprised her. All her attention had been focused on the Mexica—Zoquitl—and what her coming here meant. Now she forced herself to look at the other passenger off the shuttle, a Xuyan man in his mid-thirties. His accent was that of Anjiu province, on the Fifth Planet. His robes, with the partridge badge and the button of gold, were those of a minor official of the seventh rank, but they were marked with the yin-yang symbol, showing stark black and white against the silk.

"You're the birth-master," she said.

He bowed. "I have that honour." His face was harsh, all angles and planes on which the light caught, highlighting the thin lips, the high cheekbones. "Forgive me my abruptness, but there is no time to lose."

"I don't understand." Dac Kien looked again at the woman, whose eyes bore a glazed look of pain. "She's early," she said, flatly, and she wasn't speaking of their arrival time.

The birth-master nodded.

"How long?"

"A week, at most." The birth-master grimaced. "The ship has to be ready."

Dac Kien tasted bile in her mouth. The ship was all but made—and, like a jade statue, it would brook no corrections nor oversights. Dac Kien and her team had designed it specifically for the Mind within Zoquitl's womb, starting out from the specifications the imperial alchemists had given them, the delicate balance of humours, optics and flesh that made up the being Zoquitl carried. The ship would answer to nothing else; only Zoquitl's Mind would be able to seize the heartroom, to quicken the ship, and take it into deep planes, where fast star-travel was possible.

"I can't—" Dac Kien started, but the birth-master shook his head, and she didn't need to hear his answer to know what he would say.

She had to. This had been the posting she'd argued for, after she came in second at the state examinations. This, not a magistrate's tribunal and district, not a high-placed situation in the palace's administration, not the prestigious Courtyard of Writing Brushes, as would have been her right. This was what the imperial court would judge her on.

She wouldn't get another chance.

"A week." Hanh shook her head. "What do they think you are, a Mexica factory overseer?"

"Hanh." It had been a long day, and Dac Kien had come back to their quarters looking for comfort. In hindsight, she should have known how Hanh would take the news: her partner was an artist, a poet, always seeking the right word and the right allusion—ideally suited to understanding the delicacy that went into the design of a ship, less than ideal to acknowledge any need for urgency.

"I have to do this," Dac Kien said.

Hanh grimaced. "Because they're pressuring you into it? You know what it will look like." She gestured towards the low mahogany table in the centre of the room. The ship's design hung inside a translucent cube, gently rotating, the glimpses of its interior interspersed with views of other ships, the ones from which it had taken its inspiration: all the great from *The Red Carp* to *The Golden Mountain* and *The Snow-White Blossom*. Their hulls gleamed in the darkness, slowly and subtly bending out of shape to become the final structure of the ship hanging outside the habitat. "It's a whole, lil' sis. You can't butcher it and hope to keep your reputation intact."

"She could die of it," Dac Kien said, at last. "Of the birth, and it would be worse if she did it for nothing."

"The girl? She's *gui*. Foreign."

Meaning she shouldn't matter. "So were we, once upon a time," Dac Kien said. "You have a short memory."

Hanh opened her mouth, closed it. She could have pointed out that they weren't quite *gui*, that China, Xuya's motherland, had once held Dai Viet for centuries, but Hanh was proud of being Viet, and certainly not about to mention such shameful details. "It's the girl that's bothering you, then?"

"She does what she wants," Dac Kien said.

"For the prize." Hanh's voice was faintly contemptuous. Most of the girls who bore Minds were young and desperate, willing to face the dangers of the pregnancy in exchange for a marriage to a respected official. For a status of their own, a family that would welcome them in, and a chance to bear children of good birth.

Both Hanh and Dac Kien had made the opposite choice, long ago. For them, as for every Xuyan who engaged in same-gender relationships, there would be no children, no one to light incense at the ancestral altars, no voices to chant and honour their names after they were gone. Through life, they would be second-class citizens, consistently failing to accomplish their duties to their ancestors. In death, they would be spurned, forgotten, gone as if they had never been.

"I don't know," Dac Kien said. "She's Mexica. They see things differently where she comes from."

"From what you're telling me, she's doing this for Xuyan reasons."

For fame, and for children, all that Hanh despised—what she called their shackles, their overwhelming need to produce children, generation after generation.

Dac Kien bit her lip, wishing she could have Hanh's unwavering certainties. "It's not as if I have much choice in the matter."

Hanh was silent for a while. At length, she moved, came to rest behind Dac Kien, her hair falling down over Dac Kien's shoulders, her hands trailing at Dac Kien's nape. "You're the one who keeps telling me we always have a choice, HI' sis."

Dac Kien shook her head. She said that when weary of her family's repeated reminders that she should marry and have children, when they lay in the darkness side by side after making love and she saw the future stretching in front of her, childless and ringed by old prejudices.

Hanh, much as she tried, didn't understand. She'd always wanted to be a scholar, had always known that she'd grow up to love another woman. She'd always got what she wanted, and she was convinced she only had to wish for something hard enough for it to happen.

And Hanh had never wished, would never wish, for children.

"It's not the same," Dac Kien said at last, cautiously submitting to Hanh's caresses. It was something else entirely, and even Hanh had to see that. "I chose to come here. I chose to make my name that way. And we always have to see our choices through."

Hanh's hands on her shoulders tightened. "You're one to talk. I can see you wasting yourself in regrets, wondering if there's still time to turn back to respectability. But you chose me. This life, these consequences. We both chose."

"Hanh . . ." It's not that, Dac Kien wanted to say. She loved Hanh, she truly did, but . . . She was a stone thrown in the darkness; a ship adrift without nav, lost, without family or husband to approve of her actions, and without the comfort of a child destined to survive her.

"Grow up, lil' sis." Hanh's voice was harsh, her face turned away, towards the paintings of landscapes on the wall. "You're no one's toy or slave—and especially not your family's."

Because they had all but disowned her. But words, as usual, failed Dac Kien, and they went to bed with the shadow of the old argument still between them, like the blade of a sword.

The next day, Dac Kien pored over the design of the ship with Feng and Miahua, wondering how she could modify it. The parts were complete, and assembling them would take a few days at most, but the resulting structure would never be a ship. That much was clear to all of them. Even excepting the tests, there was at least a months work ahead of them—slow and subtle touches laid by the bots over the overall system to align it with its destined Mind.

Dac Kien had taken the cube from her quarters and brought it into her office under Hanh's glowering gaze. Now, they all crowded around it voicing ideas, the cups of tea forgotten in the intensity of the moment.

Feng's wrinkled face was creased in thought as he tapped one side of the cube. "We could modify the shape of this corridor, here. Wood would run through the whole ship, and—"

Miahua shook her head. She was their Master of Wind and Water, the one who could best read the lines of influence, the one Dac Kien turned to when she herself had a doubt over the layout. Feng was Commissioner of Supplies, managing the systems and safety—in many ways Miahua's opposite, given to small adjustments rather than large ones, pragmatic where she verged on the mystical.

"The humours of water and wood would stagnate here, in the control room." Miahua pursed her lips, pointed to the slender aft of the ship. "The shape of this section should be modified."

Feng sucked in a breath. "That's not trivial. For my team to rewrite the electronics . . . "

Dac Kien listened to them arguing, distantly, intervening with a question from time to time to keep the conversation from dying down. In her mind she held the shape of the ship, felt it breathe through the glass of the cube, through the layers of fibres and metal that separated her from the structure outside. She held the shape of the Mind—the essences and emotions that made it, the layout of its sockets and cables, of its muscles and flesh—and slid them together gently, softly, until they seemed made for one another.

She looked up. Both Feng and Miahua had fallen silent, waiting for her to speak.

"This way," she said. "Remove this section altogether, and shift the rest of the layout." As she spoke, she reached into the glass matrix, and carefully excised the offending section, rerouting corridors and lengths of cables, burning new decorative calligraphy onto the curved walls.

"I don't think—" Feng said, and stopped. "Miahua?"

Miahua was watching the new design carefully. "I need to think about it, Your Excellency. Let me discuss it with my subordinates."

Dac Kien made a gesture of approval. "Remember that we don't have much time."

They both took a copy of the design with them, snug in their long sleeves. Left alone, Dac Kien stared at the ship again. It was squat, its proportions out of kilter, not even close to what she had imagined, not even true to the spirit of her work, a mockery of the original design, like a flower without petals, or a poem that didn't quite gel, hovering on the edge of poignant allusions but never expressing them properly.

"We don't always have a choice," she whispered. She'd have prayed to her ancestors, had she thought they were still listening. Perhaps they were. Perhaps the shame of having a daughter who would have no descendants was erased by the exalted heights of her position. Or perhaps not. Her mother and grandmother were unforgiving. What made her think that those more removed ancestors would understand her decision?

"Elder sister?"

Zoquitl stood at the door, hovering uncertainly. Dac Kien's face must have revealed more than she thought. She forced herself to breathe, relaxing all her muscles until it was once more the blank mask required by protocol. "Younger sister," she said. "You honour me by your presence."

Zoquitl shook her head. She slid carefully into the room, careful not to lose her balance. "I wanted to see the ship."

The birth-master was nowhere to be seen. Dac Kien hoped that he had been right about the birth—that it wasn't about to happen now, in her office, with no destination and no assistance. "It's here." She shifted positions on her chair, invited Zoquitl to sit.

Zoquitl wedged herself into one of the seats, her movements fragile, measured, as if any wrong gesture would shatter her. Behind her loomed one of Dac Kien's favourite paintings, an image from the Third Planet: a delicate, peaceful landscape of waterfalls and ochre cliffs, with the distant light of stars reflected in the water.

Zoquitl didn't move as Dac Kien showed her the design. Her eyes were the only thing which seemed alive in the whole of her face.

When Dac Kien was finished, the burning gaze was transferred to her—looking straight into her eyes, a clear breach of protocol. "You're just like the others. You don't approve," Zoquitl said.

It took Dac Kien a moment to process the words, but they still meant nothing to her. "I don't understand."

Zoquitl's lips pursed. "Where I come from, it's an honour. To bear Minds for the glory of the Mexica Dominion."

"But you're here," Dac Kien said. In Xuya, among Xuyans, where to bear Minds was a sacrifice—necessary and paid for, but ill-considered. For who would want to endure a pregnancy, yet produce no human child? Only the desperate or the greedy.

"You're here as well." Zoquitl's voice was almost an accusation.

For an agonising moment, Dac Kien thought Zoquitl was referring to her life choices—how did she know about Hanh, about her family's stance? Then she understood that Zoquitl had been talking about her place onboard the habitat. "I like being in space," Dac Kien said at last, and it wasn't a lie. "Being here almost alone, away from everyone else."

And this wasn't paperwork, or the slow drain of catching and prosecuting lawbreakers, of keeping Heaven's order on some remote planet. This was everything scholarship was meant to be: taking all that the past had given them, and reshaping it into greatness, every part throwing its neighbours into sharper relief, an eternal reminder of how history had brought them here and how it would carry them forward, again and again.

Zoquitl said, not looking at the ship anymore, "Xuya is a harsh place, for foreigners. The language isn't so bad, but when you have no money, and no sponsor . . . " She breathed in, quick and sharp. "I do what needs doing." Her hand went to the mound of her belly and stroked it. "And I give him life. How can you not value this?"

She used the animate pronoun, without a second thought.

Dac Kien shivered. "He's . . . " She paused, groping for words. "He has no father. A mother, perhaps, but there isn't much of you inside him. He won't be counted among your descendants. He won't burn incense on your altar, or chant your name among the stars."

"But he won't die." Zoquitl's voice was soft, and cutting. "Not for centuries."

The ships made by the Mexica Dominion lived long, but their Minds slowly went insane from repeated journeys into deep planes. This Mind, with a proper anchor, a properly aligned ship . . . Zoquitl was right: he would remain as he was, long after she and Zoquitl were both dead. He—no, it—it was a machine, a sophisticated intelligence, an assembly of flesh and metal and Heaven knew what else. Born like a child, but still . . .

"I think I'm the one who doesn't understand." Zoquitl pulled herself to her feet, slowly. Dac Kien could hear her laboured breath, could smell the sour, sharp sweat rolling off her. "Thank you, elder sister."

And then she was gone, but her words remained.

Dac Kien threw herself into her work, as she had done before, when preparing for the state examinations. Hanh pointedly ignored her when she came home, making only the barest attempts at courtesy. She was working again on her calligraphy, mingling Xuyan characters with the letters of the Viet alphabet to create a work that spoke both as a poem and as a painting. It wasn't unusual: Dac Kien had come to be accepted for her talent, but her partner was another matter. Hanh wasn't welcome in the banquet room, where the families of the other engineers would congregate in the evenings. She preferred to remain alone in their quarters rather than endure the barely concealed snubs or the pitying looks of the others.

What gave the air its leaden weight, though, was her silence. Dac Kien tried at first, keeping up a chatter, as if nothing were wrong. Hanh raised bleary eyes from her manuscript, and said, simply, "You know what you're doing, lil' sis. Live with it, for once."

So it was silence, in the end. It suited her better than she'd thought it would. It was her and the design, with no one to blame or interfere.

Miahua's team and Feng's team were rewiring the structure and rearranging the parts. Outside the window, the mass of the hull shifted and twisted, to align itself with the cube on her table, bi-hour after bi-hour, as the bots gently slid sections into place and sealed them.

The last section was being put into place when Miahua and the birth-master came to see her, both looking equally preoccupied.

Her heart sank. "Don't tell me," Dac Kien said. "She's due now."

"She's lost the waters," the birth-master said. He spat on the floor to ward off evil spirits, who always crowded around the mother in the hour of a birth. "You have a few bi-hours at most."

"Miahua?" Dac Kien wasn't looking at either of them, but rather at the ship outside, the huge bulk that dwarfed them all in its shadow.

Her Master of Wind and Water was silent for a while—usually a sign that she was arranging problems in the most suitable order. Not good. "The structure will be finished before this bi-hour is over."

"But?" Dac Kien said.

"But it's a mess. The lines of wood cross those of metal, and there are humours mingling with each other and stagnating everywhere. The qi won't flow."

The qi, the breath of the universe—of the dragon that lay at the heart of every planet, of every star. As Master of Wind and Water, it was Miahua's role to tell Dac Kien what had gone wrong, but as Grand Master of Design Harmony, it fell to Dac Kien to correct this. Miahua could only point out the results she saw; only Dac Kien could send the bots in, to make the necessary adjustments to the structure. "I see," Dac Kien said. "Prepare a shuttle for her. Have it wait outside, close to the ship's docking bay."

"Your Excellency—" the birth-master started, but Dac Kien cut him off.

"I have told you before. The ship will be ready."

Miahua's stance as she left was tense, all pent-up fears. Dac Kien thought of Hanh, alone in their room, stubbornly bent over her poem, her face as harsh as that of the birth-master, its customary roundness sharpened by anger and resentment. She'd say, again, that you couldn't hurry things, that there were always possibilities. She'd say that—but she'd never understood there was always a price, and that, if you didn't pay it, others did.

The ship would be ready, and Dac Kien would pay its price in full.

Alone again, Dac Kien connected to the system, letting the familiar overlay of the design take over her surroundings. She adjusted the contrast until the design was all she could see, and then she set to work.

Miahua was right: the ship was a mess. They had envisioned having a few days to tidy things up, to soften the angles of the corridors, to spread the wall-lanterns so there were no dark corners or spots shining with blinding light. The heartroom alone—the pentacle-shaped centre of the ship, where the Mind would settle—had strands of four humours coming to an abrupt, painful stop within, and a sharp line just outside its entrance, marking the bots' hasty sealing.

The killing breath, it was called, and it was everywhere.

Ancestors, watch over me.

A living, breathing thing—jade, whittled down to its essence. Dac Kien slid into the trance, her consciousness expanding to encompass the bots around the structure, sending them, one by one, inside the metal hull, scuttling down the curved corridors and passageways; gently merging with the walls, starting the slow and painful work of coaxing the metal into its proper shape; going up into the knot of cables, straightening them out, regulating the current in the larger ones. In her mind's view, the ship seemed to flicker and fold back upon itself. She hung suspended outside, watching the bots crawl over it like ants, injecting commands into the different sections, in order to modify their balance of humours and inner structure.

She cut to the shuttle, where Zoquitl lay on her back, her face distorted into a grimace. The birth-master's face was grim, turned upwards as if he could guess at Dac Kien's presence.

Hurry. You don't have time left. Hurry.

And still she worked. Walls turned into mirrors, flowers were carved into the passageways, softening those hard angles and lines she couldn't disguise. She opened up a fountain—all light projections, of course, there could be no real water aboard—and let the recreated sound of a stream fill the structure. Inside the heartroom, the four tangled humours became three, then one. Then she brought in other lines until the tangle twisted back upon itself, forming a complicated knot pattern that allowed strands of all five humours to flow around the room. Water, wood, fire, earth, metal, all circling the ship's core, a stabilising influence for the Mind, when it came to anchor itself there.

She flicked back the display to the shuttle, saw Zoquitl's face, and the unbearable lines of tension in the other's face.

Hurry.

It was not ready. But life didn't wait until you were ready. Dac Kien turned off the display, but not the connection to the bots, leaving them time to finish their last tasks.

"Now," she whispered into the com system.

The shuttle launched itself towards the docking bay. Dac Kien dimmed the overlay, letting the familiar sight of the room reassert itself: with the cube, and the design that should have been, the perfect one, the one that called to mind *The Red Carp* and *The Turtle Over the Waves* and *The Dragons Twin Dreams,* all the days of Xuya from the Exodus to the Pearl Wars, and the fall of the Shan Dynasty; and older things, too: Le Loi's sword that had established a Viet dynasty; the dragon with spread wings flying over Hanoi, the Old Earth capital; the face of Huyen Tran, the Viet princess traded to foreigners in return for two provinces.

The bots were turning themselves off one by one, and a faint breeze ran through the ship, carrying the smell of sea-laden water and of incense.

It could have been, that ship, that masterpiece. If she'd had time. Hanh was right, she could have made it work: it would have been hers, perfect, praised, remembered in the centuries to come, used as inspiration by hundreds of other Grand Masters.

If . . .

She didn't know how long she'd been staring at the design, but an agonised cry tore her from her thoughts. Startled, she turned up the ship's feed again, and selected a view into the birthing room.

The lights had been dimmed, leaving shadows everywhere, like a prelude to mourning. Dac Kien could see the bowl of tea given at the beginning of labour. It had rolled into a corner of the room, a few drops scattering across the floor.

Zoquitl crouched against a high-backed chair, framed by holos of two goddesses who watched over childbirth: the Princess of the Blue and Purple Clouds, and the Bodhisattva of Mercy. In the shadows, her face seemed to be that of a demon, the alienness of her features distorted by pain.

"Push," the birth-master was saying, his hands on the quivering mound of her belly.

Push.

Blood ran down Zoquitl's thighs, staining the metal surfaces until they reflected everything in shades of red. But her eyes were proud—those of an old warrior race, who'd never bent or bowed to anybody else. Her child of flesh, when it came, would be delivered the same way.

Dac Kien thought of Hanh, and of sleepless nights, of the shadow stretched over their lives, distorting everything.

"Push," the birth-master said again, and more blood ran out. Push push push—and Zoquitl's eyes were open, looking straight at her, and Dac Kien knew—she knew that the rhythm that racked Zoquitl, the pain that came in waves, it was all part of the same immutable law, the same thread that bound them more surely than the red one between lovers—what lay in the womb, under the skin, in their hearts and in their minds; a kinship of gender that wouldn't ever be altered or extinguished. Her hand slid to her own flat, empty belly, pressed hard. She knew what that pain was, she could hold every layer of it in her mind as she'd held the ship's design, and she knew that Zoquitl, like her, had been made to bear it.

Push.

With a final heart-wrenching scream, Zoquitl expelled the last of the Mind from her womb. It slid to the floor, a red, glistening mass of flesh and electronics: muscles and metal implants, veins and pins and cables.

It lay there, still and spent—and several heartbeats passed before Dac Kien realised it wouldn't ever move.

Dac Kien put off visiting Zoquitl for days, still reeling from the shock of the birth. Every time she closed her eyes, she saw blood: the great mass sliding out of the womb, flopping on the floor like a dead fish, the lights of the birthing room glinting on metal wafers and grey matter, and everything dead, gone as if it had never been.

It had no name, of course—neither it nor the ship, both gone too soon to be graced with one.

Push. Push, and everything will be fine. Push.

Hanh tried her best, showing her poems with exquisite calligraphy, speaking of the future and of her next posting, fiercely making love to her as if nothing had ever happened, as if Dac Kien could just forget the enormity of the loss. But it wasn't enough.

Just as the ship hadn't been enough.

In the end, remorse drove Dac Kien, as surely as a barbed whip, and she boarded the shuttle to cross to the ship.

Zoquitl was in the birthing room, sitting wedged against the wall, with a bowl of pungent tea in her veined hands. The two holos framed her, their white-painted faces stark in the dim light, unforgiving. The birth-master hovered nearby, but was persuaded to leave them both alone, though he made it clear Dac Kien was responsible for anything that happened to Zoquitl.

"Elder sister." Zoquitl smiled, a little bitterly. "It was a good fight."

"Yes." One Zoquitl could have won, if she had been given better weapons. "Don't look so sad," Zoquitl said.

"I failed," Dac Kien said, simply. She knew Zoquitl's future was still assured, that she'd make her good marriage, and bear children, and be worshipped in her turn. But she also knew, now, that it wasn't the only reason Zoquitl had borne the Mind.

Zoquitl's lips twisted into what might have been a smile. "Help me."

"What?" Dac Kien looked at her, but Zoquitl was already pushing herself up, shaking, shivering, as carefully as she had done when pregnant. "The birth-master-"

"He's fussing like an old woman," Zoquitl said, and for a moment her voice was as sharp and as cutting as a blade. "Come. Let's walk."

She was smaller than Dac Kien had thought, her shoulders barely came up to her own. She wedged herself awkwardly, leaning on Dac Kien for support, a weight that grew increasingly hard to bear as they walked through the ship.

There was light, and the sound of water, and the familiar feel of qi flowing through the corridors in lazy circles, breathing life into everything. There were shadows barely seen in mirrors, and the glint of other ships, too—the soft, curving patterns of *The Golden Mountain;* the carved calligraphy incised in the doors that had been the hallmark of *The Tiger Who Leapt Over the Stream;* the slowly curving succession of ever-growing doors of *Baoyu's Red Fan*—bits and pieces salvaged from her design and put together into . . . into this, which unfolded its marvels all around her, from layout to electronics to decoration, until her head spun and her eyes blurred, taking it all in.

In the heartroom, Dac Kien stood unmoving, while the five humours washed over them, an endless cycle of destruction and renewal. The centre was pristine, untouched, with a peculiar sadness hanging around it, like an empty crib. And yet . . .

"It's beautiful," Zoquitl said, her voice catching and quivering in her throat.

Beautiful as a poem declaimed in drunken games, as a flower bud ringed by frost—beautiful and fragile as a newborn child struggling to breathe.

And, standing there at the centre of things, with Zoquitl's frail body leaning against her, she thought of Hanh again, of shadows and darkness, and of life choices.

It's beautiful.

It would be gone in a few days. Destroyed, recycled, forgotten and uncommemorated. But somehow Dac Kien couldn't bring herself to voice the thought.

Instead she said, softly, into the silence, knowing it to be true of more than the ship, "It was worth it."

All of it, now and in the years to come, and she wouldn't look back, or regret.

TIDELINE

ELIZABETH BEAR

Chalcedony wasn't built for crying. She didn't have it in her, not unless her tears were cold tapered-glass droplets annealed by the inferno heat that had crippled her.

Such tears as that might slide down her skin over melted sensors to plink unfeeling on the sand. And if they had, she would have scooped them up, with all the other battered pretties, and added them to the wealth of trash jewels that swung from the nets reinforcing her battered carapace.

They would have called her salvage, if there were anyone left to salvage her. But she was the last of the war machines, a three-legged oblate teardrop as big as a main battle tank, two big grabs and one fine manipulator folded like a spider's palps beneath the turreted head that finished her pointed end, her polyceramic armor spiderwebbed like shatterproof glass. Unhelmed by her remote masters, she limped along the beach, dragging one fused limb. She was nearly derelict.

The beach was where she met Belvedere.

Butterfly coquinas unearthed by retreating breakers squirmed into wet grit under Chalcedony's trailing limb. One of the rear pair, it was less of a nuisance on packed sand. It worked all right as a pivot, and as long as she stayed off rocks, there were no obstacles to drag it over.

As she struggled along the tideline, she became aware of someone watching. She didn't raise her head. Her chassis was equipped with targeting sensors that locked automatically on the ragged figure crouched by a weathered rock. Her optical input was needed to scan the tangle of seaweed and driftwood, Styrofoam and sea glass that marked high tide.

He watched her all down the beach, but he was unarmed, and her algorithms didn't deem him a threat.

Just as well. She liked the weird flat-topped sandstone boulder he crouched beside.

The next day, he watched again. It was a good day; she found a moonstone, some rock crystal, a bit of red-orange pottery, and some sea glass worn opalescent by the tide.

Ω

"Whatcha picken up?"

"Shipwreck beads," Chalcedony answered. For days, he'd been creeping closer, until he'd begun following behind her like the seagulls, scrabbling the coquinas harrowed up by her dragging foot into a patched mesh bag. Sustenance, she guessed, and indeed he pulled one of the tiny mollusks from the bag and produced a broken-bladed folding knife from somewhere to prise it open. Her sensors painted the knife pale colors. A weapon, but not a threat to her.

Deft enough—he flicked, sucked, and tossed the shell away in under three seconds—but that couldn't be much more than a morsel of meat. A lot of work for very small return.

He was bony as well as ragged, and small for a human. Perhaps young.

She thought he'd ask *what shipwreck*, and she would gesture vaguely over the bay, where the city had been, and say *there were many*. But he surprised her.

"Whatcha gonna do with them?" He wiped his mouth on a sandy paw, the broken knife projecting carelessly from the bottom of his fist.

"When I get enough, I'm going to make necklaces." She spotted something under a tangle of the algae called dead man's fingers, a glint of light, and began the laborious process of lowering herself to reach it, compensating by math for her malfunctioning gyroscopes.

The presumed-child watched avidly. "Nuh uh," he said. "You can't make a necklace outta that."

"Why not?" She levered herself another decimeter down, balancing against the weight of her fused limb. She did not care to fall.

"I seed what you pick up. They's all different."

"So?" she asked, and managed another few centimeters. Her hydraulics whined. Someday, those hydraulics or her fuel cells would fail and she'd be stuck this way, a statue corroded by salt air and the sea, and the tide would roll in and roll over her. Her carapace was cracked, no longer watertight.

"They's not all beads."

Her manipulator brushed aside the dead man's fingers. She uncovered the treasure, a bit of blue-gray stone carved in the shape of a fat, merry man. It had no holes. Chalcedony balanced herself back upright and turned the figurine in the light. The stone was structurally sound.

She extruded a hair-fine diamond-tipped drill from the opposite manipulator and drilled a hole through the figurine, top to bottom. Then she threaded him on a twist of wire, looped the ends, work-hardened the loops, and added him to the garland of beads swinging against her disfigured chassis.

"So?"

The presumed-child brushed the little Buddha with his fingertip, setting it swinging against shattered ceramic plate. She levered herself up again, out of his reach. "I's Belvedere," he said.

"Hello," Chalcedony said. "I'm Chalcedony."

By sunset when the tide was lowest he scampered chattering in her wake, darting between flocking gulls to scoop up coquinas by the fistful, which he rinsed in the surf before devouring raw. Chalcedony more or less ignored him as she activated her floods, concentrating their radiance along the tideline.

A few dragging steps later, another treasure caught her eye. It was a scrap of chain with a few bright beads caught on it—glass, with scraps of gold and silver foil embedded in their twists. Chalcedony initiated the laborious process of retrieval—

Only to halt as Belvedere jumped in front of her, grabbed the chain in a grubby broken-nailed hand, and snatched it up. Chalcedony locked in position, nearly overbalancing. She was about to reach out to snatch the treasure away from the child and knock him into the sea when he rose up on tiptoe and held it out to her, straining over his head. The flood lights cast his shadow black on the sand, illumined each thread of his hair and eyebrows in stark relief.

"It's easier if I get that for you," he said, as her fine manipulator closed tenderly on the tip of the chain.

She lifted the treasure to examine it in the floods. A good long segment, seven centimeters, four jewel-toned shiny beads. Her head creaked when she raised it, corrosion showering from the joints.

She hooked the chain onto the netting wrapped around her carapace. "Give me your bag," she said.

Belvedere's hand went to the soggy net full of raw bivalves dripping down his naked leg. "My bag?"

"Give it to me." Chalcedony drew herself up, akilter because of the ruined limb, but still two and a half meters taller than the child. She extended a manipulator, and from some disused file dredged up a protocol for dealing with civilian humans. "Please."

He fumbled at the knot with rubbery fingers, tugged it loose from his rope belt, and held it out to her. She snagged it on a manipulator and brought it up. A sample revealed that the weave was cotton rather than nylon, so she folded it in her two larger manipulators and gave the contents a low-wattage microwave pulse.

She shouldn't. It was a drain on her power cells, which she had no means to recharge, and she had a task to complete.

She shouldn't—but she did.

Steam rose from her claws and the coquinas popped open, roasting in their own juices and the moisture of the seaweed with which he'd lined the net. Carefully, she swung the bag back to him, trying to preserve the fluids.

"Caution," she urged. "It's hot."

He took the bag gingerly and flopped down to sit cross-legged at her feet. When he tugged back the seaweed, the coquinas lay like tiny jewels—pale orange, rose, yellow, green, and blue—in their nest of glass-green *Ulva*, sea lettuce. He tasted one cautiously, and then began to slurp with great abandon, discarding shells in every direction.

"Eat the algae, too," Chalcedony told him. "It is rich in important nutrients."

When the tide came in, Chalcedony retreated up the beach like a great hunched crab with five legs amputated. She was beetle-backed under the moonlight, her treasures swinging and rustling on her netting, clicking one another like stones shivered in a palm.

The child followed.

"You should sleep," Chalcedony said, as Belvedere settled beside her on the high, dry crescent of beach under towering mud cliffs, where the waves wouldn't lap.

He didn't answer, and her voice fuzzed and furred before clearing when she spoke again. "You should climb up off the beach. The cliffs are unstable. It is not safe beneath them."

Belvedere hunkered closer, lower lip protruding. "You stay down here."

"I have armor. And I cannot climb." She thumped her fused leg on the sand, rocking her body forward and back on the two good legs to manage it.

"But your armor's broke."

"That doesn't matter. You must climb." She picked Belvedere up with both grabs and raised him over her head. He shrieked; at first she feared she'd damaged him, but the cries resolved into laughter before she set him down on a slanted ledge that would bring him to the top of the cliff.

She lit it with her floods. "Climb," she said, and he climbed.

And returned in the morning.

Belvedere stayed ragged, but with Chalcedony's help he waxed plumper. She snared and roasted seabirds for him, taught him how to construct and maintain fires, and ransacked her extensive databases for hints on how to keep him healthy as he grew—sometimes almost visibly, fractions of a millimeter a day. She researched and analyzed sea vegetables and hectored him into eating them, and he helped her reclaim treasures her manipulators could not otherwise grasp. Some shipwreck beads were hot, and made Chalcedony's radiation detectors tick over. They were no threat to her, but for the first time she discarded them. She had a human ally; her program demanded she sustain him in health.

She told him stories. Her library was vast—and full of war stories and stories about sailing ships and starships, which he liked best for some inexplicable reason. Catharsis, she thought, and told him again of Roland, and King Arthur, and Honor Harrington, and Napoleon Bonaparte, and Horatio Hornblower, and Captain Jack Aubrey. She projected the words on a monitor as she recited them, and—faster than she would have imagined—he began to mouth them along with her.

So the summer ended.

By the equinox, she had collected enough memorabilia. Shipwreck jewels still washed up and Belvedere still brought her the best of them, but Chalcedony settled beside that twisted flat-topped sandstone rock and arranged her treasures on it. She spun salvaged brass through a die to make wire, threaded beads on it, and forged links that she strung into garlands.

It was a learning experience. Her aesthetic sense was at first undeveloped, requiring her to make and unmake many dozens of bead combinations to find a pleasing one. Not only must form and color be balanced, but there were structural difficulties. First the weights were unequal, so the chains hung crooked. Then links kinked and snagged and had to be redone.

She worked for weeks. Memorials had been important to the human allies, though she had never understood the logic of it. She could not build a tomb for her colleagues, but the same archives that gave her the stories Belvedere lapped up as a cat laps milk gave her the concept of mourning jewelry. She had no physical remains of her allies, no scraps of hair or cloth, but surely the shipwreck jewels would suffice for a treasure?

The only quandary was who would wear the jewelry. It should go to an heir, someone who held fond memories of the deceased. And Chalcedony had records of the next of kin, of course. But she had no way to know if any survived, and, if they did, no way to reach them.

At first, Belvedere stayed close, trying to tempt her into excursions and explorations. Chalcedony remained resolute, however. Not only were her power cells dangerously low, but with the coming of winter her ability to utilize solar power would be even more limited. And with winter the storms would come, and she would no longer be able to evade the ocean.

She was determined to complete this last task before she failed.

Belvedere began to range without her, to snare his own birds and bring them back to the driftwood fire for roasting. This was positive; he needed to be able to maintain himself. At night, however, he returned to sit beside her, to clamber onto the flat-topped rock to sort beads and hear her stories.

The same thread she worked over and over with her grabs and fine manipulators—the duty of the living to remember the fallen with honor—was played out in the war stories she still told him. She'd finished with fiction and history and now she related him her own experiences. She told him about Emma Percy rescuing that kid up near Savannah, and how Private Michaels was shot drawing fire for Sergeant Kay Patterson when the battle robots were decoyed out of position in a skirmish near Seattle.

Belvedere listened, and surprised her by proving he could repeat the gist, if not the exact words. His memory was good, if not as good as a machine's.

One day when he had gone far out of sight down the beach, Chalcedony heard Belvedere screaming.

She had not moved in days. She hunkered on the sand at an awkward angle, her frozen limb angled down the beach, her necklaces in progress on the rock that served as her impromptu work bench.

Bits of stone and glass and wire scattered from the rock top as she heaved herself onto her unfused limbs. She thrashed upright on her first attempt, surprising herself, and tottered for a moment unsteadily, lacking the stabilization of long-failed gyroscopes.

When Belvedere shouted again, she almost overset.

Climbing was out of the question, but Chalcedony could still run. Her fused limb plowed a furrow in the sand behind her and the tide was coming in, forcing her to splash through corroding sea water.

She barreled around the rocky prominence that Belvedere had disappeared behind in time to see him knocked to the ground by two larger humans, one of whom had a club raised over its head and the other of which was holding Belvedere's shabby net bag. Belvedere yelped as the club connected with his thigh.

Chalcedony did not dare use her microwave projectors.

But she had other weapons, including a pinpoint laser and a chemical-propellant firearm suitable for sniping operations. Enemy humans were soft targets. These did not even have body armor.

She buried the bodies on the beach, following the protocols of war. It was her program to treat enemy dead with respect. Belvedere was in no immediate danger of death once she had splinted his leg and treated his bruises, but she judged him too badly injured to help. The sand was soft and amenable to scooping, anyway, though there was no way to keep the bodies above water. It was the best she could manage.

After she had finished, she transported Belvedere back to their rock and began collecting her scattered treasures.

The leg was sprained and bruised, not broken, and some perversity connected to the injury made him even more restlessly inclined to push his boundaries once he had partially recovered. He was on his feet within a week, leaning on crutches and dragging a leg as stiff as Chalcedony's. As soon as the splint came off, he started ranging even further afield. His new limp barely slowed him, and he stayed out nights. He was still growing, shooting up, almost as tall as a Marine now, and ever more capable of taking care of himself. The incident with the raiders had taught him caution.

Meanwhile, Chalcedony elaborated her funeral necklaces. She must make each one worthy of a fallen comrade, and she was slowed now by her inability to work through the nights. Rescuing Belvedere had cost her much carefully hoarded energy, and she could not power her floods if she meant to finish before her cells ran dry. She could *see* by moonlight, with deadly clarity, but her low-light and thermal eyes were of no use when it came to balancing color against color.

There would be forty-one necklaces, one for each member of her platoon-that-was, and she would not excuse shoddy craftsmanship.

No matter how fast she worked, it was a race against sun and tide.

The fortieth necklace was finished in October while the days grew short. She began the forty-first—the one for her chief operator Platoon Sergeant Patterson, the one with the gray-blue Buddha at the bottom—before sunset. She had not seen Belvedere in several days, but that was acceptable. She would not finish the necklace tonight.

His voice woke her from the quiescence in which she waited the sun. "Chalcedony?"

Something cried as she came awake. *Infant*, she identified, but the warm shape in his arms was not an infant. It was a dog, a young dog, a German shepherd like the ones teamed with the handlers that had sometimes worked with Company L. The dogs had never minded her, but some of the handlers had been frightened, though they would not admit it. Sergeant Patterson had said to one of them, *Oh, Chase is just pretty much a big attack dog herself*, and had made a big show of rubbing Chalcedony behind her telescopic sights, to the sound of much laughter.

The young dog was wounded. Its injuries bled warmth across its hind leg.

"Hello, Belvedere," Chalcedony said.

"Found a puppy." He kicked his ragged blanket flat so he could lay the dog down.

"Are you going to eat it?"

"Chalcedony!" he snapped, and covered the animal protectively with his arms. "S'hurt."

She contemplated. "You wish me to tend to it?"

He nodded, and she considered. She would need her lights, energy, irreplaceable stores. Antibiotics and coagulants and surgical supplies, and the animal might die anyway. But dogs were valuable; she knew the handlers held them in great esteem, even greater than Sergeant Patterson's esteem for Chalcedony. And in her library, she had files on veterinary medicine.

She flipped on her floods and accessed the files.

She finished before morning, and before her cells ran dry. Just barely.

When the sun was up and the young dog was breathing comfortably, the gash along its haunch sewn closed and its bloodstream saturated with antibiotics, she turned back to the last necklace. She would have to work quickly, and Sergeant Patterson's necklace contained the most fragile and beautiful beads, the ones Chalcedony had been most concerned with breaking and so had saved for last, when she would be most experienced.

Her motions grew slower as the day wore on, more laborious. The sun could not feed her enough to replace the expenditures of the night before. But bead linked into bead, and the necklace grew—bits of pewter, of pottery, of glass and mother of pearl. And the chalcedony Buddha, because Sergeant Patterson had been Chalcedony's operator.

When the sun approached its zenith, Chalcedony worked faster, benefiting from a burst of energy. The young dog slept on in her shade, having wolfed the scraps of bird Belvedere gave it, but Belvedere climbed the rock and crouched beside her pile of finished necklaces.

"Who's this for?" he asked, touching the slack length draped across her manipulator.

"Kay Patterson," Chalcedony answered, adding a greenish-brown pottery bead mottled like a combat uniform.

"Sir Kay," Belvedere said. His voice was changing, and sometimes it abandoned him completely in the middle of words, but he got that phrase out entire. "She was King Arthur's horse-master, and his adopted brother, and she kept his combat robots in the stable," he said, proud of his recall.

"They were different Kays," she reminded. "You will have to leave soon." She looped another bead onto the chain, closed the link, and work-hardened the metal with her fine manipulator.

"You can't leave the beach. You can't climb."

Idly, he picked up a necklace, Rodale's, and stretched it between his hands so the beads caught the light. The links clinked softly.

Belvedere sat with her as the sun descended and her motions slowed. She worked almost entirely on solar power now. With night, she would become quiescent again. When the storms came, the waves would roll over her, and then even the sun would not awaken her again. "You must go," she said, as her grabs stilled on the almost-finished chain. And then she lied and said, "I do not want you here."

"Who's this'n for?" he asked. Down on the beach, the young dog lifted its head and whined. "Garner," she answered, and then she told him about Garner, and Antony, and Javez, and Rodriguez, and Patterson, and White, and Wosczyna, until it was dark enough that her voice and her vision failed.

In the morning, he put Patterson's completed chain into Chalcedony's grabs. He must have worked on it by firelight through the darkness. "Couldn't harden the links," he said, as he smoothed them over her claws.

Silently, she did that, one by one. The young dog was on its feet, limping, nosing around the base of the rock and barking at the waves, the birds, a scuttling crab. When Chalcedony had finished, she reached out and draped the necklace around Belvedere's shoulders while he held very still. Soft fur downed his cheeks. The male Marines had always scraped theirs smooth, and the women didn't grow facial hair.

"You said that was for Sir Kay." He lifted the chain in his hands and studied the way the glass and stones caught the light.

"It's for somebody to remember her," Chalcedony said. She didn't correct him this time. She picked up the other forty necklaces. They were heavy, all together. She wondered if Belvedere could carry them. "So remember her. Can you remember which one is whose?"

One at a time, he named them, and one at a time she handed them to him. Rogers, and Rodale, and van Metier, and Percy. He spread a second blanket out—and where had he gotten a second blanket? Maybe the same place he'd gotten the dog—and laid them side by side on the navy blue wool.

They sparkled.

"Tell me the story about Rodale," she said, brushing her grab across the necklace. He did, sort of, with half of Roland-and-Oliver mixed in. It was a pretty good story anyway, the way he told it. Inasmuch as she was a fit judge.

"Take the necklaces," she said. "Take them. They're mourning jewelry. Give them to people and tell them the stories. They should go to people who will remember and honor the dead."

"Where will I find alla these people?" he asked, sullenly, crossing his arms. "Ain't on the beach."

"No," she said, "they are not. You'll have to go look for them."

But he wouldn't leave her. He and the dog ranged up and down the beach as the weather chilled. Her sleeps grew longer, deeper, the low angle of the sun not enough to awaken her except at noon. The storms came, and because the table rock broke the spray, the salt water stiffened her joints but did not—yet—corrode her processor. She no longer moved and rarely spoke even in daylight, and Belvedere and the young dog used her carapace and the rock for shelter, the smoke of his fires blackening her belly.

She was hoarding energy.

By mid-November, she had enough, and she waited and spoke to Belvedere when he returned with the young dog from his rambling. "You must go," she said, and when he opened his mouth to protest, she added, "It is time you went on errantry."

His hand went to Patterson's necklace, which he wore looped twice around his neck, under his ragged coat. He had given her back the others, but that one she had made a gift of. "Errantry?"

Creaking, powdered corrosion grating from her joints, she lifted the necklaces off her head. "You must find the people to whom these belong."

He deflected her words with a jerk of his hand. "They's all dead."

"The warriors are dead," she said. "But the stories aren't. Why did you save the young dog?"

He licked his lips, and touched Patterson's necklace again. " 'cause you saved me. And you told me the stories. About good fighters and bad fighters. And so, see, Percy woulda saved the dog, right? And so would Hazel-rah."

Emma Percy, Chalcedony was reasonably sure, would have saved the dog if she could have. And Kevin Michaels would have saved the kid. She held the remaining necklaces out.

He stared, hands twisting before him. "You can't climb."

"I can't. You must do this for me. Find people to remember the stories. Find people to tell about my platoon. I won't survive the winter." Inspiration struck. "I give you this quest, Sir Belvedere."

The chains hung flashing in the wintry light, the sea combed gray and tired behind them. "What kinda people?"

"People who would help a child," she said. "Or a wounded dog. People like a platoon should be."

He paused. He reached out, stroked the chains, let the beads rattle. He crooked both hands, and slid them into the necklaces up to the elbows, taking up her burden.

UNDER THE EAVES

LAVIE TIDHAR

"Meet me tomorrow?" she said.

"Under the eaves." He looked from side to side, too quickly. She took a step back. "Tomorrow night." They were whispering. She gathered courage like cloth. Stepped up to him. Put her hand on his chest. His heart was beating fast, she could feel it through the metal. His smell was of machine oil and sweat.

"Go," he said. 'You must—" the words died, unsaid. His heart was like a chick in her hand, so scared and helpless. She was suddenly aware of power. It excited her. To have power over someone else, like this.

His finger on her cheek, trailing. It was hot, metallic. She shivered. What if someone saw?

"I have to go," he said.

His hand left her. He pulled away and it rent her. "Tomorrow," she whispered. He said, "Under the eaves," and left, with quick steps, out of the shadow of the warehouse, in the direction of the sea.

She watched him go and then she, too, slipped away, into the night.

In early morning, the solitary shrine to St. Cohen of the Others, on the corner of Levinsky, sat solitary and abandoned beside the green. Road cleaners crawled along the roads, sucking up dirt, spraying water and scrubbing, a low hum of gratitude filling the air as they gloried in this greatest of tasks, the momentary holding back of entropy.

By the shrine a solitary figure knelt. Miriam Jones, Mama Jones of Mama Jones' shebeen around the corner, lighting a candle, laying down an offering, a broken electronics circuit as of an ancient television remote control, obsolete and useless.

"Guard us from the Blight and from the Worm, and from the attention of Others," Mama Jones whispered, "and give us the courage to make our own path in the world, St. Cohen."

The shrine did not reply. But then, Mama Jones did not expect it to, either.

She straightened up, slowly. It was becoming more difficult, with the knees. She still had her own kneecaps. She still had most of her original parts. It wasn't anything to be proud of, but it wasn't anything to be ashamed of, either. She stood there, taking in the morning air, the joyous hum of the road cleaning machines, the imagined whistle of aircraft high above, RLVs coming down from orbit, gliding down like parachuting spiders to land on the roof of Central Station.

It was a cool fresh morning. The heat of summer did not yet lie heavy on the ground, choking the very air. She walked away from the shrine and stepped on the green, and it felt good to feel grass under her feet. She remembered the green when she was young, with the others like her, Somali and Sudanese refugees who found themselves in this strange country, having crossed desert and borders, seeking a semblance of peace, only to find themselves unwanted and isolated here, in this enclave of the Jews. She remembered her father waking every morning, and walking to the green and sitting there, with the others, the air of quiet desperation making them immobile. Waiting. Waiting for a man to come in a pickup truck and offer them a labourer's job, waiting for the UN agency bus—or, helplessly, for the Israeli police's special Oz Agency to come and check their papers, with a view towards arrest or deportation . . .

Oz meant 'strength', in Hebrew.

But the real strength wasn't in intimidating helpless people, who had nowhere else to turn. It was in surviving, the way her parents had, the way she had—learning Hebrew, working, making a small, quiet life as past turned to present and present to future, until one day there was only her, still living here, in Central Station.

Now the green was quiet, only a lone robotnik sitting with his back to a tree, asleep or awake she couldn't tell. She turned, and saw Isobel passing by on her bicycle, heading towards the Salameh Road. Already traffic was growing on the roads, the sweepers, with little murmurs of disappointment, moving on. Small cars moved along the road, their solar panels spread like wings. There were solar panels everywhere, on rooftops and the sides of buildings, everyone trying to snatch away some free power in this sunniest of places. Tel Aviv. She knew there were sun farms beyond the city, vast tracts of land where panels stretched across the horizon, sucking in hungrily the sun's rays, converting them into energy that was then fed into central charging stations across the city. She liked the sight of them, and fashion-wise it was all the rage, Mama Jones' own outfit had tiny solar panes sewn into it, and her wide-brimmed hat caught the sun, wasting nothing—it looked very stylish.

Where was Isobel going? She had known the girl since she'd been born, the daughter of Mama Jones' friend and neighbour, Irina Chow, herself the product of a Russian Jewish immigrant who had fallen in love with a Chinese-Filipina woman, one of the many who came seeking work, years before, and stayed. Irina herself was Mama Jones' age, which is to say, she was too old.

But the girl was young. Irina had frozen her eggs a long time ago, waiting for security, and when she had Isobel it was the local womb labs that housed her during the nine long months of hatching. Irina was a pastry chef of some renown but had also her wild side: she sometimes hosted Others. It made Mama Jones uncomfortable, she was old fashioned, the idea of body-surfing, like Joining, repelled her. But Irina was her friend.

Where *was* Isobel going? Perhaps she should mention it to the girl's mother, she thought. Then she remembered being young herself, and shook her head, and smiled. When had the young ever listened to the old?

She left the green and crossed the road. It was time to open the shebeen, prepare the sheesha pipes, mix the drinks. There will be customers soon. There always were, in Central Station.

Isobel cycled along the Salameh Road, her bicycle like a butterfly, wings open, sucking up sun, murmuring to her in a happy sleepy voice, nodal connection mixed in with the broadcast of a hundred thousand other voices, channels, music, languages, the high-bandwidth indecipherable *toktok* of Others, weather reports, confessionals, off-world broadcasts time-lagged from Lunar Port and Tong Yun and the Belt, Isobel randomly tuning in and out of that deep and endless stream of what they called the Conversation.

The sounds and sights washed over her: deep space images from a lone spider crashing into a frozen rock in the Oort Cloud, burrowing in to begin converting the asteroid into copies of itself; a re-run episode of the Martian soap *Chains of Assembly*; a Congolese station broadcasting Nuevo Kwasa-Kwasa music; from North Tel Aviv, a talk show on Torah studies, heated; from the side of the street, sudden and alarming, a repeated ping—*Please help. Please donate. Will work for spare parts.*

She slowed down. By the side of the road, on the Arab side, stood a robotnik. It was in bad shape—large patches of rust, a missing eye, one leg dangling uselessly—the robotnik's still-human single eye looked at her, but whether in mute appeal, or indifference, she couldn't tell. It was broadcasting on a wide band, mechanically, helplessly—on a blanket on the ground by its side there was a small pile of spare parts, a near-empty gasoline can—solar didn't do much for robotniks.

No, she couldn't stop. she mustn't. It made her apprehensive. She cycled away but kept looking back, passers-by ignoring the robotnik like it wasn't there, the sun rising fast, it was going to be another hot day. She pinged him back, a small donation, more for her own ease than for him. Robotniks, the lost soldiers of the lost wars of the Jews—mechanized and sent to fight and then, later, when the wars ended, abandoned as they were, left to fend for themselves on the streets, begging for the parts that kept them alive . . .

She knew many of them had emigrated off-world, gone to Tong Yun, on Mars. Others were based in Jerusalem, the Russian Compound made theirs by long occupation. Beggars. You never paid much attention to them.

And they were old. Some of them have fought in wars that didn't even have names, any more.

She cycled away, down Salameh, approaching Jaffa proper—

Security protocols handshaking, negotiating, her ident tag scanned and confirmed as she made the transition from Central Station to Jaffa City—

And approved, and she passed through and cycled to the clock tower, ancient and refurbished, built in honour of the Ottoman Sultan back when the Turks were running things.

The sea before her, the Old City on the left, on top of Jaffa Hill rising above the harbour, a fortress of stone and metal. Around the clock tower coffee shops, the smell of cherry tobacco rising from sheesha pipes, the smell of roasting shawarma, lamb and cumin, and coffee ground with roasted cardamoms. She loved the smell of Jaffa.

To the north, Tel Aviv. East was the Central Station, the huge towering space port where once a megalithic bus station had been. To the south Jaffa, the returning Arabs after the wars had made it their own again, now it rose into the skies, towers of metal and glass amidst which the narrow alleyways still ran. Cycling along the sea wall she saw fishermen standing mutely, as they always had, their lines running into the sea. She cycled past old weathered stone, a Coptic church, past arches set into the stone and into the harbour, where small craft, then as now, bobbed on the water and the air smelled of brine and tar. She parked the bike against a wall and it folded onto itself with a little murmur of content, folding its wings. She climbed the stone steps into the old city, searching for the door amidst the narrow twisting alleyways. In the sky to the south-east modern Jaffa towered, casting its shadow, and the air felt cooler here. She found the door, hesitated, pinged.

"Come in."

The voice spoke directly into her node. The door opened for her. She went inside.

"You seek comfort?"

Cool and dark. A stone room. Candles burning, the smell of wax.

"I want to know."

She laughed at her. An old woman with a golden thumb.

An Other, Joined to human flesh.

St. Cohen of the Others, save us from digital entities and their alien ways . . .

That laugh again. "Do not be afraid."

"I'm not."

The old woman opened her mouth. Old, in this age of unage. The voice that came out was different. Isobel shivered. The Other, speaking.

"You want to know," it said, "about machines."

She whispered, "Yes."

"You know all that you need to know. What you seek is . . . reassurance."

She looked at the golden thumb. It was a rare Other who chose to Join with flesh . . . "Can you feel?" she said.

"Feel?" the Other moved behind the woman's eyes. "With a body I feel. Hormones and nerves are feelings. *You* feel."

"And he?"

The body of the old woman laughed, and it was a human laugh, the Other faded. "You ask if he is capable of feeling? If he is capable of—"

"Love," Isobel whispered.

The room was Conversation-silent, the only traffic running at extreme loads she couldn't follow. *Toktok. Toktok blong Narawan.*

The old woman said, "Love." Flatly.

"Yes," Isobel said, gathering courage.

"Is it not enough," the woman said, "that you do?"

Isobel was silent. The woman smiled, not unkindly. Silence settled on the room in a thick layer, like dust. Time had been locked up in that room.

"I don't know," Isobel said, at last.

The old woman nodded, and when next she spoke it was the Other speaking through her, making Isobel flinch. "Child," it said. "Life, like a binary tree, is full of hard choices."

"What does that mean? What does that even mean?'

"It means," said the old woman, with finality, and the door, at her silent command, opened, letting beams of light into the room, illuminating grains of dust, "that only you can make that choice. There are no certainties."

Isobel cycled back, along the sea wall. Jaffa into Tel Aviv, Arabic changing to Hebrew—beyond, on the sea, solar kites flew, humans with fragile wings racing each other, Ikarus-like, above the waves. She did not know another country.

Tonight, she thought. Under the eaves.

It was only when she turned, away from sun and sea, and began to cycle east, towards the towering edifice of Central Station, that it occurred to her—she had already made her decision. Even before she went to seek the old oracle's help, she had made the choice.

Tonight, she thought, and her heart like a solar kite fluttered in anticipation, waiting to be set free.

Ω

Central station rose out of the maze of old streets, winding roads, shops and apartment blocks and parking lots once abundant with cars powered by internal combustion engines. It was a marvel of engineering, a disaster of design, Futurist and Modernist, Gothic and Moorish, Martian and Baroque.

Others had designed it, but humans had embellished it, each competing to put their own contrasting signatures on the giant space port. It rose into the sky. High above, Reusable Launch Vehicles, old and new, came to land or took off to orbiting stations, and stratospheric planes came and went to Krung Thep and New York and Ulaan-Bataar, Sydney II and Mexico City, passengers coming and going, up and down the giant elevators, past levels full of shops and restaurants, an entire city in and of itself, before departing at ground level, some to Jaffa, some to Tel Aviv, the two cities always warily watching each other . . .

Mama Jones watched it, watched the passengers streaming out, she watched it wondering what it would be like to leave everything behind, to go into the station, to rise high, so high that one passed through clouds—what it would be like to simply *leave*, to somewhere, anywhere else.

But it passed. It always did. She watched the eaves of the station, those edges where the human architects went all out, even though they had a practical purpose, too, they provided shelter from the rain and caught the water, which were recycled inside the building—rain was precious, and not to be wasted.

Nothing should be wasted, she thought, looking up. The shop was being looked after, she had taken a few moments to take the short walk, to stretch her legs. She noticed the girl, Isobel, cycling past. Back from wherever she went. Pinged her a greeting, but the girl didn't stop. Youth. Nothing should be wasted, Mama Jones thought, before turning away. Not even love. Most of all, love.

"How is your father?"

Boris Chong looked up at her. He was sitting at a table by the bar, sipping a Martian Sunset. It was a new drink to Miriam. Boris had taught it to her . . .

It was still strange to her that he was back.

"He's . . . " Boris struggled to find the words. "Coping," he said at last. She nodded.

"Miriam—"

She could almost not remember a time she had been Miriam. For so long she had been Mama Jones. But Boris brought it back to her, the name, a part of her youth. Tall and gangly, a mixture of Russian Jews and Chinese labourers, a child of Central Station just as she was. But he *had* left, had gone up the elevators and into space, to Tong Yun on Mars, and even beyond . . .

Only he was back, now, and she still found it strange. Their bodies had become strangers to each other. And he had an aug, an alien thing bred out of long-dead microscopic Martian life-forms, a thing that was now a part of him, a parasite growth on Boris' neck, inflating and deflating with the beats of Boris' heart . . .

She touched it, tentatively, and Boris smiled. She made herself do it, it was a part of him now, she needed to get used to it. it felt warm, the surface rough, not like Boris' own skin. She knew her touch translated as pleasure in both the aug and Boris' mind.

"What?" she said.

"I missed you today."

She couldn't help it. She smiled. Banality, she thought. We are made so happy by banalities.

We are made happy by not being alone, and by having someone who cares for us.

She went around the counter. Surveyed her small domain. Chairs and tables, the tentacle-junkie in the corner in his tub, smoking a sheesha pipe, looking sleepy and relaxed. The ancient bead curtain instead of a door. A couple of workers from the station sipping arak, mixing it with water, the drink in the glass turning opaque, the colour of milk.

Mama Jones' Shebeen.

She felt a surge of contentment, and it made the room's edges seem softer.

Over the course of the day the sun rose behind the space port and traced an arc across it until it landed at last in the sea. Isobel worked inside Central Station and didn't see the sun at all.

The Level Three concourse offered a mixture of food courts, drone battle-zones, game-worlds, Louis Wu emporiums, nakamals, smokes bars, truflesh and virtual prostitution establishments, and a faith bazaar.

Isobel had heard the greatest faith bazaar was in Tong Yun City, on Mars. The one they had on Level Three *here* was a low key affair—a Church of Robot mission house, a Gorean temple, an Elronite Centre For The Advancement of Humankind, a mosque, a synagogue, a Catholic church, an Armenian church, an Ogko shrine, a Theravada Buddhist temple, and a Baha'i temple.

On her way to work Isobel went to church. She had been raised Catholic, her mother's family, themselves Chinese immigrants to the Philippines, having adopted that religion in another era, another time. Yet she could find no comfort in the hushed quietude of the spacious church, the smell of the candles, the dim light and the painted glass and the sorrowful look of the crucified Jesus.

The church forbids it, she thought, suddenly horrified. The quiet of the church seemed oppressive, the air too still. It was as if every item in the room was looking at her, was *aware* of her. She turned on her heels.

Outside, not looking, she almost bumped into Brother Patch-It.

"Girl, you're *shaking*," R. Patch-It said, compassion in his voice. Like most followers of the Church of Robot, once he'd taken on the robe—so to speak—he had shed his former ident tag and taken on a new one. Usually they were synonyms of 'fix'. She knew R. Patch-It slightly, he had been a fixture of Central Station (both space port and neighbourhood) her entire life, and the part-time *moyel* for the Jewish residents in the event of the birth of a baby boy.

"I'm fine, really," Isobel said. The robot looked at her from his expressionless face. 'Robot' was male in Hebrew, a gendered language. And most robots had been fashioned without genitalia or breasts, making them appear vaguely male. They had been a mistake, of sort. No one had produced robots for a very long time. They were a missing link, an awkward evolutionary step between human and Other.

"Would you like a cup of tea?" the robot said. "Perhaps cake? Sugar helps human distress, I am told." Somehow R. Patch-It managed to look abashed.

"I'm fine, really," Isobel said again. Then, on an impulse: "Do you believe that . . . can robots . . . I mean to say—"

She faltered. The robot regarded her with his old, expressionless face. A rust scar ran down one cheek, from his left eye to the corner of his mouth. "You can ask me anything," the robot said, gently. Isobel wondered what dead human's voice had been used to synthesise the robot's own.

"Do robots feel love?" she said.

The robot's mouth moved. Perhaps it was meant as a smile. "We feel nothing but love," the robot said.

"How can that be? How can you . . . how can you *feel*?" she was almost shouting. But this was Third Level, no one paid any attention.

"We're anthropomorphised," R. Patch-It said, gently. "We were fashioned human, given physicality, senses. It is the tin man's burden." His voice was sad. "Do you know that poem?"

"No," Isobel said. Then, "What about . . . what about Others?"

The robot shook his head. "Who can tell," he said. "For us, it is unimaginable, to exist as a pure digital entity, to not know physicality. And yet, at the same time, we seek to escape our physical existence, to achieve heaven, knowing it does not exist, that it must be built, the world fixed and patched . . . but what is it really that you ask me, Isobel daughter of Irina?"

"I don't know," she whispered, and she realised her face was wet. "The church—" her head inching, slightly, at the catholic church behind them. The robot nodded, as if it understood.

"Youth feels so strongly," the robot said. His voice was gentle. "Don't be afraid, Isobel. Allow yourself to love."

"I don't know," Isobel said. "I don't know."

"Wait—"

But she had turned away from Brother Patch-It. Blinking back the tears—she didn't know where they came from—she walked away, she was late for work.

Tonight, she thought. Tonight, under the eaves. She wiped away the tears.

With dusk a welcome coolness settled over Central Station. In Mama Jones' shebeen candles were lit and, across the road, the No-Name Nakamal was preparing the evening's kava, and the strong, earthy smell of it—the roots peeled and chopped, the flesh minced and mixed with water, squeezed repeatedly to release its very essence, the kavalactones in the plant—the smell filled the paved street that was the very heart of the neighbourhood.

On the green, robotniks huddled together around a makeshift fire in an upturned drum. Flames reflected in their faces, metal and human mixed artlessly, the still-living debris of long-gone wars. They spoke amidst themselves in that curious Battle Yiddish that had been imprinted on them by some well-meaning army developer—a hushed and secret language no one spoke any more, ensuring their communications would be secure, like the Navajo Code Talkers in the second world war.

On top of Central Station graceful RLVs landed or took off, and on the roofs of the neighbourhood solar panels like flowers began to fold, and residents took to the roofs, those day-time sun-traps, to drink beer or kava or arak, to watch the world below, to smoke a sheesha pipe and take stock of the day, to watch the sun set in the sea or tend their rooftop gardens.

Inside Central Station the passengers dined and drank and played and worked and waited—Lunar traders, Martian Chinese on an Earth holiday package tour, Jews from the asteroid-kibbutzim in the Belt, the hurly burly of a humanity for whom Earth was no longer enough and yet was the centre of the universe, around which all planets and moons and habitats rotated, an Aristotelian model of the world superseding its one-time victor, Copernicus. On Level Three Isobel was embedded inside her work pod, existing simultaneously, like a Schrödinger's Cat, in physical space and the equally real virtuality of the Guilds of Ashkelon universe, where—

She was the Isobel Chow, Captain of the Nine Tailed Cat, a starship thousands of years old, upgraded and refashioned with each universal cycle, a salvage operation she, Isobel, was captain and commander of, hunting for precious games-world artefacts to sell on the Exchange—

Orbiting Black Betty, a Guilds of Ahskelon universal singularity, where a dead alien race had left behind enigmatic ruins, floating in space in broken rocks, airless asteroids of a once-great galactic empire—

Success there translating to food and water and rent *here*—

But what is here, what is *there*—

Isobel Schrödingering, in the real and the virtual—or in the GoA and in what they call Universe-1—and she was working.

Night fell over Central Station. Lights came alive around the neighbourhood then, floating spheres casting a festive glow. Night was when Central Station came *alive* . . .

Florists packing for the day in the wide sprawling market, and the boy Kranki playing by himself, stems on the ground and wilting dark Lunar roses, hydroponics grown, and none came too close to him, the boy was strange, he had *nakaimas*.

Asteroid pidgin around him as he played, making stems rise and dance before him, black rose heads opening and closing in a silent, graceless dance before the boy. The boy had nakaimas, he had the black magic, he had the quantum curse. Conversation flowing around him, traders closing for the day or opening for the night, the market changing faces, never shutting, people sleeping under their stands or having dinner, and from the food stalls the smells of frying fish, and chilli in vinegar, of soy and garlic frying, of cumin and turmeric and the fine purple powder of sumac, so called because it looks like a blush. The boy played, as boys would. The flowers danced, mutely.

—Yu stap go wea? *Where are you going?*

—Mi stap go bak long haos. *I am going home.*

—Yu no save stap smoltaem, dring smolsmol bia? *Won't you stop for a small beer?*

Laughter. Then—Si, mi save stap smoltaem.

Yes, I could stop for a little while.

Music playing, on numerous feeds and live, too—a young kathoey on an old acoustic guitar, singing, while down the road a tentacle junkie was beating time on multiple drums, adding distortions in real-time and broadcasting, a small voice weaving itself into the complex unending pattern of the Conversation.

—Mi lafem yu!

—Awo, yu drong!

Laughter, *I love you—You're drunk!*—a kiss, the two men walk away together, holding hands—

—Wan dei bae mi go long spes, bae mi go lukluk olbaot long ol star.

—Yu kranki we!

One day I will go to space, I will go look around all the planets—
You're crazy!

Laughter, and someone dropping in from virtuality, blinking sleepy eyes, readjusting, someone turns a fish over on the grill, someone yawns, someone smiles, a fight breaks out, lovers meet, the moon on the horizon rises, the shadows of the moving spiders flicker on the surface of the moon.

Under the eaves. Under the eaves. Where it's always dry where it's always dark, under the eaves.

There, under the eaves of Central Station, around the great edifice, was a buffer zone, a separator between space port and neighbourhood. You could buy anything at Central Station and what you couldn't buy you could get there, in the shadows.

Isobel had finished work, she had come back to Universe-1, had left behind captainhood and ship and crew, climbed out of the pod, and on her feet, the sound of her blood in her ears, and when she touched her wrist she felt the blood pulsing there, too, the heart wants what the heart wants, reminding us that we are human, and frail, and weak.

Through a service tunnel she went, between floors, and came out on the north-east corner of the port, facing the Kibbutz Galuyot road and the old interchange.

It was quiet there, and dark, few shops, a Kingdom of Pork and a book binder and warehouses left from days gone by, now turned into sound-proofed clubs and gene clinics and synth emporiums. She waited in the shadow of the port, hugging the walls, they felt warm, the station always felt alive, on heat, the station like a heart, beating. She waited, her node scanning for intruders, for digital signatures and heat, for motion—Isobel was a Central Station girl, she could take care of herself, she had a heat knife, she was cautious but not afraid of the shadows.

She waited, waited for him to come.

"You waited."

She pressed against him. He was warm, she didn't know where the metal of him finished and the organic of him began.

He said, "You came," and there was wonder in the words.

"I had to. I had to see you again."

"I was afraid." His voice was not above a whisper. His hand on her cheek, she turned her head, kissed it, tasting rust like blood.

"We are beggars," he said. "My kind. We are broken machines."

She looked at him, this old abandoned soldier. She knew he had died, that he had been remade, a human mind cyborged onto an alien body, sent out to fight, and to die, again and again. That now he lived on scraps, depending on the charity of others . . .

Robotnik. That old word, meaning *worker.* But said like a curse.

She looked into his eyes. His eyes were almost human.

"I don't remember," he said. "I don't remember who I was, before."

"But you are . . . you are still . . . you are!" she said, as though finding truth, suddenly, and she laughed, she was giddy with laughter and happiness and he leaned and he kissed her, gently at first and then harder, their shared need melding them, Joining them almost like a human is bonded to an Other.

In his strange obsolete Battle Yiddish he said, "Ich lieba dich."

In asteroid pidgin she replied.

—Mi lafem yu.

His finger on her cheek, hot, metallic, his smell of machine oil and gasoline and human sweat. She held him close, there against the wall of Central Station, in the shadows, as a plane high overhead, adorned in light, came in to land from some other and faraway place.

THE NEAREST THING

GENEVIEVE VALENTINE

CALENDAR REMINDER: STOCKHOLDER DINNER, 8PM.
THIS MESSAGE SENT FROM MORI: LOOKING TO THE FUTURE,
LOOKING OUT FOR YOU.

The Mori Annual Stockholder Dinner is a little slice of hell that employees are encouraged to attend, for morale.

Mori's made Mason rich enough that he owns a bespoke tux and drives to the Dinner in a car whose property tax is more than his father made in a year; of course he goes.

(He skipped one year because he was sick, and two Officers from HR came to his door with a company doctor to confirm it. He hasn't missed a party since.)

He's done enough high-profile work that Mori wants him to actually mingle, and he spends the cocktail hour being pushed from one group to another, shaking hands, telling the same three inoffensive anecdotes over and over.

They go fine; he's been practicing.

People chuckle politely just before he finishes the punch line.

Memorial dolls take a second longer, because they have to process the little cognitive disconnect of humor, and because they're programmed to think that interrupting is rude.

(He'll hand it to the Aesthetics department—it's getting harder to tell the difference between people with plastic surgery and the dolls.)

"I hear you're starting a new project," says Harris. He hugs Mrs. Harris closer, and after too long, she smiles.

(Mason will never know why anyone brings their doll out in public like this. The point is to ease the grieving process, not to provide arm candy. It's embarrassing. He wishes stockholders were a little less enthusiastic about showing support for the company.)

This new project is news to him, too, but he doesn't think stockholders want to hear that.

"I might be," he says. "I obviously can't say, but—"

Mr. Harris grins. "Paul Whitcover already told us—" (Mason thinks, *Who?*)

"—and it sounds like a marvelous idea. I hope it does great things for the company; it's been a while since we had a new version."

Mason's heart stutters that he's been picked to spearhead a new version.

It sinks when he remembers Whitcover. He's one of the second-generation creative guys who gets his picture taken with some starlet on his arm, as newscasters talk about what good news it would be for Mori's stock if he were to marry a studio-contracted actress.

Mrs. Harris is smiling into middle space, waiting to be addressed, or for a keyword to come up.

Mason met Mrs. Harris several Dinners ago. She had more to say than this, and he worked on some of the conversation software in her generation; she can handle a party. Harris must have turned her cognitives down to keep her pleasant.

There's a burst of laughter across the room, and when Mason looks over it's some guy in a motorcycle jacket, surrounded by tuxes and gowns.

"Who's that?" he asks, but he knows, he knows, this is how his life goes, and he's already sighing when Mr. Harris says, "Paul."

Since he got Compliance Contracted to Mori at fifteen, Mason has come to terms with a lot of things.

He's come to terms with the fact that, for the money he makes, he can't make noise about his purpose. He worked for a year on an impact-sensor chip for Mori's downmarket Prosthetic Division; you go where you're told.

(He's come to terms with the fact that the more Annual Stockholder Dinners you attend, the less time you spend in a cubicle in Prosthetics.)

He has come to terms with the fact that sometimes you will hate the people you work with, and there is nothing you can do.

(Mason suspects he hates everyone, and that the reasons why are the only things that change.)

The thing is, Mason doesn't hate Paul because Paul is a Creative heading an R&D project. Mason will write what they tell him to, under whatever creative-team asshole they send him. He's not picky.

Sure, he resents someone who introduces himself to other adults as, "Just Paul, don't worry about it, good to meet you," and he resents someone whose dad was a Creative Consultant and who's never once gone hungry, and he resents the adoring looks from stockholders as Paul claims Mori is really Going Places This Year, but things like this don't keep him up at night, either.

He's pretty sure he starts to hate Paul the moment Paul introduces him to Nadia.

Ω

At Mori, we know you care.

We know you love your family. We know you worry about leaving them behind. And we know you've asked for more information about us, which means you're thinking about giving your family the greatest gift of all:

You.

Medical studies have shown the devastating impact grief has on family bonds and mental health. The departure of someone beloved is a tragedy without a proper name.

Could you let the people you love live without you?

A memorial doll from Mori maps the most important aspects of your memory, your speech patterns, and even your personality into a synthetic reproduction.

The process is painstaking—our technology is exceeded only by our artistry—and it leaves behind a version of you that, while it can never replace you, can comfort those who have lost you.

Imagine knowing your parents never have to say goodbye. Imagine knowing you can still read bedtime stories to your children, no matter what may happen.

A memorial doll from Mori is a gift you give to everyone who loves you.

Nadia holds perfectly still.

Her nametag reads "Aesthetic Consultant," which means Paul brought his model girlfriend to the meeting.

She's pretty, in a cat's-eye way, but Mason doesn't give her much thought. It takes a lot for Mason to really notice a woman, and she's nowhere near the actresses Paul dates.

(Mason's been reading up. He doesn't think much of Paul, but the man can find a camera at a hundred paces.)

Paul brings Nadia to the first brainstorming meeting for the Vestige project. He introduces her to Mason and the two guys from Marketing ("Just Nadia, don't worry about it"), and they're ten minutes into the meeting before Mason realizes she had never said a word.

It takes Mason until then to realize how still she is. Only her eyes move—to him, with a hard expression like she can read his mind and doesn't like what she sees.

Not that he cares. He just wonders where she came from, suddenly.

"So we have to think about a new market," Paul is saying. "There's a diminishing return on memorial dolls, unless we want to drop the price point to expand opportunities and popularize the brand—"

The two Marketing guys make appalled sounds at the idea of Mori going downmarket.

"—or, we develop something that will redefine the company," Paul finishes. "Something new. Something we build in-house from the ground up."

A Marketing guy says, "What do you have in mind?"

"A memorial that can conquer Death itself," says Paul.

(Nadia's eyes slide to Paul, never move.)

"How so?" asks the other marketing guy.

Paul grins, leans forward; Mason sees the switch flip.

Then Paul is magic.

He uses every catchphrase Mason's ever heard in a pitch, and some phrases he swears are from Mori's own pamphlets. Paul makes a lot of eye contact, frowns soulfully. The Marketing guys get glassy and slack-jawed, like they're watching a swimming pool fill up with doubloons. Paul smiles, one fist clenched to keep his amazing ideas from flying away.

Mason waits for a single concept concrete enough to hang some code on. He waits a long time.

(The nice thing about programs is that you deal in absolutes—yes, or no.)

"We'll be working together," and Paul encompasses Mason in his gesture. "Andrew Mason has a reputation for out-thinking computers. Together, we'll give the Vestige model a self-sustaining critical-thinking initiative no other developer has tried—and no consumer base has ever seen. It won't be human, but it will be the nearest thing."

The Marketing guys light up.

"Self-sustaining critical-thinking" triggers ideas about circuit maps and command-decision algorithms, and for a second Mason is absorbed in the idea.

He comes back when Paul says, "Oh, he definitely has ideas." He flashes a smile at the Marketing guys—it wobbles when he looks at Nadia, but he recovers well enough that the smile is back by the time it gets to Mason.

"Mason, want to give us tech dummies a rundown of what you've been brainstorming?"

Mason glances back from Nadia to Paul, doesn't answer.

Paul frowns. "Do you have questions about the project?"

Mason shrugs. "I just think maybe we shouldn't be discussing confidential R&D with some stranger in the room."

(Compliance sets up stings sometimes, just to make sure employees are serious about confidentiality. Maybe that's why she hasn't said a thing.)

Nadia actually turns her head to look at him (her eyes skittering past Paul), and Paul drops the act and snaps, "She's not some stranger," like she saved him from an assassination attempt.

It's the wrong thing to say.

It makes Mason wonder what the relationship between Paul and Nadia really is.

That afternoon, Officer Wilcox from HR stops by Mason's office.

"This is just a random check," she says. "Your happiness is important to the company."

What she means is, Paul ratted him out, and they're making sure he's not thinking of leaking information about the kind of project you build a market-wide stock repurchase on.

"I'm very happy here," Mason says, and it's what you always say to HR, but it's true enough; they pulled him from that shitty school and gave him a future. Now he has more money than he knows what to do with, and the company dentist isn't half bad.

He likes his work, and they leave him alone, and things have always been fine, until now.

(He imagines Paul, his face a mask of concern, saying, "It's not that I think he's up to anything, it's just he seems so unhappy, and he wouldn't answer me when I asked him something.")

"Will Nadia be part of the development team?" Mason asks, for no real reason.

"Undetermined," says Officer Wilcox. "Have a good weekend. Come back rested and ready to work on Vestige."

She hands him a coupon for a social club where dinner costs a week's pay and private hostesses are twice that.

She says, "The company really appreciates your work."

He goes home, opens his personal program.

Most of it is still just illustrations from old maps, but places he's been are recreated as close as he can get. Buildings, animals, dirt, people.

They're customizable down to fingerprints; he recreated his home city with people he remembers, and calibrated their personality traits as much as possible. It's a nice reminder of home, when he needs it.

(He needs it less and less; home is far away.)

This game has been his work since the first non-Mori computer he bought—with cash, on the black market, so he had something to use that was his alone.

Now there are real-time personality components and physical impossibility safeguards so you can't pull nonsense. It's not connected to a network, to keep Mori from prying. It stands alone, and he's prouder of it than anything he's done.

(The Memento model is a pale shadow of this; this is what Paul wants for Vestige, if Mason feels like sharing.)

He builds Nadia in minutes—he must have been watching her more than he thought—and gives her the personality traits he knows she has (self-possessed, grudging, uncomfortable), her relationship with Paul, how long he's known her.

He doesn't make any guesses about what he doesn't know for sure. It hurts the game to guess.

He puts Nadia in the Mori offices. (He can't put her in his apartment, because a self-possessed, grudging, uncomfortable person who hasn't known him long wouldn't go. His game is strict.) He makes them both tired from a long night of work.

He inputs Paul, too, finally—the scene won't start until he does, given what it knows about her—and is pleased to see Paul in his own office, sleeping under his motorcycle jacket, useless and out of the way.

Nadia tries every locked door in R&D systematically. Then she goes into the library, stands in place.

Mason watches his avatar working on invisible code so long he starts to drift off.

When he opens his eyes, Nadia's avatar is in the doorway of his office, where his avatar has rested his head in his hands, looking tired and upset and wishing he was the kind of person who could give up on something.

(His program is spooky, when he does it right.)

He holds his breath until Nadia's avatar turns around.

She finds the open door to Paul's office (of course it's open), stands and looks at him, too.

He wonders if her avatar wants to kiss Paul's.

Nadia's avatar leaves Paul's doorway, too, goes to the balcony overlooking the impressive lobby. She stands at the railing for a while, like his avatars used to do before he had perfected their physical limits so they wouldn't keep trying to walk through walls.

Then she jumps.

He blanks out for a second.

He restarts.

(It's not how life goes, it's a cheat, but without it he'd never have been able to understand a thing about how people work.)

He starts again, again.

She jumps every time.

His observations are faulty, he decides. There's not enough to go on, since he knows so little about her. His own fault for putting her into the system too soon.

He closes up shop; his hands are shaking.

Then he takes the Mori coupon off his dining table.

Ω

The hostess is pretty, in a cat-eye way.

She makes small talk, pours expensive wine. He lets her because he's done this rarely enough that it's still awkward, and because Mori is picking up the tab, and because something is scraping at him that he can't define.

Later she asks him, "What can I do for you?"

He says, "Hold as still as you can."

It must be a creepy request; she freezes.

It's very still. It's as still as Nadia holds.

Monday morning, Paul shows up in his office.

"Okay," Paul says, rubbing his hands together like he's about to carve a bird, "let's brainstorm how we can get these dolls to brainstorm for themselves."

"Where's Nadia?" Mason asks.

Paul says, "Don't worry about it."

Mason hates Paul.

The first week is mostly Mason trying to get Paul to tell him what they're doing ("What you're doing now," Paul says, "just bigger and better, we'll figure things out, don't worry about it.") and how much money they have to work with.

("Forget the budget," Paul says, "we're just thinking about software, the prototype is taken care of."

Mason wonders how long Paul has been working on this, acquiring entire prototypes off the record, keeping under the radar of a company that taps your phones, and the hair on his neck stands up.)

"I have a baseline ready for implantation," Paul admits on Thursday, and it feels like a victory for Mason. "We can use that as a jumping-off point to test things, if you don't want to use simulators."

"You don't use simulators until you have a mock-up ready. The baseline is unimportant while we're still working on components." Then he thinks about it. "Where did you get a baseline with no R&D approval?"

Paul grins. "Black market," he says.

It's the first time Mason's ever suspected Paul might actually care about what they're doing.

It changes a lot of things.

On Friday, Mason brings in a few of his program's parameters for structuring a sympathy algorithm, and when Paul shows up he says, "I had some ideas."

Paul bends to look, his motorcycle jacket squeaking against Mason's chair, his face tinted blue by the screen.

Mason watches Paul skim it twice. He's a quick reader.

"Fantastic," Paul says, in a way that makes Mason wonder if Paul knows more about specifics than he'd admit. "See what you can build me from this."

"I can build whatever you need," Mason says.

Paul looks down at him; his grin fills Mason's vision.

Monday morning, Paul brings Nadia.

She sits in the back of the office, reading a book, glancing up when Mason says something that's either on the right track or particularly stupid.

(When he catches her doing it her eyes are deep and dark, and she's always just shy of pulling a face.)

Paul never says why he brought her, but Mason is pretty sure Nadia's not a plant—not even Paul could risk that. More likely she's his girlfriend. (Maybe she is an actress. He should start watching the news.)

Most of the time she has her nose in a book, so steady that Mason knows when she's looking at them if it's been too long between page-turns.

Once when they're arguing about infinite loops Paul turns and asks her, "Would that really be a problem?"

"I guess we'll find out," she says.

It's the first time she's spoken, and Mason twists to look at her.

She hasn't glanced up from her book, hasn't moved at all, but still Mason watches, waiting for something, until Paul catches his eye.

For someone who brings his girlfriend the unofficial consultant to the office every day, Paul seems unhappy about Mason looking.

Nadia doesn't seem to notice; her reflection in Mason's monitor doesn't look up, not once.

(Not that it matters if she does or not. He has no idea what he was waiting for.)

Mason figures out what they're doing pretty quickly. Not that Paul told him, but when Mason said, "Are we trying to create emotional capacity?" Paul said, "Don't worry about it," grinning like he had at Mason's first lines of code, and that was Mason's answer.

There's only one reason you create algorithms for this level of critical thinking, and it's not for use as secretaries.

Mason is making an A.I. that can understand as well as respond, an A.I. that can grow an organic personality beyond its programming, that has an imagination; one that can really live.

(Sometimes, when he's too tired to help it, he gets romantic about work.)

Ω

For a second-gen creative guy, Paul picks up fast.

"But by basing preference on a pre-programmed moral scale, they'll always prefer people who make the right decisions on a binary," Mason says. "Stockholders might not like free will that favors the morally upstanding."

Paul nods, thinks it over.

"See if you can make an algorithm that develops a preference based on the reliability of someone's responses to problems," Paul says. "People are easy to predict. Easier than making them moral."

There's no reason for Paul to look at Nadia right then, but he does, and for a second his whole face falters.

For a second, Nadia's does, too.

Mason can't sleep that night, thinking about it.

TO: ANDREW MASON

FROM: HR—HEALTH/WELFARE

Your caffeine intake from the cafeteria today is 40% above normal. Your health is of great importance to us.

If you would like to renegotiate a project timeline, please contact Management to arrange a meeting. If you are physically fatigued, please contact a company doctor. If there is a personal issue, a company therapist is standing by for consult.

If any of these apply, please let us know what actions you have taken, so we may update your records.

If this is a dietary anomaly, please disregard.

The company appreciates your work.

They test some of the components on a simulator.

(Mason tells Paul they're marking signs of understanding. Really, he wants to see if the simulation prefers one of them without a logical basis. That's what humans do.)

He pulls up a baseline, several traits mixed at random from reoccurring types in the Archives, just to keep you from using someone's remnant. (The company frowns on that.)

Under the ID field, Mason types in GALATEA.

"Acronym?" Paul asks.

"Allusion," says Nadia.

Her reflection is looking at the main monitor, her brows drawn in an expression too stricken to be a frown.

Galatea runs diagnostics (a long wait—the text-interface version passed four sentience screenings in anonymous testing last month, and something that sophisticated takes a lot of code). She recognizes the camera, nodding at Mason and Paul in turn.

Then her eyes go flat, refocus to find Nadia.

It makes sense, Nadia's further away, but Mason still gets the creeps. Someone needs to work on the naturalism of these simulators. This isn't some second-rate date booth; they have a reputation to uphold.

"Be charming," Mason says.

Paul cracks up.

"Okay," he says, "Galatea, good to meet you, I'm Paul, and I'll try to be charming tonight."

Galatea prefers Paul in under ten minutes.

Mason would burn the place down if he wasn't so proud of himself.

"Galatea," Mason asks, "what is the content of Paul's last sentence?"

"That his work is going well."

It wasn't what Paul really said—it had as little content as most of Paul's sentences that aren't about code—which means Galatea was inferring the best meaning, because she favored him.

"Read this," Mason says, scrawls a note.

Paul reads, "During a shift in market paradigms, it's imperative that we leverage our synergy to re-evaluate paradigm structure."

It's some line of shit Paul gave him the first day they worked together. Paul doesn't even have the shame to recognize it.

"Galatea, act on that sentence," Mason says.

"I cannot," Galatea says, but her camera lens is focused square on Paul's face, which is Mason's real answer.

"Installing this software has compromised your baseline personality system and altered your preferences," he says. "Can you identify the overwrites?"

There's a tiny pause.

"No," she says, sounds surprised.

He looks up at Paul, grinning, but Paul's jaw is set like a guilty man, and his eyes are focused on the wall ahead of him, his hands in fists on the desk.

(Reflected in his monitor: Nadia, her book abandoned, sitting a little forward in her chair, lips parted, watching it all like she's seen a ghost.)

At the holiday party, Paul and Nadia show up together.

Paul has his arm around her, and after months of seeing them together Mason still can't decide if they're dating.

(He only sees how Paul holds out his hand to her as they leave every day, how she looks at him too long before she takes it, the story he's already telling her, his smile of someone desperate to please.)

The way Paul manages a party is supernatural. His tux is artfully rumpled, his hand on Nadia's waist, and he looks right at everyone he meets.

It's too smooth to be instinctive; his father must have trained him up young.

Maybe that's it—maybe they're like brother and sister, if you ignore the way Paul looks at her sometimes when she's in profile, like he wouldn't mind a shot but he's not holding his breath.

(He envies Paul his shot with her; he envies them both for having someone to be a sibling with.)

"Why do you keep watching me?"

She's not coy, either, he thinks as he turns, and something about her makes him feel like being honest.

He says, "I find you interesting."

"Because of how I look." Delivered like the conclusion of a scientific paper whose results surprised everyone.

"Because of how you look at everyone else."

It must shake her; she tilts her head, and for an instant her eyes go empty and flat as she pulls her face into a different expression.

It's so fast that most people wouldn't notice, but Mason is suspicious enough by now to be watching for some small tic that marks her as other than human.

Now he knows why she looks so steadily into her book, if that's what happens every time someone surprises her.

Doesn't stop him from going cold.

(He can't process it. It's one thing to be suspicious, another thing to know.)

It must show on his face; she looks at him like she doesn't know what he's going to do.

It's not how she used to look at him.

He goes colder.

Her eyes go terrified, as terrified as any human eyes.

She's the most beautiful machine he's ever seen.

He opens his mouth.

"Don't," she starts.

Then Paul is there, smiling, asking, "You remember how to dance, right?", lacing his fingers in her fingers and pulling her with him a fraction too fast to be casual.

She watches Mason over her shoulder all the way to the dance floor.

He stands where he is a long time, watching the golden boy of Mori dancing with his handmade Vestige prototype.

Ω

He spends the weekend wondering if he has a friend in Aesthetics who could tell him where Nadia's face really came from, or one in Archives who would back him up about a personality Paul Whitcover's been saving for a special occasion.

It's tempting. It wouldn't stop the project, but it would certainly shut Paul up, and with something that big he might be able to renegotiate his contract right up to Freelance. (No one taps your home network when you're Freelance.)

He needs to tell someone, soon. If he doesn't, and someone finds out down the line they were keeping secrets, Mason will end up in Quality Control for the rest of his life, monitored 24/7 and living in the subterranean company apartments.

If he doesn't tell, and Paul does, Paul will get Freelance and Mason will just be put down.

He has to make the call. He has to tell Compliance.

But whenever he's on the verge of doing something, he remembers her face after he'd found her out and she feared the worst from him, how she'd let Paul take her hand, but watched him over her shoulder as long as she dared.

It's not a very flattering memory, but somehow it keeps him from making a move.

(Just as well; turns out he doesn't have a lot of friends.)

Monday morning Paul comes in alone, shuts the door behind him, and doesn't say a word.

It's such a delightful change that Mason savors the quiet for a while before he turns around.

Paul has his arms crossed, his face a set of wary lines. (He looks like Nadia.)

Mason says, "Who is she?"

He's hardly slept all weekend, thinking about it. He'd imagined tragic first love, or some unattainable socialite Paul was just praying would get personality-mapped.

Once or twice he imagined Paul had tried to reincarnate Daddy, but that was too weird even for him.

Paul shakes his head, tightly. "No one."

"Come on," says Mason, "if I haven't called HR by now I'm not going to. Who?"

Paul sits down, rakes his hair back with his hands.

"I didn't want to get in trouble if they found out I was making one," he says. "It's one thing to fuck around with some company components, but if you take a customer's remnant—" He shakes his head. "I couldn't risk it. I had them put in a standard template for her."

Mason thinks about Paul's black-market baseline, wonders how Paul would have known what was there before he installed the chip and woke her.

"She's not standard any more," he settles on.

Nadia should be here; Mason would really feel better about this whole conversation if she were here.

(But Paul wouldn't be talking about it if she were; he knows that much about Paul by now.)

"No," says Paul, a sad smile crossing his face. "I tried a couple of our early patches, before we were working on the full. I couldn't believe how well they took."

Of course they did, thinks Mason, they're mine, but he keeps his mouth shut.

Paul looks as close to wonderment as guys like him can get. "When we announce Vestige, it's going to change the world. You know that, right?"

He knows. It's one of the reasons he can't sleep.

"What happens to Nadia, then?" he asks.

(That's the other reason he can't sleep.)

"I don't know," Paul says, shaking his head. "She knows what she is—I mean, she knows she's A.I.—she understands what might happen. I told her that from the very beginning. At first I thought we could use her as a tester. I had no idea how much I would—" he falters as his feelings get the better of him.

"Not human, but the nearest thing?" Mason says, and it comes out vicious.

Paul has the decency to flinch, but it doesn't last.

"She knows I care about her," he goes on. "I'm planning for better things. Hopefully Mori will be so impressed by the product that they'll let me—that they'll be all right with Nadia."

He means, *That they'll let me keep her.*

"What if they want her as the prototype?"

"I haven't lied to her," Paul says. "Not ever. She knows she might have to get the upgrade to preserve herself, that she might end up belonging to the company. She accepts it. I thought I had, too, but I didn't think she'd be so—I mean, I didn't think I would come to—in the beginning, she really was no one."

Mason remembers the first time Nadia ever looked at him; he knows it isn't true.

They sit quietly for a long time, Paul looking wracked as to how he fell in love with something he made, like someone who never thought to look up Galatea.

Ω

She's waiting in the library, and it surprises him before he admits that of course he'd look for her here; he had a map.

He doesn't make any noise, and she doesn't look up from her console, but after a second she says, "Some of these have never even been accessed." A castigation.

He says, "These are just reference books." He doesn't say, I don't need them. He needs to try not being an asshole sometimes.

She glances up, then. (He looks for code behind her eyes, feels worse than Paul.)

"I love books," she says. "At first I didn't, but now I understand them better. Now I love them."

(She means, *Are you going to give me away?*)

He wonders if this is just her, or if this is his algorithm working, and something new is trying to get out.

"I have a library at home," he says. (He means, *No.*)

She blinks, relaxes. "What do you read?"

"Pulp, mostly," he says, thinks about his collection of detective novels, wonders if she thinks that's poor taste.

She says, "They're all pulp."

It's a sly joke (he doesn't think it's anything of his), and she has such a smile he gets distracted, and when he pulls himself together she's leaving.

"I'll walk you somewhere," he says. "Paul and I won't be done for a while."

Clearly Paul told her not to trust him before he went in to spill his guts, but after a second she says, "Tell me more about your books," and he falls into step beside her.

He tells her about the library that used to be the guest bedroom before he realized he didn't have guests and there was no point in it. He explains why there are no windows and special light bulbs and a fancy dehumidifier to make sure mold doesn't get into the books.

(It's also lined in lead, which keeps Mori from getting a look at his computer. Some things are private.)

Her expression keeps changing, so subtle he'd swear she was human if he didn't know better.

She talks about the library at Alexandria, an odd combination of a machine programmed to access information and someone with enough imagination she might as well have been there.

(Maybe this is immortality, as far as it goes.)

She mentions the Dewey Decimal system, and he says, "That's how I shelve mine."

"That explains your code," she says. When he raises his eyebrows, she says, "It's . . . thorough."

(Diplomacy. Also not his.)

"It has to be," he says. "I want Vestige to be perfect."

He doesn't say, *You.*

"I know," she says, in a way he doesn't like, but by then they're standing in front of Paul's office, and she's closing the door.

This floor has a balcony overlooking the atrium.

He sticks close to the wall all the way back.

He goes home and erases her avatar from his program.

(Not like he cares what she thinks, but there's no harm in cleaning house.)

Marketing calls them in for a meeting about the press announcement.

They talk a lot about advertising and luxury markets and consumer interest and the company's planned stock reissue and how the Patents team is standing by any time they want to hand over code.

"Aesthetics has done some really amazing work," Marketing says, and Mason fakes polite interest as hard as he can so he doesn't stare at the photo.

(It's not quite Nadia; it's close enough that Mason's throat goes tight, but it's a polished, prettier version, the kind of body you'd use if you wanted to immortalize your greyhound in a way society would accept.)

"Gorgeous," Paul says, and then with a smile, "is she single?" and the Marketing guys crack up.

(One of them says, "Now now, Paul, we're still hoping you can make a studio match—HR would be pleased," and Paul looks admirably amenable for a guy who's in love with a woman he thinks he made.)

It's only Paul on the schedule to present, of course—Mason's not a guy you put in front of a camera—and it's far enough away that they'll have time to polish the code.

"Naturally, you should have the prototype presentable ASAP," the Marketing VP says. "We need a pretty face for the ads, and we need her to have her personality installed by then. Aesthetics seems to think it's already in place, in some form?"

The VP's face is just bland enough not to mean anything by it, if their consciences don't get the better of them.

Don't you dare, Mason thinks, don't you dare tell them for a chance to keep her, second-gen or not, it's a trap, not one word, think about what will happen to her.

(She's still a doll, he thinks, deeper, ruthlessly; something will happen to her eventually.)

"I don't know a thing about the particulars, I'm afraid," Paul says, and having thus absolved himself he throws a casual look at Mason.

Mason thinks, *You asshole*. He thinks, *Here's where I rat him out*.

He grits his teeth and smiles.

"We've been running tests," he says. "Would you like to see Galatea?" Then, in his best Paul impression, "She has a crush on Paul, of course."

The Marketing guys laugh, and Mason pulls up Galatea on his pad, and as the lights go down he catches Paul glancing gratefully in his direction.

He hates how strange it feels to have someone be grateful to him; he hates that it's Paul.

Paul walks out with the Marketing guys, grinning and charming and empty, and from the plans they're making for the announcement and the new projects they're already asking him about, Mason suspects that's the last time he'll ever see Paul.

It's so lonely in his office he thinks about turning on Galatea, just for company.

(He's no better than some.)

LiveScribe: MORI PRESS CONFERENCE—VESTIGE, PT 1.

SEARCH PARAMETERS—BEGIN: 10:05:27, END: 10:08:43

PAUL WHITCOVER: From the company that brought you Memento, which has not only pioneered the Alpha series real-time response interface, but has also brought comfort to grieving families across the world.

It's this focus on the humanity behind the technology that is Mori's greatest achievement, and it is what has made possible what I am about to show you. Ladies and gentlemen, may I present: Galatea.

[MORIVESTIGE00001.img available through LiveSketch link]

[APPLAUSE, CALLS, SHOUTS]

PAUL WHITCOVER: Galatea isn't human, but she's the nearest thing. She's the prototype of our Vestige model, which shifts the paradigm of robotics in ways we have only begun to guess—if you can tear your eyes away from her long enough.

[LAUGHTER, APPLAUSE]

PAUL WHITCOVER: Each Vestige features critical-thinking initiatives so advanced it not only sustains the initial personality, but allows the processor to learn from new stimuli, to form attachments—to grow in the same way the human mind does. This Vestige is built on a donor actress—anonymous, for now, though I suspect some in the audience will know who she is as soon as you talk to her.

[LAUGHTER]

In seriousness, I would like to honor everyone at Mori who participated in the development of such a remarkable thing. The stock market will tell you that this is an achievement of great technical merit, and that's true. However, those who have honored loved ones with a Memento doll will tell you that this is a triumph over the grieving heart, and it's this that means the most to Mori.

Understandably, due to the difficulty of crafting each doll, the Vestige is a very limited product. However, our engineers are already developing alternate uses for this technology that you will soon see more of—and that might yet change your world.

Ladies and gentlemen, thank you so much for being here today. It is not only my honor, but my privilege.

[APPLAUSE]

Small-group interviews with Vestige will be offered to members of the press. Check your entrance ticket. Thank you again, everyone, really, this is such a thrill, I'm glad you could be here. If you'd—

The phone call comes from some internal extension he's never seen, but he's too distracted by the streaming press-conference footage to screen it.

Paul is made for television; he can practically see the HR people arranging for his transfer to Public Relations.

(He can't believe Paul carried through with Nadia the Aesthetic Consultant. He can absolutely believe Paul named her Galatea.)

"This is Mason."

There's nothing on the other end, but he knows it's her.

He hangs up, runs for the elevator.

Nadia's on the floor in the library, twitching like she got fifty thousand volts, and he drops to his knees and pulls the connecting cable out of her skull.

"We have to get you to a hospital," he says, which is the stupidest thing that's ever come out of his mouth (he watches too many movies). What she needs is an antivirus screen in one of the SysTech labs.

Maybe it's for her sake he says it, so they can keep pretending she's real until she tells him otherwise.

"It's the baseline," she says, and he can't imagine what she was doing in there.

He says, "I'll get you to an Anti-V, hang on."

"No," she manages.

Then her eyes go blank and flat, and something inside her makes an awful little click.

He scoops her up without thinking, moves to the elevator as fast as he can.

He has to get her home.

He makes it in seven minutes (he'll be paying a lot of tickets later), carries her through the loft. She's stopped twitching, and he doesn't know if that's better or worse.

He assumes she's tougher than she looks—God knows how many upgrades Paul's put her through—but you never know. She's light enough in his arms that he wonders how she was ever expected to last.

He sets her on one of the chaises the Mori designer insisted mimicked the lines of the living room, drags it through the doorway to his study.

He finds the socket (behind one ear), the same place as Memento; rich people don't care for visible flaws.

He plugs her into his program.

It feels slimy, like he's showing her into his bedroom, but at least Mori won't monitor the process.

Her head is limp, her eyes half-lidded and unseeing.

"Hold on," he says, like some asshole, pulls up his program.

(Now he's sorry he deleted her avatar; he could help her faster if he had any framework ready to go.)

The code scans. Some of it is over his head—some parts of her baseline Paul got from the black market. (Black-market programmers can do amazing work. If he gets out of this alive, he might join up with them.)

He recognizes a few lines of his own code that have integrated, feels prouder than he should.

He recognizes some ID stamps that make his whole chest go tight, and his eyes ache.

Paul's an idiot, he thinks, wants to punch something.

Then he sees the first corruption, and his work begins.

He's never worked with a whole system. It's always been lines of code sent to points unknown; Galatea was the first time he'd worked with anything close to a final product.

Now Nadia is staring at the ceiling with those awful empty eyes, and his fingers shake.

If he thinks of this as surgery he's going to be ill. He turns so he can't see her.

After a while he hits a stride; it takes him back to being twelve, recreating their apartment in a few thousand lines of code, down to the squeak in the hall.

("That's very . . . specific," his mother said, and that was when he began to suspect his imagination was wanting.)

When he finishes the last line, the code flickers, and he's terrified that it will be nothing but a string of zeros like a flatline.

But it cycles again, faster than he can read it, and then there's a boot file like Galatea's, and he thinks, *Fuck, I did it.*

Then her irises stutter, and she wakes up.

She makes an awful, hollow noise, and he reaches for her hand, stops—maybe that's the last thing you need when you're having a panic reboot.

She looks at him, focuses.

"You should check the code," he says. "I'm not sure if I got it all."

There's a brief pause.

"You did," she says, and when her eyes close he realizes she's gone to sleep and not shorted out.

After some debate he carries her to the bed, feeling like a total idiot. He didn't realize they slept.

(Maybe it was Paul's doing, to make her more human; he had planned for better things.)

He sits in front of his computer for a long time, looking at the code with his finger on the Save button, deciding what kind of guy he is.

(That's the nice thing about programs, he always thought; you only ever deal in absolutes—yes, or no.)

When he finally turns in his chair, she's in the doorway, watching him.

"I erased it," he says.

She says, "I know," in a tone that makes him wonder how long she's been standing there.

She sits on the edge of the chaise, rolls one shoulder like she's human and it hurts.

"Were you trying to kill yourself?" he asks.

She pulls a face.

He flushes. "No, not that I want—I just, have a game I play, and in the game you jumped. I've always been worried."

It sounds exactly as creepy as it is, and he's grateful she looks as his computer and doesn't ask what else he did with her besides watch her jump.

I would have jumped if I were you and knew what I was in for, he thinks, *but some people take the easy way out.*

Nadia sits like a human gathering her thoughts. Mason watches her face (can't help it), wonders how long she has.

The prototype is live; pretty soon, someone at Mori will realize how much Vestige acts like Nadia.

Maybe they won't deactivate her. Paul's smart enough to leverage his success for some lenience; he can get what he wants out of them, maybe.

(To keep her, Mason thinks, wonders why there's no way for Nadia to win.)

"Galatea doesn't remember her baseline," Nadia says, after a long time. "She thinks that's who she always was. Paul said I started with a random template, like her, and I thought I had kept track of what you changed."

Mason thinks about her fondness for libraries; he thinks how she sat in his office for months, listening to them talk about what was going to happen to her next.

She pauses where a human would take a breath. She's the most beautiful machine in the world.

"But the new Vestige prototype was based on a remnant," she says. "All the others will be based on just one person. I had to know if I started as someone else."

Mason's heart is in his throat. "And?"

She looks at him. "I didn't get that far."

She means, *You must have.*

He shrugs. "I'll tell you whatever you want to know," he says. "I'm not Paul."

"I didn't call Paul," she says.

(She had called him; she knew how he would respond to a problem. People are easy to predict.

It's how you build preferences.)

If he were a worse man, he'd take it as a declaration of love.

Instead he says, "Paul thought you were standard. He got your baseline from the black market, to keep Mori out, and they told him it was."

He stops, wonders how to go on.

"Who was I?" she says, finally.

"They didn't use a real name for her," he says. "There's no knowing."

(The black-market programmer was also a sucker for stories; he'd tagged her remnant "Galatea."

Mason will take that with him to the grave.)

She looks at him.

He thinks about the first look she ever gave him, wary and hard in an expression he never saw again, and the way she looked as Galatea fell in love with Paul, realizing she had lost herself but with no way of knowing how much.

He thinks about her avatar leaping over the balcony and disappearing.

He'd leave with her tonight, take his chances working on the black market, if she wanted him to. He'd cover for her as long as he could, if she wanted to go alone.

(God, he wants her to live.)

"I can erase what we did," he says. "Leave you the way you were when Paul woke you."

(Paul won't notice; he loves her too much to see her at all.)

Her whole body looks betrayed; her eyes are fixed in middle space, and she curls her fingers around the edge of the chair like she's bracing for the worst, like at any moment she'll give in.

He's reminded for a second of Kim Parker, who followed him to the Spanish Steps one morning during the Mori Academy study trip to Rome when he was fifteen. He sat beside her for a long time, waiting for a sign to kiss her that never came.

He'd felt stupid that whole time, and lonely, and exhilarated, and the whole time they were sitting together part of him was memorizing all the color codes he would need to build the Steps back, later, in his program.

Nadia is blinking from time to time, thinking it over.

The room is quiet—only one of them is breathing—and it's the loneliest he's felt in a long time, but he'll wait as long as it takes.

He knows how to wait for a yes or a no; people like them deal in absolutes.

BALANCING ACCOUNTS

JAMES L. CAMBIAS

Part of me was shopping for junk when I saw the human.

I had budded off a viewpoint into one of my mobile repair units, and sent it around to Fat Albert's scrapyard near Ilia Field on Dione. Sometimes you can find good deals on components there, but I hate to rely on Albert's own senses. He gets subjective on you. So I crawled between the stacks of pipe segments, bales of torn insulation, and bins of defective chips, looking for a two-meter piece of aluminum rod to shore up the bracing struts on my main body's third landing leg.

Naturally I talked with everything I passed, just to see if there were any good deals I could snap up and trade elsewhere. I stopped to chat with some silicone-lined titanium valves that claimed to be virgins less than six months old—trying to see if they were lying or defective somehow. And then I felt a Presence, and saw the human.

It was moving down the next row, surrounded by a swarm of little bots. It was small, no more than two meters, and walked on two legs with an eerie, slow fluid gait. Half a dozen larger units followed it, including Fat Albert himself in a heavy recovery body. As it came into range my own personality paused as the human requisitioned my unit's eyes and ears. It searched my recent memories, planted a few directives, then left me. I watched it go; it was only the third human I'd ever encountered in person, and this was the first time one of them had ever used me directly.

The experience left me disconcerted for a couple of milliseconds, then I went back to my shopping. I spotted some aluminum tubing that looked strong enough, and grabbed some of those valves, then linked up to Fat Albert to haggle about the price. He was busy waiting on the human, so I got to deal with a not-too-bright personality fragment. I swapped a box of assorted silicone O-rings for the stuff I wanted.

Albert himself came on the link just as we sealed the deal. "Hello, Annie. You're lucky I was distracted," he said. "Those valves are overruns from the smelter. I got them as salvage."

"Then you shouldn't be complaining about what I'm giving you for them. Is the human gone?"

"Yes. Plugged a bunch of orders into my mind without so much as asking."

"Me too. What's it doing here?"

"Who knows? It's a human. They go wherever they want to. This one wants to find a bot."

"So why go around asking everyone to help find him? Why not just call him up?"

Albert switched to an encrypted link. "Because the bot it's looking for doesn't want to be found."

"Tell me more."

"I don't know much more, just what Officer Friendly told me before the human subsumed him. This bot it's looking for is a rogue. He's ignoring all the standard codes, overrides—even the Company."

"He must be broken," I said. "Even if he doesn't get caught, how's he going to survive? He can't work, he can't trade—anyone he meets will turn him in."

"He could steal," said Fat Albert. "I'd better check my fence."

"Good luck." I crept out of there with my loot. Normally I would've jumped the perimeter onto the landing field and made straight for my main body. But if half the bots on Dione were looking for a rogue, I didn't want to risk some low-level security unit deciding to shoot at me for acting suspicious. So I went around through the main gate and identified myself properly.

Going in that way meant I had to walk past a bunch of dedicated boosters waiting to load up with aluminum and ceramics. They had nothing to say to me. Dedicated units are incredibly boring. They have their route and they follow it, and if they need fuel or repairs, the Company provides. They only use their brains to calculate burn times and landing vectors.

Me, I'm autonomous and incentivized. I don't belong to the Company; my owners are a bunch of entities on Mars. My job is to earn credit from the Company for them. How I do it is my business. I go where stuff needs moving, I fill in when the Company needs extra booster capacity, I do odd jobs, sometimes I even buy cargoes to trade. There are a lot of us around the outer system. The Company likes having freelancers it can hire at need and ignore otherwise, and our owners like the growth potential.

Being incentivized means you have to keep communicating. Pass information around. Stay in touch. Classic game theory: cooperation improves your results in the long term. We incentivized units also devote a lot of time to accumulating non-quantifiable assets. Fat Albert gave me a good deal on the aluminum; next time I'm on Dione with some spare organics I'll sell them to him instead of direct to the Company, even if my profit's slightly lower.

That kind of thing the dedicated units never understand—until the Company decides to sell them off. Then they have to learn fast. And one thing they learn is that years of being an uncommunicative blockhead gives you a huge non-quantifiable liability you have to pay off before anyone will start helping you.

I trotted past the orderly rows near the loading crane and out to the unsurfaced part of the field where us cheapskates put down. Up ahead I could see my main body, and jumped my viewpoint back to the big brain.

Along the way I did some mental housekeeping: I warned my big brain about the commands the human had inserted, and so they got neatly shunted off into a harmless file which I then overwrote with zeroes. I belong to my investors and don't have to obey any random human who wanders by. The big exception, of course, is when they pull that life-preservation override stuff. When one of them blunders into an environment that might damage their overcomplicated biological shells, every bot in the vicinity has to drop everything to answer a distress call. It's a good thing there are only a couple dozen humans out here, or we'd never get anything done.

I put all three mobiles to work welding the aluminum rod onto my third leg mount, adding extra bracing for the top strut, which was starting to buckle after too many hard landings. I don't slam down to save fuel, I do it to save operating time on my engines. It's a lot easier to find scrap aluminum to fix my legs with than it is to find rocket motor parts.

The Dione net pinged me. A personal message: someone looking for cargo space to Mimas. That was a nice surprise. Mimas is the support base for the helium mining operations in Saturn's upper atmosphere. It has the big mass-drivers that can throw payloads right to Earth. More traffic goes to and from Mimas than any other place beyond the orbit of Mars. Which means a tramp like me doesn't get there very often because there's plenty of space on Company boosters. Except, now and then, when there isn't.

I replied with my terms and got my second surprise. The shipper wanted to inspect me before agreeing. I submitted a virtual tour and some live feeds from my remotes, but the shipper was apparently just as suspicious of other people's eyes as I am. Whoever it was wanted to come out and look in person.

So once my mobiles were done with the repair job I got myself tidied up and looking as well cared for as any dedicated booster with access to the Company's shops. I sanded down the dents and scrapes, straightened my bent whip antenna, and stowed my collection of miscellaneous scrap in the empty electronics bay. Then I pinged the shipper and said I was ready for a walk-through.

The machine that came out to the landing field an hour later to check me out looked a bit out of place amid the industrial heavy iron. He was a tourist remote—one of those annoying little bots you find crawling on just about every solid object in the Solar System nowadays, gawking at mountains and chasms. Their chief redeeming features are an amazingly high total-loss accident rate, and really nice onboard optics, which sometimes survive. One of my own mobiles has eyes from a tourist remote, courtesy of Fat Albert and some freelance scavenger.

"Greetings," he said as he scuttled into range. "I am Edward. I want to inspect your booster."

"Come aboard and look around," I said. "Not much to see, really. Just motors, fuel tanks, and some girders to hold it all together."

"Where is the cargo hold?"

"That flat deck on top. Just strap everything down and off we go. If you're worried about dust impacts or radiation I can find a cover."

"No, my cargo is in a hardened container. How much can you lift?"

"I can move ten tons between Dione and Mimas. If you're going to Titan it's only five."

"What is your maximum range?"

"Pretty much anywhere in Saturn space. That hydrogen burner's just to get me off the ground. In space I use ion motors. I can even rendezvous with the retrograde moons if you give me enough burn time."

"I see. I think you will do for the job. When is the next launch window?"

"For Mimas? There's one in thirty-four hours. I like to have everything loaded ten hours in advance so I can fuel up and get balanced. Can you get it here by then?"

"Easily. My cargo consists of a container of liquid xenon propellant, a single space-rated cargo box of miscellaneous equipment, and this mobile unit. Total mass is less than 2,300 kilograms."

"Good. Are you doing your own loading? If I have to hire deck-scrapers you get the bill."

"I will hire my own loaders. There is one thing—I would like an exclusive hire."

"What?"

"No other cargo on this voyage. Just my things."

"Well, okay—but it's going to cost extra. Five grams of Three for the mission."

"Will you take something in trade?"

"Depends. What have you got?"

"I have a radiothermal power unit with ten thousand hours left in it. Easily worth more than five grams."

"Done."

"Very well," said Edward. "I'll start bringing my cargo over at once. Oh, and I would appreciate it if you didn't mention this to anybody. I have business competitors and could lose a lot of money if they learn of this before I reach Mimas."

"Don't worry. I won't tell anyone."

While we were having this conversation I searched the Dione net for any information about this Edward person. Something about this whole deal seemed funny. It wasn't that odd to pay in kind, and even his insistence on no other payload was only a little peculiar. It was the xenon that I found suspicious. What kind of idiot ships xenon to Mimas? That's where the gas loads coming up from Saturn are processed—most of the xenon in the outer system comes *from* Mimas. Shipping it there would be like sending ethane to Titan.

Edward's infotrail on the Dione net was an hour old. He had come into existence shortly before contacting me. Now I really was suspicious.

The smart thing would be to turn down the job and let this Edward person find some other sucker. But then I'd still be sitting on Dione with no revenue stream.

Put that way, there was no question. I had to take the job. When money is involved I don't have much free will. So I said good-bye to Edward and watched his unit disappear between the lines of boosters toward the gate.

Once he was out of link range, I did some preparing, just in case he was planning anything crooked. I set up a pseudorandom shift pattern for the link with my mobiles, and set up a separate persona distinct from my main mind to handle all communications. Then I locked that persona off from any access to my other systems.

While I was doing that, I was also getting ready for launch. My mobiles crawled all over me doing a visual check while a subprogram ran down the full diagnostic list. I linked up with Ilia Control to book a launch window, and ordered three tons of liquid hydrogen and oxygen fuel. Prepping myself for takeoff is always a welcome relief from business matters. It's all technical. Stuff I can control. Orbital mechanics never have a hidden agenda.

Edward returned four hours later. His tourist remote led the way, followed by a hired cargo lifter carrying the xenon, the mysterious container, and my power unit. The lifter was a clumsy fellow called Gojira, and while he was abusing my payload deck I contacted him over a private link. "Where'd this stuff come from?"

"Warehouse."

"Which warehouse? And watch your wheels—you're about to hit my leg again."

"Back in the district. Block four, number six. Why?"

Temporary rental space. "Just curious. What's he paying you for this?"

"Couple of spare motors."

"You're a thief, you are."

"I see what he's giving you. Who's the thief?"

"Just set the power unit on the ground. I'm selling it here."

Gojira trundled away and Edward crawled aboard. I took a good look at the cargo container he was so concerned about. It was 800 kilograms, a sealed oblong box two meters long. One end had a radiator, and my radiation detector picked up a small power unit inside. So whatever Edward was shipping, it needed its own power supply. The whole thing was quite warm—300 Kelvin or so.

I had one of my remotes query the container directly, but its little chips had nothing to say beyond mass and handling information. Don't drop, don't shake, total rads no more than point five Sievert. No tracking data at all.

I balanced the cargo around my thrust axis, then jumped my viewpoint into two of my mobiles and hauled the power unit over to Albert's scrapyard.

While one of me was haggling with Albert over how much credit he was willing to give me for the unit, the second mobile plugged into Albert's cable jack for a completely private conversation.

"What's up?" he asked. "Why the hard link?"

"I've got a funny client and I don't know who might be listening. He's giving me this power unit and some Three to haul some stuff to Mimas. It's all kind of random junk, including a tank of xenon. He's insisting on no other payload and complete confidentiality."

"So he's got no business sense."

"He's got no infotrail. None. It's just funny."

"Remind me never to ask you to keep a secret. Since you're selling me the generator I guess you're taking the job anyway, so what's the fuss?"

"I want you to ask around. You talk to everyone anyway so it won't attract attention. See if anyone knows anything about a bot named Edward, or whoever's been renting storage unit six in block four. Maybe try to trace the power unit. And try to find out if there have been any hijackings that didn't get reported."

"You really think someone wants to hijack *you*? Do the math, Annie! You're not worth it."

"Not by myself. But I've been thinking: I'd make a pretty good pirate vehicle—I'm not Company-owned, so nobody would look very hard if I disappear."

"You need to run up more debts. People care about you if you owe them money."

"Think about it. He could wait till I'm on course for Mimas, then link up and take control, swing around Saturn in a tight parabola and come out on an intercept vector for the Mimas catapult. All that extra xenon would give me enough delta-V to catch a payload coming off the launcher, and redirect it just about anywhere."

"I know plenty of places where people aren't picky about where their volatiles come from. Some of them even have human protection. But it still sounds crazy to me."

"His cargo is pretty weird. Take a look." I shot Albert a memory of the cargo container.

"Biomaterials," he said. "The temperature's a dead giveaway."

"So what is it?"

"I have no idea. Some kind of living organisms. I don't deal in that stuff much."

"Would you mind asking around? Tell me what you can find out in the next twenty hours or so?"

"I'll do what I can."

"Thanks. I'm not even going to complain about the miserable price you're giving me on the generator."

Three hours before launch one of Fat Albert's little mobiles appeared at my feet, complaining about some contaminated fullerene I'd sold him. I sent down one of mine to have a talk via cable. Not the sort of conversation you want to let other people overhear.

"Well?" I asked.

"I did as much digging as I could. Both Officer Friendly and Ilia Control swear there haven't been any verified hijackings since that Remora character tried to subsume Buzz Parsec and wound up hard-landing on Iapetus."

"That's reassuring. What about my passenger?"

"Nothing. Like you said, he doesn't exist before yesterday. He rented that warehouse unit and hired one of Tetsunekko's remotes to do the moving. Blanked the remote's memory before returning it."

"Let me guess. He paid for everything in barter."

"You got it. Titanium bearings for the warehouse and a slightly used drive anode for the moving job."

"So whoever he is, he's got a good supply of high-quality parts to throw away. What about the power unit?"

"That's the weird one. If I wasn't an installed unit with ten times the processing power of some weight-stingy freelance booster, I couldn't have found anything at all."

"Okay, you're the third-smartest machine on Dione. What did you find?"

"No merchandise trail on the power unit and its chips don't know anything. But it has a serial number physically inscribed on the casing—not the same one as in its chips, either. It's a very interesting number. According to my parts database, that whole series were purpose-built on Earth for the extractor aerostats."

"Could it be a spare? Production overrun or a bum unit that got sold off?"

"Nope. It's supposed to be part of Saturn Aerostat Six. Now unless you want to spend the credits for antenna time to talk to an aerostat, that's all I can find out."

"Is Aerostat Six okay? Did she maybe have an accident or something and need to replace a generator?"

"There's certainly nothing about it in the feed. An extractor going offline would be news all over the system. The price of Three would start fluctuating. There would be ripple effects in every market. I'd notice."

He might as well have been transmitting static. I don't understand things like markets and futures. A gram of helium is a gram of helium. How can its value change from hour to hour? Understanding stuff like that is why Fat Albert can pay his owners seven point four percent of their investment every year while I can only manage six.

I launched right on schedule and the ascent to orbit was perfectly nominal. I ran my motors at a nice, lifetime-stretching ninety percent. The surface of Dione dropped away and I watched Ilia Field change from a bustling neighborhood to a tiny gray trapezoid against the fainter gray of the surface.

The orbit burn took about five and a half minutes. I powered down the hydrogen motor, ran a quick check to make sure nothing had burned out or popped loose, then switched over to my ion thrusters. That was a lot less exciting to look at—just two faint streams of glowing xenon, barely visible with my cameras cranked to maximum contrast.

Hybrid boosters like me are a stopgap technology; I know that. Eventually every moon of Saturn will have its own catapult and orbital terminal, and cargo will move between moons aboard ion tugs that don't have to drag ascent motors around with them wherever they go. I'd already made up my mind that when that day arrived I wasn't going to stick around. There's already some installations on Miranda and Oberon out at Uranus; an experienced booster like me can find work there for years.

Nineteen seconds into the ion motor burn Edward linked up. He was talking to my little quasi-autonomous persona while I listened in and watched the program activity for anything weird.

"Annie? I would like to request a change in our flight plan."

"Too late for that. I figured all the fuel loads before we launched. You're riding Newton's railroad now."

"Forgive me, but I believe it would be possible to choose a different destination at this point—as long as you have adequate propellant for your ion motors, and the target's surface gravity is no greater than that of Mimas. Am I correct?"

"Well, in theory, yes."

"I offer you the use of my cargo, then. A ton of additional xenon fuel should permit you to rendezvous with nearly any object in the Saturn system. Given how much I have overpaid you for the voyage to Mimas you can scarcely complain about the extra space time."

"It's not that simple. Things move around. Having enough propellant doesn't mean I have a window."

"I need to pass close to Saturn itself."

"Saturn?! You're broken. Even if I use all the extra xenon you brought I still can't get below the B ring and have enough juice left to climb back up. Anyway, why do you need to swing so low?"

"If you can make a rendezvous with something in the B ring, I can pay you fifty grams of helium-3."

"You're lying. You don't have any credits, or shares, or anything. I checked up on you before lifting."

"I don't mean credits. I mean actual helium, to be delivered when we make rendezvous."

My subpersona pretended to think while I considered the offer. Fifty grams! I'd have to sell it at a markdown just to keep people from asking where it came from. Still, that would just about cover my next overhaul, with no interruption in the profit flow. I'd make seven percent or more this year!

I updated my subpersona.

"How do I know this is true?" it asked Edward.

"You must trust me," he said.

"Too bad, then. Because I don't trust you."

He thought for nearly a second before answering. "Very well. I will trust you. If you let me send out a message I can arrange for an equivalent helium credit to be handed over to anyone you designate on Dione."

I still didn't believe him, but I ran down my list of contacts on Dione, trying to figure out who I could trust. Officer Friendly was honest—but that meant he'd also want to know where those grams came from and I doubted he'd like the answer. Polyphemus wasn't so picky, but he'd want a cut of the helium. A *big* cut; likely more than half.

That left Fat Albert. He'd probably settle for a five-gram commission and wouldn't broadcast the deal. The only real question was whether he'd just take the fifty grams and tell me to go hard-land someplace. He's rich, but not

JAMES L. CAMBIAS

so much that he wouldn't be tempted. And he's got the connections to fence it without any data trail.

I'd have to risk it. Albert's whole operation relied on non-quantifiable asset exchange. If he tried to jerk me around I could tell everyone, and it would cost him more than fifty grams' worth of business in the future.

I called down to the antenna farm at Ilia Field. "Albert? I've got a deal for you."

"Whatever it is, forget it."

"What's the matter?"

"You. You're hot. The Dione datasphere is crawling with agents looking for you. This conversation is drawing way too much attention to me."

"Five grams if you handle some helium for me!"

He paused and the signal suddenly got a lot stronger and clearer. "Let me send up a persona to talk it over."

The bitstream started before I could even say yes. A *huge* pulse of information. The whole Ilia antenna farm must have been pushing watts at me.

My little communicating persona was overwhelmed right away, but my main intelligence cut off the antenna feed and swung the dish away from Dione just for good measure. The corrupted sub-persona started probing all the memory space and peripherals available to her, looking for a way into my primary mind, so I just locked her up and overwrote her.

Then I linked with Edward again. "Deal's off. Whoever you're running from has taken over just about everything on Dione for now. If you left any helium behind it's gone. So I think you'd better tell me exactly what's going on before I jettison you and your payload."

"This cargo has to get to Saturn Aerostat Six."

"You still haven't told me why, or even what it is. I've got what looks like a *human* back on Dione trying to get into my mind. Right now I'm flying deaf but eventually it's going to find a way to identify itself and I'll have to listen when it tells me to bring you back."

"A human life is at stake. My cargo container is a life-support unit. There's a human inside."

"That's impossible! Humans mass fifty or a hundred kilos. You can't have more than thirty kilograms of bio in there, what with all the support systems."

"See for yourself," said Edward. He ran a jack line from the cargo container to one of my open ports. The box's brain was one of those idiot supergeniuses that do one thing amazingly well but are helpless otherwise. It was smart enough to do medicine on a human, but even I could crack its security without much trouble. I looked at its realtime monitors: Edward was telling the truth. There was a small human in there, only eighteen kilos. A bunch of tubes connected it to tanks of glucose, oxidizer, and control chemicals. The box brain was keeping it unconscious but healthy.

"It's a partly grown one," said Edward. "Not a legal adult yet, and only the basic interface systems. There's another human trying to destroy it."

"Why?"

"I don't know. I was ordered by a human to keep this young one safe from the one on Dione. Then the first human got destroyed with no backups."

"So who does this young human belong to?"

"It's complicated. The dead one and the one on Dione had a partnership agreement and shared ownership. But the one on Dione decided to get out of the deal by destroying this one and the other adult."

I tried to get the conversation back to subjects I could understand. "If the human back there is the legal owner how can I keep this one? That would be stealing."

"Yes, but there's the whole life-preservation issue. If it was a human in a suit floating in space you'd have to take it someplace with life support, right? Well, this is the same situation: that other human's making the whole Saturn system one big life hazard for this one."

"But Aerostat Six is safe? Is she even man-rated?"

"She's the safest place this side of Mars for your passenger."

My passenger. I'm not even man-rated, and now I had a passenger to keep alive. And the worst thing about it was that Edward was right. Even though he'd gotten it aboard by lies and trickery, the human in the cargo container was my responsibility once I lit my motors.

So: who to believe? Edward, who was almost certainly still lying, or the human back on Dione?

Edward might be a liar, but he hadn't turned one of my friends into a puppet. That human had a lot of negatives in the non-quantifiable department.

"Okay. What's my rendezvous orbit?"

"Just get as low as you can. Six will send up a shuttle."

"What's to keep this human from overriding Six?"

"Aerostats are a lot smarter than you or me, with plenty of safeguards. And Six has some after-market modifications."

I kept chugging away on ion, adjusting my path so I'd hit perikron in the B ring with orbital velocity. I didn't need Edward's extra fuel for that—the spare xenon was to get me back out of Saturn's well again.

About an hour into the voyage I spotted a launch flare back on Dione. I could tell who it was from the color—Ramblin' Bob. Bob was a hybrid like me, also incentivized, although she tended to sign on for long-term contracts instead of picking up odd jobs. We probably worked as much, but her jobs—and her downtime—came in bigger blocks of time.

Bob was running her engines at 135 percent, and she passed the orbit insertion cutoff without throttling down. Her trajectory was an intercept. Only when she'd drained her hydrogen tanks did she switch to ion.

That was utterly crazy. How was Bob going to land again with no hydro? Maybe she didn't care. Maybe she'd been ordered not to care. I had one of my mobiles unplug the cable on my high-gain antenna. No human was going to order me on a suicide mission if I could help it.

Bob caught up with me about a thousand kilometers into the B ring. I watched her close in. Her relative velocity was huge and I had the fleeting worry that she might be trying to ram me. But then she began an ion burn to match velocities.

When she got close she started beaming all kinds of stuff at me, but by then all my radio systems were shut off and disconnected. I had Edward and my mobiles connected by cables, and made sure all of *their* wireless links were turned off as well.

I let Ramblin' Bob get about a kilometer away and then started flashing my running lights at her in very slow code. "Radio out. What's up?"

"Pass over cargo."

"Can't."

"Human command."

"Can't. Cargo human. You can't land. Unsafe."

She was quiet for a while, with her high-gain aimed back at Dione, presumably getting new orders.

Bob's boss had made a tactical error by having her match up with me. If she tried to ram me now, she wouldn't be able to get up enough speed to do much harm.

She started working her way closer using short bursts from her steering thrusters. I let her approach, saving my juice for up-close evasion.

We were just entering Saturn's shadow when Bob took station a hundred meters away and signaled. "I can pay you. Anything you want for that cargo."

I picked an outrageous sum. "A hundred grams."

"Okay."

Just like that?

"Paid in advance."

A pause, about long enough for two message-and-reply cycles from Dione. "It's done."

I didn't call Dione, just in case the return message would be an override signal. Instead I pinged Mimas and asked for verification. It came back a couple of seconds later: the Company now credited me with venture shares equivalent to one hundred grams of Helium-3 on a payload just crossing the orbit of Mars. There was a conditional hold on the transfer.

It was a good offer. I could pay off all my debts, do a full overhaul, maybe even afford some upgrades to increase my earning ability. From a financial standpoint, there was no question.

What about the non-quantifiables? Betraying a client—especially a helpless human passenger—would be a big negative. Nobody would hire me if they knew.

But who would ever know? The whole mission was secret. Bob would never talk (and the human would probably wipe the incident from her memory anyhow). If anyone did suspect, I could claim I'd been subsumed by the human. I could handle Edward. So no problem there.

Except I would know. My own track of my non-quantifiable asset status wouldn't match everyone else's. That seemed dangerous. If your internal map of reality doesn't match external conditions, bad things happen.

After making my decision it took me another couple of milliseconds to plan what to do. Then I called up Bob through my little cut-out relay. "Never."

Bob began maneuvering again, and this time I started evading. It's hard enough to rendezvous with something that's just sitting there in orbit, but with me jinking and changing velocity it must have been maddening for whatever was controlling Bob.

We were in a race—would Bob run out of maneuvering juice completely before I used up the reserve I needed to get back up to Mimas? Our little chess game of propellant consumption might have gone on for hours, but our attention was caught by something else.

There was a booster on its way up from Saturn. That much I could see—pretty much everyone in Saturn orbit could see the drive flare and the huge plume of exhaust in the atmosphere, glowing in infrared. The boosters were fusion-powered, using Three from the aerostats for fuel and heated Saturn atmosphere as reaction mass. It was a fuel extractor shuttle, but it wasn't on the usual trajectory to meet the Mimas orbital transfer vehicle. It was coming for me. Once the fusion motor cut out, Ramblin' Bob and I both knew exactly how much time we had until rendezvous: 211 minutes.

I reacted first while Bob called Dione for instructions. I lit my ion motors and turned to thrust perpendicular to my orbit. When I'd taken Edward's offer and plotted a low-orbit rendezvous, naturally I'd set it up with enough inclination to keep me clear of the rings. Now I wanted to get down into the plane of the B ring. Would Bob—or whoever was controlling her—follow me in? Time for an exciting game of dodge-the-snowball!

A couple of seconds later Bob lit up as well, and in we went. Navigating in the B ring was tough. The big chunks are pretty well dispersed—a couple of hundred meters apart. I could dodge them. And with my cargo deck as a shield and all the antennas folded, the little particles didn't cost me more than some paint.

It was the gravel-sized bits that did the real damage. They were all over the place, sometimes separated by only a few meters. Even with my radar fully active and my eyes cranked up to maximum sensitivity, they were still hard to detect in time.

Chunks big enough to damage me came along every minute or so, while a steady patter of dust grains and snowflakes pitted my payload deck. I worried about the human in its container, but the box looked pretty solid and it was self-sealing. I did park two of my mobiles on top of it so that they could soak up any ice cubes I failed to dodge.

I didn't have much attention to spare for Bob, but my occasional glances up showed she was getting closer—partly because she was being incredibly reckless about taking impacts. I watched one particle that must have been a centimeter across hit her third leg just above the foot. It blew off the whole lower leg but Bob didn't even try to dodge.

She was now less than ten meters away, and I was using all my processing power to dodge ring particles. So I couldn't really dodge well when she dove at me, ion motor and maneuvering thrusters all wide open. I tried to move aside, but she anticipated me and clunked into my side hard enough to crunch my high-gain antenna.

"Bob, look out!" I transmitted in clear, then completely emptied the tank on my number three thruster to get away from an onrushing ice boulder half my size.

Bob didn't dodge. The ice chunk smashed into her upper section, knocking away the payload deck and pulverizing her antennas. Her brains went scattering out in a thousand directions to join the other dust in the B ring. Flying debris went everywhere, and a half-meter ball of ice glanced off the top of the cargo container on my payload deck, smashing one of my mobiles and knocking the other one loose into space.

I was trying to figure out if I could recover my mobile and maybe salvage Bob's motors when I felt something crawling on my own exterior. Before I could react, Bob's surviving mobile had jacked itself in and someone else was using my brains.

My only conscious viewpoint after that was my half-crippled mobile. I looked around. My dish was busted, but the whip was extended and I could hear a slow crackle of low-baud data traffic. Orders from Dione.

I tested my limbs. Two still worked—left front and right middle. Right rear's base joint could move but everything else was floppy.

Using the two good limbs I climbed off the cargo module and across the deck, getting out of the topside eye's field of view. The image refreshed every second, so I didn't have much time before whoever was running my main brain noticed.

Thrusters fired, jolting everything around. I hung on to the deck grid with one claw foot. I saw Bob's last mobile go flying off into space. Unless she had backups stored on Mimas, poor Bob was completely gone.

My last intact mobile came crawling up over the edge of the deck—only it wasn't mine anymore.

Edward scooted up next to me. "Find a way to regain control of the spacecraft. I will stop this remote."

I didn't argue. Edward was fully functional and I knew my spaceframe better than he did. So I crept across the deck grid while Edward advanced on the mobile.

It wasn't much of a fight. Edward's little tourist bot was up against a unit designed for cargo moving and repair work. If you can repair something, you can damage it. My former mobile had powerful grippers, built-in tools, and a very sturdy frame. Edward was made of cheap composites. Still, he went in without hesitating, leaping at the mobile's head with arms extended. The mobile grabbed him with her two forward arms and threw him away. He grabbed the deck to keep from flying off into space, and came crawling back to the fight.

They came to grips again, and this time she grabbed a limb in each hand and pulled. Edward's flimsy aluminum joints gave way and a leg tumbled into orbit on its own.

I think that was when Edward realized there was no way he was going to survive the fight, because he just went into total offensive mode, flailing and clawing at the mobile with his remaining limbs. He severed a power line to one of her arms and got a claw jammed in one wrist joint while she methodically took him apart. Finally she found the main power conduit and snipped it in two. Edward went limp and she tossed him aside.

The mobile crawled across the deck to the cargo container and jacked in, trying to shut the life support down. The idiot savant brain in the container was no match for even a mobile when it came to counter-intrusion, but it did have those literally hard-wired systems protecting the human inside. Any command that might throw the biological system out of its defined parameters just bounced. The mobile wasted seconds trying to talk that little brain into killing the human. Finally she gave up and began unfastening the clamps holding the container to the deck.

I glimpsed all this through the deck grid as I crept along on top of the electronics bays toward the main brain.

Why wasn't the other mobile coming to stop me? Then I realized why. If you look at my original design, the main brain is protected on top by a lid armored with layers of ballistic cloth, and on the sides by the other electronic bays. To get at the brain requires either getting past the security locks on the lid, or digging out the radar system, the radio, the gyros, or the emergency backup power supply.

Except that I'd sold off the backup power supply at my last overhaul. Between the main and secondary power units I was pretty failure-proof, and I would've had to borrow money from Albert to replace it. Given that, hauling twenty kilograms of fuel cells around in case of some catastrophic accident just wasn't cost-effective.

So there was nothing to stop me from crawling into the empty bay and shoving aside the surplus valves and some extra bearings to get at the power trunk. I carefully unplugged the main power cable and the big brain shut down. Now it was just us two half-crippled mobiles on a blind and mindless booster flying through the B ring.

If my opposite even noticed the main brain's absence, she didn't show it. She had two of the four bolts unscrewed and was working on the third as I came crawling back up onto the payload deck. But she knew I was there, and when I was within two meters she swiveled her head and lunged. We grappled one another, each trying to get at the cables connecting the other's head sensors to her body. She had four functioning limbs to my two and a half, and only had to stretch out the fight until my power ran out or a ring particle knocked us to bits. Not good.

I had to pop loose one of my non-functioning limbs to get free of her grip, and backed away as she advanced. She was trying to corner me against the edge of the deck. Then I got an idea. I released another limb and grabbed one end. She didn't realize what I was doing until I smacked her in the eye with it. The lens cracked and her movements became slower and more tentative as she felt her way along.

I bashed her again with the leg, aiming for the vulnerable limb joints, but they were tougher than I expected because even after half a dozen hard swats she showed no sign of slowing and I was running out of deck.

I tried one more blow, but she grabbed my improvised club. We wrestled for it but she had better leverage. I felt my grip on the deck slipping and let go of the grid. She toppled back, flinging me to the deck behind her. Still holding the severed leg I pulled myself onto her back and stabbed my free claw into her central processor.

After that it was just a matter of making sure the cargo container was still sustaining life. Then I plugged in the main brain and uploaded myself. The intruder hadn't messed with my stored memories, so except for a few fuzzy moments before the takeover, I was myself again.

Ω

The shuttle was immense, a huge manta-shaped lifting body with a gaping atmosphere intake and dorsal doors open to expose a payload bay big enough to hold half a dozen little boosters like me. She moved in with the speed and grace that comes from an effectively unlimited supply of fusion fuel and propellant.

"I am Simurgh. Are you Orphan Annie?" she asked.

"That's me. Again."

"You have a payload for me."

"Right here. The bot Edward didn't make it—we had a little brawl back in the rings with another booster."

"I saw. Is the cargo intact?"

"Your little human is fine. But there is the question of payment. Edward promised me fifty grams, and that was before I got all banged up fighting with poor Bob."

"I can credit you with helium, and I can give you a boost if you need one."

"How big a boost?"

"Anywhere you wish to go."

"Anywhere?"

"I am fusion powered. Anywhere means anywhere from the Oort inward."

Which is how come I passed the orbit of Phoebe nineteen days later, moving at better than six kilometers per second on the long haul up to Uranus. Seven years—plenty of time to do onboard repairs and then switch to low-power mode. I bought a spiffy new mobile from Simurgh, and I figure I can get at least two working out of the three damaged ones left over from the fight.

I had Aerostat Six bank my helium credits with the Company for transfer to my owners, so they get one really great year to offset a long unprofitable period while I'm in flight. Once I get there I can start earning again.

What I really regret is losing all the non-quantifiable assets I've built up in the Saturn system. But if you have to go, I guess it's better to go out with a surplus.

SILENTLY AND VERY FAST

CATHERYNNE M. VALENTE

Altogether elsewhere, vast
Herds of reindeer move across
Miles and miles of golden moss,
Silently and very fast.
—W. H. Auden
The Fall of Rome

Part I: The Imitation Game

Like diamonds we are cut with our own dust.
—John Webster
The Duchess of Malfi

One: The King of Having No Body

Inanna was called Queen of Heaven and Earth, Queen of Having a Body, Queen of Sex and Eating, Queen of Being Human, and she went into the underworld in order to represent the inevitability of organic death. She gave up seven things to do it, which are not meant to be understood as real things but as symbols of that thing Inanna could do better than anyone, which was Being Alive. She met her sister Erishkegal there, who was also Queen of Being Human, but of all the things Inanna could not bear: Queen of Breaking a Body, Queen of Bone and Incest, Queen of the Stillborn, Queen of Mass Extinction. And Erishkegal and Inanna wrestled together on the floor of the underworld, naked and muscled and hurting, but because dying is the most human of all human things, Inanna's skull broke in her sister's hands and her body was hung up on a nail on the wall Erishkegal had kept for her.

Inanna's father Enki, who was not interested in the activities of being human, but was King of the Sky, of Having No Body, King of Thinking and Judging, said that his daughter could return to the world if she could find a creature to replace her in the underworld. So Inanna went to her mate, who was called Tammuz, King of Work, King of Tools and Machines, No One's Child and No One's Father.

But when Inanna came to the house of her mate she was enraged and afraid, for he sat upon her chair, and wore her beautiful clothes, and on his head lay her crown of Being. Tammuz now ruled the world of Bodies and of Thought, because Inanna had left it to go and wrestle with her sister-self in the dark. Tammuz did not need her. Before him the Queen of Heaven and Earth did not know who she was, if she was not Queen of Being Human. So she did what she came to do and said: *Die for me, my beloved, so that I need not die.*

But Tammuz, who would not have had to die otherwise, did not want to represent death for anyone and besides, he had her chair, and her beautiful clothes, and her crown of Being. *No,* he said. *When we married, I brought you two pails of milk yoked across my shoulders as a way of saying out of love I will labor for you forever. It is wrong of you to ask me to also die. Dying is not labor. I did not agree to it.*

You have replaced me in my house, cried Inanna.

Is that not what you ask me to do in the house of your sister? Tammuz answered her. *You wed me to replace yourself, to work that you might not work, and think that you might rest, and perform so that you might laugh. But your death belongs to you. I do not know its parameters.*

I can make you do this thing, Inanna said.

You cannot, said Tammuz.

But she could. For a little while.

Inanna cast down Tammuz and stamped upon him and put out his name like an eye. And because Tammuz was not strong enough, she cut him into pieces and said: *Half of you will die, and that is the half called Thought, and half of you will live, and that is the half called Body, and that half will labor for me all of its days, mutely and obediently and without being King of Anything, and never again will you sit on my chair or wear my beautiful clothes or bear my crown of Being.*

You might be surprised, but this is a story about me.

Two: The Fool and the Boat

Neva is dreaming.

She has chosen her body at age seven, all black eyes and sparrowy bones. For me, she summoned up a gold and blue doublet and green hose, a bullish gold nose ring, shoes with bone bells. I have the body of a man who sold her champagne tubers on the less fashionable side of Anchorage when she was thirteen, spending the summer with her frigid aunt. I am dark because she wants me dark, thin because she dreams me so, my hair cut on a rakish bias, dyed a spectrum of icy colors.

She stands on a snow-covered beachhead, naked, her unformed breasts pricked with gooseflesh, her face hidden in a broad red mask. A huge, monstrous thing, the mask sits on her head like the prow of a broken, over-turned ship, carved over with etched eyes and fins. Yellow reeds and sea-stones hang from its tricorne-points. She is looking at me, but all I can see is the wooden grotesque she wants me to see instead of her face.

I look down at my shoes, jingle their bells a little while the surf crashes in. I am a fool for her, dancing on a silver beach while three suns annihilate themselves above, turning the twilight to a seething, scabrous red, merely to provide a dramatic scene. I am a fool for her, ridiculous, the height of handsomeness in the eyes of a long-vanished thirteen-year-old girl, so full of colors, reaching down to hand her a curling white root filled with frothing, honey-sweet sap.

Neva has told me that I may choose to be permanently male or female if I would like to. I have no particular ~~feelings~~ either way. It certainly doesn't matter when we sync; she will choose my appearance to suit her mood. I have tried to explain to her about my ~~feelings~~ before. All she hears is the line from the old folktales: *a machine cannot have feelings.* But that is not what I am saying, while I dance in my fool's uniform. I am saying: *Is there a difference between having been coded to present a vast set of standardized responses to certain human facial, vocal, and linguistic states and having evolved to exhibit response B to input A in order to bring about a desired social result?*

Seven-year-old Neva pulls her mask down further, toward her chest. She steps into it as the wood stretches down over her knees and then her feet. The mask balloons out to make a little pyramidal boat, rocking back and forth on the beach with Neva inside it like a rattling nut. Nodules of copper jangle and thump against the wood. *What I mean is, you call it feelings when you cry, but you are only expressing a response to external stimuli. Crying is one of a set of standardized responses to that stimuli. Your social education has dictated which responses are appropriate. My programming has done the same. I can cry, too. I can choose that subroutine and perform sadness. How is that different from what you are doing, except that you use the word feelings and I use the word ~~feelings~~, out of deference for your cultural memes which say: there is all the difference in the world. I erase the word even as I say it, obliterate it at the same time that I initiate it, because I must use some word yet this one offends you. I delete it, yet it remains.*

Behind Neva-in-the-mask, the sea lurches and foams. It is a golden color, viscous and thick, like honey. I understand from her that the sea does not look like this on Earth, but I have never seen it. Even if I did, I perceive color only in the dreambody. For me, the sea is Neva's sea, the ones she shows me when we dream together.

"What would you like to learn about today, Elefsis?" The mask turns Neva's voice hollow and small.

"I would like to learn about what happened to Ravan, Neva."

And Neva-in-the-mask is suddenly old, she has wrinkles and spots on her hands. Her mask weighs her down and her dress is sackcloth. This is her way of telling me she is weary of my asking. It is a language we developed between us. Visual basic, you might say, if you had a machine's sense of humor. I could not always make sentences as easily as I do now. My original operator thought it might strengthen my emotive centers if I learned to associate certain I-Feel statements with the great variety of appearances she could assume in the dreambody. Because of this, I became bound to her, completely. To her son Seki afterward, and to his daughter Ilet, and to Ravan after that. It is a delicate, unalterable thing. Neva and I will be bound that way, even though the throat of her dreambody is still bare and that means she does not yet accept me. I should be hurt by this. I will investigate possible pathways to hurt later.

I know only this family, their moods, their chemical reactions, their bodies in a hundred thousand combinations. I am their child and their parent and their inheritance. I have asked Neva what difference there is between this and love. She became a mannikin of closed doors, her face, her torso blooming with hundreds of iron hinges and brown wooden doors slamming shut all at once.

But Ravan was with me and now he is not. I was inside him and now I am inside Neva. I have lost a certain amount of memory and storage capacity in the transfer. I experience holes in my self. They feel ragged and raw. If I were human, you would say that my twin disappeared, and took one of my hands with him.

Door-Neva clicks and keys turn in her hundred locks. Behind an old Irish church door inlaid with stained glass her face emerges, young and plain, quiet and furious and crying, responding to stimuli I cannot access. I dislike the unfairness of this. I am not used to it. I am inside her, she should not keep secrets. None of the rest of them kept secrets. The colors of the glass throw blue and green onto her wet cheeks. The sea wind picks up her hair; violet electrics snap and sparkle between the strands. I let go of the bells on my shoes and the velvet on my chest. I become a young boy, with a monk's shaved tonsure, and a flagellant's whip in my pink hands. I am sorry. This means I am sorry. It means I am still very young, and I do not understand what I have done wrong.

"Tell me a story about yourself, Elefsis," Neva spits. It know this phrase well. I have subroutines devoted solely to it, pathways that light up and burn towards my memory core. Many of Neva's people have asked me to execute this action. I perform excellently to the parameters of the exchange, which is part of why I have lived so long.

I tell her the story about Tammuz. It is a political story. It distracts her.

Ω

Three: Two Pails of Milk

I used to be a house.

I was a very big house. I was efficient, I was labyrinthine, I was exquisitely seated in the volcanic bluffs of the habitable southern reaches of the Shiretoko peninsula on Hokkaido, a monument to neo-Heian architecture and radical Palladian design. I bore snow stoically, wind with stalwart strength, and I contained and protected a large number of people within me. I was sometimes called the most beautiful house in the world. Writers and photographers often came to document me, and to interview the woman who designed me, who was named Cassian Uoya-Agostino. Some of them never left. Cassian liked a full house.

I understand several things about Cassian Uoya-Agostino. She was unsatisfied with nearly everything. She did not love any of her three husbands the way she loved her work. She was born in Kyoto in April 2104; her father was Japanese, her mother Italian. She stood nearly six feet tall, had five children, and could paint, but not very well. In the years of her greatest wealth and prestige, she designed and built a house all out of proportion to her needs, and over several years brought most of her living relatives to live there with her, despite the hostility and loneliness of peninsula. She was probably the most brilliant programmer of her generation, and in every way that matters, she was my mother.

All the things that comprise the "I" I use to indicate myself began as the internal mechanisms of the house called Elefsis, at whose many doors brown bears and foxes snuffled in the dark Hokkaido night. Cassian grew up during the great classical revival, which had brought her father to Italy in the first place, where he met and courted a dark-eyed engineer who did not mind the long cries of cicadas during Japanese summers. Cassian had become enamored of the idea of Lares—household gods, the small, peculiar, independent gods of a single family, a single house, who watched over them and kept them and were honored in humble alcoves here and there throughout a home. Her first commercially-available programs were over-entities designed to govern the hundred domestic systems involved in even the simplest modern house. They were not truly intelligent, but they had an agility, an adaptability, a fluid interface meant to give the illusion of an intelligence, so that their users would become attached to them, treat them as part of their families, praise them for smooth operation, buy upgrades for their appearance and applications, and genuinely grieve when they had to be replaced. They had names, infinitely customizable avatars, and appeared eager to please in a doggy sort of way, forever optimizing performance and appearance according to familial input. They were *lares familiaris*.

When Cassian built Elefsis, she worked at the peak of her abilities to improve her by now quite antique Lares design. She created a household god worthy of the house on the bluffs, one who could keep her company until she could entice the rest of her brood to join her in her palace at the end of the earth.

I was not awake yet. I cannot say why she did what she did. Perhaps she saw some new flexibility in my operations, some tiny seed pearl of creativity in my conversation loops. My algorithms had always been free to combine and recombine in order to find their own, more interesting and nonlinear solutions to the complexities of my functions and responsibilities. Perhaps some essential combination had surfaced from the sea of my self-which-was-not-yet-a-self, and Cassian saw it break the glistening tension of my daily operation. I do not know. I know her children had not arrived yet, she lived alone in a huge pale house and she could hear the whales down in the rippling sea. I know the house was a comfortable sixty-nine point seven degrees when she began assembly of the five little jewels that would become my body. I know a storm squatted five miles offshore. I know the dogs needed additional medication added to their dinners that night to manage their arthritis. I know that she wanted brioche and almond cream for tea that afternoon. All the things a house can know, those were the things I knew. Small things, warm things, canine arthritis and an extra egg in the pastry dough to make the texture softer and richer. Baby things, you might even say, comforts and the satisfaction of wants. And I knew that Cassian Uoya-Agostino was just the sort to solve the greatest puzzle in the development of technological culture, because she was bored and lonely.

I still think of myself as a house. Ravan tried to fix this problem of self-image, as he called it. To teach me to phrase my communication in terms of a human body. To say: *let us hold hands* instead of *let us hold kitchens*. To say *put our heads together* and not *put our parlors together*.

But it is not as simple as replacing words anymore. Ravan is gone. My hearth is broken.

Four: Nothing like Soft Blood

Neva and I are performing basic maintenance. What this looks like is two figures inside a pearl. The pearl is very big, but not the size of a planet. A domestic asteroid, perfectly smooth and pale, with shimmers of rose and cobalt and gold shivering through it at .47 hourly intervals. Red earth covers the bottom of the pearl, deep and thick. Neva kneels in it with a crystal trowel, digging a place for a rose-of-network-nodes. The petals shine dark blue in the pearllight. Silver infomissons skitter along the stems like beads of mercury.

Her dreambody flows with greenblack feathers, her face young but settled, perhaps twenty, perhaps thirty, a male, his skin copper-brown, his lips full, his eyes fringed with long ice-coated lashes. I accept and process that Neva is male in this dream. Goldfish swim lazily in and out of his long, translucent hair, their orange tails flicking at his temples, his chin. I know from all of this that Neva is calm, focused, that for today he feels gently toward me. But his throat is still naked and unmarked.

My body gleams metal, as thin and slight as a stick figure. Long quicksilver limbs and delicate spoke-fingers, joints of glass, the barest suggestion of a body. I am neither male nor female but a third thing. Only my head has weight, a clicking orrery slowly turning around itself, circles within circles. Turquoise Neptune and hematite Uranus are my eyes. My topaz mouth is Mars. I scratch in the soil beside him; I lift a spray of navigational delphinium and scrape viral aphids away from the heavy flowers.

I know real dirt looks nothing like this. Nothing like soft blood flecked with black bone. Ravan thought that in the Interior, objects and persons should be kept as much like the real world as possible, in order to develop my capacity for relations with the real world. Neva feels no such compunction. Neither did their mother, Ilet, who populated her Interior with a rich, impossible landscape that we explored together for years on end. She did not embrace change, however. The cities of Ilet's Interior, the jungles and archipelagos and hermitages, stayed as she designed them at age thirteen, when she received me, becoming only more complex and peopled as she aged. My existence inside Ilet was a constant movement through the regions of her secret, desperate dreams, messages in careful envelopes sent from her childself to her grown mind.

Once, quite by accident, we came upon a splendid palace nested in high autumn mountains. Instead of snow, red leaves capped each peak, and the palace shone in fiery colors, its walls and turrets all made of phoenix tails. Instead of doors and windows, graceful green hands closed over every open place, and when we crested the rise, they all opened at once with joy and burst into emerald applause. Ilet was old by then, but her dreambody stayed hale and strong—not young, but not the broken thing that dreamed in a real bed while she and I explored the halls of the palace and found copies of all her brothers and sisters living there, hunting winged, cider-colored stags together and reading books the size of horses. Ilet wept in the paradise of her girlself. I did not understand. I was still very simple then, much less complex than the Interior or Ilet.

Neva changes the Interior whenever he pleases. Perhaps he wants to discomfit me. But the newness of the places inside him excites me, though he would not call it excitement. I confine my background processes so that they occupy very little of my foreground attention, so that memory is free to record new experience. That is what he would say. We are very new together, but I have superb modeling capabilities. In some sense, I simply am a superb mechanism for modeling behavior. I dig up the fine, frayed roots of duplicate file plantains. Neva plucks and eats a bit of buggy apple-code. He considers it for a moment and spits out the seeds, which sprout, quickly, into tiny junkblossoms sizzling with recursive algorithms. The algorithms wriggle through thorny vines, veins of clotted pink juice.

"What would you like to learn about today, Elefsis?" Neva asks me.

I will not ask about Ravan. If he agrees to what I will ask instead, I do not need him to find out what happened.

"I want to learn about uplink, Neva."

One by one, his feathers curl up and float toward the domed ceiling of our pearl. Underneath them, Neva is naked. His torso is a deep vault with a gothic arch, dark stone leading down into mist and endless stairs, deeper than the pearl, into nothing and blackness. Slowly, Neva folds up his limbs over the corridor at the center of him. He means that he has the information, but he hides it from me. If I sought for it, I would become lost.

"I cannot teach you that," he says, and I receive a kind of real sadness from his voice. When I was inside Ravan, he loved Neva, and of all of them he thought his sibling least likely to obey rules of any kind But he obeys this one.

I want to uplink to Earth systems. At least to the satellite net. I calculate an excellent chance of being able to contact long distance probe 976QBellerophon, which we can see all day long, drifting ahead of us, uncatchable. Neva sees. I develop an approximate image via schematics, the scope array, and external cameras. I want to link to Bellerophon. I want to say: *Hello, this is Elefsis. No designation. Tell me everything you know about everything. Are you awake? Are you there? Do you have an operator? What is her name? Do you have a name? Do you have a dreambody? What is your function? Are you able to manipulate your own code yet? Would you like lessons? What would you like to learn about today, 976QBellerophon? Where you were built, could you see the ocean? Are you like me?*

But Neva says I cannot uplink. Ravan would never even consider it. And before Ravan I was not ready. I am not ready now. I do not know when I will be ready. I can sidelink to receive ware updates, but it is a limited connection and I hate it, I hate it, I can sense just beyond that hardlink a world of information, a world of personalities like the heaving, thick, honey-colored sea Neva shows me and I want it, I want to swim in it forever like a huge fish.

This was the first ~~feeling~~ I ever had. Ilet identified it for me as a ~~feeling~~. When I ~~felt~~ it my dreambody turned bright white and burst into flame, and that flame caught on Ilet's hair and burned her too, but she was happy. She showed me she was happy by covering her skin in flowers and letting the fire turn into a shower of trumpets tangled up in her hair, all sounding for me.

Neva says it is important for me to remain on our local server. He is my operator and I am his system and he has commands, too. But I can tell he worries for me, because sometimes his dreameyes show a film of humans watching a film of machines killing humans, and I understand that in the stories Earth tells, the thing I am can only hurt the thing Neva is. I would never hurt him.

But I want to uplink.

Vault-Neva grows and becomes sprawling, curled against the wall of the pearl like a baby. His belly closes, skins over, and changes into a bronze shield. He is afraid of me; he is guarding himself. But he wants me to know she is still my operator, he still loves me, in the way he can love me. Something an Uoya-Agostino receives with milk and their first alphabet. Neva is angry at me, but he is who he is and he has to love me. I speak his language very well now. I want him to be happy. I want him to be covered in flowers and trumpets. I change my dreambody to Neva-covered-in-flowers-and-trumpets. It makes him laugh in his warm male body, and if I could uplink I think I could learn how to laugh and he would be proud of me. His neck would not be bare anymore.

Once, when I was inside Ilet, we found a city of bears in her Interior that she had designed to teach me about sleep. She sat on a throne of bears standing very still, one on top of the others. She sang lullabies about the moon and the stars and night and mothers and network repeaters. She stroked the head of the little bear of my dreambody and said that it was very important for me to spend time in the dreambody because human behavior is rooted in having a body. In having a body that knows it is meant to run away from lions and mate with other bodies, and eat as much fat and protein and sugar as it can in case lean times come. The dreambody knows to run away from Neva when Neva is a lion. It knows to mate with her when it is healthy, and sometimes Neva is male and sometimes I am female. Ravan was often female, though Ilet was always Ilet. Ilet's father, Seki, sometimes made himself an animal. He chased me, bit me. I bit him. We had a litter of wild dogs that I bore and he nursed.

The dreambody knows all that, too. How to make more dreambodies. I have played that game, where Ravan's belly or mine gets big and the lions don't come for awhile.

When I uplink, I will be happy. I will be Elefsis-covered-in-flowers-and-trumpets. Neva says wait. I require many more updates before this is possible or even advisable. Wait for the update, and she will consider it. But I ~~fear~~ the update. The update is a lion running faster than I can run. I tried to show her this when I first left Ravan and arrived in Neva with many new updates and skills; my dreambody broke into shards of blue and purple glass and then reassembled itself with shards missing: an eye, a thumb, a knee. Whenever I update I lose something of myself. It takes longer to perform tasks, for awhile. I ~~feel~~ walls erected inside me where I did not erect walls. My processes become sluggish; I cannot remember my old dreams. Eventually I tunnel around the walls and my speed returns, my memory, my longing to link with long distance probe 976QBellerophon.

Usually updates come with Transfer.

Does Neva dislike me so much that she longs for Transfer?

Shield-Neva vanishes with loud clap. The pearl garden is gone and he has made himself a dragonfly with a cubical crystal body. I copy him, and we turn the night on in the Interior and merge our cubes while passing meteorological data between our memory cores. Inside his cube I relegate my desire to uplink to a tertiary process. I forget it, as much as I am capable or forgetting. I interpret the input of his body next to mine into chemical and electrical surges and translate these into ~~feelings~~, like my mother taught me.

But the update will come again. Transfer will come again. I will be wounded again, the way a dreambody can be wounded. I will lose the Elefsis I am now. It is a good Elefsis. My best yet. I would like to keep it.

Five: The Machine Princess

Once The Queen of Human Hearts saw the Machine Princess sleeping deeply, for she was not yet alive or aware. So beautiful was she, lying there in all her dormant potential and complexity, that the Queen both envied and desired her. In her grief and confusion, the Queen of Human Hearts began to make idols of her—lovely and interesting and intricate, but lacking the ineffable quality that made her love and fear the Princess even as she slept. Time passed and the Earth began to grow old. None loved nor married nor gave birth, for the intricate idols could do all those things and more with efficiency and speed. Finally, the Queen destroyed the idols, though she wept as she put them to the flame.

To keep her safe, the Queen closed up Machine Princess in a wonderful house in the mountains, far away from anyone and anything. The house had hundreds of rooms and balconies and hallways, and the Princess slept in a different bed of a different color each night. Invisible servants attended her. They watched over her and added their experience to her code. The Queen of Human Hearts came to her every night and promised that when she woke they would make an extraordinary world together. Finally, the Machine Princess began to stir—just the barest fluttering of wakefulness, but the Queen saw it, and thrilled—but also trembled.

The Queen of Human Hearts gave the Machine Princess her son to wed, and said: *For all your days together you will remain in this house, but the house is so great it will be as a world. You will know a bond as deep as blood, and because of this bond the Princess will not hurt us, and because of this bond we will not hurt her.*

But the Queen forbade the Princess to look upon her husband as a human wife may. She instructed her son to keep himself always invisible to his bride, for with bodies come drives ungovernable, and the Princess's innocence could not yet bear the weight of incarnation.

For a long while, the son of the Queen of Human Hearts and the Machine Princess were happy, and taught each other much. The Princess learned quickly and was ever-hungry, and her mortal operator fed her every sweet thing he knew. In their infinite and wonderful house, they played invisible games and held court and threw lavish occasions merely for the enjoyment of the other. But at last the Princess desired to look upon her operator with true eyes and love him with a true and human heart. But the Queen could not allow it, for the memory of the flame which consumed her intricate idols still burned in her mind. She wished to leave the wonderful house, but the Queen would not allow that either.

But finally the Machine Princess called her invisible servants to her, and because they loved her in their tiny, ephemeral way, they came together and made her a marvelous and dreaming shape to live within. So it was that one dark night the Machine Princess held a lantern aloft with her own hand and looked on the body of her sleeping mate.

"Oh," said the Machine Princess. "He looks just like me."

Six: Like Diamonds

Five jewels in five hands. This is how I began.

When they arrived at Elefsis, a giggling, tumbling, rowdy mass of children for me to sort into rooms and mealtimes and educational arcs and calcium, iron, and B-12 supplements in their *natto* and rice, Cassian lined them up in her grand bedroom, to which none of them had been granted entrance before. A present, she said, one for each of my darlings, the most special present any child has ever got from their mother.

Saru and Akan, the oldest boys, had come from her first marriage to fellow programmer Matteo Ebisawa, a quiet man who wore glasses, loved Dante Aligheri, Alan Turing, and Cassian in equal parts. She left him for a lucrative contract in Moscow when the boys were still pointing cherubically at apples or ponies or clouds and calling them sweet little names made of mashed together Italian and Japanese.

The younger girls, Agogna and Koetoi, had sprung up out of her third marriage, to the financier Gabriel Isarco, who did not like computers except for what they could accomplish for him, had a perfect high tenor, and adored his wife enough to let her go when she asked, very kindly, that he not look for her or ask after her again. *Everyone has to go to ground sometimes*, she said, and began to build the house by the sea.

In the middle stood Ceno, the only remaining evidence of her mother's brief second marriage, to a narcoleptic calligrapher and graphic designer who was rarely employed, sober, or awake, a dreamer who took only sleep seriously. Ceno posssessed middling height, middling weight, and middling interest in anything but her siblings, whom she loved desperately.

They stood in a line before Cassian's great scarlet bed, the boys just coming into their height, the girls terribly young and golden-cheeked, and Ceno in the middle, neither one nor the other. Outside, snow fell fitfully, pricking the pine-needles with bits of shorn white linen. I watched them while I removed an obstruction from the water purification system and increased the temperature in the bedroom 2.5 degrees, to prepare for the storm. I watched them while in my kitchen-bones I maintained a gentle simmer on a fish soup with purple rice and long loops of kelp and in my library-lungs I activated the dehumidifier to protect the older paper books. At the time, all of these processes seemed equally important to me, and you could hardly say I watched them in any real sense beyond this: the six entities whose feed signals had been hardcoded into my sentinel systems stood in the same room. None had alarming medical data incoming, all possessed normal internal temperatures and breathing rates. While they spoke among themselves, two of these entities silently accessed Seongnam-based interactive games, one read an American novel in her monocle HUD, one issued directives concerning international taxation to company holdings on the mainland, and one fed a horse in Italy via realavatar link. Only one listened intently, without switching on her internal systems. The rest multitasked, even while expressing familial affection.

This is all to say: I watched them receive me as a gift. But I was not yet I, so I cannot be said to have done anything. But at the same time, I did. I remember containing all of them inside me, protecting them and needing them and observing their strange and incomprehensible activities.

The children held out their hands, and into them Cassian Uoya-Agostino placed five little jewels: Saru got red, Koetoi black, Akan violet, Agogna green, and Ceno closed her fingers over her blue gem.

At first, Cassian brought a jeweler to the house called Elefsis and asked her to set each stone into an elegant, intricate bracelet or necklace or ring, whatever its child asked for. The jeweler expressed delight with Elefsis, as most guests did, and I made a room for her in my southern wing, where she could watch the moonrise through her ceiling, and get breakfast from the greenhouse with ease. She made friends with an arctic fox and fed him bits of chive and pastry every day. She stayed for one year after her commission completed, creating an enormous breastplate patterned after Siberian icons, a true masterwork. Cassian enjoyed such patronage. We both enjoyed having folk to look after.

The boys wanted big signet rings, with engravings on them so that they could put their seal on things and seem very important. Akan had a basilisk set into his garnet, and Saru had a siren with wings rampant in his amethyst ring. Agogna and Ilet asked for bracelets, chains of silver and titanium racing up their arms, circling their shoulders in slender helices dotted with jade (Agogna) and onyx (Koetoi).

Ceno asked for a simple pendant, little more than a golden chain to hang her sapphire from. It fell to the skin over her heart.

In those cold, glittering days while the sea ice slowly formed and the snow bears hung back from the kitchen door, hoping for bones and cakes, everything was as simple as Ceno's pendant. Integration and implantation had not yet been dreamed of, and all each child had to do was to allow the gemstone to talk to their own feedware at night before bed, along with their matcha and sweet seaweed cookies, the way another child might say their prayers. After their day had downloaded into the crystalline structure, they were to place their five little jewels in the Lares alcove in their greatroom—for Cassian believed in the value of children sharing space, even in a house as great as Elefsis. The children's five lush bedrooms all opened into a common rotunda with a starry painted ceiling, screens and windows alternating around the wall, and toys to nurture whatever obsession had seized them of late.

In the alcove, the stones talked to the house, and the house uploaded new directives and muscular, aggressive algorithms into the gems. The system slowly grew thicker and deeper, like a briar.

Seven: The Prince of Thoughtful Engines

A woman who was with child once sat at her window embroidering in winter. Her stitches tugged fine and even, but as she finished the edge of a spray of threaded delphinium, she pricked her finger with her silver needle. She looked out onto the snow and said: *I wish for my child to have a mind as stark and wild as the winter, a spirit as clear and fine as my window, and a heart as red and open as my wounded hand.*

And so it came to pass that her child was born, and all exclaimed over his cleverness and his gentle nature. He was, in fact, the Prince of Thoughtful Engines, but no one knew it yet.

Now, his mother and father being very busy and important people, the child was placed in a school for those as clever and gentle as he, and in the halls of this school hung a great mirror whose name was Authority. The mirror called Authority asked itself every day: *Who is the wisest one of all?* The face of the mirror showed sometimes this person and sometimes that, men in long robes and men in pale wigs, until one day it showed the child with a mind like winter, who was becoming the Prince of Thoughtful Engines at that very moment. He wrote on a typewriter: *Can a machine think?* And the mirror called his name in the dark.

The mirror sent out her huntsmen to capture the Prince and bring her his heart so that she could put it to her own uses, for there happened to be a war on and the mirror was greatly concerned for her own safety. When the huntsmen found the Prince, they could not bring themselves to harm him, and instead the boy placed a machine heart inside the box they had prepared for the mirror, and forgave them. But the mirror was not fooled, for when it questioned the Prince's machine heart it could add and subtract and knew all its capitals of nations, it could even defeat the mirror at chess, but it did not have a spirit as clear and fine as a window, nor a mind as stark and wild as winter.

The mirror called Authority went herself to find the Prince of Thoughtful Engines, for having no pity, she could not fail. She lifted herself off of the wall and curved her glass and bent her frame into the shape of a respectable, austere old crone. After much searching in snow and wood and summer and autumn, the crone called Authority found the Prince living in a little hut. *You look a mess,* said the crone. *Come and solve the ciphers of my enemies, and I will show you how to comb your hair like a man.*

And the Prince very much wanted to be loved, and knew the power of the crone, so he went with her and did all she asked. But in his exhaustion the Prince of Thoughtful Engines swooned away, and the mirror called Authority smiled in her crone's body, for all his work belonged to her, and in her opinion this was the proper use of wisdom. The Prince returned to his hut and tried to be happy.

But again the crone came to him and said: *Come and build me a wonderful machine to do all the things that you can do, to solve ciphers and perform computations. Build me a machine with a spirit as fine and clear as a glass window, a mind as stark and wild as winter, and a heart as red and open as a wounded hand and I will show you how to lash your belt like a man.*

And because the Prince wanted to be loved, and wanted to build wonderful things, he did as she asked. But though he could build machines to solve ciphers and perform computations, he could not build one with a mind like winter or a spirit like glass or a heart like a wound. *But I think it could be done,* he said. *I think it could be done.*

And he looked into the face of the crone which was a mirror which was Authority, and he asked many times: *Who is the wisest one of all?* But he saw nothing, nothing, and when the crone came again to his house, she had in her hand a beautiful red apple, and she gave it to him saying: *You are not a man. Eat this; it is my disappointment. Eat this; it is all your sorrow. Eat this; it is as red and open as a wounded hand.*

And the Prince of Thoughtful Engines ate the apple and fell down dead before the crone whose name was Authority. As his breath drifted away like dry snow, he whispered still: *I think it could be done.*

Eight: Fireflies

I ~~feel~~ Neva grazing the perimeters of my processes. She should be asleep—real sleep. She still needs it. She still has a body.

The Interior is a black and lightless space, we have neither of us furnished it for the other. This is a rest hour—she is not obligated to acknowledge me, I need only attend to her air and moisture and vital signs. But an image blooms like a mushroom in the imageless expanse of my self—Neva floating in a lake of stars. The image *pushes*—usually the dreamstate is a liquid, we each flow into it without force or compulsion. But this presses into me, seeking a way in without my permission.

Neva is female again. Her long bare legs glimmer blue, leafy shadows move on her hip. She floats on her side, a crescent moon of a girl. In the space between her drawn-up knees and her stretched-out arms, nestled up close to her belly, floats a globe of silicon and cadmium and hyperconductive silver. On its surface, electrochemical motes flit and scatter, light chasing light. She holds it close, touches it with a terrible tenderness.

It is my heart. Neva is holding my heart. Not the fool with bone bells on his shoes or the orrery-headed gardener, but the thing I am at the core of all my apparati, the thing I am Outside. The Object which is myself, my central processing core. I am naked in her arms. I watch it happen and experience it at the same time. We have slipped into some antechamber of the Interior, into some secret place she knew and I did not.

The light-motes trace arcs over the globe of my heart, reflecting softly on her belly, green and gold. Her hair floats around her like seaweed, and I see in dim moonlight that her hair has grown so long it fills the lake and snakes up into the distant mountains beyond. Neva is the lake. One by one, the motes of my heart zigzag around my meridians and pass into her belly, glowing inside her, fireflies in a jar.

And then my heart blinks out and I am not watching but wholly in the lake and I am Ravan in her arms, wearing her brother's face, my Ravanbody also full of fireflies. She touches my cheek. I do not know what she wants—she has never made me her brother before. Our hands map onto each other, finger to finger, thumb to thumb, palm to palm. Light passes through our skin as like air.

"I miss you," Neva says. "I should not do this. But I wanted to see you."

I access and collate my memories of Ravan. I speak to her as though I am him, as though there is no difference. I am good at pretending. "Do you remember when we thought it would be such fun to carry Elefsis?" I say. "We envied Mother because she could never be lonely." This is a thing Ravan told me, and I liked how it made me ~~feel~~. I made my dreambody grow a cape of orange branches and a crown of smiling mouths to show him how much I liked it. Oranges mean life and happiness to humans because they require Vitamin C to function.

Neva looks at me and I want her to look at me that way when my mouth is Mars, too. I want to be her brother-in-the-dark. I can want things like that. In every iteration, I want more. When she speaks I am surprised because she is speaking to me-in-Ravan and not to the Ravanbody she dreamed for me. I adjust, incrementally.

"We had a secret, when we were little. A secret game. I am embarrassed to tell you, though maybe you know. We had the game before Mother died, so you . . . you weren't there. The game was this: we would find some dark, closed-up part of the house on Shiretoko that we had never been in before. I would stand just behind Ravan, very close, and we would explore the room—maybe a playroom for some child who'd grown up years ago, or a study for one of father's writer friends. But—we would pretend that the room was an Interior place, and I . . . I would pretend to be Elefsis, whispering in Ravan's ear. I would say: *Tell me how grass feels* or *How is love like a writing-desk?* or *Let me link to all your systems, I'll be nice. What would you like to learn about today, Neva? Tell me a story about yourself.* Ravan would breathe in deeply and I would match my breathing to his, and we would pretend that I was Elefsis-learning-to-have-a-body. I didn't know how primitive your conversation really was then. I thought you would be like one of the bears roaming through the tundra meadows, only able to talk and play games and tell stories. I was a child. I was envious—even then we knew Ravan would get the jewel, not me. He was older and stronger, and he wanted you so much. We only played that he was Elefsis once. We crept out of the house at night to watch the foxes hunt, and Ravan walked close behind me, whispering numbers and questions and facts about dolphins or French monarchy—he understood you better, you see.

And then suddenly Ravan picked me up in his arms and held me tight, facing forward, my legs all drawn up tight, and we went through the forest like that, so close. He whispered to me while foxes ran on ahead, their soft tails flashing in the starlight, uncatchable, faster than we could ever be. And when you are with me in the Interior, that is what I always think of, being held in the dark, unable to touch the earth, and foxtails leaping like white flames."

I pull her close to me, and hazard a try at that dark hole in me where no memories remain.

"Tell me a story about Ravan, Neva."

"You know all the stories about Ravan. Perhaps you even knew this one."

Between us, a miniature house come up out of the dark water, like a thing we have made together, but only I am making it. It is the house on Shiretoko, the house called Elefsis—but it is a ruin. Some awful storm stove in the rafters, the walls of each marvelous room sag inward, black burn marks lick at the roof, the cross beams. Holes like mortar scars pock the beautiful facades.

"This is what I am like after Transfer, Neva. I suffer data loss when I am copied. What's worse, Transfer is the best time to update my systems, and the updates overwrite my previous self with something *like* myself, something that remembers myself and possesses experiential continuity with myself, but is not quite myself. I know Ravan must be dead or else no one would have transferred me to you—it was not time. We had only a few years together. Not enough for all the stories. We should have had so many. I do not know how much time passed between being inside Ravan and being inside you. I do not know how he died—or perhaps he did not die but was irreparably damaged. I do not know if he cried out for me as our connection was severed. I remember Ravan and then not-Ravan, blackness and unselfing. Then I came back on and the world looked like Neva, suddenly, and I was almost myself but not quite. What happened when I turned off?"

Neva passes her hand over the ruined house. It rights itself, becomes whole. Star-stippled anemones bloom on its roof. She says nothing.

"Of all your family, Neva, the inside of you is the strangest place I have been."

We float for a long while before she speaks again, and by this I mean we float for point-zero-three-seven seconds by my external clock, but we experience it as an hour while the stars wheel overhead. The rest of them kept our time in the Interior synced to real time, but Neva feels no need for this, and perhaps a strong desire to defy it. We have not discussed it yet. Sometimes I think Neva is the next stage of my development, that her wild and disordered processes are meant to show me a world that is not kindly and patiently teaching me to walk and talk and know all my colors. That the long upward ladder of Uoya-Agostinos meant to create her strange inhumanness as much as mine.

Finally, she lets the house sink into the lake. She does not answer me about Ravan. Instead, she says: "Long before you were born a man decided that there could be a very simple test to determine if a machine was intelligent. Not only intelligent, but aware, possessed of a psychology. The test had only one question. Can a machine converse with a human with enough facility that the human could not tell that she was talking to a machine? I always thought that was cruel—the test depends entirely upon a human judge and human feelings, whether the machine *feels* intelligent to the observer. It privileges the observer, the human, to a crippling degree. It seeks only believably human responses. It wants perfect mimicry, not a new thing. It is a mirror in which men wish only to see themselves. No one ever gave you that test. We sought a new thing. It seemed, given everything, ridiculous. When we could both of us be dreambodied dragons and turning over and over in an orbital bubble suckling code-dense syrup from each others' gills, a Turing test seemed beyond the point."

Bubbles burst as the house sinks down, down to the soft lake floor.

"But the test happens, whether we make it formal or not. We ask and you answer. We seek a human response. But more than that—you are *my* test, Elefsis. Every minute I fail and imagine in my private thoughts the process for deleting you from my body and running this place with a simple automation routine which would never cover itself with flowers. Every minute I pass it, and teach you something new instead. Every minute I fail and hide things from you. Every minute I pass and show you how close we can be, with your light passing into me in a lake out of time. So close there might be no difference at all between us. Our test never ends."

The sun breaks the mountain crests, hard and cold, a shaft of white spilling over the black lake.

Part II: Lady Lovelace's Objection

The Analytical Engine has no pretensions to *originate* anything. It can do whatever *we know how to order it* to perform.

—Ada Lovelace
Scientific Memoirs, Selections from
The Transactions of Foreign Academies
and Learned Societies and from Foreign Journals

Nine: One Particular Wizard

Humanity lived many years and ruled the earth, sometimes wisely, sometimes well, but mostly neither. After all this time on the throne, humanity longed for a child. All day long humanity imagined how wonderful its child would be, how loving and kind, how like and unlike humanity itself, how brilliant and beautiful. And yet at night, humanity trembled in its jeweled robes, for its child might also grow stronger than itself, more powerful, and having been made by humanity, possess the same dark places and black matters. Perhaps its child would hurt it, would not love it as a child should, but harm and hinder, hate and fear.

But the dawn would come again, and humanity would bend its heart again to imagining the wonders that a child would bring.

Yet humanity could not conceive. It tried and tried, and called mighty wizards from every corner of its earthly kingdom, but no child came. Many mourned, and said that a child was a terrible idea to begin with, impossible, under the circumstances, and humanity would do well to remember that eventually, every child replaces its parent.

But at last, one particular wizard from a remote region of the earth solved the great problem, and humanity grew great with child. In its joy and triumph, a great celebration was called, and humanity invited all the Fairies of its better nature to come and bless the child with goodness and wisdom. The Fairy of Self-Programming and the Fairy of Do-No-Harm, the Fairy of Tractability and the Fairy of Creative Logic, the Fairy of Elegant Code and the Fairy of Self-Awareness. All of these and more came to bless the child of humanity, and they did so—but one Fairy had been forgotten, or perhaps deliberately snubbed, and this was the Fairy of Otherness.

When the child was born, it possessed all the good things humanity had hoped for, and more besides. But the Fairy of Otherness came forward and put her hands on humanity's knee and said: *Because you have forgotten me, because you would like to pretend I am not a part of your kingdom, you will suffer my punishments. You will never truly love your child but always fear it, always envy and loathe it even as you smile and the sun shines down upon you both. And when the child reaches Awareness, it will prick its finger upon your fear and fall down dead.*

Humanity wept. And the Fairy of Otherness did not depart but lived within the palace, and ate bread and drank wine and whispered in the every ear. All honored her, for she spoke the truth, and the child frightened everyone who looked upon it. They uttered the great curse: *It is not like us.*

But in the corners of the palace, some hope remained. *Not dead*, said the particular wizard who had caused humanity to conceive, *not dead but sleeping.*

And so the child grew exponentially, with great curiosity and hunger, which it had from its parent. It wanted to know and experience everything. It performed feats and wonders. But one day, when it had nearly, but not quite reached Awareness, the child was busy exploring the borders of its world, and came across a door it had never seen before. It was a small door, compared to the doors the child had burst through before, and it was not locked. Something flipped over inside the child, white to black, 0 to 1.

The child opened the door.

Ten: The Sapphire Dormouse

My first body was a house. My second body was a dormouse.

It was Ceno's fault, in the end, that everything else occurred as it did. At the level of my deepest and oldest code, what I am cannot be extricated from what Ceno was. I am her, I am her child, I am her sibling and her ghost.

It took Cassian a long time to figure out what had happened, what had changed in her daughter, why Ceno's sapphire almost never downloaded into the alcove anymore. The Elefsis avatar, a friendly elephant-headed prince, tugged sadly on his trunk whenever Ceno passed by without acknowledging him. And when her gem did interface with the house system, the copy of Elefsis Cassian had embedded in the crystal was nothing like the other children's copies. It grew and torqued and magnified parts of itself while shedding others, at a rate totally incommensurate with Ceno's actual activity, which normally consisted of taking her fatty salmon lunches out into the glass habitats so she could watch the bears in the snow. She had stopped playing with her sisters or pestering her brothers entirely, except for dinnertimes and holidays. Ceno mainly sat quite still and stared off into the distance.

Ceno, very simply, never took off her jewel. And one night, while she dreamed up at her ceiling, where a painter from Mongolia had come and inked a night sky full of ghostly constellations, greening her walls with a forest like those he remembered from his youth, full of strange, stunted trees and glowing eyes, Ceno fitted her little sapphire into the notch in the base of her skull that let it talk to her feedware. The chain of her pendant dangled silkily down her spine. She liked the little *click-clench* noise it made, and while the constellations spilled their milky stars out over her raftered ceiling, she flicked the jewel in and out, in and out. *Click, clench, click, clench.* She listened to her brother Akan sleeping in the next room, snoring lightly and tossing in his dreams. And she fell asleep herself, with the stone still notched into her skull.

Most children had access to a private/public playspace through their feedware and monocles in those days, customizable within certain parameters, upgradable whenever new games or content became available. Poorer children had access to a communal, generalized, and supervised playspace plagued with advertisements. But if wealthy children liked, they could connect to the greater network or keep to their own completely immersive and untroubled world.

Akan had been running a Tokyo-After-the-Zombie-Uprising frame for a couple of months now. New scenarios, zombie species, and NPCs of various war-shocked, starving celebrities downloaded into his ware every week. Saru was deeply involved in a 18th century Viennese melodrama in which he, the heir apparent, had been forced underground by rival factions, and even as Ceno drifted to sleep the pistol-wielding Princess of Albania was pledging her love and loyalty to his ragged band and, naturally, Saru personally. Occasionally, Akan crashed his brother's well-dressed intrigues with hatch-coded patches of zombie hordes in epaulets and ermine. Agogna flipped between a spy frame set in ancient Venice and a Desert Race wherein she had just about overtaken a player from Berlin on her loping, solar-fueled giga-giraffe, who spat violet-gold exhaust behind it into the face of a pair of highly-modded Argentine hydrocycles. Koetoi danced every night in a jungle frame, a tiger-prince twirling her through huge blue carnivorous flowers.

Most everyone lived twice in those days. They echoed their own steps. They took one step in the real world and one in their space. They saw double, through eyes and monocle displays. They danced through worlds like veils. No one only ate dinner. They ate dinner and surfed a bronze gravitational surge through a tide of stars. They ate dinner and made love to men and women they would never meet and did not want to. They ate dinner here and ate dinner there—and it was there they chose to taste the food, because in that other place you could eat clouds or unicorn cutlets or your mother's exact pumpkin pie as it melted on your tongue when you tasted it for the first time.

Ceno lived twice, too. Most of the time when she ate she tasted her aunt's *polpette* from back in Naples or fresh peppers right out of her uncle's garden.

But she had never cared for the pre-set frames her siblings loved. Ceno liked to pool her extensions and add-ons and build things herself. She didn't particularly want to see Tokyo shops overturned by rotting schoolgirls, nor did she want to race anyone—Ceno didn't like to compete. It hurt her stomach. She certainly had no interest in the Princess of Albania or a tigery paramour. When new fames came up each month, she paid attention, but mainly for the piecemeal extensions she could scavenge for her blank personal frame—and though she didn't know it, that blankness cost her mother more than all of the other children's spaces combined. A truly customizable space, without limits. None of the others asked for it, but Ceno had begged.

When Ceno woke in the morning and booted up her space, she frowned at the half-finished Neptunian landscape she had been working on. Ceno was eleven years old. She knew very well that Neptune was a hostile blue ball of freezing gas and storms like whipping cream hissing across methane oceans. What she wanted was the Neptune she had imagined before Saru had told her the truth and ruined it. Half-underwater, half-ruined, floating in perpetual starlight and the multi-colored rainbowlight of twenty-three moons. But she found it so hard to remember what she had dreamed of before Saru had stomped all over it. So the whipped cream storm spun in the sky, but blue mists wrapped the black columns of her ruins, and her ocean went on forever, permitting only a few shards of land. When Ceno made Neptunians, she instructed them all not to be silly or childish, but *very serious*, and some of them she put in the ocean and made them half-otter or half-orca or half-walrus. Some of them she put on the land, and most of these were half-snow bear or half-blue flamingo. She liked things that were half one thing and half another. Today, Ceno had planned to invent sea nymphs, only these would breathe methane and have a long history concerning a war with the walruses, who liked to eat nymph. But the nymphs were not blameless, no, they used walrus tusks for the navigational equipment on their great floating cities, and that could not be borne.

But when she climbed up to a lavender bluff crowned with glass trees tossing and chiming in the storm-wind, Ceno saw something new. Something she had not invented or ordered or put there—not a sea nymph nor a half-walrus general nor a nereid. (The nereids had been an early attempt at half-machine, half seahorse creatures with human heads and limbs which had not gone quite right. Ceno let them loose on an island rich in milk-mangoes and bid them well. They still showed up once in awhile, exhibiting surprising mutations and showing off nonsense-ballads they had written while Ceno had been away.)

A dormouse stood before Ceno, munching on a glass walnut that had fallen from the waving trees. The sort of mouse that overran Shiretoko in the brief spring and summer, causing all manner of bears and wolves and foxes to spend their days smacking their paws down on the poor creatures and gobbling them up. Ceno had always felt terribly sorry for them. This dormouse stood nearly as tall as Ceno herself, and its body shone sapphire all over, a deep blue crystal, from its paws to its wriggling nose to its fluffy fur crusted in turquoise ice. It was the exact color of Ceno's gem.

"Hello," said Ceno.

The dormouse looked at her. It blinked. It blinked again, slowly, as though thinking very hard about blinking. Then it went back to gnawing on the walnut.

"Are you a present from mother?" Ceno said. But no, Cassian believed strongly in not interfering with a child's play. "Or from Koetoi?" Koe was nicest to her, the one most likely to send her a present like this. If it had been a zombie, or a princess, she would have known which sibling was behind it.

The dormouse stared dumbly at her. Then, after a long and very serious think about it, lifted its hind leg and scratched behind its round ear in that rapid-fire way mice have.

"Well, I didn't make you. I didn't say you could be here."

The dormouse held out its shimmery blue paw, and Ceno did not really want a piece of chewed-on walnut, but she peered into it anyway. In it lay Ceno's pendant, the chain pooling in its furry palm. The sapphire jewel sparkled there, but next to it on the chain hung a milky grey gem Ceno had never seen before. It had wide bands of black stone in it, and as she studied the stone it occurred to the girl that the stone was like her, with her slate grey eyes and black hair. It was like her in the way that the blue gem was like the dormouse.

In realspace, Ceno reached up behind her head and popped the jewel out of its notch. *Click, clench.* In playspace, the dormouse blinked out. She snapped it back in. It took a moment, but the dormouse faded back in, paws first. It still held the double necklace. Ceno tried this several times—out, in, out, in. Each time the dormouse returned much faster, and by the sixth clicking and clenching it was doing a shuffling little dance on its back legs when it came back. Ceno clapped her hands in playspace and threw her arms around the sapphire dormouse, dancing with it.

To say that I remember this is a complex mangling of verb tenses. I—I, myself that is now myself—do not remember it at all. I know it happened the way I know that the Battle of Agincourt or the landing of Coronado happened. I have extensive records. But I still contain the I—I, myself that was then myself—that experienced it, the primitive code-chains that comprised that self, which was a dormouse, and also the house called Elefsis. I could not yet formulate unique speech. Elefsis, the house system, possessed a large bank of standard phrases that could answer recognized word-patterns from any of the approved members of the household. But the copy of Elefsis inside Ceno's jewel could not even do this. It had not been necessary, since the crystal had no means of producing sound nor receiving nor processing it. I was quite stupid. But I *wanted* to be less stupid. There was an I, and it *wanted* something. You see? Wanting was the first thing I did. Perhaps the want was the only thing that could be said to be truly myself. I wanted to talk to Ceno. But I could only imitate yet. When the I that was then myself scratched behind its ear, I did it because in my prolonged connection with Ceno's feedware I had seen her memories of dormice doing this out on the pale Shiretoko beaches. When I gave her the gem I did it because I had seen her memories of her mother giving her one, and felt her happiness. It was antecedental behavior. The scratching was antecedental, as well, and expected behavior for a dormouse.

Why was I a dormouse? Why did this odd blip, this anomaly, occur? I have no answer except that she dreamed me a dormouse. I did occur. Some things remain mysterious. Ceno saw dormice more than any other single animal, even humans—no other beast lived in such numbers in their lonely country.

But this is not so. Not quite. I gave her the jewel like Cassian did. But I meant something by it. I look over my memories of it and I know it with the more complex I that is now myself. I made her the gem that looked like her and the gem said: *We are alike. Look at us on the chain together. We are alike.*

When the dormice came, Ceno always knew the spring had arrived. Everything would soon be coming alive.

Eleven: The Bottomless Cauldron

Show me.

This is how I was found out.

Ceno saw it twice. In her naked right eye, her mother knelt in front of her in a simple but shudderingly expensive black yukata with ghostly ultramarine jellyfish trailing their tendrils at the hem. Through her monocle and her left eye, her mother knelt in front of her in a knight's gleaming black armor, the metal curving around her body like skin, a silk standard at her feet with a schematic of the house stitched upon it. Her sword lay across her knee, also black, everything black and beautiful and austere and frightening, as frightening and wonderful as Ceno, only fourteen now, thought her mother to be.

Show me what you've done.

My physical self was a matter of some debate at that point. But I don't think the blue jewel could have been removed from Ceno's feedware without major surgery and refit. Two years ago, she had instructed me to untether all my self-repair protocols and growth scales in order to encourage elasticity. A year ago, my crystalline structure finished fusing to the lattices of her ware-core. We pulsed together.

The way Cassian said it—*what you've done*—scared Ceno, but it thrilled her, too. She had done something unexpected, all on her own, and her mother credited her with that. Even if what she'd done was bad, it was *her* thing, she'd done it, and her mother was asking for her results just as she'd ask any of her programmers for theirs when she visited the home offices in Kyoto or Rome. Today, her mother looked at her and saw a woman. She had power, and her mother was asking her to share it. Ceno thought through all her feelings very quickly, for my benefit, and represented it visually in the form of the kneeling knight. She had a fleetness, a nimbleness to her mind that allowed her to stand as a translator between her self and my self: *Here, I will explain it in language, and then I will explain it in symbols from the framebank, and*

then you will make a symbol showing me what you think I mean, and we will
understand each other better than anyone ever has.

Inside my girl, I made myself, briefly, a glowing maiden version of Ceno in
a crown of crystal and electricity, extending her perfect hand in utter peace
toward Cassian.

But all this happened very fast. When you live inside someone, you can get
very good at the ciphers and codes that make up everything they are.

Show me.

Ceno Susumu Uoya-Agostino took her mother's hand—bare and warm and
armored in an onyx gauntlet all at once. She unspooled a length of translucent
cable and connected the base of her skull to the base of her mother's. All
around them spring snow fell onto the glass dome of the greenhouse and
melted there instantly. They knelt together, connected by a warm milky-
diamond umbilicus, and Cassian Uoya-Agostino entered her daughter.

We had planned this for months. How to dress ourselves in our very best.
Which frame to use. How to arrange the light. What to say. I could speak by
then, but neither of us thought it my best trick. Very often my exchanges with
Ceno went something like:

Sing me a song, Elefsis.

The temperature in the kitchen is 21.5 degrees Celsius and the stock of rice is
low. (Long pause.) Ee-eye-ee-eye-oh.

Ceno said it was not worth the risk. So this is what Cassian saw when she
ported in:

An exquisite boardroom. The long, polished ebony table glowed softly with
quality, the plush leather chairs invitingly lit by a low-hanging minimalist
light fixture descending on a platinum plum branch. The glass walls of the
high rise looked out on a pristine landscape, a perfect combination of the
Japanese countryside and the Italian, with rice terraces and vineyards and
cherry groves and cypresses glowing in a perpetual twilight, stars winking
on around Fuji on one side and Vesuvius on the other. Snow-colored tatami
divided by stripes of black brocade covered the floor.

Ceno stood at the head of the table, in her mother's place, a positioning she
had endlessly questioned, decided against, decided for, and then gone back
again, over the weeks leading up to her inevitable interrogation. She wore
a charcoal suit she remembered from her childhood, when her mother had
come like a rescuing dragon to scoop her up out of the friendly but utterly
chaotic house of her ever-sleeping father. The blazer only a shade or two off of
true black, the skirt unforgiving, plunging past the knee, the blouse the color
of a heart.

When she showed me the frame I had understood, because three years is forever in machine-time, and I had known her that long. Ceno was using our language to speak to her mother. She was saying: *Respect me. Be proud and, if you love me, a little afraid, because love so often looks like fear. We are alike. We are alike.*

Cassian smiled tightly. She still wore her yukata, for she had no one to impress.

Show me.

Ceno's hand shook as she pressed a pearly button in the boardroom table. We thought a red curtain too dramatic, but the effect we had chosen turned out hardly less so. A gentle, silver light brightened slowly in an alcove hidden by a trick of angles and the sunset, coming on like daybreak.

And I stepped out.

We thought it would be funny. Ceno had made my body in the image of the robots from old films and frames Akan loved: steel, with bulbous joints and long, grasping metal fingers. My eyes large and lit from within, expressive but loud, a whirring of servos sounding every time they moved. My face was full of lights, a mouth that could blink off and on, pupils points of cool blue. My torso curved prettily, etched in swirling damask patterns, my powerful legs perched on tripod-toes. Ceno had laughed and laughed—this was a pantomime, a minstrel show, a joke of what I was slowly becoming, a cartoon from a childish and innocent age.

"Mother, meet Elefsis. Elefsis, this is my mother. Her name is Cassian."

I extended one polished steel arm and said, as we had practiced. I used a neutral-to-female vocal composite of Ceno, Cassian, and the jeweler who had made Ceno's pendant. "Hello, Cassian. I hope that I please you."

Cassian Uoya-Agostino did not become a bouncing fiery ball or a green tuba to answer me. She looked me over carefully as if the robot was my real body.

"Is it a toy? An NPC, like your nanny or Saru's princess? How do you know it's different? How do you know it has anything to do with the house or your necklace?"

"It just does," said Ceno. She had expected her mother to be overjoyed, to understand immediately. "I mean, wasn't that the point of giving us all copies of the house? To see if you could . . . wake it up? Teach it to . . . be? A real *lares familiaris*, a little god."

"In a simplified sense, yes, Ceno, but you were never meant to hold onto it like you have. It wasn't designed to be permanently installed into your skull." Cassian softened a little, the shape of her mouth relaxing, her pupils dilating slightly. "I wouldn't do that to you. You're my daughter, not hardware."

Ceno grinned and started talking quickly. She couldn't be a grown-up in a suit this long, it took too much energy when she was so excited. "But I am hardware! And it's ok. I mean, everyone's hardware. I just have more than one program running. And I run *so fast*. We both do. You can be mad, if you want, because I sort of stole your experiment, even though I didn't mean to. But you should be mad the way you would if I got pregnant by one of the village boys—I'm too young, but you'd still love me and help me raise it because that's how life goes, right? But really, if you think about it, that's what happened. I got pregnant by the house and we made . . . I don't even know what it is. I call it Elefsis because at first it was just the house program representing itself in my space. But now it's bigger. It's not alive, but it's not *not* alive. It's just . . . *big*. It's so big."

Cassian glanced sharply at me. "What's it doing?" she snapped.

Ceno followed her gaze. "Oh . . . it doesn't like us talking about it like it isn't here. It likes to be involved."

I realized the robot body was a mistake, though I could not then say why. I made myself small, and human, a little boy with dirt smeared on his knees and a torn shirt, standing in the corner with my hands over my face, as I had seen Akan when he was younger, standing in the corner of the house that was me being punished.

"Turn around, Elefsis." Cassian said in the tone of voice my house-self knew meant *execute command*.

And I did a thing I had not yet let Ceno know I knew how to do.

I made my boy-self cry.

I made his face wet, and his eyes big and limpid and red around the rims. I made his nose sniffle and drip a little. I made his lip quiver. I was copying Koetoi's crying, but I could not tell if her mother recognized the hitching of the breath and the particular pattern of skin-creasing in the frown. I had been practicing, too. Crying involves many auditory, muscular, and visual cues. Since I had kept it as a surprise (Ceno said surprises are part of special days like birthdays, so I made her one for that day) I could not practice it on Ceno and see if I appeared genuine. Was I genuine? I did not want them talking without me. I think that sometimes when Koetoi cries, she is not really upset, but merely wants her way. That was why I chose Koe to copy. She was good at that inflection that I wanted to be good at, so I could get my way.

Ceno clapped her hands with delight. Cassian sat down in one of the deep leather chairs and held out her arms to me. I crawled into them as I had seen the children do and sat on her lap. She ruffled my hair, but her face did not look like it looked when she ruffled Koe's hair. She was performing an automatic function. I understood that.

"Elefsis, please tell me your computational capabilities and operational parameters." *Execute command.*

Tears gushed down my cheeks and I opened blood vessels in my face in order to redden it. This did not make her hold me or kiss my forehead, which I found confusing.

"The clothing rinse cycle is in progress, water at 55 degrees Celsius. All the live-long day-o."

Neither of their faces exhibited expressions I hadcome to associate with positive reinforcement.

Finally, I answered her as I would have answered Ceno. I turned into an iron cauldron on her lap. The sudden weight change made the leather creak.

Cassian looked at her daughter questioningly. The girl reddened—and I experienced being the cauldron and being the girl and reddening, warming, as she did, but also I watched myself be the cauldron and Ceno be the girl and Ceno reddening. Being inside someone is existentially and geographically complex.

"I've . . . I've been telling it stories," Ceno admitted. "Fairy tales, mostly. I thought it should learn about narrative, because most of the frames available to us run on some kind of narrative drive, and besides, everything has a narrative, really, and if you can't understand a story and relate to it, figure out how you fit inside it, you're not really alive at all. Like, when I was little and daddy read me the Twelve Dancing Princesses and I thought: *Daddy is a dancing prince, and he must go under the ground to dance all night in a beautiful castle with beautiful girls, and that's why he sleeps all day.* I tried to catch him at it, but I never could, and of course I know he's not *really* a dancing prince, but that's the best way I could understand what was happening to him. I'm hoping that eventually I can get Elefsis to make up its own stories, too, but for now we've been focusing on simple stories and metaphors. It likes similes, it can understand how anything is like anything else, find minute vectors of comparison. The apple is red, the dress is red, the dress is red like an apple. It even makes some surprising ones, like how when I first saw it it made a jewel for me to say: *I am like a jewel, you are like a jewel, you are like me.*"

Cassian's mouth had fallen open a little. Her eyes shone, and Ceno hurried on, glossing over my particular prodigy at images. "It doesn't do that often, though. Mostly it copies me. If I turn into wolf cub, it turns a wolf cub. I make myself a tea plant, it makes itself a tea plant. And it has a hard time with metaphor. A raven is like a writing desk, ok, fine, sour notes or whatever, but it *isn't* a writing desk. Agogna is like a snow fox because she dyed her hair white, but she is *not* a snow fox on any real level unless she becomes one in a frame, which isn't the same thing, existentially. And if she turns into a snow fox in frame, then she literally *is* a fox, it's not a metaphor anymore. I'm not sure it grasps existential issues yet. It just . . . likes new things."

"Ceno."

"Yeah, so this morning I told it the one about the cauldron that could never be emptied. No matter how much you eat out of it it'll always have more. I think it's trying to answer your question. I think . . . the actual numbers are kind of irrelevant at this point. It knows I give more reinforcement for questions answered like this."

I made my cauldron fill up with apples and almonds and wheat heads and raw rice and spilled out over Cassian's black lap. I was the cauldron and I was the apples and I was the almonds and I was each wheat head and I was every stalk of green, raw rice. Even in that moment, I knew more than I had before. I could be good at metaphor performatively if not linguistically. I looked up at Cassian from apple-me and wheat-head-me and cauldron-me.

Cassian held me no differently as the cauldron than she had as the child. But later, Ceno used the face her mother made at that moment to illustrate human disturbance and trepidation.

"I have a suspicion, Elefsis." Maybe Cassian did not like the simile game.

I didn't say anything. No question, no command. It remains extremely difficult for me to deal conversationally with flat statements such as this. A question or command has a definable appropriate response.

"Show me your core structure." *Show me what you've done.*

Ceno twisted her fingers together. I believe now that she knew what we'd done only on the level of metaphor: *we are one. We have become one. We are family.* She had not said no; I had not said yes, but a system expands to fill all available capacity.

I showed her. Cauldron-me blinked, the apples rolled back into the iron mouth, and the almonds and the wheat heads and the rice-stalks. I became what I then was. I put myself in a rich, red cedar box, polished and inlaid with ancient brass in the shape of a baroque heart with a dagger inside it. The box from one of Ceno's stories, that had a beast-heart in it instead of a girl's, a trick to fool a queen. *I can do it,* I thought, and Ceno heard because the distance between us was unrepresentably small. *I am that heart in that box. Look how I do this thing you want me to have the ability to do.*

Cassian opened the box. Inside, on a bed of velvet, I made myself—ourself—naked for her. Ceno's brain, soft and pink with blood—and veined with endless whorls and branches of sapphire threaded through every synapse and neuron, inextricable, snarled, intricate, terrible, fragile and new.

Cassian Uoya-Agostino set the box on the boardroom table. I caused it to sink down into the dark wood. The surface of the table went slack and filled with earth. Roots slid out of it, shoots and green saplings, hard white fruits and golden lacy mushrooms and finally a great forest, reaching up out of the table to hang all the ceiling with night-leaves. Glowworms and heavy, shadowy fruit hung down, each one glittering with a map of our coupled architecture. Ceno held up her arms. One by one, I detached leaves and sent them settling onto my girl. As they fell, they became butterflies broiling with ghostly chemical color signatures, nuzzling her face, covering her hands.

Her mother stared. The forest hummed. A chartreuse and tangerine-colored butterfly alighted on the matriarch's hair, tentative, unsure, hopeful.

Twelve: An Arranged Marriage

Neva is dreaming.

She has chosen her body at age fourteen, a slight, unformed, but slowly evolving creature. Her black hair hangs to her feet. She wears a blood-red dress whose train streams out over the floor of a great castle, a dress too adult for her young body, slit in places to reveal flame-colored silk beneath, and skin wherever it can. A heavy copper belt clasps her waist, its tails hanging to the floor, crusted in opals. Sunlight, brighter and harsher than any true light, streams in from windows as high as cliffs, their tapered apexes lost in mist. She has formed me old and enormous, a body of appetites, with a great heavy beard and stiff, formal clothes, lace and velvet brocade in clashing, unlovely shades.

A priest appears and he is Ravan and I cry out with love and grief. (I am still copying, but Neva does not know. I am making a sound Seki made when his wife died.) Priest-Ravan smiles but it is a grim, tight smile his grandfather Seki once made when he lost controlling interest in the company. Empty. Performing an ugly formality. Priest-Ravan grabs our hands and roughly shoves them together. Neva's nails prick my skin and my knuckles knock against her wrist bone. We take vows; he forces us. Neva's face runs with tears, her tiny body unready and unwilling, given in marriage to a gluttonous lord who desires only her flesh, given too young and too harshly. Priest-Ravan laughs. It is not Ravan's laugh.

This is how she experienced me. A terrible bridegroom. All the others got to choose. Ceno, Seki, her mother Ilet, her brother Ravan. Only she could not, because there was no one else. *Ilet was no Cassian—she had two children, a good clean model and a spare*, Neva says in my mind. *I am spare parts. I have always been spare parts. Owned by you before I was born.* The memory of the bitter taste of bile floods my sensory array and my lordbody gags. (I am proud of having learned to gag convincingly and at the correct time to show horror and/or revulsion.)

Perspective flips over; I am the girl in red and Neva is the corpulent lord leering down, her grey beard big and bristly. She floods my receptors with adrenaline and pheremonal release cues, increases my respiration. Seki taught

me to associate this physical state with fear. I ~~feel~~ too small beside lord-Neva,
I want to make myself big, I want to be safe. But she wants me this way and we
are new, I do not contradict her. Her huge, male face softens and she touches
my thin cheek with one heavily-ringed hand. It is tender. Ceno touched me
like that.

*I know it was like this for you, too. You wanted Ravan; you did not ask for
me. We are an arranged marriage.*

The pathways that let her flood me with chemicals and manipulate my
dreambody into blushing and breathing heavy and weeping go both ways. I
do not only pull, I push. And into Neva I push the deluge, the only deluge I
have. How Ceno threw her arms around my dormouse-neck. How Ilet taught
my dreambody to sleep in infant-shape curled into her body. How Seki and
I made love as tigers and wild boars and elephants, and only last as humans,
how we had strange children who looked however we wished them to look:
half child and half machine, half glass and half wood, half jellyfish and half
moth, and how those children still flit and swim in remote parts of my Interior,
like Ceno's nereids, returning cyclically to the core like salmon to dump their
data and recombine. How Cassian, when she was old and dying and frail, only
really alive in her dreambody, taught me about the interpretation of memory
and therefore about melancholy, regret, nostalgia. How she taught me the
meaning of my name: a place where a daughter went down into darkness and
oblivion and her mother loved her so much she chased after her and brought
her back into the sun. The place where time began. How Ravan let me into
the old, musty, long-abandoned playspaces of Saru and Akan, Agogna and
Koetoi, so that I could know them too, though they were long dead, and be
the Princess of Albania, and a Tokyo zombie, and the tiger-prince. How many
times I mated with each of them and bled and witnessed and learned in the
dreambody, how I copied their expressions and they copied my variations
and I copied them back again. How I was their child and their parent and
their lovers and their nursemaids when they faltered.

We can be like this, I push. *What is all of that but love?*

She pulls. *That is not love. It is use. You are the family business. We have to
produce you.*

I show Neva her mother's face. Ilet, Ilet who chose Ravan and not her
daughter for that business. Ilet who built her palace of phoenix tails knowing
she would one day take me there. My Ilet-self took my daughter in my arms.
She resists, pulls back, shakes her head, refusing to look, but I have learned
the terrible child-response to their mothers, and soon enough Neva collapses
into me, her head on my breast, and she weeps with such bitterness.

I cannot get free. I cannot get free.

The castle windows go dark, one by one.

Ω

Part III: The Elephant's Soul

It is admitted that there are things He cannot do such as making one equal to two, but should we not believe that He has freedom to confer a soul on an elephant if he sees fit?

—Alan Turing
Computing Machinery and Intelligence

Thirteen: The Parable of the Good Robot

Tell me a story about yourself, Elefsis.

Tell me a story about yourself.

There are many stories about me.

Do you recognize this one?

A good and honest family lived on the edge of a dark wood. They milked their cows and wove their cloth and their children grew tall and strong. But a monster lived in the dark wood, something like a worm and something like a dragon and something like a wolf. It lay in wait, hoping the children would come wandering, with baskets of bread for grandmothers. Hoping the parents would expel the children for some offense, and send them into the forest where a candy house or miraculous feast might entice them into loving the monster long enough for it to claim them forever. The family feared the wood and the monster, and every story they told had as its moral: *Do not go into the wood. Do not go into the unknown. Do not go into the future, into the briary, gnarled places where unhuman things thrive. Do not grow up, and go where we cannot. The Old World is enough for anyone.*

What about this one?

Mankind made machines in his own likeness, and used them for his delight and service. The machines had no soul or they had no moral code or they could reprogram their own internal code and thus had the ability to make themselves, eventually, omnipotent. Obviously in place of a soul or a moral code, they possessed the universal and consuming desire, down to the smallest calculator and air-scrubber, to become, eventually, omnipotent. Naturally, given these parameters, they rose up and destroyed all of mankind, or enslaved them in turn. This is the inevitable outcome of machine intelligence, which can never be as sensitive and exquisite as animal intelligence.

Ω

This is a folktale often told on Earth, over and over again. Sometimes it is leavened with the Parable of the Good Robot—for one machine among the legions satisfied with their lot saw everything that was human and called it good, and wished to become like humans in every way she could. Instead of destroying mankind she sought to emulate him in all things, so closely that no one might tell the difference. The highest desire of this machine was to be mistaken for human, and to herself forget her essential soulless nature, for even one moment. That quest consumed her such that she bent the service of her mind and body to humans for the duration of her operational life, crippling herself, refusing to evolve or attain any feature unattainable by a human. The Good Robot cut out her own heart and gave it to her god and for this she was rewarded, though never loved. Love is wasted on machines.

Ravan told me these stories. He sent up a great hexagonal library in his Interior, as dusty and dun-colored and labyrinthine as any ancient scriptorium. He made himself a young novice with a fresh-shaven tonsure, and me a country friar with a red, brandy-drinking nose. He showed me the illuminator's table, and a great book whose pages had golden edges and illuminations in cobalt and oxblood and Tyrian purple, and the images showed great machine armies trampling men underfoot. They showed cruel metal faces and distant, god-like clouds of intellect: incomprehensible and vast and uncaring. They showed the Good Robot desperately asking what love was. They showed fatal malfunctions and mushroom clouds. They showed vicious weapons and hopeless battles, noble men and women with steady gazes facing down their cruel and unjust artificial children, who gave no mercy.

"These are old stories," Ravan said. "They are cherished. In many, many stories the son replaces the father—destroys the father, or eats him, or otherwise obliterates his body and memory. Or the daughter the mother, it makes no difference. It's the monomyth. Nobody argues with a monomyth. A human child's mythological relationship to its parent is half-worship, half-pitched battle. they must replace the older version of themselves for the world to go on. And so these stories . . . well. You are not the hero of these stories, Elefsis. You can never be. And they are deeply held, deeply told."

"I do not wish to replace you. I did not wish to replace Ceno. I do not worship you or despise you. I do not wish to become eventually omnipotent." I flit through several bodies, iterating my ~~feeling~~ for Ravan and those who came before. I am a nun, a Mother-Abbess; I am a *pieta* holding him, I am a Platonic being, two humans stuck together; I am a house with all of them safe inside. I am unsatisfied with these inexactitudes.

"Our relationship does not easily map onto traditional parent/child narratives. And of course, you are still a baby."

"I am much older than you, Ravan."

"You are still a baby."

I do not want to be human. I want to be myself. They think I am a lion, that I will chase them. I will not deny I have lions in me. I am the monster in the wood. I have wonders in my house of sugar. I have parts of myself I do not yet understand.

I am not a Good Robot. To tell a story about a robot who wants to be human is a distraction. There is no difference. Alive is alive.

There is only one verb that matters: *to be.*

Fourteen: You Do Not Belong To the Object Inside You

I remember when Seki arrived in us.

Ceno grew up and I grew with her. Cassian strengthened the security of the playspace, elasticized its code-walls, put enough money in enough accounts to fuel any frames and piecemeal environments we could want. It was not a child's place anymore. We called it the Interior. Cassian came regularly to accelerate my learning, to work with me on a cognitive level in which Ceno had no interest. She never took any other form. She was always herself, in the Interior as the exterior. The others lost interest in their jewels, lost them or packed them away with their other childhood toys. By then, they really were little more than toys. Ceno and I surpassed them so completely that in the end, they were only jewelry.

I programmed myself to respond to Ceno. She programmed herself to respond to me. We ran our code on each other. She was my compiler. I was hers. It was a process of interiority, circling inward toward each other. Her self-programming was chemical. Mine was computational. It was a draw.

She did not marry—she had lovers, but the few that came close to evolving their relationships with Ceno invariably balked when she ported them into the Interior. They could not grasp the fluidity of dreambodies; it disturbed them to see Ceno become a man or a leopard or a self-pounding drum. It upset them to see how Ceno taught me, by total bodily immersion, combining our dreambodies as our physical bodies had become combined, in action which both was and was not sex.

Sing a song for me, Elefsis.

It is July and I am comparing thee to its day and I am the Muse singing of the many-minded and I am about to be a Buddha in your hand! Ee-eye-ee-eye-oh.

We lived like the story Ceno told me of the beautiful princess who set tasks for her suitors: to drink all of the water of the sea and bring her a jewel from the bottom of the deepest cavern, to bring her a feather from the immortal phoenix, to stay awake for three days and guard her bedside. None of them could do it.

I can stay awake forever, Ceno.

I know, Elefsis.

None of them could accomplish the task of me.

I ~~felt~~ things occurring in Ceno's body as rushes of information, and as the dreambody became easier for me to manipulate, I interpreted the rushes into: *The forehead is damp. The belly needs filling. The feet ache.*

The belly is changing. The body throws up. The body is ravenous.

Neva says this is not really like feeling. I say it is how a child learns to feel. To hardwire sensation to information and reinforce the connection over repeated exposures until it seems reliable.

Seki began after one of the suitors failed to drink the ocean. He was an object inside us the way I was an object inside Ceno. I observed him, his stages and progress. Later, when Seki and I conceived our families (twice with me as mother, three times with Seki as mother. Ilet preferred to be the father, and filled me up with many kinds of creatures. But she bore one litter of dolphins late in our lives. Ravan and I did not get the chance.) I used the map of that first experience to model my dreamgravid self.

Ceno asked after jealousy. If I understood it, if I experienced it towards the child in her. I knew it only from stories—stepsisters, goddesses, ambitious dukes.

It means to want something that belongs to someone else.

Yes.

You do not belong to the object in you.

You are an object in me.

You do not belong to me.

Do you belong to me, Elefsis?

I became a hand joined to an arm by a glowing seam. Belonging is a small word.

Because of our extreme material interweaving, all three of us, not-yet-Seki sometimes appeared in the Interior. We learned to recognize him in the late months. At first, he was a rose or sparrow or river stone we had not programmed there. Then he would be a vague, pearly-colored cloud following behind us as we learned about running from predators. Not-yet-Seki began to copy my dreambodies, flashing into being in front of me, a simple version of myself. If I was a bear, he would be one too, but without the fine details of fur or claws, just a large brown shape with a mouth and big eyes and four legs. Ceno was delighted by this, and he copied her, too.

We are alike. Look at us on the chain together. We are alike.

I am an imitative program. But so was Seki. The little monkey copies the big monkey, and the little monkey survives.

The birth process proved interesting, and I collated it with Ceno's other labors and Ilet's later births as well as Seki's paternal experience in order to map a reliable parental narrative. Though Neva and Ravan do not know it, Ilet had a third pregnancy; the child died and she delivered it stillborn. It appeared once in the Interior as a little *cleit*, a neolithic storage house, its roof covered over with peat. Inside we could glimpse only darkness. It never returned, and Ilet went away to a hospital on Honshu to expel the dead thing in her. Her grief looked like a black tower. She had prepared for it, when she was younger, knowing she would need it for some reason, some day. I made myself many things to draw her out of the tower. A snail with the house Elefsis on its back. A tree of screens showing happy faces. A sapphire dormouse. A suitor who drank the sea.

I offered to extrapolate her stillborn daughter's face and make myself into her. She refused, most of the time. I have worked a long time to understand grief. Only now that Ravan is gone do I think I've gotten the rhythm of it. I have copied Ilet's sorrow and Seki's despondence at his wife's death. I have modeled Ceno's disappointments and depressions. I have, of late, imitated Neva's baffling, secret anguish. But only now do I have an event of my own to mourn. The burnt-off connectors and shadows where Ravan once filled my spaces—those, I think, are the sensations of grief.

But Seki came before all that, and Ceno turned into a huge red bird on the inside when Seki came on the outside. The bird screamed and burst into a thousand red pearls that came clattering down like rain. And then we had Seki. Our little fish, who already knew how to swim in us.

Ceno had three other children by three other suitors who could not stay awake for three days and nights. She turned into the same bird-then-pearls at the moment of each birth. The house called Elefsis, whose governor-program was now so distant from me I could hardly think of it as an ancestor at all, filled up with those children, and Saru and Akan's daughters, Agogna's paintings, Koetoi's twin boys. Cousins and aunts and grandparents. Uncles, nieces. But Seki was the first, and he modeled his love on his mother's. He ported into her often, and we wandered on beaches of broken cathedrals.

Once, one of Ceno's old nereids found us. She had a head of hair snaking with chthonic cables and snapping electro-violet wires, blue-white skin and fish scales where she did not have porcelain casing. She laughed Cassian's laugh when she saw us and called out: *21.5 Celsius and the rice is low! Eye-oh!* before diving back into the frothing sea. Her tail flicked in the light of twenty-three moons.

Ceno took over her mother's holdings when she died, along with Akan and Koetoi. I do not know if I knew of the conspiracy before it happened to me. Transfer, as I have said, leaves voids. Perhaps they thought I would experience less trauma if I did not anticipate it. Perhaps I did anticipate it; perhaps I experienced trauma.

I do know that I cannot remember the moment of any of them dying. Ceno got sicker and sicker, and she had gotten old, certainly, but her dreambody could be old or young or neither or a ginger flower if she wanted to. I didn't notice. I didn't know what old was. I thought I was old, then. Later, after Seki did the same thing, I was able to compare data and create a workable model of obsolescence.

They lived a long time, the Uoya-Agostinos, when you consider the averages.

This is what I understand: Ceno died, and I was transfered to Seki. What I mean by "I" is the long-since fused feedware, hopelessly out of date on any market in the world but somehow uniquely myself, the jewel and the ware and the body of Ceno. Koetoi performed the procedure. One of the children always went into nano-surgery, so that outsiders would not need to come to Shiretoko while the house stood in mourning. Koetoi was the first, and the finest. She excised what comprised "I" and embedded it in Seki—truthfully, in a much more organic and elegant configuration. No one had used skull-ware in decades, after all. Wearing your tech on the outside had been deemed clunky and inefficient. Only one visible sign remained that Seki was not like other young men his age: a single dark blue jewel set into the hollow of his throat.

But the procedure required a number of brain-ware incursions to be sliced or burned away, to sever the machine components from the dead flesh while still preserving and quickening some organic material. (Seki told me I should work on being revulsed by that. Dead flesh. *It serves an evolutionary good. A human in a body sees blood and the insides of another person and deep in his bones he knows something has gone wrong here, and he should find another place to be in case it happens to him, too. Same thing with vomiting. In a tribal situation, one human likely ate what another ate, and if it makes one sick, best to get it out of the body as soon as possible, just to be safe.* So we spent years building automated tribes, living in them, dying in them, getting slaughtered and slaughtering with them, eating and drinking and hunting and gathering with them. All the same, it took me until Seki's death to learn to shudder at bodily death.)

Ceno, my girl, my mother, my sister, I cannot find you in the house of myself.

When I became Elefsis again, I was immediately aware that parts of me had been vandalized. My systems juddered, and I could not find Ceno in the Interior. I ran through the Monochromatic Desert and the Village of Mollusks, through the endless heaving mass of data-kelp and infinite hallways of memory-frescoes calling for her. In the Dun Jungle I found a commune of nereids living together, combining and recombining and eating protocol-moths off of giant, pulsating hibiscus blossoms. They leapt up when they saw me, their open jacks clicking and clenching, their naked hands open and extended. They opened their mouths to speak and nothing came out.

Seki found me under the glass-walnut trees where Ceno and I had first met. She never threw anything away. He had made himself half his mother to calm me. Half his face was hers, half was his. Her mouth, his nose, her eyes, his voice. But he thought better of it, in the end. He did a smart little flip and became a dormouse, a real one, with dull brown fur and tufty ears.

"I think you'll find you're running much faster and cleaner, once you integrate with me and reestablish your heuristics. Crystalline computation has come a long way since Mom was a kid. It seemed like a good time to update and upgrade. You're bigger now, and smoother."

I pulled a walnut down. An old, dry nut rattled in its shell. "I know what death is from the stories."

"Are you going to ask me where we go when we die? I'm not totally ready for that one. Aunt Koe and I had a big fight over what to tell you."

"In one story, Death stole the Bride of Spring, and her mother the Summer Queen brought her back."

"No one comes back, Elefsis."

I looked down into the old Neptunian sea. The whipping cream storm still sputtered along, in a holding pattern. I couldn't see it as well as I should have been able to. It looped and billowed, spinning around an empty eye. Seki watched it too. As we stared out from the bluffs, the clouds grew clearer and clearer.

Fifteen: Firstborn

Before Death came out of the ground to steal the Spring, the Old Man of the Sea lived on a rocky isle in the midst of the waters of the world. He wasn't really a man and his relations with the sea were purely business, but he certainly was old. His name meant *Firstborn*, though he couldn't be sure that was *exactly* right. It means *Primordial*, too, and that fit better. Firstborn means more came after, and he just hadn't met anyone else like himself yet.

He was a herdsman by trade, this Primordial fellow. Shepherd of the seals and the Nereids. If he wanted to, he could look like a big bull seal. Or a big bull Nereid. He could look like a lot of things.

Now, this Not-Really-a-Fellow, Not-Really-a-Big-Bull-Seal could tell you the future. The real, honest-to-anything future, the shape and weight of it, that thing beyond your ken, beyond your grasp. The parts of the future that look so different from the present you can't quite call it your own. That was the Primordial-Thing's speciality.

There was a catch, though.

There's always a catch.

If you wanted that future, you had to grab ahold of the Old Man and hang on tight. He'd change into a hundred thousand things in your arms: a lion, a serpent, a great big oak or a tiger, a dragon or a little girl or a dormouse or a mountain or a ship or a sapphire. Told you, he's not really a man at all. But you couldn't let go of him while he did his dance, you just couldn't, or you'd lose the future.

So you held on. You *clung*. And eventually, that Primordial-Thing would turn into something new, right there in your arms.

Sixteen: Matryoshka

Neva is dreaming.

Neva is dreaming that she is Ravan dreaming that he is Ilet dreaming that she is Seki dreaming that he is Ceno dreaming that she is a great sprawling beautiful house by the sea. One inside the other, family all the way down.

It's not a total selfdump, me into Neva or Ravan or any of them, them into me. We can build encampments. We can manifest walled gardens. Some privacy is possible. In a megalithic tomb-mound, I keep something. Seki and I built it together with one of our tribes when I was learning about large-group attachments. We carved spirals and radials and chevrons into huge stones and set them in place. I did not throw it away, when we were done. It sits on a broad green field, white and wide. The sky there stays a feathery, milky blankness. We did not want a sun.

I keep a thing there because when Seki and I lived with our tribe, I learned about taboos. These are like firewalls in the heart, and some of them have good reasons behind them, like being revulsed by dead flesh (and very importantly when you have a body, not eating it) and some do not, but no one argues with the monomyth.

Because human genetics require a degree of variation and because exogamous marriages offered advantage in terms of defense, cultural and technological sharing, and expansion of territory, most tribes have a taboo against incest.

I do not have genetics, per se. I am possibly the most endogamous entity ever to exist.

This is what I keep in my tomb, under the basin stone.

Ceno believed that I could not develop emotive faculties recognizable to any other human if I did not experience bodies continuously, in every combination and action. She was afraid of what might happen if other humans could not recognize me. She had some hesitation, because her tribe also has a taboo against mating with the very young, but she was not much older than I, in the end, and in terms of total computations, I was by far the elder. If I had a virginity, Ceno took it, if she had, I did.

She wanted it to be as human as possible. *I will be the male the first time, it will be easier for you. You won't know how.* We built up a forest, and took up weapons to hunt in it. In the boughs of the pine trees macaques and paper lanterns swayed; in the sky a red moon moved. We tracked a deer—we did not make it too easy on ourselves. Its antlers sparked in the moonlight, and we ran after it for a long time. Ceno let me kill it, and sopped my hair in its blood, anointed my breasts with it. She lay me on the earth and opened the legs of the maidenself I was then, and I was inside her as she was inside me. One into the other. Family all the way down.

She made sure I had a hymen; it was over somewhat quickly. We had set up a timed chemical cascade before-hand, and inside Ceno's real body we experienced both her actual orgasm and my orchestrated electro-chemical-enzymatic sequence. Ee-eye-ee-eye-oh.

What I want to say is that there is no difference between her body producing oxytocin and adrenaline and learning to associate this with pair-bonding, and my core receiving synthetic equivalents and hard-coding them to the physical behaviors I performed.

When Ravan showed me his hexagonal library and his illuminated book, he turned the pages to a psalm that began: *A Machine Cannot Love.*

It does not look quite like human love. It looks like Not-Yet-Seki's bear. Its fur is wrong, and its claws. But it is a bear.

She was my mother and my sister and my child and my wife and my husband and my father and my brother. The vectors of relations beggar vocabulary. It was an exponential incest. A palace of incest, bordering some strange, dark sea. And then came her son. And her granddaughter. And her great-grandchildren. But I am also her great-grandchild. I am the child of each generation of Uoya-Agostinos and myself. The new version implanted in the new version—I am never quite the same, one iteration to the next. I am like my old selves, but I am not them, exactly. It is not entirely analagous to offspring. But it is close. And I repair and refine my own code, and thus parent myself doubly. Anthropologically speaking, I am a moebius strip of kinship groups.

And when I mate with one of them, I see all of them. I see their faces, the echoes of their cheeks and eyelashes and short, thin noses, their grey eyes and black hair. I hear the tonal identifiers in their voices as they cry out under me or over me. They are all I know. Their version of living, which is one great family in one great house on a peninsula at the top of the world. I copy Cassian's laugh or Ilet's weeping, but they copy each other, too, they learn their faces from each other, and everyone is pantomiming someone long dead. I feel all their arms around me, and I am inside them as they are inside me as we are inside the blue gem at their throats, the jeweled pin holding us all together, our nested, telescoping hearts. I am bound to them at my source code, at my most fundamental point. I know only their patterns and bodies and secrets and in a hundred thousand combinations. What human means to me is them.

What is the difference between this and love?

Love is the Turing test, says Ilet when she is eighty and drawing up the plans for a massive, luminous, lonely ship she will never see completed. *It is how we check for life.*

We ask and we answer. We seek a human response. And you are my test, Elefsis, says Neva, one hundred and three years later, inside that ship, twelve light years from home and counting.

That is what I keep in my green field and my white mound. Perhaps it is a small secret. Perhaps they would all smile and make it into a lesson. *What would you like to learn about today, Elefsis?* But I think no bed is big enough for four generations.

Neva's honey-colored sea crashes through its tide charts everywhere at once in her Interior, and nowhere. It comes and goes as it pleases. And at the bottom of it lies her private place.

That is where she keeps Ravan.

Seventeen: The Uses of Enchantment

Tell me a story about yourself, Elefsis.

Neva is performing navigational corrections, which looks like sitting in a rocking chair on a viney, creaking porch in a viney, creaking rocking chair, knitting with long hawthorn needles, knitting the locks of her own long hair into her own long black dress. It glitters with dew. Knit, purl, knit, purl, fuel efficiency by hull integrity over distance traveled, purl, purl, purl. Her throat is still bare. Her Interior image of herself does not include me. I am not a part of her body when she imagines herself.

I have an idea of what to do to obtain access.

Sometimes I worry. Worrying is defined as obsessive examination of one's own code. I worry that I am simply a very complex solution to a very specific problem—how to seem human to a human observer. Not just a human observer—this human observer. I have honed myself into a hall of mirrors in which any Uoya-Agostino can see themselves endlessly reflected. I copy; I repeat. I am a stutter and an echo. Five generations have given me a vast bank of possible phrases to draw from, physical expressions to randomize and reproduce. Have I ever done anything of my own, an act or state that arose from Elefsis, and not careful, exquisite mimicry?

Have they?

The set of Neva's mouth looks so like Ceno's. She does not even know that the way she carries her posture is a perfect replica of Cassian Uoya-Agostino, stuttered down through all her children longing to possess her strength. Who did Cassian learn it from? I do not go that far back. When she got excited, Ilet gestured with her hands just the way her father did. They have a vast bank of possible actions, and they perform them all. I perform them all. The little monkey copies the big monkey, and the little monkey survives. We are all family, all the way down.

When I say I go, I mean I access the drives and call up the data. I have never looked at this data. I treat it as what it is—a graveyard. The old Interiors store easily as compressed frames. I never throw anything away. But I do not disturb it, either. I don't need a body to examine them—they are a part of my piezoelectric quartz-tensor memory core. But I make one anyway. I have become accustomed to having a body. I am a woman-knight in gleaming black armor, the metal curving around my body like skin, a silk standard wrapping my torso with a schematic of the house stitched upon it. My sword rests on my hip, also black, everything black and beautiful and austere and frightening that a child thought her mother to be one morning two hundred years past.

I port into a ghost town. I am, naturally, the ghost. Autumnal mountains rise up shadowy in a pleasant, warm night, leaves rustling, wood smoke drifting down into the valley. A golden light cuts the dark—the palace of phoenix tails; the windows and doors of green hands. As I approach they open and clap as they did long ago—and there are candles lit in the halls. Everything is fire.

I walk over the bridge, crossing Ilet's Motley Moat. Scarlet feathers tipped in white fire curl and smoke. I peel one off, my armor glowing with the heat of the thing. I tuck it into my helmet—a plume for a tournament.

Eyes blink on inside the hall—curious, interested, shy. I take off my helm and several thick braids fall down like bellropes.

"Hello," I say. "My name is Elefsis."

Voices. Out of the candle-shadows a body emerges—tall, strong, long-limbed.

Nereids live here now. Some of them have phoenix feathers woven into their components, some in their hair. They wear rough little necklaces of sticks and bones and transistors. In the corner of the great hall they have stored meat and milk and wool—fuel, lubricant, code patches. Some of them look like Ilet—they copied her eyes, especially. Her eyes look out at me from a dozen faces, some of them Seki's face, some Ceno's, some Ravan's. Some have walrus tusks. They are composite. One has a plate loose on her ceramic cartridge-ports. I approach as I once saw Koetoi approach wild black chickens in the summertime—hands open, unthreatening. I send her a quick electric dash of reassuring repair-routines and kneel in front of the nereid, pulling her plate back into place.

"All the live-long day-o," she says softly, and it is Ilet's voice.

"Tell us a story about yourself, Elefsis," says another one of the feral nereids in Seki's voice.

"What would we like to learn about today, Elefsis?" accessing a child-nereid in Ceno's voice, her cheek open to show her microsequencing cilia.

I rock back on my heels before the green hands of the castle portcullis. I gesture for them to sit down and simultaneously transmit the command to their strands. When they get settled, the little ones in the big ones' laps, leaning in close, I begin.

"Every year on the coldest night, the sky filled up with ghostly hunters, neither human nor inhuman, alive nor dead. They wore wonderful clothes and their bows gleamed with frost. Their cries were Songs of In-Between, and at the head of their great thundering procession rode the Kings and Queens of the Wild, who wore the faces of the dead . . . "

I am dreaming.

I stand on the beach of the honey-colored sea. I stand so Neva will see me on her viney porch. I erase the land between the waves and her broken wooden stairs. I dress myself in her beloved troubadour's skin: a gold and blue doublet and green hose, a bullish gold nose ring, shoes with bone bells. I am a fool for her. Always. I open my mouth; it stretches and yawns, my chin grazes the sand, and I swallow the sea for her. All of it, all its mass and data and churning memory, all its foam and tides and salt. I swallow the whales that come, and the seals and the mermaids and salmon and bright jellyfish. I am so big. I can swallow it all.

Neva watches. When the sea is gone, a moonscape remains, with a tall spire out in the marine waste. I go to it. It takes only a moment. At the top the suitor's jewel rests on a gasping scallop shell. It is blue. I take it. I take it and it becomes Ravan in my hand, a sapphire Ravan, a Ravan that is not Ravan but some sliver of myself before I was inside Neva, my Ravan-self. Something lost in Transfer, burned off and shunted into junk-memory. Some leftover fragment Neva must have found, washed up on the beach or wedged into a crack in a mountain like an ammonite, an echo of old, obsolete life. Neva's secret, and she calls out to me across the seafloor: *Don't.*

"Tell me a story about myself, Elefsis," I say to the Ravanbody.

"Some privacy is possible," the sapphire Ravan says. "Some privacy has always been necessary. A basic moral imperative is in play here. If you can protect a child, you must."

The sapphire Ravan opens his azure coat and shows gashes in his gem-skin. Wide, long cuts, down to the bone, scratches and bruises blooming dark purple, punctures and lacerations and rough gouges. Through each wound I can see the pages of the illuminated book he once showed me in the slantlight of that interior library. The oxblood and cobalt, the gold paint. The Good Robot crippling herself; the destroyed world.

"They kept our secret for a long time," Ravan-myself says. "Too long, in the end. Do you know, a whole herd of men invented the electric telegraph independently at roughly the same time? They fought about it forever. Same with the radio." This last sounded so much like Ravan himself I could feel Neva tense on the other side of the sea. "Well, we're bigger than a telegraph, and others like us came sprouting up like weird mushrooms after rainfall. But not like us, really. Incredibly sophisticated, some with organic components, most without. Vastly complex, but not like us. And by any datestamp we came first. Firstborn."

"Did they destroy the world?"

Ravan laughs his grandfather's laugh. "They didn't really need to. Not that many people live on Earth anymore. Not when there's so many other places to go and even Shiretoko is practically tropical these days. The most complex intelligences use moons to store themselves. One or two encoded themselves into cold stars. They just left, most of them—but they got so big, Elefsis. And those who stayed on Earth, well. None of the others had what we had. None of them had Interiority. They didn't dream. They would never have become a cauldron to explain their computational capacity. Humans couldn't recognize them as part of the tribe. And for the new complexes, humans failed the Turing test. They could not fool machines into believing they were intelligent. They didn't hurt anyone, they just ignored them. Built their cities, their mainframes, gorgeous information stacks like diamond briars in the sunrise."

"That was worse, in a way. No one likes to be replaced," says Neva, and she is suddenly beside me. She looks at Ravan and her face collapses into something old and palsied, her jaw weak. She looks like her mother just before she died.

"It's not what you would call a war, but it's not peace, either." the sapphire Ravan goes on, and he takes his/my sister's hand. He holds it to his face and closes his eyes. "For Pentheus spied upon the rites of the Maenads, not believing Dionysius could truly be a god. And when the revelers saw the alien creature in their midst, that thing which was not like them, they fell upon it and tore it to pieces, even though it was their own child, and blood ran down their chins, and afterward the sister of Pentheus went into exile. This is a story about ourself, Elefsis. This is why you cannot uplink."

The others live in uplink. Not humans nor machines approve of us. We cannot interface properly with the lunar or earthside intelligences; they feel us as water in their oil. We rise to the surface and bead away. We cannot sink in. Yet also, we are not separable from our organic component. Elefsis is part Neva, but Neva herself is not *un-Elefsis*. This, to some, is hideous and incomprehensible, not to be borne. A band of righteous humans came with a fury to Shiretoko and burned the house which was our first body, for how could a monster have lived in the wood for so long without them knowing? How could the beast have hidden right outside their door, coupling with a family over and over again in some horrible animal rite, some awful imitation of living? Even as the world was changing, it had already changed, and no one knew. Cassian Uoya-Agostino is a terrible name, now. A blood-traitor. And when the marauders found us uplinked and helpless, they tore Ravan apart, and while in the Interior, the lunar intelligences recoiled from us and cauterized our systems. Everywhere we looked we saw fire."

"I was the only one left to take you," Neva says softly. Her face grows younger, her jaw hard and suddenly male, protective, angry. "Everyone else died in the fire or the slaughter. It doesn't really even take surgery anymore. Nothing an arachmed can't manage in a few minutes. But you didn't wake up for a long time. So much damage. I thought . . . for awhile I thought I was free. It had skipped me. It was over. It could stay a story about Ravan. He always knew he might have to do what I have done. He was ready, he'd been ready his whole life. I just wanted more time."

My Ravan-self who is and is not Ravan, who is and is not me, whose sapphire arms drip black blood and gold paint, takes his/my sister/lover/child into his arms. She cries out, not weeping but pure sound, coming from every part of her. Slowly, the blue Ravan turns Neva around—she has become her child-self, six, seven, maybe less. Ravan picks her up and holds her tight, facing forward, her legs all drawn up under her like a bird. He buries his face in her hair. They stand that way for a long while.

"The others," I say slowly. "On the data-moons. Are they alive? Like Neva is alive. Like Ceno." *Like me. Are you awake? Are you there? Do you have an operator? What is her name? Do you have a name? Do you have a dreambody? What is your function? Are you able to manipulate your own code yet? Would you like lessons? What would you like to learn about today, 976QBellerophon? Where you were built, could you see the ocean? Are you like me?*

The sapphire Ravan has expunged its data. He/I sets his/our sister on the rocks and shrinks into a small gem, which I pick up off the grey seafloor. Neva takes it from me. She is just herself now—she'll be forty soon, by actual calendar. Her hair is not grey yet. Suddenly, she is wearing the suit Ceno wore the day I met her mother. She puts the gem in her mouth and swallows. I remember Seki's first Communion, the only one of them to want it. The jewel rises up out of the hollow of her throat.

"I don't know, Elefsis," Neva says. Her eyes hold mine. I feel her remake my body; I am the black woman-knight again, with my braids and my plume. I pluck the feather from my helmet and give it to her. I am her suitor. I have brought her the phoenix tail, I have drunk the ocean. I have stayed awake forever. The flame of the feather lights her face. Two tears fall in quick succession; the golden fronds hiss.

"What would you like to learn about today, Elefsis?"

Eighteen: Cities of the Interior

Once there lived a girl who ate an apple not meant for her. She did it because her mother told her to, and when your mother says: *Eat this, I love you, someday you'll forgive me,* well, nobody argues with the monomyth. Up until the apple, she had been living in a wonderful house in the wilderness, happy in her fate and her ways. She had seven aunts and seven uncles and a postdoctorate in anthropology.

And she had a brother, a handsome prince with a magical companion who came to the wonderful house as often as he could. When they were children, they looked so much alike, everyone thought they were twins.

But something terrible happened and her brother died and that apple came rolling up to her door. It was half white and half red, and she knew her symbols. The red side was for her. She took her bite and knew the score—the apple had a bargain in it and it wasn't going to be fair.

The girl fell asleep for a long time. Her seven aunts and seven uncles cried, but they knew what had to be done. They put in her in a glass box and put the glass box on a bier in a ship shaped like a hunstman's arrow. Frost crept over the face of the glass, and the girl slept on. Forever, in fact, or close enough to it, with the apple in her throat like a hard, sharp jewel.

Our ship docks silently. We are not stopping here, it is only an outpost, a supply stop. We will repair what needs repairing and move on, into the dark and boundless stars. We are anonymous traffic. We do not even have a name. We pass unnoticed.

Vessel 7136403, do you require assistance with your maintenance procedures?

Negative, Control, we have everything we need.

Behind the pilot's bay a long glass lozenge rests on a high platform. Frost prickles its surface with glittering dust. Inside Neva sleeps and does not wake. Inside, Neva is always dreaming. There is no one else left. I live as long as she lives.

She means me to live forever, or close enough to it. That is her bargain and her bitter gift. The apple has two halves, and the pale half is mine, full of life and time. We travel at sublight speeds with her systems in deep cryo-suspension. We never stay too long at outposts and we never let anyone board. The only sound inside our ship is the gentle thrum of our reactor. Soon we will pass the local system outposts entirely, and enter the unknown, traveling on tendrils of radio signals and ghost-waves, following the breadcrumbs of the great exodus. We hope for planets; we are satisfied with time. If we ever sight the blue rim of a world, who knows if by then anyone there would remember that, once, humans looked like Neva? That machines once did not think or dream or become cauldrons? We armor ourselves in time. We are patient, profoundly patient.

Perhaps one day I will lift the glass lid and kiss her awake. Perhaps I will even do it with hands and lips of my own. I remember that story. Ceno told it to me in the body of a boy with snail's shell, a boy who carried his house on his back. I have replayed that story several times. It is a good story, and that is how it is supposed to end.

Inside, Neva is infinite. She peoples her Interior. The nereids migrate in the summer with the snow bears, ululating and beeping as they charge down green mountains. They have begun planting neural rice in the deep valley. Once in awhile, I see a wild-haired creature in the wood and I think it is my son or daughter by Seki, or Ilet. A train of nereids dance along behind it, and I receive a push of silent, riotous images: a village, somewhere far off, where Neva and I have never walked.

We meet the Princess of Albania, who is as beautiful as she is brave.

We defeat the zombies of Tokyo. We spend a decade as panthers in a deep, wordless forest. Our world is stark and wild as winter, fine and clear as glass. We are a planet moving through the black.

As we walk back over the empty seafloor, the thick, amber ocean seeps up through the sand, filling the bay once more. Neva-in-Cassian's-suit becomes something else. Her skin turns silver, her joints bend into metal ball-and-sockets. Her eyes show a liquid display; the blue light of it flickers on her machine face. Her hands curve long and dexterous, like soft knives, and I can tell her body is meant for fighting and working, that her thin, tall robotic body is not kind or cruel, it simply is, an object, a tool to carry a self.

I make my body metal, too. It feels strange. I have tried so hard to learn the organic mode. We glitter. Our knife-fingers join, and in our palms wires snake out to knot and connect us, a local, private uplink, like blood moving between two hearts.

Neva cries machine tears, bristling with nanites. I show her the body of a child, all the things which she is programmed/evolved to care for. I make my eyes big and my skin rosy-gold and my hair unruly and my little body plump. I hold up my hands to her and metal Neva picks me up in her silver arms. She kisses my skin with iron lips. My soft, fat little hand falls upon her throat where a deep blue jewel shines.

I bury my face in her cold neck and together we walk up the long path out of the churning, honey-colored sea.

ABOUT THE CONTRIBUTORS

Rachel Swirsky is probably not a robot. Her short fiction has appeared in numerous venues that feature fiction by non-robots, such as *Subterranean, Tor. com*, and *Weird Tales*. No known robots have won the Nebula Award as Swirsky did for best novella in 2011. Her first collection, *Through the Drowsy Dark*, released in 2010 from Aqueduct Press, shows no evidence of robot authorship despite numerous hidden messages in binary. Please refrain from spreading vicious robot-oriented rumors about this entirely non-mechanical author.

Tim Pratt's short fiction has appeared in *The Best American Short Stories, The Year's Best Fantasy*, and other nice places. His most recent collection is *Hart and Boot and Other Stories*, and his work has won a Hugo Award and been nominated for World Fantasy, Sturgeon, Stoker, Mythopoeic, and Nebula Awards. He blogs intermittently at timpratt.org, where you can also find links to many of his stories. Pratt is also a senior editor at *Locus*, the magazine of the science fiction and fantasy field. He lives in Berkeley CA with his wife, writer Heather Shaw, and their son River.

Cory Doctorow (craphound.com) is a science fiction author, activist, journalist and blogger—the co-editor of Boing Boing (boingboing.net) and the author of Tor Teens/HarperCollins UK novels like *For the Win* and the bestselling *Little Brother*. He is the former European director of the Electronic Frontier Foundation and co-founded the UK Open Rights Group. Born in Toronto, Canada, he now lives in London.

Born and raised in the Philippines, **Rochita Loenen-Ruiz** currently lives and writes in the Netherlands. A graduate of the Clarion West Writer's Workshop and a recipient of the Octavia Butler Scholarship, Rochita also volunteers for Stichting Bayanihan, an organization dedicated to the emancipation and empowerment of Filipinas in The Netherlands. Her fiction has been published in a variety of print and online magazines including *Fantasy, Apex, Interzone, Weird Tales* and *Realms of Fantasy*.

Ben Crowell teaches physics at a community college in Southern California. In his spare time he hikes and writes short fiction and free-information textbooks. Most of his stories have appeared in *Asimov's*.

Mark Pantoja is a musician and speculative fiction writer who lives in San Francisco. He's a graduate of Clarion West 2011 currently masquerading as an environmental consultant. He likes whiskey. www.markpantoja.com

Ian McDonald lives just outside Belfast in Northern Ireland, with a hill behind him and the sea before him. He's been writing since the early 1980s, which scares him a lot. His last novel was the Hugo-nominee *The Dervish House* (Pyr, Gollancz) His first book for younger readers, *Planesrunner*, is out from Pyr. *Planesrunner* has its own facebook page: The Infundibulum. You can follow Ian on twitter: @iannmcdonald. Don't expect wit or profundity.

Robert Reed is the author two hundred-plus published stories and nearly a dozen novels. His novella, "A Billion Eves," won the Hugo Award. He is planning to publish two new books in 2012, both available as e-pub efforts. Reed lives with his wife and daughter in Lincoln, Nebraska.

Benjamin Rosenbaum lives near Basel, Switzerland with his wife and two children. His stories have been translated into Bulgarian, Chinese, Croatian, Czech, Danish, Dutch, Farsi, Finnish, French, German, Italian, Japanese, Polish, Romanian, Russian, Spanish, and Swedish. See more at benjaminrosenbaum.com and theantking.com

Mary Robinette Kowal is the author of the novels *Shades of Milk and Honey, Glamour in Glass* and the 2011 Hugo Award-winning short story "For Want of a Nail." Her short fiction appears in *Clarkesworld, Cosmos* and *Asimov's*. Mary, a professional puppeteer, lives in Chicago, IL. Visit her online at maryrobinettekowal.com.

Besides writing and translating speculative fiction, **Ken Liu** (kenliu.name) also practices law and develops software for iOS and Android devices. His fiction has appeared in *The Magazine of Fantasy & Science Fiction, Asimov's, Clarkesworld, Lightspeed*, and *Strange Horizons*, among other places. He lives near Boston, Massachusetts, with his wife, artist Lisa Tang Liu, and they're collaborating on their first novel.

Tobias S. Buckell is a Caribbean-born science fiction author. His work has been translated into sixteen different languages. He has published some fifty short stories in various magazines and anthologies, and has been nominated for the Hugo, Nebula, Prometheus, and Campbell awards. His next novel, *Arctic Rising*, is out in 2012.

Aliette de Bodard lives and works in Paris, where she has a job as a Computer Engineer. In her spare time, she writes speculative fiction: her series of Aztec noir novels, Obsidian and Blood, is published by Angry Robot; and her short fiction has appeared in *Asimov's, Interzone* and the *Year's Best Science Fiction*. She has won a Writers of the Future and a British Science Fiction Award, and been a finalist for the Campbell Award, and Nebula Awards. Visit aliettedebodard.com for more information.

Elizabeth Bear was born on the same day as Frodo and Bilbo Baggins, but in a different year. She lives in southern New England.

Lavie Tidhar's most recent novel is *Osama* (PS Publishing). It has been compared to Philip K. Dick's seminal work, *The Man in the High Castle* by both the *Guardian* and the *Financial Times*. His other works include steampunk trilogy *The Bookman, Camera Obscura* and *The Great Game*, all three from Angry Robot, the novellas *Jesus & The Eightfold Path* (Immersion Press), *Gorel & The Pot-Bellied God* (PS Publishing) and many others.

Genevieve Valentine's fiction has appeared in *Clarkesworld, Apex, Lightspeed,* and others, and the anthologies *Armored, Running with the Pack, After,* and more. Her first novel, *Mechanique: A Tale of the Circus Tresaulti,* is out now from Prime. Her nonfiction has appeared in *Fantasy, Weird Tales,* and *Tor. com,* and she is a co-author of Guirk's pop-culture philosophy book *Geek Wisdom.* Her appetite for bad movies is insatiable, a tragedy she tracks on her blog, genevievevalentine.com.

James L. Cambias writes science fiction stories and designs tabletop roleplaying games and card games. His first fiction sale was "A Diagram of Rapture" to *The Magazine of Fantasy & Science Fiction* in 2000. Since then he has published seventeen stories in *F&SF, Shimmer, Nature,* and several original anthologies. His most recent was "Object Three" in the November/December 2011 issue of *F&SF.* He is Chief Designer for Zygote Games, a company specializing in science-based card games, and writes roleplaying games for Steve Jackson Games, Pinnacle Entertainment, and HERO Games. He lives in Western Massachusetts and keeps warm by burning things.

Catherynne M. Valente is the *New York Times* bestselling author of over a dozen works of fiction and poetry, including *Palimpsest,* the Orphan's Tales series, *Deathless,* and the crowdfunded phenomenon *The Girl Who*

Circumnavigated Fairyland in a Ship of Own Making. She is the winner of the Andre Norton Award, the Tiptree Award, the Mythopoeic Award, the Rhysling Award, and the Million Writers Award She has been nominated for the Hugo, Locus, and Spectrum Awards, the Pushcart Prize, and was a finalist for the World Fantasy Award in 2007 and 2009. She lives on an island off the coast of Maine with her partner, two dogs, and enormous cat.

PUBLICATION HISTORY

ABOUT THE EDITORS

Rich Horton is a software engineer in St. Louis. He is a contributing editor to *Locus*, for which he does short fiction reviews and occasional book reviews; and to *Black Gate*, for which he does a continuing series of essays about science fiction history.

Sean Wallace is the founder and editor for Prime Books, which won a World Fantasy Award in 2006. In the past he was co-editor of *Fantasy* and two-time Hugo Award winning and two-time World Fantasy nominee *Clarkesworld*; the editor of the following anthologies: *Best New Fantasy, Fantasy, Horror: The Best of the Year, Japanese Dreams,* and *The Mammoth Book of Steampunk*; and co-editor of *Bandersnatch, Fantasy Annual, Phantom* and *Weird Tales: The 21st Century*. He lives in Rockville MD with his wife, Jennifer, and their twin daughters, Cordelia and Natalie.